Ojo

Ojo

Donald Mengay

Saddle Road Press

Saddle Road Press
Ithaca, NY
saddleroadpress.com

ISBN 9798990054325
Library of Congress Control Number 2024940587

Design by Don Mitchell
Cover image by Donald Mengay

Books by Donald Mengay
The Lede to Our Undoing

v.1.0

CONTENTS

For Linda Warren

LAS HORMIGAS

LOS DIOSES SE MEARON POR EL TERRENO, duchando las montañas con oro. Tommy impregnates me with the idea, gasps in my ear, jerks to present matters, our heads drifting toward drunk divines showering the world—with autumn. Or is it fall? My fall. From grace to this. Cheek to earth. Soil around. In my nose. Tommy hovers with a mouthful of dirt while glass lengthens from the two of us, mirroring up. Watercolors sit, a day gone amiss.

What a thing to say. To think of drunk divines gilding the earth. With—this guy takes liberties. Does he think he's a god or is he on some kind a kick? Across the reservoir I spy fishers with lines arrayed in inverted Vs. They extend on an axis of webbed chairs that shrinks toward a point, engaged in talk more sober than what's coming from Tommy, I'm sure—

—Should we be—?

—Relaaaax—

The liquefaction of skin, pine whiff, the transition to musk. The effect is golden in a sense, enough to raise the eyebrows of a body passing by, but who's here to see or recognize—fourteen hundred miles from Laurentine? Not Florrie or Harry, Ghost or Marks, Rauch with his telling tongue, Diablo or Cin, and god knows you, having left me on the other side of Eisenhower Tunnel as I hurtled toward the light. You either, Wren. Or you, Mollykins.

It's just me, a roadie, with a hitcher on my back.

God knows if his name jibes with the one he gave.

I'm untethered in an existential though not literal way, a seed helicoptering down. Would it matter if the earth swallowed me? This dude does his thing no matter what.

What are we anyway? A duo void of jeans, tees, and everything else, doffed in godless haste on a makeshift patch, the spot where I pondered my state behind a veil, smearing pigments on a wheel, only to find myself engaging color in a different sense.

I was sure I was alone, at last, that I evaded the world—that was my mantra, evasion. To timidly go where others fail to tread, as far as I possibly could. Later Tommy'll tip me off to a local chestnut, namely that I stumbled on a piney version of what in a future life I'll hear referred to as The Brambles, on another green, in the middle of a bustling city. The place seemed anonymous enough, and like I say distant. Whether by will or oblivion I didn't eye the others pooling around, Tommy most of all, trapped as I was in an inward-turn—he caught me. Never mind he wasn't fishing.

At the moment I have more pressing matters to attend to—he persists. My resolve misfires like a carburetor begging for air at these altitudes, having been set for sea- or lake-level. Several times I consider calling a halt to the proceedings until again I get the drift from Tommy, Chiiillll, niño. Who cares? If we do this or anything?

Watercolor the lake, enjoy a picnic of chips, or chuck our jeans?

For his part steam is gaining like a truck down a grade. I remind myself that for now it's just this guy on my back, him an' me. The ants. Lodgepole pines huddling in a brake, sheltering us loosely, the human warmth around me fending off the late September air. Everything and everyone else—you, Wren; you, Molly; and you, Peacoat, most of all—you've all left. Or have I left you? What do I know about life in thin air? About rays that blister even as the world turns icy, shifts at a rate this time of year. Succumbs to events, quick as a piston shooting in a cylinder?

Tommy's having a day.

Rolling toward Pandemonium spruces meet where mountains angle up. Even traveling at sixty you catch hummingbirds wheeling by, whistling on a flight to Chihuahua or points south, where the sun dangles in the sky. Where the highway turns true my foot eases the gas, having a mind of its own. How many times have I pulled aside to take in this view, stick still, only to be deflated? As though standing were the best way to ruin a thing—sometimes the best prospects present only at speed. Stop and they vanish. Track on and they maintain, spark awe as you shoosh by. Not unlike a bighorn. So long as you avert your gaze you're good, but a bare-naked glance and it scats away.

What does the Forest City offer compared to this? How could Harry or Florrie conceive it, a ground of giants rising up, toward a different god than the one they worship? The sight-lines slope to this stand of pines, thick as pubic hair, exuding earth. The terrain offers company only when you can't suffer your own another day. No driver tails or hassles you at the moment, lays on their horn to shake you; when you slow down the world deaccelerates too—it vanishes. I hit the pedal though I have nowhere to go; I'm driving. Anywhere but east.

Problem is, when you commit yourself to a goal, including never to set one, when you give up looking— searching, discovering, or uncovering; finding, locating, or advancing; growing, or, god forbid, improving—when you get it together enough to decide all that you still gotta keep going, it turns out, because an object without motion is dead. Dead, dead, dead. Even a rock lives, rising and falling with earth—it tells a story. Of heat and cold. Lichens.

Accordingly if you harbor a rock in your chest, devoid of will, drive, or purpose, it, too, is prey to circumstance. Never mind time and its twists. If these rocks here were to have a will—say, to suck in this view, whiff this crotch of firs—it'd be possible only because it's the nature of things. They've been doing it longer than me, looking.

As the Fiat rattles on Harry eyes me, him and Florrie both, two passengers who haven't stopped tracking me since I left. I've been trying to lose them for over fourteen hundred miles, since I left Laurentine, but every time I glance back they're there in the rear-view, worse than a couple a cops in Kansas, getting you on a trumped-up technicality but refusing to reveal the nature of the infraction, forcing you to pay one way or another. In lieu of cash I didn't have.

Harry and Florrie have been dogging me the whole way. You'd think once you took leave no would mean no, that they'd get the message that I don't want them in my life and back off. But the two hang here as though they had a bevy of selves to split. If life were the way it is in books I'd turn into a lark, flit outta here. But things remain stubbly the same. Eyes take up position as I signal toward the Pandemonium exit. Harry and Florrie, Rauch and Marx, Cin and Diablo, perch where once a welter of things jumbled around, junk I snatched at the last minute. Peacoat, a corpse coughed by the lake, leathery and worn, slumps next to me. I adjust the mirror so I can't see the crowd in the back.

I'm not much good at gazing forward either as it turns out—it feels I'm riding a momentum bigger than me. All that vanishes though as I take in the leafy streets of Pandemonium, rolled in a symmetry, a geometry that must've come from a will to tame the rudeness of the valley where the town rests. They threw a net over nature to subdue it; it wilted but in a half-assed way. The gentle grid only roughly domesticates the place, overlays it with a veneer of order after the raucous early days, on the heels of a rush. It's dotted with gingerbread now—rows of houses that gather on a road stretching, unpaved, from one side of the valley to the other.

The goal a century on seems to be formaldehyding the past, after the insanity of the early days when it was a lawless gathering of tents, just like the other towns nearby, including Ojo Caliente where I live, but in a different way, having opted for a more respectable look. Here in Pandemonium evidence of a constant turning-back smacks you in the face, not just in the homes but the post office, town hall, and clinic; the Hotel de Paris; grade school, jail, hardware, and liquor stores; bars, eateries, churches, and cafes—four churches and ten cafes to be exact, for a town of eight hundred. A storybook village whose founders lie unmissed, unloved, and unknown in Alvarado Cemetery, just a piece down Frontage Road.

A cousin of Ojo, there's no Safeway, no golden arches, or ten-gallon neon rotating over a steak-house, no motels luring drivers off I-70. There are no tin cans like the one I call home, no rock shops just across; no defunct mines bilking tourists panning for gold. On foot Pandemonium opens as you trod the pavers—they must date back to the time the cornerstone was set. Part of an effort to lift soles from vulgar earth, elevate souls above the devil wilderness, up from mud with its knack for tagging every cuff, hem, and seam, smudges that must have reminded them of their fate one day. The brazen goal was to lose the earth and in some way feminize it, given the froufrou everywhere. If men wrangled the rowdiness that was here originally, pinned it into submission, held it at gunpoint, women delivered another blow with the proliferation of ornaments, everywhere you look. Including the copper tricks holding up the bar just there.

I take it in, shops and wares. Hand-wheeled crockery, the colored glass, crystals diffusing light; silver-and-turquoise displays; kiosks of seeds, columbine, Indian paintbrush, and edelweiss; hummingbird feeders in unnatural reds; hyped hues too in paintings on gallery walls; photos of this or that peak, ambered in light.

Tables inside the Happy Looker align in tight rows, inside and out, an effort to pack them in. The whiff of corn oil and waffle batter crisping. Fairies wheel overhead, whistle while bee-lining to plastic blooms under the Looker's eves. How is it possible such a trifle can thrive beyond the borders of the town, in air so harsh, so vertical? How do they escape raptors, daughters of dinosaurs, spiraling on thermals overhead, craning to make a kill? Two hummingbirds buzz by, buzz each other, then part until they rush each other again. It's difficult to tell if they're mating on the wing or warring for nectar.

The lacy columbine—how does it do it? A shaky vulnerability, braving spaces where giants step. Everything here's named in its honor, streets and churches, emporiums, inns, and restaurants—a flouncy, showy gaiety that muscles its way through the culture.

I'm struggling to hang on 'til noon.

After three quarters of an hour, drifting through side-streets, I return to Main. The sun emerges from its closet finally—I catch the pre-glow over the crest.

You from 'round 'ere?

A man silhouettes before overhead rays.

Do I look like I wanna talk? Uhh, no.

Where you from then?

What business is it a yours? And why you wanna know?
From some'ere.

No news there, son. Everyone's from some'ere. First time
here?

I'll say it again: Why don' you min' your own business? Yep.
You on a vay-cay-tion?

Florrie isn't here to admonish you about rudeness, that
there's no excuse for it, so just walk away. Split. Make
tracks—I don't even gotta answer. Be polite. And yet here
I hang as if cemented, despite the fact I know this guy
already, through and through, even though he and I never
met. I read the pressed trousers and cuffs, polished shoes
and fresh haircut, the whole look, rendered unique by a
bolo touch. Everything else shouts familiar territory on a
day like nothing else, in a town recognizable only in story-
books—or better yet a movie. Like some black-and-white I
might a seen on TV with Harry, eons ago, just before he got
a buzz on and flamed out. If it weren't for the clothes this
guy'd blow his cover with the book, flammable with the
strike of a match.

I'm Dan!

And your point is?

Whistle.

Huh—?

Dan Whistle.

Well, Whistle, le' me alone—I take his hand.

What's yer name, son?

An enormous spider's made a killing between the picture
window and casing next to me. She's shrouding the thing
with her forelegs, twirling and mummifying it. I wonder
how it is that both she and her prey escaped the frost last
night—it dipped that low in Ojo, just a stone's throw away.
I shivered under a sleeping bag because the usual blankets
didn't suffice.

How has she endured?

Dan's hand meanwhile holds mine, caresses it. I say, son, what's your name?

Persistent as ants, your kind. Gunnin' for souls, pocketbooks, or is it somethin' else? Name's Peacoat.

The man's eyes slit, squint, study mine. The spider finishes wrapping her prey and suspends it in place. What kind a name's that?

A dead one.

What's that s'posed to mean?

—.

Well, Peacoat, I'd like t'invite you t'an hour a worship. Just up the road yonder—see that buildin'?

I've never seen a structure so dwarfed before, huddled at the foot of a vertical, its spire gesturing skyward, copying the peak overhead. It cowers, small and lowly, and at the same time crouches with a net to nab you, like this über-chatty guy whose words epoxy me to the spot.

I got other plans.

Which way you goin'?

I already got a carful if you're fixin' to bum a ride, a crowd in the back and a stiff in front—. Dunno. Maybe west.

West?? Or to The West? As in coast. Big difference, son.

One by one cars arrive, line Columbine Street. A couple piles out of a sedan and the two take each other's hands robotically as they stroll, as though they'd cease to exist if they unhitched. A family with two, three, no, four children pours out onto the bluestone as well. Two women arrive keeping a healthy distance. A convertible tools past with a gray-hair behind the wheel, adjacent to a twenty-something. The top is down, and I see his hand on her knee.

West means west.

You live 'round here?

Against my will and judgment he manages to extract from me a general geographical map of my current address in Ojo, which I told myself I had no interest in divulging.

You headed to Vail? Lots a people head there this time a year. Leaf-peepers lookin' for aspens, golden this time a year. You goin' t' Frisco? Not to be confused with San Fran—who don' love that place? Silverthorne? Lovely town, that. Breckenridge?

The sidewalks start to swell with day-trippers from the Mile High City, stopping on their way to someplace else. Dan's eyes stray past me from time to time as he continues to calculate, tot up totals, beyond just bodies to fill pews, I remind myself, but dollars to fill coffers. And yet again is he sussing spiritual or financial quarry? Or is it something else? He lets my hand fall finally and cranes his neck back and around to take in the scene. After the grip of his hand I wonder about the size of his congregation in this postcard-picture of a town, a gingerbread façade with German logos in driveways. I half expect I might enter through the doors of these places, only to be greeted by timber framing and rude nature on the other side. A movie set.

Dan backs a pace or two, I assume to eye some guy more flush than me. When he moves away in earnest it's not toward what's congregating on the sidewalk but up the hill.

Maybe I'll see you around sometime! he yells from across the way. Also, if you want a good time try Dodgson! He disappears inside what looks like a maquette for a church.

Dodgson?!?

Many of the newly arrived aim toward the Happy Looker, which stands loosely catty-corner from the church on a road ascending the foot of the peak. I contemplate spending my last couple bucks on a pile of flap-jacks then reconsider. Hummingbirds buzz the restaurant veranda, hover over awestruck diners while other day-trippers queue for a table. It's no breakfast for me, or, god knows, lunch. All I have is a bag of potato chips to sustain me. Whatever money jingles in my pocket I'll use to flip for gas, enough to extend west a bit, before returning to Ojo.

After that, who knows?

At the filling station on the edge of town I contemplate how for one thousand four hundred miles I pressed on in search of a thing I couldn't name, visualize, or hear echo back. I simply drove until I couldn't catch the whites of the eyes following me. It wasn't until I ramped toward Ojo that I saw nothing but stuff in the back. Junk really. And books. Effects you throw in your car on the run. By the time I reached Ojo that was all I saw, so I stopped. Where eyes no longer followed.

For a few days at least. Maybe even a week. I didn't know zombies need time to catch up—they track you, no matter what. Make you think they're gone, only to re-emerge, as they did this morning, just as I was beginning to think I could get through a day without those hangers-on. They look more than a touch out of their element here, like they're from Mars. There or Laurentine.

As I pile into the Fiat I realize they split up while I was harassed by the church guy. They toured the place but now are reconvening in their usual spots, there in the back. There's Diablo, of all people, and Cin, perennially holding Diablo's hand. Here's Romeo drawing his usual puss. Harry and Florrie press together as they scoot the others over, and there pouts Peacoat, perching in position beside me, eyes yellow and vitreous, trained on me silently, the deathly skin, water-logged, Army-issue jacket and ghastly look.

Weren't nothing I could a done, I plead. Billy told me t' get lost and you bid me go.

He stares at me without blinking the way the living dead do, a look of unguarded vulnerability blaming me while the vehicle fills with water, enough to drown the lot of us. The others disappear and it's just me and Peacoat now in a viscous flow, the two of us below the surface. I'm shifting with him toward the open lake, drifting like perch through the frigid medium, dead leaves and branches, vegetable rot fertilizing the water, rotting us too. Our dreams. If I'd a known what was about to go down I would a never left.

I promise.

Peacoat stares blankly back, a wounded puppy, so unlike the gaze that locked on me in that room on Chester. I wanna dwell on that moment, the thrill of it in our living days, so unlike this, when it seems we're both lilting toward—only he knows for sure. We were in the process of filling a prescription for what ailed us. In a room named Possibility. Florrie reappears and opens the back door of the Fiat from outside. Erie water drains and the others pile back in, resume the positions they had the whole trip. We head west.

Emerging from Eisenhower, birth canal of a range transecting the terrain from north to south, I eye the Continental Divide skirting the rear-view. Emerging is difficult—I squint into light. The sun slaps you into breathing, offers little hope of adjusting as you issue from safety to vulnerability. I wasn't expecting to be born this way, thrust to the other side. For all intents and purposes I've come out alone, the living dead—look!—have abandoned me again, somewhere in the blackness behind. Who knows how long it'll last, but for now I'm free. Even the Fiat seems to feel the difference. It rides lighter without the dead to weigh it down. Accelerates faster, though not fast enough. Other cars gain speed as I readjust the rear-view upward, glance to see the tunnel opening shrink in the mirror.

I rise in the seat, sense I'm more lissome without the hangers-on. A road sign approaches, reading the distances from where I am to the place that Whistle guy mentioned, and more. The thighs of the valley widen and I fly out. Double lines yellow and curve with the arc of the pavement, a snaking unusual at lower elevations given the pressures of getting from A to B in this endless, open country. Leading from the ever-climbing prairie to the mountains. The space is so vast in the flatlands and the time required to get anywhere so pressing that straight-and-narrow rules. Unlike these roads beside river runs that dodge and twist in hair-pins, clover-leafs, and loop-de-loops, forcing traffic to crawl at times, until again you come to a straight-away not unlike at lower elevations.

Though I'm in no rush I'm champing at the bit behind an old fart in front, doing forty in a fifty-five. Normally it wouldn't matter but cars are slowing after the tunnel, with traffic down to two lanes. A car tails me as though I were the culprit; he nudges closer, almost pressing my rear. Then another, and another, and another still until a proper train has formed behind the Fiat, through no fault of my own. One thing Harry used to stress if he stressed anything, is don't tail a body. You never know if he's gonna smash the brake or if some critter'll dash out, force you to stop when it's too late. Fuzz come it's yer fault, sure as shit. Even though he's gone now in the rear-view, his voice plays in my ear. He used to caution, Some'ns on yer ass, tap yer brake, force 'im t' hang back. All of which sounds easy. But the line behind me is close, and antsy. One by one it takes over the opposite lane, reserved for oncoming cars, as opportunity allows. Vehicle after vehicle dashes across the temporary double-line, sailing by, leaving me to doddle behind the slowpoke.

The sun doesn't stand long in these passes—the reality dawned on me soon after I settled. Especially this time a year. Light drains early from the valley walls, timeworn as crockery, and it's already past noon. I'm eager to get a move on so I sail toward the line, eyeing no oncoming cars and hoping the guy ahead will figure he's the problem, moving at a glacial pace, then yield. So I and—what is it, eight, ten, twelve cars yet behind me?—can all slide by.

I wanna get going—me—probably the only schlump in the country who prefers the fifty-five requirement that took effect during the gas shortage. Now even I feel the burn in my blood, fanned by frustration as I advance at a speed typical a half century ago, the double line holding firm, refusing to budge, until finally—at last!—a break! Directed by a series of cones, oncoming traffic must shift to what was the eastbound shoulder while westbound traffic takes over the eastbound lane. At last I make my move and it's me neck-and-neck with the geezer, who's somehow, now, no longer toodling along. The road elbows into a straightaway and I floor it—beside the gray-beard I float, light as a hummingbird. I glance at the man and realize he's so short his head barely clears the dashboard. Then just as I'm about to pass he lilts forward. I attempt to slip in front of him, but it isn't long before he's moved up, putting us door-to-door. I increase my speed even more and he copies me, as though we're a couple Blue Angels roaring, like the time Harry got the notion it'd be a bonding experience for me and him to attend the air-show at Burke Lakefront, father and son—I must have been what? Four? Five?—inducing not awe in me but tears from the growl of the jets as they swooped down, close enough to give Harry a shave.

In the distance a vehicle approaches in my lane so I let up on the gas, beating a retreat. But the line of cars trailing the codger has tightened and there's no way to shoehorn the Fiat back in. What's more, when I ease the pedal the man to my right does the same, toggling his speed, unaware of his surroundings—or is he completely aware? I realize my only option is to dive like a kite in free-fall in hopes I can outpace the Impala, yet when I give it the gas once again he gains speed.

What was a speck in the distance grows in size, rushing dead toward me, hurtling so quickly my palms turn soggy. Flustered, I avert my gaze long enough to catch the dead-pan look of the guy keeping pace. The vehicle aimed toward me presses near, then nearer, more and more distinctly, offering no plausible option but to ditch into the guardrail to my left, hopefully sparing me from the embankment, boulders, and river below, the car in front so close I don't have time to catch its make. The Fiat shimmies and shakes at a speed it hasn't achieved since the Valiant died somewhere in Indiana, with me in it.

I'm not going to make it! I realize. The laws of gravity and the car manual too stipulate that an engine can perform only at X speed for X amount of time, and the crank next to me has opted to test the limits.

In the press of circumstance it isn't lost on me that death is staring down my throat with its sweaty, grabby hands, but I have no will to call on a divine. Rather I'm thinking of you, Molly, and you, Wren, the two I ran out on; the two, I pray, who'll blame me the least. You too, Peacoat, who—look!—has decided to ride shotgun all of a sudden, observing me if you can call it that, in my final moments, the ones in which I see our fates dove-tailing, forcing me to a different kind of watery grave than the one he knew, the oncoming vehicle approaching at an evil speed, the driver, like me, slated at birth to drown and not hang, strangers engaged in the casualty of chance.

As if magic were possible after all, the car ahead suddenly disappears from view—POOF!—at the same time my hands have risen up, over my face, such that if I'm to bid so long this way the last thing I want to do is observe the event, like a scene in an American movie elevating violence, the gratuitous kind, an inevitability you know sure as shit the moment you plunk your money at the booth, the meaningless gore announced in advance by the music, lighting, and cutaways, the frenzied mix of shots—none of which I could match let alone watch. And yet an eternity, or a couple seconds, later I'm aware that a physicality remains, endures, integrated and not atomized, the perspiring weight of it, that and the pull of the wheel to the right. The man next to me lays on his horn and I jerk the Fiat over, finally, only to perceive from a glance in the rear-view that the car once on a collision course with me and destiny is pulling out of an emergency turn-off, having jetted out of the way at the last moment, cheating fate and in a sense me, of an expedited, guiltless passing, one the folks back in Laurentine would cast as tragic, unlike the one I often contemplate that would give them cause to shake their heads and remark, See, I told you!—chatter sentencing me to the depths in their eyes. This-here situation though, as it turns out, has preserved me to exist another day, me and the driver to the right whom I eye almost in slo-mo as he flips me the bird, just before he slows enough for me to tuck the Fiat in front, as though nothing were amiss on this most ordinary of days.

As soon as I'm positioned securely on the legit side of the road the car behind diminishes, just as the orange cones and yellow line return us to the usual side of the road. The highway now swerves south and the Fiat begins to complain about a climb. There's not a soul behind me now; it's just me and these hairpins, not to mention a basket full of paradoxes resting on the seat, commencing with, What just happened there? What if I'd been killed? Would I be happier? More attuned? Or merely flat-lining? Oblivious. A nothing. What's it like where you are?—you there, Peacoat. Say something instead of just staring that way. Affectless. And what about the other driver? Never mind the geezer—no doubt he would've just slipped from the scene, gone his way as though nothing happened. The others on the road ahead? Would the tragedy—the gore—make their day the way it does for American movie-goers, as the emergency personnel pulled me and my death-partner from the rushing river, a watery crypt? What about the rubber-neckers, braking involuntarily to a crawl even as cops motion them furiously to move on, the rubber-neckers slowing to the speed of flies on road-kill, so close, the view all the more juicy because of the serenity of the scene? Could there be anything more alluring, more mesmerizing for The People than a grisly sight, in which I was one of the main players?

I'm forced to end these musings in order to engage in yet another kind of awareness. We, all of us peopled vehicles coming and going, must look sharp as we negotiate the switchbacks we're climbing, in some places only a car wide, with dizzying drops just beyond the passenger door.

When I set my shoe on bare earth I feel the sun singling me out. I can't stop thinking about the fact that unlike Peacoat, who I discover waiting for me, incarnating out of the blue as he does, I was thrown toward then snagged from the pit. The fact of my physicality overwhelms me, nudges me toward tears, however delayed, toward the authority of pines commanding the air. My legs wobble as I retrieve a blanket from the trunk, the same one Peacoat and I used to throw over leaves in the woods south of Laurentine. I whiff his presence other than I used to, minus the water-logged air that usually haunts me, an offense that lives in the nose forever. In fact it's the same blanket Romeo and I unfolded back in the Dark Ages before he was usurped. I considered running it through a wash cycle lest it tattle, release my past. To no avail. It wasn't so easy to oust Romeo from the knit of the spread that Ruby and Miss Glasby gifted me one Christmas, must a been when I was seven or eight. Even at the time I thought it a wrong fit for someone of my sensibilities, marked with scenes from the prairie. Cowboys and Indians, horses and bison. Nevertheless it's followed me from the moment it no longer spread across my bed, when Romeo argued it'd do for what he had in mind, down by the lake. From that point on I slept on a naked bed so to speak, the spread having assumed a more culted purpose, including two bodies among a field of rough-riders.

It's looking more than threadbare these days, as it was when Peacoat adopted it. It felt shameless, given how your history hounds you. But necessity topped sense, so Peacoat and I went with it. If he had anything in common with Romeo it came down to one thing, and that is he didn't nitpick when push came to shove. On the contrary he adopted the thing, fondly, tied it to me and what was between us. He groused if I forgot to bring it, all those times outdoors, as though it belonged to him, like me.

The gravel crunches as I walk. The height of the pines, close up, surprises. Slim lodgepoles furring the valleys around the reservoir. Water yawns wide in a bowl similar to the one Pandemonium and Ojo rest in, though several times the size. My eye traces the perimeter, numbering the fishermen setting in a loose chain. Although some are lithe and upright, casting their lines repeatedly, most are portly and slouch in chairs, poles anchored in the sand beside them, heads nodding as though fishing were a ruse. Others dot the rim in the distance, though the reservoir is so enormous I realize it must take an effort to bushwhack there—which is what I'm determined to do, bushwhack. Trek into unpeopled territory on the edge of which I spot an opening that leads to a trail, a network of them that delivers me to a clearing where I consider unfurling the blanket, until I determine to press on.

Pressing on seems to be the running theme. Moving, hair on fire. Making a hell of heaven the way the dark place follows you, demons in tow. After Peacoat disappeared Florrie used to tell me I focus too much on trouble, by which I think she meant trauma, to which I replied, On the contrary, mommy dear. Trauma focuses too much on me.

To have left her and that ghoulish lot on the far side of the tunnel, all except Peacoat who slipped through, being drawn to water I suppose. When you run for your life it's just a matter a time before fatigue sets in. I'm only gone a few weeks and the will to stop, cease everything, eats at me.

Still I pad farther around the lake, undetected by spectator or specter so far as I can tell, giving Peacoat too the slip on an elk path through the under-brush, a route that must be hundreds or even thousands of years old, gazing back from time to time until my Fiat, yellow as the sun and visible from a mile or more, fades from view. Pine fills the air, beds of grass open here and there. Needles cushion my feet—the smell.

A squirrel gives notice that this terrain is taken. A gray jay slips in and out of view, hammering the stillness. At my feet ants track across the forest floor in a frenzy—in less than a month they'll be gone. Scrub oaks battle for a patch of sun. Even through my jeans I feel them go after me as I clamber for the perfect opening, a blanket wide, where I can enjoy a different kind of high than the one I experienced with Cin, Diablo, Rauch, and Marks, Romeo too, just west along the lake from Laurentine.

At the point I think I'm happily lost the path reappears and I conveyor onto it. I imagine a line of mule deer advancing, dwarfing me. The thick under-brush gives way once again to patches of grass that are bare in places save for a sprinkle of needles, until I find myself standing on the far rim of the reservoir where solid and fluid meet. I spot a trout, a pink pole that not only doesn't flick away but angles nearer. Through the clear water I spot her slippery back dark against the sand; when she arches around she flashes scarlet.

In the absence of a god to attribute such beauty I go with chance. Luck void of divine or human hand, unspoiled in that way. I unbuckle Peacoat's old belt, the one he strapped around the blanket to keep it neat, before he morphed into a monster. He formed it in a tidy roll, seems a millennium ago—I unroll the thing, and after losing my second skin land on it, revive Peacoat, contemplate the pink fish, black ants, green canopy, and blue awning overhead, a sky trafficking in sugar-clouds that flatten on the surface of the lake. The lust of firs. When I sit up the rainbow's disappeared—was the unfurling blanket too much like a net? She didn't read me right—if she had she'd a known she had nothing to worry about with me, unlike the others. Anyway she split, though I feel her still. I close my eyes, commune with her spirit a moment, my mother now, until the ants begin to top me. I have no real gripe, but it takes discipline to ruminate as they patter here and there, as if you've entered not a secluded patch but an anty version of Times Square, where the locals tramp, avert each other and, from time to time, come to blows. I swish them aside in order to take in the world unmolested.

Water laps, air whooshes, jays hammer. The world reduces to aural and olfactory cues, raw sensation, light washing over my eyelids as the lodgepoles fuss in the breeze, admitting and blocking light. When it slips in the world goes orange; when blocked it shades lavender; the mantra of sense. For the first time since Peacoat and I pealed down to the flesh I feel myself slacken. An ant surveys my beard, lips, and cheeks until it deboards on my shoulder, arm, hand, then the blanket. My skin melts. Interior and exterior morph into moot borders, an untold number of times greater than the blanket below me, this patch, the reservoir, my naked state, the globe, and solar system—they stretch out. The only thing that interrupts the moment is the flick of a fin. Is it the rainbow? Reaching from the dark, seizing my testicles, tugging them, surrounding my penis.

I let it go, as if it were detachable. I sense my testicleness and penisness a new way, acknowledge their existence after having sworn them off. I grant them a moment, verging on enjoyment, as though blessed by—

—Who are you??

Silencio, amigo. Disfrútalo.

I scramble upright.

—Where'd you come from?!

A finger rests on my lips, muting me, foreshadowing another kind of fish. I can't speak or protest. His belt unbuckles with a mind of its own then slicks away. The zipper trains down, denim slides. A shirt slats up, exposing something untoward, too beautiful to exist in this reality. I'm a beetle bugged on its back, my legs helpless, unable or unwilling to move as hands and lips survey the territory. I grow rigid, expose myself to the fall.

I come to, pull myself away. Twice more I wonder Who are you Where'd you come from, and twice I get the silencio treatment—

—Shshshshshshshshshshsh—

The giant pine I repaired to dwarfs me, its needles feather down, brush my skin.

Decades later I'm still not sure why I let myself be jacked that way, a pink trout in cold water, resistance ebbed, except to say I was hooked from the get-go, enough for Tommy to boast to Polly later, Sissy! I did th'impossible! Shut the gringo down! For a moment a'least. Which in retrospect I realize is true. Defenses and tongue both, reduced to nada, a big-fat O, for maybe the first and—who knows?—last time. Preserving my tongue for more fruitful things—that was his take-away. The hammer-head on my brain, still today, parts not normally exposed to the sun. Coffee or toffee—how to describe him? The skin. The candy Harry used to spring for on a Saturday at Euclid Beach, after he'd come away from the refreshment stand with a cup foaming, handing me and Wren a sack with the dark treat, which we over-ate to the point of puking though we blamed the Rotor and Flying Turns, the Racing Coasters, uneager as we were to deny Harry the joy of the gesture. Blame it on too much toffee. I didn't think it at the time, but I see in my brain more than ever my paleness pressed against Tommy's skin, a divergence that spoke not hell but heaven.

I nailed 'im, Sissy!

That'll fix Harry.

EL BURRO

Is that yer pimp? A man shifts his eyes from one to the other. How much she cost a hour? How much you wan' for a night?

Billie, get 'n the car.

Donald nears a guy who sways like a thistle, attempting to stay erect in the wind. He cocks his head, attempts to lock his gaze while the other studies him in turn—

Donald! Leave 'im be! Get 'n the car! Wren pleads from the passenger seat, from the window she's rolled down despite the dust tramping the road, adjacent field, and entire landscape. It never seems to rest, hefting earth upward, slant-wise and parallel with a surface that rolls as far as the eye can see. The alarm in her voice. She's seen Donald like this before and knows—

—He's drunk! Why waste yer energy?

Donald leans forward until he's practically nose-to-nose with the man.

Daddy!

Two voices beg, cry, and whine while the man face-to-face with Donald shifts from foot to unsteady foot, struggling to stop the swaying. Car voices continue to importune Donald, whose gaze is locked like a monument defying sun, rain, drought, and desertification, the two facing off in a winner-take-nothing game, hopeless as the terrain. Meanwhile feet traffic by. One or two try their luck at panhandling but the two pay no mind, as though only the other existed. Steely silence now marks the confrontation, beyond the pleas from the vehicle.

An eternity passes until the nature of the situation dawns on Donald. His gaze relaxes.

I ain't 'er pimp, man.

The man squints, his body slacks and doubles over then falls back; he cackles then breaks in a bellied roar, displaying gaps in his teeth as he rises up finally—You got a cig'rette?

Donald's neck untenses. He cranes it, swivels his jaw from side to side.

No. I ain' got a cig'rette.

He backs away, yanks the handle of a door that wails as it shuts.

The man follows him to the side of the vehicle, sets two weathered mitts on the glass and leans in. Sure y'ain't got a cig'rette?

Apples, bananas, crepes.... Dumplings. Eggs...then—

—Eff—

I know!!

Fffffaaaa!

Don't tell! Fffffaaaa—

Your faaavvvorite!

Fava beans!

Good! Gee for good!

Mmmmoooommm!

OK, you do it then.

Gggggoood.... No, gggooooo.... Gooseberries! Then harrycots verts—

Good!

Then—ice cream! ...

And???

Jackfruit...

Annnnddd? Kkkkkaaan you guess what's next?

Kola nuts!

Now you add one. Ell—
Mommmmmy!
Let 'er do it on her own.
Just a li'l help—
—She don' need no hel'—
Llllliicorice!
Aintchoo smart.

Donald mums, eyes trained on the lane line, firm as a resolution after only a day, maybe two, in response to what seemed unsolvable and was in that way pernicious, with no good options. He only half hears the game Billie and Wren have been playing. Blankness rolls in every direction, flat as Donald's mood as they hurtle along Rte. 160.

Your turn, mommie!

Wren cycles through the letters, from A to L, lickety split, apples to kola nuts...licorice.

And mmmmiillliik!

Milik?

Ancient jalopies gear past in the opposite direction, some with two in the front and others packed with citizens from another country. For the most part you'd never know you were on a reservation. If the land looks otherworldly to a pair of urbanites, it wasn't so much that they were strangers in a strange land as the terrain itself provokes anxiety, bodes a struggle. It's querulous. Tetchy and demanding. Never mind foreign and in that way alluring. Yet even then, to a traveling band used to strip malls, discount stores, bowling alleys, and factories—anything but endless sky—it feels off-putting. Wren's chattiness, a reaction to the glumness weighing the air down, a funk Donald's been feeding since they left Gallup—is it a reaction to the miserly hand of the landscape? Billie mirrors the tension, beyond the usual sullenness. The three jumpy as locusts.

From the moment Donald and Wren met, on those afternoons when they stole time after school before heading home in opposite directions, they discussed coming here, not just because Wren had seen it on *Jim Doney's Adventure Road* but because Donald had read so much about it. About a history not unsimilar to that of his own people. It was the anti-South, Birthplace of Bondage, and the anti-North, that Great Disappointment—an independent country within the bounds of a patched-together experiment gone awry. For Donald the motive was as much about solidarity, standing with others dealt an equally bad hand by whites, maybe worse, if comparisons are ever apt. A pair of bad hands dealt by cheaters.

The goal was to be in this land, striated with color, deepened by rivers tracing eons. And yet in every town they stopped the story was too familiar, too close to home—never mind the terrain. Disappointment upon disappointment—the way expectations betray you. Hit you up for cash, a cigarette, a drink, though you've got nothing to give.

A cloud menaces the car as the passengers take in the dwellings on wheels, ramshackle and dotting the landscape, grouped few and far between like a series of fiefdoms without fiefs, that is if you're only counting humans, barren empires with out-buildings slatted in back, a donkey grazing idly, ribs on view.

Billie trips her way through the series of letter-words. Nnnnuttybars! she crows.

Thass a good one! Wish I had a nutty-bar right now. It's hot out here, ain' it?

The vehicle slows to a halt and a gate looms open.

Think it's worth it? Donald's pulled the car over in order to let other vehicles pass. Ahead the arms, torso, and head of a ranger hang through the opening of a booth, hand outstretched.

You willin'?

I dunno.... I mean how's it right to charge for a view? Who knew lookin' ain't free? I mean, it's jus' space.

We're foreigners to 'ese parts. Ain' you been noticin'? Sure looks like they, whoever they are, could use the cash.

I wanna see, daddy!

Who asked you, little girl?

I'm not a little girl.

Then what are you? A duck?

A mountain line.

Donald finally cracks a grin at his daughter's remark, cranes his neck this way and that, struggles to survey what lies on the other side of the entrance gate in order to determine if it merits shelling out—How can it top what we a'ready seen? Wren commences to cycle through the alphabet, and Billie lisps her way in turn, a budding word-worshiper.

A vehicle flashes his lights at Donald and the Honda advances; the decision has been made for them in a sense. They don't drive far beyond the entrance gate when the road drops down. Three pairs of eyes take in what must be the broadest view on the planet. The road extends under spikes of red pointing skyward.

Oh. My. God.

Shii-it.

Donald.

Look a' that, daddy! Billie gestures toward a row of monuments and eroded mesas, seasoned warriors, and Donald eases the car onto the shoulder to take it in. The child unbuckles her belt and scrambles out of her car-seat. She stands between driver and passenger until they decide to remove themselves from the vehicle once again. On the berm beside the road they survey what stretches ahead.

Aleast they got sumpin' for gettin' so screwed. Can't grow crap here, I'm sure. Cain't even graze a cow. But it ain't nothin', even empty like this.

An' yet, where does a view get you?

The first roof over my head after I walked free was the shell of a Valiant. In contrast these digs are luxe. The weather use to creep up on the Shagaran, southeast of Laurentine and due south of East Shagaran, there on the lake. The sweltering heat of the thaw that time, freakishly early and just ahead of a refreeze; the electrical storms so near, and again so unseasonable, shearing branches from cottonwoods, renting the warp of the roof fabric; the limbs dropped like severed hands, fingers poking through the roof. If it were me, solo, it would a been one thing. But accompanied by another that life wasn't a fit response to the query, Where will you lay your head tonight? It didn't take long to realize—was it me or Wren who drove home the point?—that it weren't fair to Molly to drag her on what turned out to be a personal, in some ways whacky journey, which didn't go the way I planned or imagined, implicating Molly in a life pocked with unknowns, overcast with the urge to split, to get as far away from the state as possible.

Still, whenever I climb the steps to this place here, fight the key, the lock, shoulder this door across the sill, I can't dodge the sense I dumped her. Dumped Molly. Nor can I escape how far I've come, from her and the Valiant both, perched like I say on the Shagaran, all the way to this tin of a dwelling on Main in beautiful Ojo Caliente. My couch-wide paradise.

If living in a sardine can in a neon mountain town isn't what I had in mind when I vowed to scramble, leave the state, go for good, on any of those rides along Liberty, pickled in silence because of Harry's state—if it wasn't what I pictured it could be worse. What does it matter if it feels like a prison sometimes? I could instead be doused by a downpour in a deep sleep, under the roof of a vehicle that found its resting place somewhere in Indiana, a state named after the ones the whites robbed, drove out, or killed.

Fifteen strides take me from bow to stern, where I come bang against a wall or a concavity, reminding me of my below-deck existence. Forget the fact that the windows strike a mutinous air, that I'm forced to retrieve them some mornings, covered in dew, drag and mask them back in place. Who cares about this whiney door that complains every time I pass? The heater that bails when you need it most. Toilet that joins the insurrection, crusts over when the temperature dips below freezing. Unlike my time on the Shagaran I have a heater. A toilet. And windows, however mutinous. Nothing's bailed for good, yet. They or any of the other nonfunctioning parts—the wiring!—which I return to service with several flicks whenever it goes AWOL. If, like I say, it wasn't what I pictured back in Laurentine maybe the flaw's in me, my imagination, what it means to futurize a world, which is another way of saying flesh out a ghost. What's more, to all those naysayers—to wit, one Harry, Florrie, or Diana, whose role in life is to query every choice I make—to them I can only counter doubts by pointing out that this is a good sight better than anything they offered. Better than Harry's bottled replies or Florrie's ices, if that's the standard. I got air in my tires and gallons in the tank. I can take off anytime.

All of which is to say when you've taken your leave of everything and everyone, settled in foreign parts, alien not just to you but everyone you left behind, the trouble isn't too little me-space but too much. I mean if you lived in a telephone booth on the busiest corner in Manhattan you'd still hear your voice echo in a void if you know no one. And yet I have no complaints, no matter the rudeness of my guest, who's less impressed than me with my newfound wealth.

You live *aquí* amigo?!

Wha's wrong with it.

Nuthin'. Supongo. Pero—

—Well?

Well, ...jeesh!

Jeesh, what? Did you see my rock garden? I planted it myself. The chamomile, poppies—and columbines! I draw the door shut, back down the stairs, nudge Tommy out of my way, point to my handiwork, which I set about the day I moved in, quelling the rebellion of weeds in this slip of green that serves as my Eden. Home for a Fiat and me. All mine, in a manner of speaking. So long's I don't forget the rent.

I'll take it, I told Jeanette, the landlady, soon's as I saw it. It'll be my home. Mine, mine, mine. All mine. How much more could a body want? I didn't bother to unpack before laying out the rock garden, establishing what I'd look on, under the picture window, such as it is. From which I spotted you as you, Tommy, you lout, drove up. Only to trash my handiwork. I mean, I gathered the rocks myself, transported the soil from where the skirt around the trailer broke and left an opening, there between the back of the trailer and the motel wall it abuts, stucco crumbling. I sorted the sedum and rerooted it, here among the rocks, interspersing chamomile, the closest I came to something cultivatable, watering it all with a soda bottle, one of the many chucked under my living quarters by earlier tenants, who knows how long ago?

Well? I s'pose es un jardín of sorts. Pero—

—What d'you mean you s'pose?

37

I know well how appearances can trip a person up, the way people mistake outside for in. Marking my surprise, dismay, not to say hurt, Tommy leaves his disparagements and commences a different tune, once I strong-arm the door over the sill, letting the two of us in.

Past the gate the vehicle dips, overlooks monuments intrepid as Native women defying time, temperature, and what-not, wearing with the elements, ogled by outsiders passing through as if staking a claim by their sheer numbers, accosted by a dry wind over ancestral soil, as though trying to unburden the locals of land and soul both. Still the monuments stand, rocks carved by wind and water, again like women teasing a life from stone, millenniums before white people became white people, before they tattooed others with a name.

A fiction.

What a view!

It's pretty, I'll give you that. But somehow it don' seem right.

What don' seem right? How could anything be wrong? I mean, the colors! The space. Like it goes forever, in every direction, without a thing on it.

Heh-heh. May be. But it ain' empty. Wha'd'you call them homes over there, this road? Like a serpent about t' strike.

A road don't count. No one lives on a road.

Cars do. People. That ain't nothin'.

But we're all just passin' through.

We are. But the cars are constant. People too. A presence that don't stop. If this is my land, I'm thinking I gotta accept the fact that strangers live with me three-sixty-five days a year whether I wan' 'em or not. Like this valley is no longer my land. Like they almos' own it more'n me.

Well we paid. So they're gettin' somethin'.

Judas money.

Looky, mommy! A pony! Can we stop?

Looks like someone's yard, so maybe not little girl.

I'm not a girl.

Wheels rumble over rubble, prodded by another vehicle tailing the bumper. Donald eases the car right so it can slip by. Billie persists, I wanna pet the pony, I wanna pet the pony, I wanna pet the pony, daddy!

It's someone's home, girly girl.

You think someone lives in that? Looks like that ol' Harley ain't been rid in a cent'ry.

They ain't been aroun' that long. Have they?

Y' know what I mean.

Once the three set foot to turf the terrain opens into a maze of grama grass, scrub cactus, and cholla, forcing the trio to their toes. Again Donald expresses reservations about nosing around.

An animal don' stay put 'less someone look after 'im.

Well that someone's fallin' on the job—look how thin she is! You can count the ribs.

That's 'cause there ain' nothin' t' eat.

Can I pet 'im?

Wren tells Donald to hold onto Billie. She dances to the car over the spiny terrain, and when she returns she holds out her hand.

Give 'er this.

Billie takes the carrot, one that's been sitting in cooler-water for days, succeeding several rounds of ice from a daisy chain of gas stations stretching many hundreds of miles, a snack Wren said would be better than the crap you find on the road, from which she was bound and determined to spare Billie, in a battle she lost. Junk food and Donald prevailed. In part because, as he argued, We're on veecation—. Time t' splurge! It ain't gonna kill 'er. He averred they both grew up on a diet a crap—An' look how we turned out. Let 'er have 'er fun.

The animal moves away as the child approaches, until she extends the orange root, a hue way too primary for this landscape, if you discount the evening sky. Her hooves advance around a patch of opuntia.

Here! Billie advances, followed by Wren. Hold it out futher. Grab it toward the back so she don' bite.

The animal nears and the child loses nerve, flopping the thing to the ground. The three stand watching as sturdy lips surround the thing, work magic on it. It could be day-glo lavender or lime green it seems so out of place. Until it disappears.

Wren hands Billie another and suggests she hold it firmer this time.

She ain' gonna hurt you.

Let 'er work it out.

Well she gotta try.

Billie takes the carrot and wields it like a weapon as she sheeps her way forward, toward an animal who also appears unsure, stepping slowly toward the child despite the fact she enjoys a size advantage. The more the gap is narrowed the greater Billie's anxiety grows, and once again she appears on the verge of tossing the thing down, backing away, until Wren intervenes, firms her grip. She muscles the thing still as the animal works it with powerful teeth and jaws, snapping off pieces, nibbling almost to Billie's hand and then stopping until it's set free.

She can't a eaten in a month. Poor thing.

Can I help you?

Almost in unison Donald, Wren, and Billie start, swivel their heads in the same direction like a row of prairie dogs. Before Donald can get a word out Wren is explaining the situation, starting from where they're from, where they've been, where they're headed, and how the three of them ended up here, separated from their vehicle on what is no doubt, they now realize, private land.

It's so beautiful here.

Is this your property? I hope you don' mind.

A woman peers at the trio and says nothing in response. Her skin is the color of the landscape and mildly crevassed.

You live here? Donald repeats. He holds his hand out and the other responds in kind.

In a manner a speakin'.

Wren opines the horse looks a li'l underfed.

She ain't a horse. And what business is it of yours? She's standin', ain' she?

Above the zipper on the woman's jeans a buckle flashes in the afternoon sun. It's dotted with blue like the sky.

Is this yer house?

You call that a house?

Is it a trailer?

It's my property if that's what you mean.

It's very nice.

The woman lowers her head, eyes Wren suspiciously. She lifts the front rim of her hat long enough to let air flow over her hair, then rests it again.

Which way you headed?

Donald is the directions man, and he responds in the short term, not their ultimate destination, toward the Forest City.

I need t' get t' Bluff.

I don' know where that is.

It's on yer way.

The three follow the woman as she paces back to the trailer. They watch as she disappears inside the door then survey the terrain around the dwelling, such as it is, the field of metal, wood, and glass that emanates like space debris. An automobile's been disassembled, its parts strewn like offerings to the gods. Donald instructs Billie and Wren to take their positions in a pair of bucket seats, plopped willy–nilly atop the ground, so he can snap their pics. They stand out amid the array of other bits and bobs that have been discarded before a hogback in the distance, framing the trailer. The two oblige Donald who orders them not to smile.

Who could a ever dreamed a this?

Put on your stubborn face! he instructs Billie, who struggles to draw a long jaw. He orders, No smiles! Which is the most expedient way to coax a grin, in her and Wren both.

In the cross-hairs Donald frames the duo in such a way it appears they're time travelers in the cab of a comet, sailing through time, drawing a tail in their wake. After he's snapped the image the three survey the trash more closely, five-gallon buckets and dried paint tins. They discover rolls of insulation, strips of aluminum, assorted engine parts. Trailer parts too. All have lost their shine in the unrelenting sun. There are pipe fittings and a rusted transmission, half-buried decades ago, and hundreds of other objects the uses of which neither Wren nor Donald can guess.

I suppose when you got no neighbors....

Still. In a landscape like this—

—OK ready.

The woman makes a beeline to the car while the others suss where their shoes will land. She jackknifes the door and slips in, setting her bag between the seats, then rolls her window down.

Y'all might wanna mind th' rattlers.

October 18, 19—

Molly, I swear. If you were here I'd
know. What to do. I'd read your eyes,
tell the ethical from the lowdown way.
You always knew what to do and say. Until
I hightailed it outta there, let you
down. Me a all people.

I did my best. Stuck it out long's
I could until my guts started to rot.
Brain. Heart most a all. Turned to jelly
by the side of the river. I felt it in my
groin. Everything uncoiling. Drying up.
You watch it happen, so you get it more'n
anybody. Why I had to — plus, would you a
really liked it here?

Be honest.

Now here I am, in the clouds it's so
high, this guy constantly next to me, the
air so thin I can hardly breath at times.
The way is uncertain as the air, Moll,
when mist snakes through the valley.
They call this god's country, but to be
honest it can be hell. A fallen state —
what did god ever do but rob me a the
ones I love. Including you. And after how
many years? Who knew you can be fragile
as a eggshell. The two a us conjoined
for the most part — sometimes I used to
think it was you that everyone liked,
that they just tolerated me. Everyone
thought you were soooo cute, a cutie
patootie Cin used to say, the quiet one
whose expressions I translated for them,
a language only Wren an' me knew. Except
the look you shot at me as I drove away.
That was new — I couldn't make hide or
hair of it. I did my best not to look
back — I worried I'd turn to salt, there
at the wheel. Turn to tears is more like

43

it. But I couldn't help myself. You were
running along the car, trying to bark
my attention, and I was yelling at you
to get back — Leave me alone! Forget
about me! For good!
  Like that's possible.
  I'm still trying to figure whose
interest I had at heart. You must
a followed me a mile, shadowed by
Harry trying to snag you, yammering
something, limping farther and farther
behind. I saw you, but I didn't get the
look. Not until today when Wren called
to say you passed.
  At leas' you're with me now, I'm sure.
Come all the way from the Forest City,
to these mountains, this tin can, and
me. We got things to discuss.

Just as the road relaxes after a series of bends, a wall
appears. It stretches to the ether, the kind of barrier
bigots fantasize erecting, high enough to keep foreigners
out. This-here wall is impossible to circumvent, either by
climbing, catapulting, ramming, or tunneling. It's too airy,
dense, and ubiquitous for one, the kind of structure you
can't escape, and it's moving in our direction fast. Straight
for the vehicle.
  What in the world?
  Damn!
  I never seen anythin' like it in my life! Not on *Jim
Doney's Adventure Road* for sure.
  It sure is somethin'!
  Sh'we keep driving? Stop? Or turn around?
  Let's stop, mommy!
  To do what?

To see.

The kid's right. No sense tryin' t' outrun it. Ain't gonna work.

It's the first words out of the passenger's mouth since we've been driving. Donald maneuvers the vehicle to the shoulder, and a pick-up, trailed by a caravan like a line of ants, whisks impatiently by. After a short time another car whizzes past, then another. The silence inside and outside the vehicle is audible. So is the advancing darkness, thick as fear. If only they could direct the car perpendicularly, flee not along this two-lane affair, south to north, now a frontage road to a mobile fortification advancing steadily over prickly pear, sage, and cholla. If they could only head east, to outrun the inevitability of what's coming.

Best t' cover yer noses with sumpin.

But we're in th' car.

Dust don't care. Nothin' gonna stop it gettin' in. We all gonna be covered 'fore this is done, even in here. Better get that thing covered too. Lest you don't mind a broken cam'ra.

Donald has slipped the thing from under the seat and is clicking at a rolling red cloud, advancing at a clip, a bumper of dust as broad as the horizon. Cars fly by in an effort to outpace it, but it's gaining.

How did people do it before cars? Outside? How'd they survive a century ago?

A hunderd years ain't nothin'.

Wha' that mean?

The passenger doesn't reply.

Fine powder, the advance guard, strays through the windows as the wind kicks up and envelopes the car. Donald checks his window and Wren does the same, cutting off the breeze despite the heat. Wren pulls a Kleenex from the box beside her and instructs Billie to breathe through it.

How often this happen?

Anough.

What d'y'all do?

What d'you think?

What about the horsey mommy??

Yeah, what will she do?

Burro ain't no dummy. Nothin' she ain't seen b'fore.

The ruckus of dust and debris now swallows the vehicle. Cars ditch the idea of driving, line the shoulder in front and back of the rental car, emergency lights flashing. A layer of powder settles on everything this side of the windshield—dashboard, upholstery, hair, and clothing, lashes and brows, aging everyone—before another wave slips in. Billie has her nose pinched tight and coughs from breathing through her mouth. Wren holds the tissue and tells her to take air in through her nostrils. In no time the world inside is washed in red.

Welcome t' Naabeehó Bikéyah.

Huh?

The woman peers at Donald then the others and cracks a smile, toggling into a laugh. Her tongue flashes pink in an otherwise red world, and Donald can't seem to stop focusing on it. It fascinates him, and now he too begins to laugh at the commonality of pinkness, until he and the stranger land in a fit, lips red as pomegranates, faces checking the two in the back then glancing at each other, breaking in a roar, another round of cackling, tittering, and full-boiled laugh, as though they'd stumbled on a truism, hilarious as they always are, not limited by geography or origin. The woman uses her bandana not as a mask but a hankie to blow her nose and cough up phlegm, then places another over her face below the eyes.

When the darkness arrives for real it appears there's no outside. Powder lighter than air, dust, and soot infiltrate the space, continue their assault, breech the seals of doors and windows, the undercarriage—grit finds a way. Billie begins to cough again and Wren pulls another tissue from the box, holding it over mouth and nose.

Breathe through this.

What d' we do??

Stay put.

Just as she speaks a car careens by, flashing hazard lights in panic, blinking on and off, the headlights bootless.

Bilagáana.

Donald cracks a grin. I don't know what that means. But I like you.

Billie coughs yet again and Wren places another clean tissue, such as it is, over her face, along with her own.

Take one.

Donald places a Kleenex over his nostrils, and Wren remarks, How long this gonna last?

Tommy lets the door flap against the aluminum, a man on a mission. I dreamt of you again last night, Mollykins, as I do most nights since I left, more now since I got Wren's call. I almos' wish she wouldn't a done it, phoned from the middle a nowhere, not a minute after hanging up with Auntie Midge. Even in a wakeful state I find myself thinking a you, never mind the circumstances, you and me—as it should be, Mollykins. Leashed to my dreams and waking hours both with so much time to think, about you and me, our life together, chained as we were, and then he comes barking in. Jerking me from my thoughts. Lording the space and filling it with scent, bulk too, head bruising the ceiling. He ogles me but doesn't speak, he nor I, until—

—Is it Jack?

The sweetness of chamomile in the air, that and Tommy's sweat, while I'm steeped in a potpourri of rotting thoughts.

About propriety, number one. And two, how he found my hide-away. He says he parked the car a ways away, complains it ain't easy to find a place with no address. Just a tire dip off the road with cat-food tins strewn here and there. For a while he goes on complaining, accusing me of not being very specific when I told him where to find me that day, if he was interested, and now he drops the subject, just like that, plants himself in front of me, my brain stalled.

His hand finds my legs and under-parts. He works intently and, granted, knowingly at this point given our experience, never mind he hasn't mastered my name. Still he's into discovery, under my T-shirt, belt, jeans, and socks, filching my second self until I'm perched on the sofa and like you, dearly departed, naked to the very skin. Neither of us speaks. I remain motionless while hands, fingers, lips, and breath do their thing, plead with me to join in.

In fact it doesn't seem to matter where my mind is, whether I make it easy or hard, fast or slow, which in this circumstance, thinking of you, Molly, what you would counsel in the situation, whether to go with it or demur. Nothing hinders Tommy, his appetite. As though he's exercising a right, the same one that licensed him to barge through the door behind me, derailing my thoughts.

A tussle ensues, and I'm lost, a doe in the grass, in part because my emotions are on edge, the thoughts streaking through my head as his hands caper about. I view the unfolding as a spectator, the memories, Molly, not only in my head but body too, the same one that Tommy engages to the nth degree. Here's a guy who gets commitment, focus, and yet his efforts are directed toward a facsimile of me, a likeness he's trying to breathe life into, as though giving life to marble, speaking earnestly now, desperately too, on a day in the throat of Indian summer. Lips and beard abrade my skin, peal me like a tangerine—

—Tommy stops.

You sorta seem into it? And sorta not. I ain't sure.

Don' mind me.

Seguro?

Huh.

You sure?

Yeah—I'm into it.

Pienso que solo una parte de ti.

Huh?

I hear my neighbor's pick-up crunch the gravel then come to a stop. I listen as the engine cuts and a door creaks open. He slips in, followed by another, and I can't help craning my neck a bit, far enough to spy a woman. What is it now, one o'clock? Two in the afternoon? And yet here he is, back from Safeway, toting a six-pack and someone different than the one that left this morning. As they slip into the darkness a Persian gray shoots out and rests on the landing, licking her paw. She suns, in no apparent hurry to be anywhere else but outside—she peers at a cloudless sky. Two hands raise the sash beside the door and slip a beer can under to prop it. Black Sabbath trails from there to here, a sound that plays on Tommy, inducing him to leave chatter behind as though it were a waste anyway— he returns to where he left off, moving in sync to *Heaven and Hell*.

I wonder where I am. If sometimes it's best to pass on being romeoed, even when the one that comes for you does it so unassumingly, say in an army-issue coat. Or toffee skin, all over. And yet again maybe sometimes it's best to seize the moment, act now, think later. Otherwise why not halt these shenanigans, call them off in order to take things a tad slower, enough to learn each other's names to start with—and then what? Forfeit a second chance?

Over a formality?

Too many questions. So I play along. It's difficult to tell who's having the better time, this brown beauty or the pair next-door. Given the narrowness of the corridor between us, a pick-up wide, we four are mixing business, sharing notes in real time like a form of recitative. To complicate things I'm gunning to figure what stems from the heart versus what's mere instinct, what lives for the moment but'll be curtained in time, like the sparrow the Persian left on my stoop two days ago. And yet can I even think about any of that under the circumstances? I mean, I'm juggling enough, what with the news about Molly and this other story breaking over me.

You don't waste no time.

La vida es corta. ¿Te gusta?

Huh?

Tommy's sweating, his chest heaving on autopilot as he slips into a rhythm, deals with the hand he's got, the George-Washington part of me that can't tell a lie, whether it's enjoying the party or not, whether my partner has solidified my attentions, riveting him to me, or whether they've scattered like circus cats.

For chrise sake don' make me stop.

Maybe Molly's spirited herself into this guy, come to comfort me in my grief in her bardo phase, indicating, It's gonna be OK my boy—life goes on. I mean who would've thunk he'd return today of all days? After assuring he'd find me—y pronto. Yet how long's it been? Like a fool I hung out waiting. For how many weeks?

—You OK amigo?—

—You tell me.

Not 'til Wren called from the desert or wherever they are, after I'd all but given up, does he come packing in—

Maybe can we stop for just a minute?—Lemme catch my breath?—

But Tommy's on a mission, trailing momentum, working the moment—unlike me he knows his own heart, my throat, saliva mingling—Me gusta, niño. Mucho. His lips hover over mine before going in again. He has me stretched on the couch at the head of the trailer. He lifts himself above me and peers toward the dwelling next-door.

I think we got a audience.

That's such a pretty bracelet.

The woman reaches for a tumbler, supersized and ruby-plastic, some of its contents having been spilled by the waitress as she plopped it down. Water puddles on the table. She reaches into the icy mix and extracts a lemon, which she drops on the formica. Sun streams through glass and water both, rosing her wrist, the silver band tooled with floral motifs and studded with stones that shade purple in the light.

Where'd you get it?

Where'd you think?

I have no idea.

Wren, think about it.

You made that? Wren's eyes widen.

Noooo, I didn' make it. It's from a friend. No big deal.

But it is! I've never seen anything like it!

A blond interrupts, What can I git y'all?

Do you have anything without meat? Donald shifts his weight on the banquette, gazes at a ridge spanning the length of the horizon. He takes in the view that appears empty and jam packed. With his middle finger he brushes off dust from the tip of his nose, leftover from the storm. He peers at the waitress almost apologetically.

Well.... Let's see. Wren holds her menu open and the woman runs the butt of her pen down the options. Don' look like much. I could have them make up a bowl a rice an' beans for y'.

Are the beans cooked with stock?

What kind a stock?

Chicken or beef. Pork?

I'll ask. The waitress rolls her eyes upwards then disappears, and the woman across from Wren remarks, You ain't one a them are you?

One a what?

Loosey-gooseys.

I hope not—not sure what that is.

Y' know. One a them.

There's pork in th' beans.

I'll take jus' rice in that case. Maybe a egg on top?

You wan' a egg on toppa a bowl a rice.

That'd be great. Thanks. Same fer her.

Billie complains she wants a hamburger, and Wren replies, You'll have what I'm having.

Donald remarks, What's the big deal? Let 'er.

The waitress stands, her pen poised, and Wren reiterates, We'll have the same thing.

The woman seated across orders the Sky's-the-Limit burger, and Donald proclaims he'll have the same. As the waitress walks away Wren rests her cheek on the back of her hand, gazing out the window. She goes quiet then rouses herself—That burger's named after you! How in the world did anyone ever make that? she queries, looking at the woman's wrist.

Take too long t'explain.

Did she make it at the place we met?

You kiddin'? Can't make nothin' there. It's me and my dad's place, though he stays in Kayenta mos'ly. Comes back t' check on the burro, only one left. I crash when I'm passin' through.

Where'd you live?

Wren—thousan' questions. Skye ogles Donald who lets out a laugh ending in a hack, the kind you hear after someone's ingested dust.

No worries. I live in the City Different.

You got a car?

Let it go.

I ain't got nothin' t' hide. Skye takes a swill from the giant tumbler and taps it back on the table. Long story. My father stole it basically.

So sorry. He's right—it's none a my business.

Tried to say it was his, that he bought it and let me borra it, but I paid every cent. Ain't my problem he ran his in a ditch. Then he invites me t' Kayenta, only to tell me I'm drivin' his car an' he wants it back.

That's a bummer. What kind a father—

—Best to zip it.

Now I'm stuck having t' figure out a way home, like I'm fifteen an' hitchin' again.

You hitch-hiked? Ever go cross-country?

Ain't you?

Sorry that happened.

He's up there in years. Mind's goin'. Or he's rotten. Ain't sure.

I wouldn't understand. I had a peach of a dad.

He die or somethin'?

In a way.

Can't do nothin' about parents.

Ain't that the truth.

What about you, mister?

What about me?

You got a father?

No. I come from a rock.

I figured s'much. Donald lets out an uncomfortable laugh.

53

I like you, Skye. Are you married?

You two?

The waitress arrives, a flying saucer hovering over her shoulder, which she sets on a stand. She passes dishes around and Donald remarks she mixed up his and Skye's orders. She looks flustered for a moment, checks the order, then dons a perturbed look, juts her lower lip and blows bangs from her eyes—

—Just kiddin', Donald replies, but the waitress fails to crack a smile.

This guy's a man after my own heart, suggests Skye, lifting a stack of bun, meat, and toppings. Yer funny, she blurts, mouth full, the sound muffled as she chews.

We are married.

For good or for ill. Now Donald takes up a burger and bites. God I was starved.

So it's like that, huh?

Like what?

Like you two.

What's that mean? And what about you?

Why is it people always go there first? Like the most important thing to know about somebody is if they're—

I didn't mean—

—I mean, of a thousand, maybe million questions a person could ask, first thing come out is—

Again, I didn't mean—

—Am I married? Yes an' no—it's complicated. Not sure we would if we could.

No need to—

—Trust me, I been there. A couple times.

Sorry to hear.

'Cause you think marriage is the only way?

No, 'cause it didn't work. More'n once, as you said.

I blame men—Skye looks at Donald, who draws a long face all of a sudden. It's all your fault.

Think I'm gonna defend?—

—What's life like out here?

Wren—

—Where's out here?

—Out here, out here. It's so open, so enormous.

Donald shoots a look.

Leave me alone—I can ask whatever I want. I mean here. Where we met you.

You mean on the res?

I mean, it's so pretty. Rough too.

Oh, it's real pretty. What's it like where you're from?

Where do I begin?

My point azackly.

Billie tugs at Donald's arm, resting on the table. Can I have some?

Ask your mommy.

Why you goin' t' Bluff if you live in—?

Perched beside her on the banquette, next to the picture window, Billie appears crestfallen, mutters to herself, oblivious to adults. She points at the ravens bouncing in the lot at the edge of an expanse, scavenging left-overs diners discarded, food and wrappers, cans, bottles, and trash that's migrating across the terrain.

If I said I was goin' all the way to the City Different you'd a said it's too far. Bluff's a stone's throw—everybody gotta go there.

We can take you! Can't we? To the City Different.

Donald douses a fry in a pool of red and brings it to his lips. I never been, so why not?

That a make things a helluva lot easier. I never imagined I'd be 'thout wheels.

I succumb, go with the wave topsy-turvying me, legs high. I do my best to adjust to the nature of things, a chain of events, leaving me to contemplate again how I got here and what it means. Circumstances throw you. You can stand up—true—declare enough's enough already with this depraved state of affairs! But if I can muscle it without being bruised; if a slice of me relishes it deep down; if the one getting his Irish up is burdened with scruples millenniums old; if people that haven't been in a situation like this can never understand what it's like; if swallowing scruples is my other mantra, dodging that hook; and most important if I and this lout here consent to the thing—then scruples be damned. Even on the heels of a death. Maybe Molly would want me to suspend grief for a time because timing is everything in life, and as I say you don't get a second chance—is there ever a convenient time for death? Wouldn't Molly want me to seize the moment, this guy's body, yield to another kind of death—I mean would death have deterred her if she had the chance? To nab a piece of meat?

I yield. To this guy's athleticism, his physique, raining sweat, imposing himself on the air in the room, my nostrils, as though he were born with a knack for dominating space, and me, lurching us toward a kind of completion.

When can we do this again?

Well—we're not even—

—I'm lovin' this—

—Can we chat?—I'm still panting, though not as heavily as him. For a minute?

—See me leavin'?

The chorus next-door works toward a thickening. This woman's got a set of pipes compared to the one yesterday who barely sounded a peep. He does too this time around, as though he's trying to outdo her. I'd like to join in, belt out something of my own, but maybe that ship has sailed.

—There's no rush.

Great.

Relax, niño.

I'm too—

—You can never be too relaxed. Pero—

On the side of the cupboard over Tommy's shoulder hangs a photo under glass of Peacoat and Molly that time on the lake. Literally on it, perched on the jagged surface, frozen, taken during a wild-hair trek across the ice to Canada, at least that was the plan. A black-and-white world, it's miles removed from the colored universe I'm tight with at the moment, Tommy's face, chest, shoulder, and neck, hemming me near, a world suffused with flesh. The figures in the flat world inside the frame, more vital to me now than ever in a sense. It hasn't escaped me that Peacoat's been watching— me, us—from the corner, next the sink, two vacancies following our every move, the view he adopted when we crossed the state line, a face and presence that persists, a form gelled out in a perpetual thawing, as though you could keep the past from defrosting. It's him and Molly, there in the rectangle, hanging in this closet of a room, alive but in a different way, secreted from everyone but me, rendering me half alive compared to Tommy, who's torso presses robustly now, his lips plying my neck and cheek in an avalanche of kisses, unaware of the grisly specter past his shoulder, the scene under glass, two figures having come to life and aggregated around me. The vital dead. The moribund scene under my skin, in my chest. Pine persists through the window along with the ruckus from next-door, where they seem to have concluded kicking up a fuss, or killed it, after conjuring a spirit the way Tommy's attempting to conjure me. I can't figure a way around it, haunted as I am, an image framing the unknowable.

Tommy lowers himself as in benediction then raises his head. Outside I hear a car scrape to a stop. Gravel gnaws at tires. A door creaks and slams shut.

Could this be it??

You tell me!

Looks like th' pitcher.

Ain't that th' new car?

How would I know when I never saw it?

You saw the pitcher.

I heave Tommy away, and he falls on the floor.

Up!

What gives?

Up, up, up! Ay-sap!

I don't wait for the guy to catch the drift of what's happened, is happening—of all things! I spring to action, don much of what trails across the floor, including Tommy's tee, forcing him to stuff himself in mine—stomach hairs showing over the buttons of his jeans. We start at the inevitable knock.

Jake??

Shit, shit, shit.

Shit, what?

The door swings open on its own or some other accord. Wren! Donald! L'il Billie!

As his twin angles the door wide, she remarks, Did we catch you at a bad time?

I wouldn't necessarily call it tha—

—This is my friend—um—

I peer at Tommy for help, his head framed by the door and the side of the trailer next-door. My gaze draws to the hairy field extending from the bottom of the tee, reminding, inviting, promising. I motion for Tommy to stand closer, shift away so the three—oh no, it's four—can pile up from the landing and inside, in a caravan. The look on Tommy's face suggests an urge to shoot toward the bedroom at the back, climb the mountain of books and slip out the mutinous window, as though the fuzz had arrived.

Wren and Donald, trailed by Billie and a stranger, single-file into my living-slash-kitchen-slash-dining-room and instantly we're a crowd at capacity.

This is Skye! We met her in Mon'ment Valley. We've been having a grand time.

The woman tips her Stetson and peers around, sizing the place.

Place looks older'n mine and my Daddy's, if that's possible. Third the size. Short people only. Indeed, her, Tommy's, and Donald's heads scratch the ceiling. I peer at Wren, feel her eyes scanning me, reading with the accuracy of a twin. She glosses the situation, critically I fear, tracking the pheromones in the air, glancing at Tommy then at me, sussing the tee situation. I do my best to project the message, Later. Maybe never?

We interrupted you.

Again I take a stab at introductions, not just between Tommy and the newcomers, but for all intents and purposes between Tommy and me as well.

He volunteers, Me llamo Tomás. I'm Tommy.

Names jump like magpies on power-lines that sag low, looks exchanged when no one knows what to say. Wren tots up the situation, and Donald's tots up Wren's expression, and now everyone seems loath to speak, everyone but Tommy paradoxically. The air introduces him, a part of him they may have never known otherwise, a side everyone but Billie comprehends. I pipe up, ask if the latter wants to see my rock garden, and she opts to go along, but only after being nudged by Wren.

59

I gotta get on the road.

Don't you wanna stay? A couple days? We can take you home after.

We would a been here a lot sooner if it weren't for this guy drivin' the way he did—Skye pokes Donald, elbows him in the stomach. Thanks but I gotta go. You got my address. Don' hesitate t' stop. An' give my info t' this guy, indicating me with a lift of a hat rim, though it may have been Tommy she meant, or him and me both.

Go with Uncle Jake to see the garden. I'll come in a minute—I wanna see th' place. Min' if I look around?

Actually, yes....

Ain't much t' see, Tommy remarks, tugging at the hem of his too-short tee, attempting to cover the hair around the navel. Lotta books.

Can I get a glass a water?

Jake, you go with the kid. I'll get 'im one, assures Tommy. You wan' one too—is it Reina?

Wren.

The last thing I wanna do is leave these three, but Skye throws the door open and Billie tugs at my hand as she aims to descend the stairs.

Feel free to stop by anytime, I comment.

You too. Your sister's got my address.

I watch as the woman ascends the road, past the trailer next-door, two over from my neighbor and his present lover. She doesn't waste a minute before extending her thumb toward the line, unbothered by a train of cars filing by. She turns around and proceeds toward 1-70, as if she were planning to walk to Eldorado. I'm below the front window, pointing at wild poppies while taking in the chatter inside the trailer, the moment souls meet across a dividing line—I perceive the engine of sociability lubricating, kicking into gear so long as Wren's in the mix.

They're adults. I can't worry about it. What is and isn't passing without me, too much to fathom and out of my control. I look to a child I don't know, sprouted by my other self and for that reason my own flesh and blood. I tell myself she's too young to remember this, so I'm safe from mucking things up. I hope. And besides, even if the moment were to impress itself on her in an eidetic sense, how much could it register beyond a random, shadow image, without language to color it, footnote the moment your twin, her husband, and their child meet their bespoke uncle, out of his element, in the throes of entertaining a gentleman caller bent on making an impression, full talent on display, on the heels of a death that hovers over things the way only Molly could, asserting herself despite the fact she never spoke a word, not in any conventional way.

I choose to let it go, for now, focus on what's before me. I realize I don't know a thing about child-speak—talk about alien-life. I may have been there once but blotted it out, as though nature designed it that way—I don't know whether to baby-talk her the way Florrie does or offer her a drink à la Harry.

We saw the Gran' Canyun, Jake!

Did you see flowers like these?

Uhn-uhn.

Did you see any other kind?

Bed-der.

Inside, Donald bro's Tommy, a thing I recognize having been bro'ed myself, including on the banks of the Shagaran in one of my less-than-stellar moments.

Oh—better?! OK....What kind a flowers did y' see?

Billie looks at the ground while Wren slips into gear.

Do you live in Ojo Caliente too? queries Wren. Is that how you two met?

Pickly pear.

Is that a plant—?—oh yes! they're real pretty.
Oh god, no.
You mean the flower or the fruit?
I live in the Mile High City.
Flar.
You just up for the day then?
What other kind a flower did you see?
I guess you could put it that way.
Injun pain' brush.
That's another pretty one. What else?
Does your family live there too?
Bellflar.
We have some of them around here's well.
Wren, leave the guy alone. Stop with th' inquisition.
But not here.
Sorry—no harm meant.
No hay problema.
Huh? How did you and Jake meet then?

In my head I can see Wren telegraphing to Donald, the way she does when she's been shushed. I take Billie's hand.

I guess it's not much of a garden after all, not compared to what you saw. Did you like it?

What?

The trip. Where-all did you go?

Our feet echo on the metal stairs as we clomp inside.

Mon'men Balley.

The others go silent when we enter. Why don' we go for a bite? You must be starved.

Speakin' a starved, you should a seen some a the animals we passed.

On the range?

Yeah an' no. Not the range really, though not penned up. Not roamin' neither. More like scratchin' an existence. In all that heat.

This one wanted t' take 'em all home.
We met a *burra*!
Too bad Skye couldn' a joined us.

A plate of clear glass rests atop a weaving on the table at Las Dos Hermanas. Raw hues jump like the paintings on the walls. Color is the theme it seems, a surfeit of it in naked tones, not just in the visual but the aural and olfactory sense. I doubt there's anything like this in the Forest City, Wren opines.

I pass this place on my way to the freeway, but it's off-limits the way all restaurants are after the outlay of cash for the Fiat. It nearly wiped me out, shrank my options. I know better than to hang around the center of Ojo Caliente, if you can call it that, where a palm is always upturned and extended. So I drive by, until today. Here we are, south of the border, or the Ojo version of it. I sit kitty-corner to Donald and butt-next to Tommy, stranger and intimate both.

Do you believe we're here?!
Wren, it's just a restaurant.
I mean here-here! With Jake! In Ojo Calyentie! Ever since you left I knew we had t' come. We wanted to make it a s'rprise.

She's been planning this. Donald points his thumb in hitchhike fashion toward Wren.

You definally surprised me! The both a us.
Pero todo está bien—it's all good! Tommy shoots Jake a look, either to scold or pull him into their first, private joke. Excitement. Razor's edge.

A waitress approaches and sets a plastic cup first in front of Wren, then Billie and Jake, followed by Tommy and then Donald. Mariachi music swells past the void of looks around the table as the waitress sets down a basket of chips and salsa, followed by menus. Eyes burrow in options, everyone's but Jake's, who offers Billie the lemon wedge from his glass. She sucks on it and her eyes bulge; her mouth crests in a frown.

Drink water, that'll help, advises Wren.

Leave 'er alone—how else she gonna learn? Why you do dat, little girl?

I'm not a little girl.

When the waitress comes for Wren's order, she begs a bit more time—Can you take theirs first. The server backs away and circles around to where I'm seated.

I need more time, too.

Tommy volunteers he'd like los tacos al pastor. Carne todavía viva. Still kicking. Donald passes his gaze from top to bottom over the menu, then closes it. I'd like the same. Whatever he said. His eyes were traveling the options, ones we don't encounter in the Forest City, on a menu or anywhere. The waitress scribbles on her pad as she moves back toward Wren.

I don' ea' meat.

OK.

You got anythin' without?

The woman extends her neck, cocks it—I need t' ask. She disappears, and after an eternity she returns. How 'bout bean tacos?

Sounds great. The waitress is poised to write it on her pad until Wren queries, Are they cooked in stock?

The waitress clears her throat. Without saying anything she pads away, through the double doors then back.

In stock. A course.

I guess I'll take a salad. And plain rice. Same for her.

Billie traces imaginary lines along the colors in the fabric under glass. Red, green, purpo, green, red, yel-lo, brown....

The waitress circles toward me. You ready?

I'll take the same's them two.

How you want your meat cooked?

No, I mean them. Salad an' rice.

That makes it easy, Wren enthuses. Doesn' it, ma'am?

So no carne.

Huh?

Tommy turns in his chair. Talk about gringos.

Weeelllll ....

If the shoe fits.

We don' got nothin' like this where we're from.

Don' even get me started, quips Donald. The two a them. A couple a rabbits.

Who's makin' you eat anything?

No carne, amigo? Verda'? Could a fool me.

Out of the blue Molly comes to me. Her and me, camped on the Shagaran, how she'd probably say it's impossible to survive without it. Meat, that is. The larded kind that Florrie used to slip her when I wasn't looking, causing her to thicken around the waist, so much so that the difference was noticeable when Wren and Donald paid me a visit, after she'd gone without her lardoons and everything else for— how long was it? Forty days or forty years? Wren scolded, said it was too much, that the two of us were gonna starve. And yet here we are—I am. Though not my Moll, who went back to meat soon's we returned to Laurentine.

Well I don' eat certain kinds a meat. Not the animal kin'. I eye Tommy.

You don' eat no meat, period. You an' Wren both.

In the old days they used to call veggies meat.

No carne, amigo? Verdad?

Huh?

Is it true?

It is.

How boring.

Tell me 'bout it.

It's complicated, Wren opines.

No it ain't. God made animals t' eat.

We made it this far. Ain't we Jake?

I push back my chair and the legs complain atop the floorboards. I rise up, slide my chair under the table then head for the doors marked Caballeros and Mujeres and pick one randomly.

I hear Donald signaling the waitress, who replies from across the room, What kin I get you? He orders a beer, and Tommy adds, make that two—or three, one for me and my gringo—motioning toward my chair.

I'll have a pop. An' a pop for her.

A pop?

Un refresco I think.

We're from the Forest City, can you tell? We drink pop there. When I return, Tommy holds his bottle toward the middle of the table, and the others, me included, cheeks flush and moist whether I like it or not, join a toast.

Hold up your glass. Wren nudges Billie.

Salud!

Salloo, reply the others.

Glass clinks glass as Tommy rests his hand on my thigh. ¡A ti, amigo, y a tu nueva vida aquí! His hand slips further under the tablecloth. He cradles me. Wren ventures the corner of a tortilla in the salsa while Donald reaches a whole one in, dragging it fulsomely through the bowl, crunches the thing, chews to the music, then reaches quickly for his beer.

So Tommy, what does your father do? How many kids you got in the family?

Wren—

—I got brothers. Three.

They live here too?

Nearby.

And your parents? Do they live—?

—Where?

I guess here, in the States.

Where else?

Wren, what is this?

¡Está bien! They live not far away. Near Loveland.

What a funny name!

Again Wren raises the question of Tommy's father's profession. He peers at me. Le's just say he works with animals.

That's great! We love animals, don't we Billie? Jake?

How many kids in your family?

Two girls an' a BOY! Billie remarks, eyeing me.

Entonces tu madre tenía tres niñas.

Huh?

Tommy translates and Donald doubles over. Wren chuckles, and Tommy attempts to suppress a smile.

Meanwhile I take a bite of chip and it's like eating a cookie with enchanted powers. A world pops up, inducing a rush. I take another then follow it with a swig that goes down in a different idiom. Tommy's hand speaks a language I understand. I give his foot a tap and he retracts it, then rests his arm across the back of my chair.

Billie and Wren take notice but only Wren looks away. She suggests the scenery they saw on their way here was the prettiest she's ever seen.

Jake, it's too much to describe. So huge! I mean endless. Completely open!

Bienvenido a mi mundo—

Huh?

Welcome to my world.

I can' b'lieve you grew up in it.

Well, not exactly, but close. The land of mis abuelos.

You don' think about it when you're from here.

You would if you were from Laurentine. Huh, Jake?

Jake rests his palm on Tommy's knee, squeezes and massages it.

You're always romanticizing.

Well you just can' compare our world t' this.

We live on a big lake, Jake explains. Or I did. It can be endless in a way, only there's no road across it. I guess it's the end a the road. Was for me at least. Jake eyes Peacoat as he circles around the table, moving near and perusing Tommy.

Jake—. Wren reaches over and clenches his free hand, inducing him to draw the other back.

You mean you lived on a lake—'til you run off, corrects Donald.

Be nice.

We got mierda where I'm from too. Literalmente.

What's that mean?

Mierda?

Wren glances at Billie, who continues to study colors under glass.

I mean literalmente.

Mierda de vaca—I grew up with cows. A lotta cow shit. Literally.

You grew up on a farm?? How cool! I'd love t' take Billie.

Not quite a farm. But there were cows. A lotta them comin' an' goin'. Not sure you'd like it—

But I love animals! We both do! Wren pats Jake's hand.

I take a sip and feel myself anesthetize to the situation. The waitress brought Wren a beer by accident, which has been sitting untouched, and I begin to down it.

Don't forget, Jake. We got the whole evenin' ahead a us.

Donald takes his bottle and offers Tommy a toast. Here's to mierda debacle! She could use it in her garden. We ain' got any barn animals roamin' around 'cept chickens.

We got more a it than we know what t' do with, seguro. No barn though. Jus' plenny a mierda. An' open air, lots a that.

How can you have cows without a barn? Billie drones.

[The world has lost its glow. It began with an earthquake.]

Tomás: Oye, despierta . . .
Jake: Huh? Shhhh. You'll wake 'em.

[Tommy grabs and tugs to rouse me. He slips his hand between my thighs and finds his target.]

Jake: Iss a little early, in't it?
Tomás: No better time a day if y'ask me. Th'early bird catches the—

[I'm not awake enough to protest. Before I know it Tommy has me on my stomach, legs splayed.]

Tomás: Niiiiññño.

[The bed complains as he works to a rhythm. He's tossed the pillows on the floor—I heard first one then another slump down, submit to gravity the way I submit to Tommy, flatten out as though a cushion myself, stabbed, my head a cushion too banging against the wall between the bedroom and bathroom, shaking the floor, I swear, rocking it, waking up the dead. Tommy never seems unsure of his intentions.]

Tomás: Amigo...te amo . . .
Jake:...Hhhh...Hhhh.

[Tommy's head lowers, nears mine, maintains a presence inside me, my brain, as he scooches my body lower, toward the foot of the bed to avoid banging his head the way mine has been doing all this time. His sweat trails down my neck, cheek, and chin, infiltrates my beard as he labors. Hair tickles my shoulder, the side of my face.]

Jake: Tommy.

Tomás: Sil-en-ci-o—

[The toilet flushes and almost instinctually I struggle to rise.]

Tomás: ¡*No te muevas!* Don' *move,* gringo!

[A gentle knock. A voice filters through the door in hushed tones]:
Jake?

Jake *[In equally hushed but frantic tones.]:* Just a minute!

Tomás: Mi amor—hhhhhhhhhhh—hhhhhhhhhhh—hhhhhhhhhhhhhhhhh.

Wren: Jus' wan' you t' know we're goin' for a run. Billie's asleep, so if you can keep an eye....

Tomás (*whispering*): No te muevas ....

Jake: We'll watch—have a good—

[Tommy softens despite his will to elongate the moment, stretch it forever. Is that what he always says at times like this—? Te amo...? Or is it unique to me? Is it spur-of-the-moment? Or practiced, a door prize for his latest trick? Met without objection. Breeding expectations, and at such an ungodly hour. I mean is this how he rolls?]

Jake: I got a kid t' watch.

Tomás: She said she's still sleepin'.

Jake: You mean you actually heard?

Tommy has his way, not unlike Romeo. Unlike Romeo though he's unabashed about it, even matter-of-fact. Which from Dodgson to now amounts to something I didn't know existed.

Jake: I didn't think you heard any a that, lost as you were—

Tommy remains unmoved, then flips and reorients me, his back against the sheet and me looking down. Hands move expertly, work me to a white sweat, huff and puff, a verge—I wanna cry but his tongue stifles until the drama's over, after which he lengthens against me on the mattress, lifts a pillow from the floor and sets it under my head.

At which point he skedaddles. He slips on jeans and raises a salute while I struggle to crack my lids. By the time I'm fully awake, sometime around six, he's hurtling down I-70, past Mother Cabrini Shrine on his way to Loveland. Pressed to be out the door myself in less than an hour, Jake remembers himself, his charge, never having had this type of responsibility before.

He noses the pillow where Tommy lay. Conversations from the night before return through the morning haze. Tommy's tirelessness. The flak when the waitress brought Donald's meal.

I ordered tacos like his, gesturing toward Tommy.

You ordered a burrito.

No es verdad, señora. He ordered tacos al pastor. Como los míos.

Huh?

Forget it.

Back and forth the three went until the waitress fetched the chef, moonlighting after his regular job. It says right here one tacos al pastor and one burrito plate. Are you bein' difficult?

Donald glances at Billie then Wren, Tommy, and me. I know I ordered tacos. I wanted the same as him—but never mind.

The waitress and moonlighting chef disappear, shaking their heads.

The customer's always right, Wren injects.

It's not about that. I know what I ordered.

Gringos. That's what they are. Parading as—

—What's that?

Wha' d' you think?

Tommy glances around. Next time you're here I'll show you the real deal. Good choice, Jake. He cracks a smile.

I never did anything like this, so it's all good.

The neighbor's pick-up crunches the gravel on his way to work. When Jake splits the blinds he spies a world gone lavender. He cracks the door to check the life in the other room, an extraterrestrial for all he knows but in a way his own flesh and blood, too much to consider so early, the way the child links him to Donald, an overdue embrace—more than an embrace. A discourse in blood, though god knows it's been happening for centuries, under the radar, in the open too for anyone able to see, under different stars. Again, it's too much to think about, and yet so simple, so elementary. Dandelion, prairie dog, cricket, and fruit bat. Slug, gray jay, monarch, and bighorn. A life's a life. Vulnerable. Like that slug in the corner who's had his day but can't seem to give up the ghost, the sad one with the dour face that won't stop reminding me—

—Where's my mommy?

Oh! Hi! Mornin'! She—they'll—be right back. Come with me and look outside. What color is that?

Jake squeaks the stubborn door, takes Billie's hand and leads her, still in her pajamas, onto the metal landing—Do you believe this?! What color is it?

Pur-po.

Purple it is! Some might call it lavender. Some pink.

Is it possible a hand could be so small, the features of a face? Eyes chestnut, skin coffee cream?

Would you let me draw your picture?—

—Oh my god! Is it like this every morning? Wren jogs up from the road. Billie, what are you doing out here in your bare feet?

My fault. We only been out a minute.

Wow! Jake! Never saw anything like this!

Now Donald jogs up, and even he, always chill as mountain run-off, can't mask the thrill of a world washed in hybrid hues, from the direction of a sun that refuses to step out and show its face, as though even it isn't ready to get outta bed, bending from the east, shading to pink in the opposite direction.

It's sumpin' else! A purple sky!

It's lab-en-der.

OK smarty pants. Lavender then. Have you ever seen anythin' like it!

The ornamental lines around the upper and middle edges of the trailer shift from blue to black in the light, as have the pines in the distance, but the sky and everything else, including the aluminum structure behind Jake, all blushes.

I can't believe you're a carpenter. Jake sets down his belt and the tools lie lifeless.

I'm a framer. Sorta the same. But diffren'.

Mommy, we have frames.

That's right. Wren wiggles her glasses in place, up and down, and Billie mirrors her, almost knocking them off her face.

Can you find another frame?

Billie's eyes rummage through the room in an impromptu game of I Spy, followed by her body tumbling over the sleeping bags strewn here and there between the living room couch and cupboards. The area is as pipsqueak as the kid, but she towers over it. She nearly slips a couple of times on the array of reading and coloring books, the box of crayons and tablet of paper.

Here's one! Billie stretches toward an object near the cupboard but it's out of reach. His head almost brushing the ceiling near the door, Donald steps across the sea of bedding and books as if on water, lifts the image off the nail and hands it to Billie. Here you go little girl.

—.

Who's that?

It's the same guy as him. The one grimacing in the corner, giving me hell for last night, this morning too. That's who you're looking at, the love of my life and my tormentor. The only one I'll never get over, free of, the only real thing beside Wren. Her and Molly.

He's Uncle Jake's special friend.
Was.
Where is he?
He wen' away.

He morphed into a squishy, rotten slug, a memory decomposed, transformed, suspended in a hybrid state. In perpetuity.

Why did he go?
He had to.
Where did he go?
Too far to come back.

On the contrary. He's too, too near, trailing me here and everywhere, in every situation, no matter what kind, leering—Mr. Doleful—wherever I go—don't you see him just there, the corpse in the living room? Or are you, all of you, oblivious, like Tommy, who generally doesn't mind a prying eye or two. He even seems to enjoy it, in the woods. Here. Or anywhere.

Look, Daddy! Millie!
You mean Molly.
Why isn't he here?
Jake takes the frame to rehang it on the hook, but opts instead to lay it on the counter, face-down.
She—
I wanna see Molly!
Uncle Jake is feeling a little sad right now.
Whhhhy?
Because his friend went away.

Friends. Plural.

How come?

Sadly for Jake the words "just because" can never escape Wren's lips according to her parenting play-book, hers and Donald's both. "Just because life's shitty that way." "Just because life sucks." "Just because life's unfair." "Just because life's out to rob you of everything you love, or everyone." It's not as though either of them lacks the cause to be bothered—on the contrary. Though the reasons vary, they're both armed with arrows of complaint. Yet they refrain from reaching back, drawing one out, nocking, and letting it fly. Whether by agreement or instinct, it's as if they've grown oblivious to them, or as if they'd made a pact, at least around Billie. As though a child has to grow into "just because."

We'll talk about it later—on the ride home maybe. How does that sound?

Donald stretches himself on the couch, toes and scalp just about defining the width of the trailer. His head and toes reach to the arms of the thing—C'mere little girl.

I'm not a girl.

Then what are you? An aardvark?

—.

Donald lifts Billie and sets her on his stomach. He reaches for a coloring book and box of crayons. Can you fill this in for me?

Uncle Jake is gonna draw my pitcher.

Scent of potatoes wafts through the door from the stovetop.

Breakfast is his thing. What he cooks best.

Lucky you.

I can't complain. How 'bout you?

What about me?

You finding what you want out here?

Ha! What do I want?

You tell me.

We're lying forehead to forehead under the covers—how long has it been? Two books lie on the bedspread near my feet.

You didn't need to bring anything.

Iss just a cookbook. And—. Got 'em on Coventry.

—That's one place I miss. I bought the *Bhagavad Gita* there. *Narcissus and Goldmund*. The *Gulag* too.

So you know how much I paid.

It's weird to think about a city you reviled. Once you get away it alters from what you thought you left, reminds you what you overlooked, things that come to you only when you're away. You recall finally the sweet and not just bitter fruits. But when you're there the more you reach for them the more they fade, like a punishment in hell. Then again, Wren—here you are, in the flesh.

You think this is it? The end a the road? That you'll make a go of it here?

I miss Molly. As quickly as the words slip from my mouth I realize she's present, like that lug over there, the corpse in the room, who no one can bear to name save Wren, the news too much really, threatening to throw a blanket on the visit—she's here for sure. Tommy too, though differently, his essence in the fabric, the sheets, testosterone that I swear he emits through pores, tagging everything, including the molecules in the air—I whiff them as discerningly as Molly would were she here. The living Molly, who capers about even out of body, though neither Wren or I can bring ourselves to touch her in extended conversation, as if her memory were made of glass. So we lie, forehead to forehead, after a morning run, somewhere, the two of us blind but seeing too, twins in the womb communicating through a phantom cord severed decades ago yet never not connected, like that ever-present figure—there are times when speaking is downright gross. Could there be a better way, this forehead-to-forehead thing?

Wren drifts off. Post-drive, post-sleep, and post-run—the expense of motherhood. No doubt it was like this in the womb as well. She was always the better sleeper, stuck with a squirmy, flailing neighbor who bucked the very idea of confinement, the way he bucks the sky.

A knock at the door jolts me to.

It's ready.

Seated at the table only two steps from the stove, it's apparent there wouldn't be room even if Wren were awake. I slinked out of bed without disturbing her, only to find myself face to face with two strangers.

Looks like you landed on your feet—Billie, don't make a mess! Not on the rug!

Where is Wren when you need her?

No need to worry about that—that thing must a been here since this can was built—when d'you think that was?

Fifties? Forties?

Maybe thirties? When did car culture begin?

For who?

Got it.

Seems 'bout right though. Whenever white folk got to ownin' the road. OK not just white folks—that's about the time my parents got antsy too, though they didn't own no car. Trailer. Looks like this thing was more for gettin' than stayin' away.

Its travelin' days are over.

Look like.

Nothin' but four flats below. Don' look like they seen air in ages.

Billie, I said watch what you're doing! You're getting that on the rug. The goal is to stay on the paper with the crayons.

Where's the fun'n that?

You're no help. Remember, you rentin'.

In more ways than one.

What's that s'pose t' mean? Billie, stop! Gimme the crayons! Donald shouts in muted tones. The child tosses them across the room. You're gonna wake up mommy! Let's let her sleep. Jake lifts himself from the chair and starts to collect the colors.

Let her do it.

It's no prob—

—Really, Jake. I want her t' do it.

Jake releases his grip and a fistful of hues tumble. Donald sits the child on a chair, locks his gaze, eye to eye, talks in one way or another, about decorum basically, which later he'll pronounce a dead art, a line the child may or may not be taking in. Her legs swing in the air below her, eyes wandering, until Donald corrals them, herds them back— Tell Uncle Jake you're sorry.

Really it's no—

—Let her say it!

An eternity passes as Billie's foot rocks like the pendulum of a cuckoo, hands gripping the sides of the chair, steady as counter-weights—

—I'm waiting. After a time the child finally lets out a trilogy of syllables, soft and dulcet as a marsh tit and weighty as a bison under the circumstances.

Now go and color nicely.

I want mommy!

Well, we ain't gonna wake 'er. Color your book. Donald swings his head back and points toward the sofa with his chin. Mommy'll be here soon enough.

Jake looks to be on the verge of tears, as though he were the one scolded.

Life really is the shits. An' it starts early.

Donald reaches toward the sink, spilling cold tea from his cup. He stretches toward the stove and switches on the flame, then observes the coils at the bottom of the kettle until they glow orange. Wan' another cup?

I'll make something for you to eat later—I'll wait on another cup. Otherwise I'll get the jitters.

God knows we don' wan' that. You jittery enough. Donald sets a mug in the light that streams across a checkerboard cloth, red and white, steam rising, curlicuing in the sun beaming from the ridge on the east side of town, illuminating the vapor in zebra stripes as it ascends before the venetians. Jake tugs on a mum in the vase at the edge of the table. Withered, he separates it from its stem. He plucks the dried petals unconsciously, one by one, lets them fall in a heap. Billie sits absorbed in a book, muttering to herself, oblivious to Jake beheading the blossom—

Everything goes, sooner or later.

Ha!

It finds you, trouble does. It's different for you—you got parents.

Think so?

Well it's different than Wren an'—

—I'll never know what it's like to pack a toddler. Run with the clothes on your back. Hop a train, in the South, which you never done before. Shake the only place you ever know, family too, who been there hunderds a years, longer than most white folk. Only to end up in a city in the North where nobody wants you. Includin' your and Wren's daddy. Try t' make a life there 'cause there ain't no goin' back.

You trying t' say—?

—Alabama's foreign t' me. Forest City was foreign t' them, an' it stayed foreign. It's true, we talk, unlike you and Wren with your folks. But—

Billie toddles over with her book and Donald lifts her to his lap.

You don't know what it's like to be me.

Pfft! Once you say that, then what?

What I was trying to say—

What were you tryin' t' say? Sense I got, you think you got it—

Oh my god it smells good in here!

Mommy!

Jake, gold!

Call him Uncle Jake.

Gold, Jake!

The mine's a racket if there ever was one. Donald sports a cowboy hat that barely fits. Perches is more like it.

Jake, we got a peek a the mine.

Sure it ain't fool's gold?—

It's amazing what you find. What life must a been.

Billie lifts the vial above her head and Jake takes it, lifts it toward his eyes, shakes it and watches the particles filter down in the clear liquid, catching the light. Probly all planted. And worthless.

Jake—be nice. She had a ball. By the way, Donald's right. How'd they do it back then? It's so dark down there.

In an underground world uncovered by the Utes, centuries ago, and who knows who before them, in this place where I'm naked and floating on the fire-breathing water, blind as the womb, my eyes shut, I feel my toe toed as it floats above the surface. In the dim light I spy a man towering over me, aroused by something down here.

Well, I'll be. Must be kismet.

He moves to enter the basin where I am, and I swivel my feet down, feel my heel graze the granite, back slowly toward the edge where I rest my behind on a chiseled ledge. The intruder slides first one and then the other foot in, rests on the upper lip of the pool, thighs spread. He's flying a flag in a sense, but for who? For what country? The nether-world down here? A place hidden from prying eyes and light of day? Public scrutiny? He sports the perkiness of a teenager in a body more than twice my age.

One of life's great pleasures, this place, eh? He slinks in the water like a seal, creating a wave. Is it Peacoat?

Peacoat?! I feel my face flush.

I believe you tol' me yer name's Peacoat.

An' you remembered, a course. I scratch the back of my neck as though a bug bit me, wonder how in the world—. I guess it goes with his line a work, in which remembering a name is money in the bank.

My real name's—

Well, Jake, nice to see you again, more completely.

If I had my druthers—

—Did you ever make it t' Dodgson?

Now the other Peacoat with his walrus skin, or like a fiend on call, conjured at a moment's notice, establishes himself next to the two of us.

I did.

You enjoy it? His eye sockets, orange in the light, laser mine, catch flame. Again I feel myself blush. I figured you for the type who would.

How would you know?

So you had a good time.

I feel a foot brush against my leg as it paddles around the sulfurous bath. It grazes the inside of my thigh, first one then the other, dilly-dallies there too long to be an accident, until my knees clam shut. It's impossible not to notice the shift as Dan's expression deflates, swiveling his head in the direction of Peacoat, as though he eyed him too.

Well I like to get out there from time to time, when's too hot t' come here. Check out the action—it's amazing the people y' meet! I probly would a accompanied you that day if I didn' have other things—

—So you like to fish.

In a manner a speakin'. Reverend Whistle reaches for a wash-rag, dunks it in the black pool then then lifts and squeezes, anointing himself. Meet all kinds there. Day-trippers, back-packers, run-aways, and truck-drivers. Lotta married men—. Fathers. Like me. A convict or two. Once I met a pastor. Had a family.

You think a it as a min'stry?—I mean, what's this guy gettin' at?

Are we talkin' about the same thing?

We had a ball, him 'n me! Trus' me—the experience was blessed. Truly. Dan breaks out in a smile he can't suppress. Yep. A hellova good time. If we only lived closer, instead a a thousand miles away.

Are we talking about the same thing?

You tell me.

No, you tell me.

Well then we are. Irenaeus. The glory a god. Man fully alive.

If you say so.

Doing what men've always done. Women too, I'm sure.

Ohhhkaaay.

My guess is if we took a vote down here, polled the splayed and sweltering in these rocky cavities on this Tuesday night for men only, in a place that branded the town with a name of a particular kind, with a particular meaning—several—men lounging in the viscera of a mountain rising from the earth's molten core—if we fielded a vote the majority would come down on the side of not spelling things out too nakedly.

If Romeo could hear me now.

Dan lets both the topic and his foot drop, slumping as though I've killed something.

Time passes.

How you gettin' along? If I remember right you just moved down here from—was it Iowa?

Down here?

Over, up, in here—whatever. You managing? Did you find work?

D'you ever think a minding your own business? Or are you constitutionally nosy—are you that way because a your line a work?

Here 'n there.

I got a parishioner lookin' for help—not just a parishioner, a close friend—young guy. Only thing is you gotta be on time. Ever'day. He can't seem t' find nobody reliable, which means punctual. An' long term. Too many transients here, passin' through—really nice guy, Emilio. Four kids. So he needs t' hustle.

Billie takes the vial with the magic flakes in it—Gold, Jake!

Billie what'd I say?

I hope it din't cost a arm an' leg.

When we ever gonna be back this way?

She had a ball.

I got a pan, Jake!

You got soaked is what you got. Jus' look't you, little girl.
—.

We gotta get you in dry clothes.

Wren unlatches a suitcase that takes up half the floor when opened. Donald slips off Billie's blouse and tee, then her pants and underthings and immediately she tears through the trailer, front to back, freely, like her DNA commanded it. She hops on Jake's bed, leaping up and down until Donald arrests her, picks her up wriggling and squirming and carries her back to the front of the dwelling where he sets her down next to a stack of clothes that Wren has laid out. From the trailer next-door adult noises filter through the venetian blind—

—Oh my! remarks Wren. They ain't that discrete.

He's home for lunch.

Soun's like quite a meal.

Billie rebels against the idea of donning clothes, having had a moment of enjoying life without them. Wren engages in a full-on struggle against arms and legs—

—I don't wan' to!

Well, you gotta, little girl.

I'm not a little girl!

I hear you, girlfriend. About the clothes. And you're a big girl, aren' you.

No I'm not!

Without skipping a beat Wren leads Billie kicking and screaming to Jake's room in the back and eases the door shut.

I made this for you to take on the road.

That's awesome!

My landlady gave me a ton of it, enough to make a hundred pies, I swear. Jake takes out a bundle from the bottom shelf of the fridge and holds it out.

I can't believe this came from that.

Earth, rich and black, clings to the blood-red stalks and oversized leaves, covered where rain shot dirt upward, casting a net over the frilly greens—It's amazing to think these could make you sick if they ain't red.

It's amazing to think anyone ever thought a eating it—one. And—two—who came up with the idea of a pie? An' yet here it is—look what Jake made while we were at Del Oro.

Wren comes padding out softly with Billie, light on her tail. Oh look! There's *The Joy of*—you don't skip a beat, Jake! At least I won't have to worry about you starving. Don't forget the other thing I brought—

—Wren, later!—Billie, look! Uncle Jake here made this for us to take in the car. I say we eat it now. What d'you say little girl?

I want pie!

Noooowww? It's gonna spoil her app'tite. An' ours.

Y'only live once. And we on veecation.

I want pie!

Jake takes out the only four plates he owns, which he bought at the Goodwill, mismatched, along with an equal number of forks, also not from the same set.

Oh my god, I loooove—y'know, Jake, I grow it in my yard. But so far I've only canned it. I thought a makin' a pie. Jam. But, you know—Wren glances at Billie—the sugar.

Like I say, y'only live—

Jake extracts a carving knife from the drawer, another semi-rusted, second-hand find, and begins slicing thinnish wedges, until Donald commandeers the thing—

—I always say if yer gonna eat pie then eat *pie*! Lots a it.

Donald—

—Why be shy?

In no time the disk is divided in four, divvied up semi-evenly, semi-democratically, without any preference regarding age, gender, race, class, sexual orientation, ability, religion, or lack thereof—Billie succumbs to the giggles just at the sight of what's on her plate. Even at her age she's savvy enough to know how over-the-top her portion is, the idea of all that sugar, which each slice contains, off-limits in the normal course of things.

This is obscene. She'll never eat all that, not in a million years. Never mind lunch.

It won't go t' waste. Trus' me. We got a long drive ahead, an' we gotta fuel up.

Once the frenzy begins, it's Billie who takes the lead, downing her portion with focus in an effort to prove the adults wrong. She begins by letting the fork lie in its spot next to her plate, peeling away the top with her fingers, downing it, then working the filling. She's exposed the gooey pinkness inside and is working that now too, setting the braided part of the crust aside, scooping up the filling in handful after handful—

—You got more on your face little girl than in your mouth!

An' I jus' changed you.

Looks like Billie might win after all! Jake abandons his fork and begins to stuff his face the way humanity did before decorum was invented, forks too, following the lead of youth—and now Wren copies her twin, dropping her fork on the plate in her lap and letting out a giggle. Now here goes Donald's fork—

—Thank god Tommy's not here to see this!—what would he think a us?

Huh? queries Donald, his face covered with sweetness.

Huh? remarks Billie, smiling with rhubarb-red teeth, appearing toothless.

Huh indeed! laughs Wren.

Huh, laments Jake. Am I ever gonna see him again?

But the others aren't paying attention, caught as they are in the moment, casting glances around, at the life of rhubarb, worn as much as ingested—

—I won! Billie declares.

Looks like you did, little girl.

I won, I won, I won!

Later at the Great Rocky Mountain Pizza Company a giant pie of another kind will confront diners less giddy than the foursome here, seated on the floor in a makeshift circle, plates and forks abandoned. In the spirit of the morning they'll be troopers, polish off the savory version of a pie, but dolefully. Jake and Donald will make up for Billie and Wren—We're taking one for the team, Jake announces when Wren complains she doesn't wanna see a slice a anything, ever again.

By the time everyone is packed, and everyone but Jake is perched on a car seat, about to launch on a journey, food is the last thing on anyone's mind.

I can't believe we gotta go.

That's the bummer about a job.

Wren nudges Billie to give her uncle a kiss when he pokes his head inside the vehicle, and when it's her own turn she melts like snow on the south face of the mountain. I can' believe we're gonna leave you to this place.

Jake's a big boy.

It's jus'—

—Leave it. He'll be fine. Won't you?

Jake hugs Donald, who kisses Jake's cheek. He pats Jake on the back instinctively, then they disconnect.

Thank you for comin' so far outta your way.

We would'n a missed it, you.

It wan't that far, Jake.

Wren brushes under her glasses as the others remain mum as statues. She comments on the clouds quilting the sky. She bids Billie, Wave bye t' Uncle Jake, who backs away as the car starts to roll. The tires complain while scraping the gravel. The neighbor's pick-up rumbles past. The woman they heard at lunch perches on the passenger side— the neighbor dips the rim of his hat as he drives by. Wren blows kisses and Donald points at Jake before throwing the transmission into drive. As the car grates toward Main, Wren cranes her head out the window and gazes back, as though abandoning a loved one to a city about to go down in flames, touching her hand to her mouth and pushing it away, the salt coming on, as Jake catches the mechanical regularity of the sign overhead, a neon derby, revolving above the steak-house next door.

Los Conejos

IF A SQUALL BLOWS IN on a Sunday in December, marooning you in your trailer; if a mood cold and gray as the sky descends at the same time; if you realize even if you had friends you'd be unfit company on a night like this—in that case you still have to figure how to get by in your own company, your own skin. After all, you've already split, shot outta Dodge, and there's nowhere else to go. You've got to make do, find a way to get through the rest of the day. The next hour. Minute. Whether to eat. Or not. Whether tomorrow will come let alone next week. Next year. A lifetime. If you'll deal with humans again. I mean—the way things will play out is all the less certain when you have no one to answer to, and on a Sunday when church and its rote responses to life's knottiest questions no longer suffice.

Long stretches of time expire, as though they never occurred, even as you observe the seconds tick by, trying as a bad high. Blink and an afternoon, day, week, or month came and went, but where? As though there were a skip in the record of time.

Options oppress, especially on a Sunday for some reason, one like today when the sky's gone bleary. When you're between books and unsure where to go next—wait for a volume to crook its finger? When the view beyond the window, limited and expansive, blues beyond the orange inside. When your neighbor's just led through the door the fourteenth, or is it the twenty-fourth, caller in a fortnight and here you sit, alone, having drawn the shades in order to spy on all the goings and comings—over there—without let-up. When the Persian he's been feeding in a daisy chain of tins from his trailer to yours, terminating under your stoop in a heap of rusting metal, without signifying home to the thing, still, after a duration of days, the animal mewing at this very moment not outside your but his door, despite his many efforts to palm her off—I mean that is home. She licks her paws in a mix of wet and snow. He knows she's there, and after he's had his fun he'll admit her again, his many efforts be damned.

Some make a home for others that they can't undo no matter how hard they try. Some make a space unbearable for anyone to live in. When you perch on a couch listening to the sounds next-door, jeans around your knees, it's easy to let the feline of care sit out there because it'll still be there tomorrow, in six months, a year from today. Maybe forever. Waiting to be let in. One thing's for sure: you can choose to admit or not admit her, but not choosing is a non-option because to exist is to be snowed with decisions, leading to decision-exhaustion.

Dec. 3, 19—
I'm alone, let's face it. The state
everyone runs from, hair on fire. On the
Shagaran I had Molly at least, her and
the rumblings in my gut. I was close
to Laurentine, which of course was the
problem, in earshot of so much crowing
and cawing — it found me, Laurentine.
Dragged me back. But I'm on a lake now,
floating, with nothing to tie me here
or anywhere. No Harry with his empties

clinking as they topple beside the
armchair. No Diana with her fire-brick
opinions about things, her love affair
with green — The only thing in the world
that won't ever let you down, she argued
after shedding the habit, is money. No
Florrie to hound me with other people's
sad-face, nudging me toward services she
had no interest in performing herself.
None of Florrie's hard-luck tales that she
frumped on all three of us because she
considered a pensive child a dangerous
thing. Like a loaded firearm. Going
against some cosmic law: Never allow a
child to rest, take a moment to catch
his breath — god forbid. So we were
prodded. If you don't have anything to
do I know plenty a people who are worse
off than you, mister. People who'd give
anythin' for your youth and vitality.
Like poor Mrs. Wantmore whose lawn I
swear to god is going to reach her roof.
Poor thing can't manage now that she's
lost her husband — for the life of me I
don't know how she gets by. Shall I call
her and tell her you're bored and that
you'd just love to mow her grass for her?
Or the poor sisters. The flower-beds in
front of the convent are so packed with
weeds they pra'tically can't get in the
door. How you think it'd look for the
poor things to be out in the blazin' sun,
on a sweltering day like today, an' in
coal-black, wearin' gloves and sneakers,
sweating to beat the band and gettin'
their habits filthy? You think that's OK,
mister? Poor nuns got a lot better things
t' do than pull dandelions. Like pray for
your soul, for one. And jus' think a poor
Miss Irene, stuck in that big, old house

alone on the lake because her husband
ain't never aroun'. The lake is devouring
the poor woman's prop'ty — it's eating it
up! No wonder she got a heart condition —
I'd have one too if my prop'ty were bein'
consumed like that, day after day, foot
by foot, and by water a all things. Your
father'd never go off and leave me like
that! Rumor got it he's ten sheets t' the
wind every time she see him — god knows
where he goes. Wouldn't you like to keep
the poor thing comp'ny?

In fact, no. I didn't want to keep her
comp'ny. Her or anyone. Yet off I went,
guilt-tripped into it. Florrie had her
phone-finger ready. The more I whined the
quicker it hit the dial, rotating. It'll
do you both good. When Miss Irene spotted
me through the screen her face fell,
withered from having lost the battle
with Florrie about what she needed and
didn't need — Oh. It's you. Florence's
boy. Again. Tell yer mom I got better
things t' do than babysit. Why don't she
look after her own kid? — that's what her
face said. Her mouth was another story.
Hello dear. How nice of your mother to
drive you. I don't really have anything
for you, though. I hope you don't get
bored. You only need t' stay a li'l bit
— like we both understood the deal. That
it wasn't about me or her but Florrie's
yen for identifying charity cases.
Knotted knuckles clutched the handle of
Miss Irene's oxygen caddy, as though it
were a thick cane on training wheels. I
suppose it can't hurt, you bein' here.
But please don't touch nothin' — the
cleaning lady was just here, and I'd like
to keep the place in shape a li'l while

at least. She backs from the door and
allows me to pass. With her free hand
she gestures toward an overstuffed chair
in the living room. I sit and observe
as she eases into hers, across from me,
light as a leaf, and closes her eyes.
Without unclosing them she whispers, You
stay there now. I'm afraid I might pass
out a while. And indeed she did pass out.
As in lost consciousness. Still as the
broken clock on the mantle, motionless,
a still life I wanted to draw if I only
had I a pad, a pencil. The tubes resting
on her cheekbones, trailing to her upper
lip, exhaled in one long breath from
the tank at her feet that I listened to
for well over two hours, observing her
silently, a rabbit frozen and afraid to
move, wondering what was passing in her
breast. A broken heart? Florrie used to
let that out, freely, in low tones to
anyone who'd listen. Her wheezing's so
spotty I wondered at times if it'll flame
out, like a candle under a jar, shut
from the volume of air in the room and
outside the door, a vacancy reaching
to Canada, having betrayed her in some
way, gone AWOL like her husband, Bootsy.
Or so Florrie used to say. In fact one
time Bootsy returned early from his job
while I was there resting, unseen and
unheard as befitting a child back then,
studying the lines of Miss Irene in her
oxygen-stupor. Before shooing me out he
impressed me with the way he held her
hand, cooing at her and calling her to,
soliciting what she needed. I need a
drink, she replied when she came to. Can
you pour me a gin? I could hear cubes
clinking in the glass from the kitchen at

the back of the grand old home, listened
to them tinkle as Bootsy made his way
from there to Miss Irene's side. I've
been waiting all day for this. It's been
stressful — she raised her chin ever so
slightly in my direction as she spoke.
Time to run along now, Bootsy remarked.
As I passed through the screen-door he
muttered, Tell your mother the show's
over for today.

She's gone now, Miss Irene. Like Miss
Glasby, dearly departed. Once she passed,
Florrie phoned Aunt Midge to say, Jake'd
be happy to come and sit with you if
you need comp'ny. I know Leo's gone and
left you high and dry, but Jacob'd be
happy to come. I was shaking my head
vehemently. I even scribbled on the
back of an envelope, NO NO NO! But the
following week there I was, perched next
to Midge because Leo had better things
to do. Molly and I had only just returned
from the Shagaran, before I started up
again at Geist, so I wasn't working.
Florrie didn't skip a beat. Thought it'd
do me good, normal me up she said, make
me stop thinking about myself all the
time, that guy that disappeared. What
made those mercy missions all the worse
was the way Florrie prevented Molly from
accompanying me, as though she wanted her
all to herself, for keeping her company
when no one else was home, practically
speaking. And Molly seemed content to
take Florrie's bribes, the endless supply
of egg, cheese, and bacon, bread dredged
through fat. Spurring me to wonder if
Molly was happier with her than me after
all, because what did I have to offer? —
grass and dirt, and she had catching up

to do. She seemed content to be with a
woman who didn't want me to bring her
in the house initially, when I carried
her home the first time. Don't even let
that thing through the door! I believe
she cried, though she denied it later. I
said it was too late, that there was no
taking her back because I got her from
a stranger. Like pure chance brought us
together. It's impossible to go back for
her now, though I admit I fantasized
about it when she was still with us.
About helicoptering in and rescuing her
from not just the three of them but
Laurentine most of all. Wren said Diana
said Molly spent half the day after I
split with her head through the curtains,
nose marking the glass as though looking
for something. Someone. But how could I
bring her here, even if it were possible,
subject her bones to these conditions,
thin air and temps bottomed-out, cramped
space and the lack of creature comforts,
especially after Florrie spoiled her so?
She became her baby from what I hear,
after Florrie lost her other two. No, the
door on opportunity closed shut on the
option of bringing Molly here, leaving me
with just thoughts to pet, them and this
empty sketchbook that Wren left under
my pillow. Thought I might draw in it,
rekindle a part of me that's dead, like
Miss Irene. Instead of drawing I'm trying
to sketch my thoughts — I can scribble
on any surface. Let a part a me shoot
out leaves, and in the middle of winter.
I hope to draw again at some point. All
it takes is a box of charcoals, which
I thought I left behind but only just
discovered. Some used oils. Beyond the

set of watercolors I've relied on so
far. If Peacoat were in the flesh and not
slinking around like a zombie I'd draw
him. Buck naked. Not the way he sits
over there now but the way he visits my
dreams. Warm, dark, and vibrant. The way
I used to sketch him, exposed to me and
god — Reverend Billy ok'd it initially
because, as he said, drawing a naked lady
might a given rise to sin. That would
a been a defilement a god's wishes. So
Peacoat stripped down because the lord
saw no danger in it we determined, free
of Pastor Billy. In that way Peacoat
lives, in renderings of him in his birth
suit, before we dove into each other.
They contradict the person sitting there
now, mostly devoid of a covering.

Would it also end in calamity if I
were to draw Tommy that way, if he were
ever to come around? Just seeing him
today was a shocker, though I know he's
never coming back. So why question it?
He seemed to make that clear. It wasn't
my fault that we run into each other,
there in Pandemonium. As though he were
the Kris Kringle of my dreams, definitely
a more handsome devil than the official
guy in red. Wearing a granny wig under
his chin. Actually Tommy wore not red but
black, head to toe, his jacket absorbing
the sun and smelling as though it had
just come off the cow. He looked almost
apologetic in that get-up when he saw
me, munching on a corn dog, him and his
friend. When he introduced me I wanted
to turn tail and run, wondering what
she knew about me, what she didn't know.
Tying stories to a face always produces
a jolt, the things that get left out. I

could a sworn she shed tidbits about me
with every breath, crystalized as they
were in the cold air, that Tommy was
betraying me too as he remarked, L'Dell
and I decided to drive up for the day.
She'd never been to Pandemonium, being
strictly a city girl, and she had much to
say about it, which I not only tolerated
but indulged, anything but talk to Tommy.
For his part he stared me up and down,
like I was a stranger and intimate both
— I wasn't sure which. L'Dell blurted
she wanted to get another corn dog and
asked Tommy if he wanted one too. After
she went off he asked, You still not
eatin' meat? Livin' in that tin can? I
watched a cloud rise from the concession,
smelling of franks and cider — the vapor
trailed all the way to where we stood.
That sardine can on wheels, the width of
a sofa — I remember it well. Remember
what, do you? I says. I don't know why
you do it. Because I like it. Children in
heavy coats trapped us in the middle of
a game of keep-away, darting as they were
for a bundle of paper plates rolled and
jammed in a Styrofoam cup, that is until
their parents warded them off. You like it
probably a little too much. What's that
supposed to mean? Kris Kringle, a hired
hand, proved a bigger incitement for the
kids once he arrived than their parents'
admonishments, pulling trinkets from a
sack as if a trainer, tossing herring
to a pack of seals. You love to deprive
yourself, like you're tryin' to be a
saint. I wouldn't call what we did self-
denial. Or saintly. Still. L'Dell returns
and hands Tommy a stick with a hunk of
breaded meat on the end. Want me to get

you one? No come carne. Oh? — is that a
thing? That's weird! I'd rather give up
sex than that — actually, they the same,
ain't they? L'Dell cackles at her own
joke then proceeds to catalogue all the
things she could never give up along with
bacon. A fat burger. Pot roast falling off
the bone. Ribs swimming in sauce. City
chicken — she outlined a laundry list she
absolutely could not live without, under
any circumstance. I fantasized she'd been
ruminating on that list a while, that
Tommy tipped her off about me, the meat
thing, but it was he who called off her
game of Meat-Meat-Gotta-Have-Meat, her
checklist of My Favorite Meat Conquests,
her book of Meats to Eat When You're
Depressed. He got his reasons. Just then
a man taller even than Tommy waltzes up
and takes his hand. He too is covered
in black, his upper lip darkened by a
moustache in the shape of a pine marten,
belly-up. Over Kris Kringle's baritone
Ho-Ho-Ho's Tommy tries to introduce us,
but the guy goes, I'm Polly. AKA Polly
Purebred. AKA Polly Morphous. AKA Polly
Morphously Perverse. But La Duquesa to
you, girl. She asks me how long I known
Alicia. Who's that? Tommy blushes. How'd
the two a yous meet? You never told me
you had a straight friend. Polly laughs
and Tommy copies her with a belly-laugh.
What about me? L'Dell protests. You know
what I mean, girlfriend.
  Alicia, huh?
  Don't mind her.
  We met on a hike. At Dodgson.
  Oh, a course. Got it.
  Polly looks at me in a manner that
bespeaks surprise, but simultaneously

says, Try as you may to hide it, I got
you figured out, girlfriend. Got what,
L'Dell insists? Tommy tells Polly to cool
it, to which Polly replies, We should
skedaddle. I wanna get back in time for
Battlestar Galactica.

And that was that. Tommy exited
Pandemonium and my life, no doubt for
good this time, and not without a rebuke
for what I eat, or don't eat. Not without
a hand down my jeans too that dallied for
a time, long enough to get my attention,
cloaked as we were by the crush of
festival-goers. I miss this thing, he
whispers. I admit. I even dream about it.
As though "this thing" were separate from
me. And then, after his friends had done
an about-face, he pulls his hand out and
backs away. I watched as they braved the
unpaved surface on Main, took his place
beside the other two on the banquette of
his pick-up. I saw him glance back in the
side-view, wait a moment as though trying
to locate me before pulling away. Leaving
me alone-alone in the most existential
way, a way I don't ever remember,
Shagaran or no Shagaran. Not like this.
Is it possible to live comme ça in
perpetuity? Is it advisable? Healthy?
Lawful? No one to hold or distract you,
leaving you smack up against yourself
most of all. That pit. That and your
principles — whoop-de-doo. What are they
worth when push comes to shove?

I had my hopes for Tommy, but now
that I've given the idea of me and him
an airing I don't know why. What did
we know about each other? A lot on the
one hand, too much to unknow. Like me
and Romeo after that first night. Though

Tommy's turned out to be a tougher nut,
immune to my charms or he'd be here.
I thought I had him — I let him take
the lead. If I learned anything from
Florrie's speeches to Diana and Wren
on the subject of men it's You gotta
let them set the pace a things. Never
be the one t' act. Never mind that her
advice fell on deaf ears in Diana's
case, and in Wren's too in a sense. If
fate played tricks on Florrie one of the
biggest would have to be the degree to
which I internalized lessons in a way my
siblings never did. Which — look where
it got me. One thing Florrie never held
forth on was how to keep a man once
he was interested. So it's just me and
my principles barb-wiring me in, too
barbed Tommy probably thinks, assigning
me to the quick and dead of ex-dom.
Extinguished like the flame I discovered
I had for you after all, Tommy. To whom
I bid goodbye.

A block of freshly laid cement, cured overnight despite the temps, like a gessoed canvas or a page before a pen. Emil glances at his watch then back at Jake.

Seven means seven.

It ain' even daylight!

Emil shoulders a stack of two-by-fours, bones of a dwelling stacked in parallels in the shape of a plinth. Jake joins the hauling, belatedly, threads a board under his arm and totes it near the foundation, followed by another, making a series of trips, a board at a time.

This is the easy part, pal. We wanna get 'em moved 'fore Chrissmus.

Jake chuffs over the terrain as vapor crystalizes around him. While yesterday the sun softened the earth, turning it slick, the moon last night rigidified it with its breath, which Jake externalizes—huff, huff, huff. The mundane bending and shouldering of materials ordered by someone with-it enough to requisition only what's needed to skeletalize a place, bone it out with little waste, from a yard stacked with timber felled in mountains, milled and kilned. A crew drew stock and fork-lifted it on a bed. A driver gassed up a rig, wheeled the timbers from there to here—wherever there is—off-loaded them with steel tines. Never mind the effort of soil and water to convert a shoot to an arboreal tower that could kill a body if it fell amiss. Never mind the sun-work, shy and aggressive in equal parts at these altitudes, nestled in valleys, extending the life of pines that wait on a solar visit. The chemical magic shuttling from root to leaf. The stubborn attitude, braving fire, cold, and heat; pine beetles; lightening; downpour and blizzard. A parched tongue, that's what I'm thinking as I mule two-by-fours back and forth, I mean the tedium of it. To carry a thing from that place to this like I were Emil's wood-man, avoiding liquid glass that shatters under your shoe. The idea of the trade-off, mindless work for a roof at night—rule number one. A sack of potatoes from Safeway. Gas to get.

Hustle is Emil's middle name. He outpaces me in every way, moving the pile bit by bit to the pad that he and I are going to do what on? With just this? A pile a wood? Twitch our noses and something shakes into place? After the original pile by the road shrunk and the one nearer the site grew, Emil starts to lay out two-by-fours in a 3D drawing. Then he stops to explain to the novice how you build a house. In a nutshell, methodically. Not at all random. Nothing slapped together, everything planned.

There's a right 'n wrong way for everything, Jake. Just so—my daddy taught me that, who learned it from his daddy. When my sons are big enough I'll pass it on t' them. But for the time being it's just me an' you.

Emil explains a two-by-four ain't a two-by-four, though it started life that way. After it's milled and kilned it shrinks— An' we know what a difference half a inch make. Then he unravels how studs are aligned, how to eye a crooked from a straight. How to hammer for maximum drive—From here! He pivots my elbow in repeated ups and downs.

Framing is the opposite of detail-work, where you swivel with a limp wrist. He's flexing my fist now in a series of motions, as if a tool were in my hand.

And to think I considered only piece-work repetitive, not raising a house for sure. Having said that, I learn more than muscle makes the work. True, there's the robo-repeat of work by seven, home by four, because the sun's so finnicky in these parts, especially this time a year. It forbids you to work more even if you wanted, no matter how much you need the cash. For that reason instead of five days you do six, depending on the sky, though not the temperature—it's never too cold to hammer.

Beyond those basics, it requires brains to build an abode. That and heart.

December flakes away as a house roughs in, fast as the white that's falling. I've graduated from toting to cutting, though I'm told measuring is still a long ways off. If we both wanna get paid, last thing we can afford is waste, Emil explained. Novices are known for that.

So it's more toting, cutting, and driving—that's it. And for what? A few bucks at the end of the week? For who is the better question. Some banker or oilman, CEO, or shop-owner, I'm told. So he can bag a buck, lop off his head and mount it on a wall. Indulge a primal fantasy in this hunter's hideaway we're building, a place for avoiding wife and kids. Where he can spend a weekend with the guys, all the way from Texas, Kansas, or Nebraska. Maybe even the Mile High City.

The macho draw of the place, bred in its bones by Emil who enthuses about his own time in the bush, sporting camo he wore in the war while taking down deer, elk, moose, or bear—anything he can shoot. His home is a natural history museum the way he pictures it, peopled with specimens his children helped mount. How many times has he gone on about weekends with the guys, and me not having set eye on Tommy since Pandemonium? What do he and the wife do at night, without a TV?

Whoever thought that when you arrive in the Rockies you landed in a cloister in the sky? That aloneness would poke its wet nose at you repeatedly, begging for attention. Not that I'm alone completely, far from it—I got that guy to keep me company. Sometimes I meditate on my solitariness up here, how the thin air gives you terrors at night, oxygen-deprived dreams that make you leap out of bed, wondering your name, who and where you are. Whether you're alive or dead. In a dream or reality—everything fuses together. Or used to early on, before I adjusted to the air, though it took a while. Causing Tommy to roll over on his side that night, contorted in a fetal position, laughing. He blurted, You were calling out for Jesus, of all things. Jesus! Help me, Jesus! Oh, Jesus! As I peed, delirious, in the next room he continued his mimicry, making me testy given it was nothing I'd be caught dead uttering in the light.

A bad dream's a bad dream, so shud-dup.

It was a dream alright! You sounded like a preacher! Gimme your blessing, padre! Bless me father for I have sinned. I've eaten a lot of meat lately.

OK, Tonto.

Estás loco!

Do Emil and his wife sing out in the night. Or are they acclimated? What with his taste for slaying things and how many kids? Does his daily duty, family, and familiarity have an effect on his sleep?

The wife drops by from time to time to leave lunch, a diminutive thing who moved here from Jersey, though not the one the cows are named after. For a person of her stature she's tall in the offspring department. When Emil tops her with his lithe, muscular frame, does he turn into a grasshopper, his buttocks tightening as he thrusts, goatee tickling her cheek, hands callused and abrading her skin? Obliging her because fertility is her power, her agency? Does he drift off, still on top, beat from the demands of the day, from so much muscle- and brain-work?

A thermos of tea is all I've seen him with, unlike other men I've met on sites like this after I first arrived in the area. Day laborers who down a beer or two and sometimes three after the lunch wagon rolls in, before returning to power-tools. Men who cover a nostril with a thumb before blowing, ejecting what's inside. By contrast when the time arrives here Emil and I hop in his pick-up. He unfolds a handkerchief from his pocket, takes time to clean the sawdust and snot in his nose, then re-pleats it and stashes it away. He unfolds another hankie from the glove compartment onto the seat between us and sets a spoon and napkin on top; two cups are arrayed, the caps of two thermoses.

Want some? I watch as soup streams from a mercury lip. Steam of beef-broth fills the cab.

I don't eat meat.

No meat!? No wonder you're so thin. I mean that's peculiar, ain't it? Well, if y' change yer mind. It's more'n I can eat.

As I bite into my PBJ, I wonder if it'd be the same as eating meat if Emil and I kissed. I mean if stock were mixed with saliva, would it compromise me?

Lunch wrappings fall across the floor of the cab, windows obscured by vapor from a series of quick, short breaths. I'm straddling Emil, our mid-sections heaving. Huge hands wedge under my belt, the back of my jeans, discover I've gone commando as they pet warm flesh. His tongue and mine enjoy a feast, one that could be labeled meaty—Emil's freed up what's below and the two of us press flesh to flesh, causing me to frot the horn in rhythmic beats, the sound intensifying on this barren spit below I-70.

Have you ever eaten meat? You don' know what you're missing.

Not in ages.

I couldn't live without it—that explains things about you!

He has me plastered against the passenger door, my leg draped over his shoulder as he goes in. My jeans scrunch around the other foot, draped to the floor. The guy works expertly, as well as Peacoat and better than Romeo as he slides in and out, his goatee buried in my face. Then he slicks my jeans away and lifts both legs, resting them over his shoulders, banging my head against the door. He skinnies his jeans off too and for the first time I eye what's been out of sight, what he's been keeping from me, now brazenly exposed. He's panting like a steer. I hesitate but he takes command, forces himself then moans long, not unlike the elk you hear from time to time nearby.

It sounds a little fruity.

What's that supposed to mean?

God made animals t' eat. Much as we want.

I wonder what it's like in the middle of the night when Emil and the Mrs. discover they're awake, the two of them. Do they kiss? Do his kisses taste meaty? Do they do anything? Or do they simply roll back off a mountain of dreams?

One thing you learn out here is that building a house isn't unlike erecting a capital or a metropolitan seat, like Rome. There's the planning, including the requisitioning of materials, as well as the assembly of a thousand raw elements that you could strew across a football field, including some things you have to over-order because you never know exactly what you'll need. Like two-by-fours and -sixes, four-by-fours, trim-boards, shims, and plywood. There's the braces keeping the thing true that'll only be tossed after. Boxes of masonry—common, penny, ten-penny, and casing nails—a mountain of them. Hammers specialized for an array of tasks—framing, sledge, and claw. Cat's paws, plumb bobs, and chalk reels. Measuring tapes—who knew there were so many? Circular, miter, hack, and rip saws. All employed to raise a structure that'll survive a quarter, third, or half as long as any tree—if you're lucky. Like empires, a dwelling's doomed to fail someday. The expense of cash to fulfill a dream or satisfy a whim. Some wild hair. Or more accurately, if I overheard the owner right, under contract and mortgaged to his ears, the manly pleasure of owning a hideaway, a hunting lodge. Never mind that I, against places like this in principle, will one day seek out the structure from the roadway above, pointing to it as I fly by, boasting, I built that! Me'n another guy—just the two've us! Long after I've again become a foreigner to these parts. I'll glance at this affair on the outskirts of Ojo, here on the banks of Clear Creek, not quite able to grasp the reality of the thing, squaring it in my mind.

We're finally closed to the elements, a milestone Emil's been chattering about. As though that were possible, to be closed to the elements. Naked plywood plays roof for now, the entire outer skin, supporting sheets of melting whiteness that piss on us as the afternoon sun heats the exterior. Inside we're raising walls, Emil and I, the two of us closed in. I get a whiff of breakfast in my beard. I brush away a crumb or two nesting in my moustache, which has grown to some length, as though I've taken a leaf from a hare's notebook. What would Tommy, or is it Alicia, think? Would he love or hate it, if he were around? Would he even notice with his single-minded eye? Hot for who-knows-what, or -whom? Was I right to hang myself out there, or should I have zipped it the way I was taught? Never reveal too much, Florrie warned Diana and Wren, which I gather includes if you don't eat meat. Save it for later, when it's too late for him to turn back.

Let's firm this thing up, Emil comments. He measures an interior wall at cross-angles. Jake taps the corners toward ninety degrees, in tune to his partner's hand signaling this way or that, pulling things close or pushing them away.

Gimme a skosh—just a tad!

While struggling to keep the wall square, Jake observes Emil's wrist as he moves the hammer up and down. Nail after nail drives into the brace that will hold not just the wall but the structure until time and gravity have gained on it, them or some future version of progress. After checking his work Emil taps a sledge delicately, then worries, No, that's too much! Lemme kick it back. When the bubble is finally on the money, he finishes the job by hammering through the free end of a two-by-four, tracking diagonally across the studs, and after a giant heave the two have set another wall in place.

Jake you never talk about no girlfriend.

Huh?

Why not? You scared or sumpin'?

Huh?

Don't you get horny?

Huh?

—Look't Pastor Dan. The life he got. Don't you aspire to a life like that?

Pastor Dan?

Still penetrable to the eye, the walls will block what's beyond them someday, define an inside and outside once it's sheeted—taped, mudded, and painted—providing cover for any number of indiscretions, the kind people wall away, short- or long-term, practically or frivolously, never mind the snow above.

I jus' loss someone. Reason I move here. Gotta give it time.

I'd go outta my mind without it. Ain't that what it all come down to? A pink hole?

I guess that's one—

We move on to the next wall, studs laid out. Tools jingle from Emil's belt. I mean, I gotta have it!

—.

I don't know how you go without it for a week. Weird as not eatin' meat.

Emil cackles at his joke. You ain't a fruitcake are you? I wouldn't be caught dead, alone here with a fruitcake.

I do like fruitcake.

Emil cackles at Jake now—That's what I'll call you. Fruitcake!

Thus Emil and Fruitcake compartmentalize things within a labyrinth of walls that, void of sheet-rock, seem a forest still, dense but see-through, revealing walls and not-walls. The place in Laurentine must a looked like this once. With nothing to hide behind. Then came the closing-off and god-knows-what was hidden—it requires violence to break through a finished wall. A fist or sledge, foot if you're lucky. From wattle-and-daub living where dozens crammed in a room, to the bourgie Dutch house, individuals locked in solitary spaces, secreted from others. To be secreted here with Emil, despite his bluster, or better yet Tommy, who's never coming back after I went striding my high horse, Principle. Committed the sin of talking straight.

So you never eat meat, amigo? *Ever?* And you don't plan on it at some time en el futuro?

He smelled of al pastor and beer as he whispered while he did his thing. He reached his arms under me, steadying himself, and clenched me tightly.

Not really.

Not really or not—

—Aghhh!—

—Lo siento!—at all? You're not against...taking it, though. His voice was coming out in pants and spurts.

I realize now that was my cue to lie, move like some tired cliché. Say I didn't mean it when I said I never wanted to eat meat, ever again. But I couldn't bring myself, couldn't even crack a smile at a time I knew I was walkin' on ice, despite the heat in Tommy's moves. I grunted, Why does it matter?

Uggggh! Matter what?

Owww!! What I eat.

Tommy groaned then seemed to forget me and the topic, sweating then collapsing, burying me under dead weight as though he'd landed an animal sacrifice. I felt his heart galloping, his beard muzzling me.

I pull away. Why does it matter?

Let it go. He empties his lungs.

But I wanna talk about it.

Silencio, mi amor. Tengo mis razones—I got my reasons.

Silence came. Separating our voices, bodies too. After he gasped te amo of all things, in the morning. He lay a while, heaped on me, as if loath to go. I ran my hand along his spine to see if it were there, felt the fluff toward the bottom until his temperature began to drop, as though he were going dead on me.

Sorry I said anythin', I groan.

We're adults—say what you wan'.

You brought it up.

It ain' the only thing I brought up.

I did my best.

Then I owe you.

You don' owe nothin'. A little honesty, why it matters. If it didn' matter you would'n a brought it up. I mean've all times.

Tommy stands. I said f'get it. There don't have t' be a reason. It just slipped out, like this thing. But it ain't normal, niño.

Jake stretches then lays flat on his back, staring at the ceiling.

Think what we do is normal?

I do f' sure. Tommy reaches for Jake, clenches his hand around him, tugs, then lets him go.

It ain't where I come from.

I grew up with animals so I seen plenny. One thing I never seen is someone that don' eat meat.

There's always a firs' time.

Good luck with that.

If I could survive Laurentine—

—My god the roof's a sieve—it's really comin' through.

So much for bein' closed t' the elements.

Get a push broom.

Melted snow pools on the concrete, so much so that Jake wonders when it'll ever be dry. He swishes toward the door then shooshes the water out through the opening where stairs are slotted to rise. The broom-handle burns against his palms as it moves back and forth. Blood beads at the ends of his fingers where they've split. He sucks a drop of red from his thumb which smarts from the salt.

The question is how much it matters.

Matters how?

With regard t' you 'n me.

Me an' you, what?

Y' know.

No, I don't.

About us.

Who said there was an us?

You came all this way, for what reason?

And your point is?

What d'you call this then? I complained. Ain't it a pattern?

Ain't now, this minute, enough? Who said anything about t'morrow?

—.

It takes all kinds, Jake—it's a big, bad world out there. Do what you gotta do. Far be it from me—

—Where're you in this big, bad world?

At the moment I was just—. Tommy belches and Jake whiffs beer and taco sauce. After that, who knows?

Not to beat a dead horse, but one of the biggest trials for human animals is a moment, let alone months, of solitude. I mean the real article. Monks champion it as the place to meet the divine, though you gotta wonder if they fly that flag based on experience or some script, given all the diversions out there, ways of avoiding having to be solo for a minute let alone any length of time. For the majority, time-alone mounts to hell on wheels. Not unlike a dog chained to a stake, isolated from her pack that's warming itself around a fire, inside, while she curls in a C outdoors. Or maybe it's like being an ant-stowaway, marooned on a pant-leg, dragged to a place where they speak another chemical language. As bad as a traveler abroad, in a country where no one knows you. You can bob on a sea of people and the isolation can crush you, reduce you to tears.

I knew a priest who decided to do the noble thing, leave parish comforts and labor alongside the saint of Calcutta. After a matter of weeks he suffered a breakdown, because, A, the culture was so alien; B, all his usual comforts—trusty car, prepared meals, nightly scotch—were stripped away; C, for all his sermons raising poverty to godliness the real thing proved a grotesque demon; D, he encountered social ills that he never dreamed of and realized they could visit him someday, reduce him too to a charity case; E, it seemed impossible for a loving god to allow such crushing dearth to take place, ever—if there were a god, he, she, it, or they; and F, suffering makes you solitary, and that's what really does you in, makes you wanna do yourself in. The many forms of lack, he discovered, everywhere you look, staring at you naked, revealing the lie of every sermon he ever gave about god's fullness. Far from his surroundings, alone, god vanished from the earth. When he returned, finally, unable to stick it out, he saw joy leach from him, along with his accustomed comforts. He left the ministry. Town as well. I never saw him again, not after he relayed to me his story.

In no way does it take extremes like that, I'm learning, to rattle a body. Mind too. To the core. Isled in this tin can on wheels Jake slumps, peers at an overly-familiar, deadly-quiet interior. He sighs. It's yet again what people call the lord's day, one per week, a day earmarked for reading and journaling, but, as has been the case for some time, heavy-thinking more than anything, trapped in a tourist town in a foreign state at a foreign altitude. The pit in the stomach grows after force-swallowing the pill of aloneness. Again, at least on the Shagaran there was Molly. What's worse, it's one thing to be banished from a place like an emperor, exiled on an island on the other side of the world, eking a living in a rat-infested dwelling on a remote hill, far from the nearest town, turning days with hollow memories of past heroics. It's another thing to exile yourself, up and leave by choice, astride a high horse, only to find yourself on another gray Sunday in what seems like a month of them, just so you can wonder for the umpteenth time the whys and wherefores of a move, where matters stand at the moment, and where they might turn. If they'll turn. Jake gazes at Peacoat in the corner, at him and Molly in 2D under glass.

It's at that moment, coming late on a solemn Sunday, that he begins to pick away at the scab of deceit. That isn't to say he stopped blaming the Forest City for his present state—it'd only been how long since he left after all? But with the panoramic vision that distance provides, he begins to admit there may have been things he missed. Or messed. He even thinks about phoning Romeo, engaging in the kind of word games the two enjoyed back in the day, speaking code as Florrie, Harry, and Diana lazed nearby with their big, elephant ears, trying to read between the lines.

After all, the hours he worked overtime for Emil afforded him not just rent, bills, gas, and eats but a slim extra to spend as he wished. Enough to upgrade the old, split-wired and staticky rotary to a sleek princess-dial, with push buttons and clearer sound, which he could pick up at any time and give Romeo a buzz, slip into their old tongue with his wife nearby, completely unaware. Given Wren's last letter, which she wrote after running into him, he suspected Romeo'd welcome it, and who knows what else, despite their past. Tell that bum of a brother not to be a stranger, he groused. Is he so hard up he can't pay t' dial? Tell him he better or I'm gonna go down there and give him what-for. After all, it's hard to forget how he headed after me on the beach that time, stood at attention as we relieved ourselves, surprising me after everything that went down, confusing him too, so much that he begged Molly off from the direction she was headed to come help us find something on the beach to burn, in order to warm the group in the wee hours, just before they discovered—Jake peers across the room. He caught Romeo's drift alright, the effort to snag him, as if he were a form of driftwood. So why not call, even if it were the last thing in the world he would've imagined back then.

Sometimes life pushes you. Turns you into a punk—

—A knock at the door.

Jake! Thunder in the silence. He squeaks the door open.

So this is it? This is where you live?

Oh—it's you. Yep, this is my home.

The lord loves all kinds.

Wan' a cup a tea?

I wouldn' mind—got anything else? A little stronger maybe—mind if I look around?

Ain't nothin' t' look at.

The figure usually skulking around the place looks alarmed at the intrusion, morphing two into three, like a mouse at the sight of the neighbor's cat. Dan noses here and there, checking the closet, the closet-sized bathroom, sleeping quarter large enough to accommodate a bed and that's it, that and a mess of books.

From the tiny four-burner where Jake fires the kettle he observes his guest crane his neck out the blinds as though there were something to see. He runs his fingertips along the cuffs of the shirts in the closet, lifts and smells one of the sleeves.

Never seen you in this before. Doesn't even look your size.

It belonged to a friend. Jake eyes the other figure.

The visitor's eyes peer through the stacked volumes, spine by spine, bending until he's read a title pressed against the floor. He separates the slats of the blinds in the bedroom and Jake discerns him checking out the Del Oro Mine, floodlit in the darkness. It hugs the mountain on the opposite side of the valley, towering over the town, an erstwhile cash-cow now turned into a tourist-trap. The Black Hat sits to the south along Main, attached to the motel next door, in the opposite direction of the town center. The derby-shaped neon flashes above.

BEST STEAKS IN THE ROCKIES!
SURF-N-TURF TUESDAY!

To the north, just barely in view, sits Columbine Rock Shop, or a shell of it, its doors shuttered this time of year, waiting for warm weather and the crowds. Next to it stands the Ojo Diner, renowned for its **RED-EYE BREAKFAST, STEAK AND EGGS, ALL DAY, EVERY DAY, FROM 6:00 TO 3:00.** The cafe's the only place walkable with a working toilet on bone-rattling mornings, the spot Jake shambles to when his own commode has crusted over. Farther to the north there's a string of motel signs with their chain of ~~NO~~ VACANCY notices, unblinking this time of year, operations down on their luck even during the tourist season, stucco crumbling, paint flaking, parking lot moldering, waiting for a sprucing come spring. Tommy suggested he and Jake rent a room sometime—How expensive can it be? he wondered. So the two could make their own mark on a space that hosted thousands of couples unlike them, though with a purpose not unsimilar, here in the coniferred air.

Dan takes it all in.

It ain't Pandemonium by a longshot, Dan declares. Though just down the highway—what is it, ten, fifteen minutes? I've gone through the other end a town on my way to the hot-springs, but I never been down here.

Then how d'you eat? Only one Safeway 'tween the two towns.

Ginny takes care a that. Her or th' housekeeper.

How 'd'you know where to find me?

You said it was the trailer court on the strip. Only one a them. Also how many yellow Fiats out there?

At a table suitable for two, two paces from the stove, Jake shimmies into a chair, his back to the furnace while Dan takes his spot by the door.

You'd think a girl lived here. Look a' the tablecloth. The dishes.

They cost two bucks.

Checker tablecloth, red 'n white. Honey-pot. Matchin' mugs—handmade. You come inta money? Vase with real flowers. In the middle a winter.

No big deal.

Nothin' t' get defensive about.

Then what's your point?

I'm just observin'.

Why'd you come?

Dan lifts the lid of the honey-pot and extracts the dipper, loaded and oozing, casting amber in the gray light, twirls it in order to keep it balled until he places it over his cup and lets it string downward. You got anything to stiffen this up?

Like what?

You know, a stiffener.

Steam rises as the honey lengthens into a thread. Dan's about to use the dipper as a stirrer until Jake taps his hand—Don' do that! He jumps up and grabs a spoon from the drawer by the sink.

Here—. An' no, I don't got no stiffener. What'm I gonna do, drink alone?

'Scuse me, Auntie Em. Dan tinkles the tip of the spoon on the bottom of the mug in circular motions. To answer your question, Jake—he crosses his legs then raises the edge of the cup to his lips, sucking air as the tea goes down.

Damn.

T'answer my question....

To answer your question.... Hard t' say. I don' really know why I'm here. Been thinkin' about it for a while I guess. Since I run inta you at the springs. I been thinking about you generally after that time—

—Not a very interestin' subject.

Actually, I find you fascinating.

Pfff!

Dan reaches over and rests his hand on Jake's. Hair lines the wrist where it juts from the sleeve. Jake tries to slip his hand away but Dan doubles his grip.

I find you very attractive.

What happened at the springs—that was a mistake—

—Or god's work.

Dan pushes away from the table and pulleys the venetian down. Before he can be stopped he begins removing his shirt, undershirt, and trousers. He stands naked as a tomcat, aroused, as though Jake were in heat.

Ain't gonna happen.

How can you turn it away?

Sorry.

Undaunted, due to confidence or experience, track record, habit, cluelessness, or just used to getting his way,

Dan stretches out on the sofa under the picture window. He pats the cushion—Come!

Jake approaches.

Take your clothes off. I know you like it—you weren't shy at the springs that time.

I don' trust you.

What if I promise not to touch? If we just sat undressed a while?

That'll happen, I'm sure.

For a reason Jake can't explain, he begins to remove one article after another, his audience eyeing every move. As jeans flop to the floor Jake observes the Persian dart from under the trailer next-door.

Such a beautiful boy.

Remember the deal.

Not even a tiny touch?

Jus' one—that's it.

Look what you do to me.

Hard to miss.

And look what I do to you.

A rubber tire'd do—

—The pleasure of youth, you dog. Lie with me.

You lie—there. I'll be back. Remember the deal.

I'm all yours.

Don't move.

. . . .

You wanna draw me? Like this?

Why not?

I never—likenesses are hard, so why not. If I agree, will you lie with me?

If I did that, would you pose for me again?

If that's the deal—.

Jake moves charcoal over a field of white.

—So tell me—

—No talking—

—Why would someone so young, with everything going for him, leave his family and come all this way, from—is it Iowa?—settle in a dump like this, like Ojo, with all its ugly optics, a has-been town, an abortion really—and you an artist—why would you come here and take up residence in a dumpy trailer a million years old, take up framing—of all things!—which you know not a damn thing about, sitting on a mountain a books back there like it's a dragon hoard—you come all this way, not knowing a soul, and with your—proclivities no less. I mean it just don' make sense.

Don't move. And no talking.

I don't get it.

Dan rests, perched on the couch, propped like an odalisque against a bank of cushions, tattered and worn, his left arm draped over the back of the sofa, body relaxed. As he speaks, his eyes search, survey Jake for answers.

We all have our—I mean, look't you! Like yer one t' talk.

A sheet of naked paper catches charcoal dust after Jake commits to his subject, blocking in the form, letting the tip run, first in geometrical shapes then expanding volumes projecting from the page—or does the background recede into nether-space, as though the frame of the page were a window in which a figure is birthed—

—What's that suppose t' mean?

If you need me t' spell it out. Way you just read me—

It's true we all have our contradictions, depending on your point a view. If we're talkin' convention—

—Is that what we're talkin'?

If we're talkin' convention, then—

—You ain't no stranger t' convention, insists Jake.

Nor an advocate, as you can see. Speaking of which, I hope you're not the slave-to-realism type. Dan casts his gaze down.

What would I know about reality?

I'll bet you know plenty—I mean. I don't know why a person like you would come—

You gonna try and save me?

This'd be a novel way a doin' it. For a preacher. Do you need saving? Like just about ever'body else who rolls through here—and trust me, that's what they all do. Roll through. As though Ojo were a way station. You'll do it too someday, I'm sure.

Is this yer way a doin' god's work?

Don't be mean.

I'm sure this-here—Jake gestures with the tip of his charcoal toward Dan then toward himself—this-here ain't your first rodeo. As he speaks Jake can feel Peacoat's gaze burning a hole in his back—he could practically feel the breath if he had one as he surveys the drawing, what Jake has opted to include and omit from the borders of the page.

Whether this is my first of five hundredth rodeo ain't the point. I never known anyone like you. I'm not sayin' the others are a blur. But I ain't gonna forget this.

You said the same at the springs.

Don' remind me a that. It's just you ain't run a the mill.

I might a believed you, before the springs. But—well, look! Again he lifts his charcoal from the page and directs it like a pointer.

He pulls away from the drawing, wrestles himself from tight quarters between the table and furnace, shooing Peacoat away, who induced him to mumble, I'm sorry, to which Dan replies, For what? You got me on the ropes— more naked'n I wanna be. He reaches between his thighs and tugs—

—Who said you could move?

Dan lengthens his legs, cranes his neck, first to the right then left, arches his back then eases into the pose Jake set.

The latter surveys the scene. Dan's body fills the contours of the space below the picture window. His torso dominates. His right hand rests delicately on his thigh, atop hairy flesh.

What would your parishioners think?

What would I think if you told me your secrets?

You'll never know.

Nor my parishioners this.

Such power.

That's true. You got it—I give you Exhibit A—

—If I were you I'd be worried.

And yet I'm not.

Is this guy out of his mind? I mean he connected me with Emil, a guy who calls me Fruitcake and who attends Dan's church, and here he is, telling me he ain't worried.

So you'n me connected, one time. That was a mistake.

Who knows the reasons we do things.

I'm not the person I was when I arrived. I accept my fate now. But to call me intriguing, me of all people. Like I'm that gullible, t' be sweet-talked like that. I don' need to hear it, one, especially from you—I mean I ain't that desperate.

You need t' come up with a more convincing line than that.

Jake approaches the couch, the drawing leafing from the pad. The pick-up of his neighbor rumbles by, spinning the gravel under the tires as it circles around, between the trailers. Jake slides apart two slats of the venetian, spies a woman Jake has never seen pop from the cab—

—Have I ever eyed the same one twice?

Huh?

Jake watches as she waits at the foot of the stairs for the guy. When he's at the door she reaches her hands, up around his neck, and he plants his lips on hers, the volume of his beard obscuring the lower half of her face. Holding his mouth there he reaches with his free paw and turns the handle of the door, allowing the Persian to shoot inside. Holding hands, the two chain into the interior, shutting the door behind then cracking it just enough for two hands to toss the feline out. She sits on the landing and takes in the orange of the streetlights, it and the gun-metal clouds.

Dan swivels his torso around, splaying his thighs and trapping Jake. He runs the back of his hand along Jake's belly, trails it down until Jake steps away.

Let's see the drawing.

Jake unfurls it like Old Glory, obscuring his midsection.

Oh no!

What's wrong?

You said you weren't a realist!

I didn't say I wasn't after somethin' real.

Well this is too-too—

The goal was to capture you.

You got too much a me.

Jus' what's there. It's not my fault if—

—It's almost too much to bear.

How can there be too much—flesh is flesh.

It's not my point.

Dan lifts himself from the couch and treads a few feet, leaning over the sink while lengthening his neck. He draws a glass from the cupboard and fills it. From the window he observes the shadows of the couple in the back of the trailer.

They don't waste any time! He's already on toppa her.

Dan shrinks his neck and runs his hand behind the nape as he turns toward Jake. Retaking his position on the couch, next to the wall, he pats the cushion.

Have a seat. Let's study this thing—I'm tryin' t' wrap my head around it.

Jake revolves the chair that played the role of Easel, sets the pad on it and clips the drawing to steady it.

You might wanna gimme me notice next time.

About what?

About the perils a bein' drawn by you. Naked no less. It's me, I give you that. More'n I wanna see. But who's the other figure off to the side?

You tell me.

No, you tell me.

It's just a drawing. We can take a match to it, set it on fire. Toss it outside—it's jus' paper.

And yet it weirds me out, like I almost can't look. Like it's dangerous. I mean, I'm no dummy. I know it's me. And somehow I don't reco'nize myself. Meanwhile, what about our deal?

What about it?

In the moment Jake couldn't help remembering the time he turned Rauch down—how could he forget? The trouble you invite when you've come to a point and then say no. There's always hell to pay, as though he were bound despite the façade of freedom. Like he were ripe for any picker, any Tom, Dick, or Harry—just because. Like there's no such thing as agency, changing your mind. The thought casts a cloud.

Talk to me.

Solitude made me do it.

Can we let things rest as they are?

Can I give you a kiss?

If books could speak here's what they'd say: We're nothing you'll ever find in Laurentine. I had to come all the way to Pandemonium to glimpse a library, the real thing, not owned by a municipality or faked on a movie set, the way you might spot in a single's flat rented by some starlet. Real books about this and that, lined in a row like a gathering of atheists, reaching to the ceiling, and not just tossed like corpses in the corner, amassing dust, some ajar, some marked, many tattered, topping and growing out of furniture like spirits rising or laid in squat piles in front of the door, serving as stops. This here—the idea of an entire, ordered wall, a giant folio-sheet unfurled, an alphabet of authors arranged from A to Z and not simply thrown in a jumble McPhee Carson Stone Moore-Lappé Reich Balfour Vogt Fuller Osborn Ehrlich Leopold and Schumacher, part hay-stack and part smoke-stack that could go up in flames any time, a quasi-organized lump that resists systematizing, there in the back of the trailer.

Unlike here.

In fact it isn't just this wall that's morphed into a kind of book writ large, parts mimicking the whole, but the other walls too, although they read in a different way.

Praise God from Whom All Good Things Come.
When life gets too hard to stand, Kneel.
Prayer is the road to Heaven, but Faith opens the door.
Trust the Lord with all thine Heart; and lean not unto thine own understanding. In all thy ways acknowledge Him, and He shall direct thy paths.

These lines hover over unbooked walls, seemingly random though not without design, in some places coming for you and in others stenciled in font so small you have to draw near to read. Later Jake will glean on the ceiling above the toilet *Faith is not believing that God can, It is knowing that he will.*

Wanna drink?

I'll wait a bit.

C'mon the day's young! We'll have coffee before you hafta drive. You can also stay over if you like. We're having manhattans.

He's having manhattans. For some of us it's chardonnay.

My wife, Ginny. Ginny, Jake.

Sorry—I was trussing the bird when you arrived. So you're the famous Jake.

Voila Jake!

Famous? Oh my god no.

He showed me your drawing.

You look so familiar—d' we know each other?

Am I the only one having a manhattan? Jake, I'll get you one.

Dan disappears and Jake remarks yet again, Have we met? You're not from—

—We haven't met, I'm sure. I get that a lot though. Jake, tell me about your art—when did you start? And where did you study?

I love the color of your blouse—is it velvet?

Ginny tosses off a comment, remarks she's had it ages— must be decades. Living here we don't get out a lot. Like there's anything to get dressed for—it's not like LA! But tell me, where did you learn to draw? That sketch you made. Of Daniel—

Jake reddens—

—No worries. We're all adults here. Tell me your background.

There ain't nothing t' tell.

Well I'd like to talk to you about it sometime. The bell rings and Ginny glances aside, excuses herself, and leaves Jake and Dan together just as he's returning with a drink.

I can't believe you showed the drawing. It's practically porn.

What do you mean practically? By the way, she loves it. Like me, she was also weirded out by it, the figure in the corner. Like it's wrapped in seaweed or god-knows-what. It haunts me still.

It haunts me too.

She thought it was a statement about patriarchy—and power. She thought you were onto something with the figure on the couch, regal, and clearly lookin' for a thrill. The terrible contrast between the two figures. Like the one is commenting on the other.

Dan seizes the moment to kiss Jake, runs his hand along the spine—

—Oh my god no. Not here.

It's all good—there's nothing to hide—cheers, Jake! I'm so glad you came.

The room lights up as Ginny swings the door wide. Cold flows through the space, heated by a roaring fire—it rushes in with three, no four children tearing here and there, followed by one adult after another—

—Fruitcake!

—Emil!

Who knew you'd be here?!

Oh—that's right, remarks Ginny. I forgot Jake works for you.

Ginny orders the newly arrived to toss their coats in the den, and after Emil's collected an armful of wraps, ordering the older ones to assist the younger, he reaches his free arm and waits while the woman he's with removes her jacket.

This is Fruitcake! he comments to her, gesturing toward Jake.

I'm Caren. I'm guessing it's one of his inventions and not your real name.

Dan embraces Caren, who stands lifeless during the duration, then hugs Emil in warm, bearish fashion. After he releases him he grasps his biceps with both hands—You two been workin' I see. What can I get you?

Emil requests a cerveza and Caren replies, Soda-water for me. Someone's gotta remain sober. She turns to Jake, the obvious newcomer in the group, and comments, I use t' be able to pack it away like the best a them. But with four kids an' him unable t' control hisself—

—Fruitcake, I'm surprised t' see you here.

Jake responds, Lotta books, eh?

Yeah we got one or two.

And a lotta writing. Everywhere.

That's my handiwork. A woman emerges from the den where she's apparently been hiding, followed by a man, the two flushed out by kids and an onslaught of coats. She steps forward and reaches her hand.

I painted them myself. One by one.

She's the religious one in the family. A saying by Sade won't cut it—

—Who's that?

—Mione, never mind, offers Ginny.

Jake channels Florrie, compliments the woman on her work no matter what he thinks, everyone's tastes being so unique. He praises her skill-set whether or not he'd allow a word to be stenciled on the walls of his trailer, infecting the space like a virus, in such a way that the eye is kept working, trying to find a place to land, or hide.

It's funny but I hardly notice it, Dan muses. I guess y' get use t'it.

You don' notice a lotta things.

Dan introduces his daughter and son-in-law, Hermione and Steve, a little man with thinning hair and tortoise glasses who's already seated himself on the sofa at the end of the room. Squealing erupts from a bedroom off the parlor, adding sound to the visual cacophony there.

Pipe down! commands Caren. Emilio, vigílalos. Keep them from destroyin' the place! But before he can say anything three kids whiz out, buzzing the legs of the adults, two in hot pursuit of a front-runner who's holding a wooden cow.

A child's hand or six bang against Jake's legs as the tinny sound of keys tink on a toy piano in the other room. Caren jumps up from Dan's chair and marches to the door, steadying her hand on the trim. She leans in.

Why th' racket?! Keep it down! She attempts to corral the moppets tearing around the parlor, directs them back to what was once a bedroom but has since been converted into a playroom.

Wan' another drink, Jake?

I haven't finished this'n yet! He raises his glass and ice tinkles.

I'll take one, Emil quips, having put away a beer. I'm ready to switch.

Emilio! We jus' got here. Why not try an' take it easy.

It's a holiday! Dan responds. The guy works hard—Jake can testify, can't you?

—.

Dan returns from the kitchen and hands a glass to Emil.

Here's to you, Fruitcake! I never thought when you started we'd get that thing up. But we did it, you'n me! Now comes the best part.

Ginny yells from the kitchen it must be satisfying to build a house. Like a giant 3D sculpture that people live in.

More surfaces to paint, comments Hermione.

It's a hunters' cabin, informs Jake.

Virginia's voice emerges again from the kitchen. She orders Dan and a couple strong ones to clear space for the table along the middle of the room. Hermione hints at Steve that he might get off his behind and lend a hand, and Dan directs him and Emil to portage the coffee table into the den, along with two side-tables, as well as the love-seat Steve rested on. Two folding-tables, the type you find in church halls, are fetched from outside and set in place, followed by the table the kids have been congregating around, flushing the four of them into the parlor all of a sudden, that is until Caren rounds them up and directs them back to the playroom to sit on the rug.

In a matter of minutes an elongated surface is staged from one end of the space to the other, the regular furniture removed or shunted aside. Ginny hands Dan an immense tablecloth, dishes, silver, and cutlery, along with everything else that defaults on a dinner table, all of which he passes on to Emil who in turn passes things to Jake to pass to Caren and Hermione until everything has finally been set.

A child tugs at my pant leg and offers a figure. Moo-moo! he cries.

Jake, drink up. The day's young.

Yes, I see. Moo-moo. Do you like moo-moos?

A head nods slowly.

What else you got there?

Ba-a-a.

Ba-a-a. A very pretty ba-a-a. Do you like ba-a-as too? Again a nod. Me too. That's a cute little lamby.

Ginny pads from the kitchen. Look who's here! I thought I heard a car!

The knob of the front door revolves and heads turn. Two women make their way from bright light to the softer tones inside. I was worried you weren' gonna come!

You always say that. When've we ever missed?

You always do say that, copies Hermione.

After the introductions, Elizabeth and Doris make the rounds, hugging Ginny and Dan, followed by Caren and Emil—

—You must be Jake! We've heard about you.

Boring subject.

Somethin' tells me we got stuff to talk about—Mione, Steve. Elizabeth acknowledges the two across the room who are now sheltering under the door to the den, as though a tornado were imminent.

The full company having been joined, apparently, guests are directed to grab a folding-chair from the foyer and assume their places. Ginny air-lifts hors d'oeuvres and appetizers from kitchen countertops. The complex ritual of getting things on the table after such a protracted process, days long given the shopping then chopping—mixing, seasoning, and baking—all distilled in a moment. Down to the toast points, just grilled, that go with an assortment of spreads.

Seated at the head of the table Ginny raises a goblet full to the brim, nods at each one while looking her directly in the eye—Thanks for coming, everyone! Here's to friends and family, old and new—and to wine!

Mom! marks Hermione.

Let her be, snips Elizabeth. It's her show.

Mind your own business.

Dan's placed himself in the middle of the assembled, sandwiched between Emil and Jake, his thigh pressed against the latter's as he intones a prayer at Hermione's bidding, an official blessing from the Man of the House—Let's not forget the reason we're here, she admonished, after her mother's toast, a gesture that moved the group to raise their glasses and swill a second time, before acknowledging the source of so much bounty.

It's about a birth after all.

Dan squeezes Jake's thigh under the cloth, in the middle of the invocation, an oration that lasts until Elizabeth pipes up, Amen! cutting him short.

Let's eat! enthuses Emil.

Ginny calls for more bottles of wine to be stationed at intervals, for glasses to be topped off, giving some two drinks to tend to, and Doris, seated across from Dan, as if on cue, hovers the lip of a cabernet over Jake's glass and requests, Wan' a touch?

How can it hurt?

There you go, my boy—how can it? What was it Franklin said? In wine there's—

—We know, dad! whines Hermione. How many times we gotta hear it? In wine there's wisdom, freedom in beer, bacteria in water—you need a new script.

You girls always bring the best stuff, shifts Ginny, gazing at Elizabeth and Doris.

Girls, repeats Elizabeth, glancing beside her.

Once a daughter—you know what I mean.

—I don' mind, Doris intones, working her way from glass to glass.

Glad you don't.

Caren drops chunks of cheese and leaves of dressed lettuce on the kids' plates.

Force a habit, apologizes Ginny. You'll always be my girls, all three a you.

So there's more'n two? wonders Jake.

Our other daughter lives back east. Wish they could be here.

Me too, Elizabeth quips, slanting an eye across the table. If you can get into a habit you can get out've it, mom—it's the same thing. Doris reaches her hand toward Elizabeth and rests it on her forearm.

Meanwhile the wine begins to work its magic. I could swear I know you! repeats Jake, gazing in Ginny's direction. Are you sure you're not from the Forest City? To which not just Dan but Ginny, the daughters, their partners, and even Emil and Caren break in a laugh.

What's so funny?

I'm not from Forest City, wherever that is—I can assure you.

Well then how do we know each other?

Twenty questions, Emil intones. Go for it, Fruitcake!

I never saw you before today, Ginny assures. Though it's possible we've seen each other at Safeway.

I go there like twice a month. Maybe less.

That's why you're so thin and I'm so—

Fleshy? interjects Dan.

Fleshy!

You ain't as thin as Fruitcake, that's for sure, remarks Emil.

Why d'you call him that? Doris appears miffed.

He likes fruit-cake! Why'd you think?

He thinks he's funny, complains Caren. I wish I could break him of it. If I had my druthers—

—You been warned, Dan interjects, patting Emil's thigh.

Plates fill after a large bird and two roasts are portaged from the oven, after having rested. Jake winces as Dan does the honors of carving, spurred by Hermione. Blood pools at the bottoms of platters, and Elizabeth enthuses, Just the way I like it! Still breathin'! Jake takes a sip from his glass, a carved crystal. After plates circulate he spies the children dangling slabs of meat over their mouths, half in and half out in a makeshift game. Jake swills his glass. He wonders if Emil or Caren will reprimand them but both are too busy spearing chunks of this and that onto their own plates. Meanwhile after the mashed potatoes come around, finally, followed by platters of sautéed greens, beans, mushrooms, and cranberries, he now shovels them on. Emil reaches in front of him and implores Elizabeth to pass the gravy, the boat Jake passed on and Doris holds in front of her.

Fruitcake, you don't know what you missin'!

D'you want me to pour some on your potatoes? requests Dan, commandeering the gravy boat.

He don't eat no meat! Emil informs the table.

Are you allergic?

Is it a medical condition?

I wish I would a known, Ginny frowns. I could a made you tortellini or somethin'.

Jake protests he's happy with what he has.

How can you survive on that? queries Dan. No wonder you're skin an' bones!

Boy ain't gettin' his protein.

I'm sure Jake's gettin' his protein.

I gotta have my meat! pipes Steve.

Once platters of sliced beef make the rounds again, Dan nabs one, spearing tranches onto his newly-emptied plate. Red swirls around the bottom of the dish as he cradles it in the crook of his arm.

Jake, you ain' got nothin' on your plate.

Wha'd'you call this?

That ain't food—have some stuffin' a'least—everyone loves stuffin'. Maybe a little gravy? That ain't meat.

Dan, stop pesterin' the guy. He's an adult.

Ain' he though.

I'll pass—so thankful to be here. That's the point, ain't it?

Here's to being together! Doris cheers, raising a glass.

I'll drink to that! adds Ginny.

I'm sure you will, mutters Hermione.

Glasses are lifted, by all except Caren, Hermione, and Steve, who raise their fists in place of goblets—Here's to the spirit of the thing, after which the usual table chatter dissipates, leaving the tap of tines and serrated edges against porcelain.

....

Seriously, Jake. You got some kind a allergy? Dan pipes.

Uhn-uhn.

Then what gives?

Boring subject. Let's leave it.

I'm sure it is! But try me—I'm open.

Too open, complains Hermione.

Is it part of your religion? You a Buddhist or sumpin'! Ha!

Then you have no religion? queries Ginny.

Almost simultaneously Doris and Elizabeth gaze across and to the left of Jake as Caren admonishes the oldest child for slapping one of the younger ones.

He's prob'ly already got two parents to pester him about it so leave 'im be.

But I'm curious, defends Ginny. And, Lizzie, I wonder why your father never told me about the meat thing. I feel like a bad host.

Emil spears a turkey thigh to his plate then smothers it in gravy, carves off a bit and brings it to his lips, taking some with his fork and some with his fingers, followed by stuffing which he also smothers. Dan too manages to filter out anything green, red, or white, opting for a brown palette. He rests his hand on Jake's knee.

Don' mind me. Eat wha' you want.

We're just curious s'all, remarks Ginny. It's in both our natures, why we lasted all these years. Girls'll tell you that.

They're curious all right.

Mione.

Don' worry, Fruitcake. So long's you can pound a nail.

I had a dog, Jake remarks.

Why past tense?

We had one too!

Had to put 'im down, though—it was devastating.

I'm still not over it.

Here's to Chocolate!

Glasses raise.

To Chooooocolate!

Such a pet, laments Elizabeth. Owned him for years. Practically a member of the family.

Practically?

You know what I mean.

We had six or seven breeders back in Oklahoma, pipes Doris. All bull-dogs.

Who took care a them?

Doris launches into a speech on Four-H—I was just a kid. Had all kind a animals. Cows, pigs, chickens, turkeys, rabbits—you name it.

And?

And what, Jake?

Just wondered what it was like. Usually people who grew up on a farm have a lot t' say about it. Most people have no clue.

I guess I have nothin' else t' say. Other'n we had 'em.

She ain't tellin' you the half a it. They got herds, big ones, her family. Far as a eye can see. Thank god there aren't too many people like you, Jake, or they'd go belly-up.

Can we change the subject?

Let the guy eat.

Fruitcake ain' botherin' me none! I see a cow, I think a steak. Roast. Like this! Emil holds up Exhibit A.

Did you eat this good back in Okie country? Caren holds up a fork with a hank of breast on it.

Hermione remarks, I don' understand the thing about the dog, Jake. What's that got t' do with anything?

Jake, we got somethin' in common—

—Don't you mean someone?

Daniel—

—No need to blush, Jake.

135

Ginny lifts her glass and Dan responds in kind. Jake eyes two animal figures beneath Ginny's chair then lifts his glass as well. Here's to things in common?

To things in common!

The three sip from goblets elevated not with hands but finger-tips. Jake observes as legs run down the inside of the glass, tracking toward the stem.

Daniel's right—someone. Not sure our eldest would approve—she's barely civil to her sister. But that's their problem.

You don't wanna go wading into them waters.

Moo for cow and baa for sheep, bovine and ovine. Moo and ba, simple's that.

So tell me, Jake. What were you trying to say in your drawing?

Oh that. Boring subject.

It's clearly no coincidence.

If I tell you will you tell me how I know you?

Oh that! Talk about boring—

I'll tell!—

—Daniel.

Ginny's an actor. Not unfamous.

Was.

Can you guess?

Wowwww. Not a clue.

None?!

The moo and ba of existence, the way we shove them aside, think about them then run.

No, no clue whatsoever.

She, my dear, was the house-keeper on *The Honeycut Clan.*

No way!

It's true.

I can't believe it. I knew I knew you!

You'd have to been raised by wolves not to.

To be honest it's a curse—it follows you everywhere. Including Pandemonium.

So all that's in the past?

Yes and no. We're still in contact, all of us—prob'ly will be forever. Though we're spread out these days. You know the father, Barry—he's gay. That's how I met Daniel. He and Barry—

—No need to go into that—

—So you're saying the country's most clean-cut, wholesome dad—*the* icon of what it means to be—

—No surprise there, Jake. Not in that business. Out of it too, I guess—Ginny gives Dan a kiss. But never mind—it's your turn now, Jake. What were you trying to say?

But I have a million questions about *The Honeycut Clan*.

Maybe another time. So—the drawing. Tell me—it haunts me.

Like I say, boring subject. I wasn't trying to say nothin'. It's just a drawing.

That all you gotta say? You can do better'n that.

See what I mean about him?

Sounds like a cop-out—it's much more than "just a drawing," Jake—Ginny crooks fingers in air while she speaks. She rests one leg over the other—it disturbs him and me both. Wasn't that your intention—what entered your head, apart from what was before you?

My intention was to get things down, best I could.

But there are two figures there, and you only had one model, who, I must say, wasn't on his best behavior—but that's between the two of you.

How to explain there were three figures present at the time, including me, and four this moment, two when I'm alone, me and the one frumped on the love-seat there. Where Steve and

Mione tried to fade into the woodwork, avoiding Elizabeth and Doris once the table was broken down, a mountain of dishes having just been scrubbed by an army crammed in a tiny kitchen, growing cooler by the moment, a group sorted into washers, dryers, carriers, and stackers? Bowls of left-overs rested on the dinette, next to mincemeat pies waiting to be enjoyed by everyone present, given the misnomer of the name, after which everything remaining could be parceled out into to-go bags, nearly all gone presently, though the spirits of the attendees remain, including echoes of children with wooden toys that no doubt Elizabeth and Hermione animated decades ago, now come to rest under Ginny's chair, the voice of the toddler after pulling on my pant-leg, moo-mooing and ba-ba-a-ing, the sounds haunting the stillness, they and the real-life animals that were devoured, the bloody platters challenging the bourgeois civility in the room, three of the four figures currently sipping port, a new one for me, chatting about this and that, serving post mortems—tensions between Elizabeth and Hermione, Hermione and Steve, Caren and Emil—the general cacophony of the day ringing on despite the audible sound of the mantel clock amid a tidy arrangement of sofas and chairs now returned to their former order, turning the room into a space more conducive to reading than the earlier ruckus. Emil's tall, looming presence, his booming voice, Caren's frequent admonishments, the asides of the daughters to their respective partners—they're all here and not-here, nearly but not quite as present as Peacoat.

I don' know what t' say. Where it came from.
It's like death broods over Daniel, has his eye on him.
Or is it on me?
On you, Jake? Don't be silly. You're practic'ly a boy.
Trust me, he ain't no—
—Spare me.
The figure's ghastly—the contrast between him and Daniel, still in the pink of life, if I can put it that way.

The pink of life—

—You know what I mean, Jake—it can't be just chance. You must a had something in mind, something you wanted to say.

It felt right.

I don't believe it. Or it's not enough.

I wouldn't want to live in your dreams.

I don't remember them anyway. Most times.

Well what are you going to do with your talent?

My talent?

He has more than one—

—Daniel! Yes, with your talent.

I guess I never saw it that—

The doorbell chimes and Ginny jumps—Oh yay! She made it!

By what quirk of chance or no-chance did I draw that?—god only knows. By what chance am I here? To think of the first time I set eyes on Pandemonium, a town that ironizes its own name in its current state, masking its beginnings, tents thrown like discarded bones in the bowl of a valley, now so prim and orderly, just below the switchbacks that carry you skyward in a series of hairpins, up and over Guanella Pass to Grant. The town shrinks the higher you ascend until it disappears, a place that at eye level is as inviting and impenetrable as a fortress.

A handsome woman enters. She has salt-and-pepper hair pulled back in a long braid, framing weathered skin. She sports cowboy boots and jeans, an embroidered denim shirt and flowered kerchief that reveal themselves, along with silver-and-turquoise accents, once she hands over her coat.

Jake, Vida, Vida, Jake. The two shake hands and Dan offers Vida a kiss.

How are you, love?

Vida, I saved you a plate. Ginny embraces the woman, rests her coat on a hook in the foyer, then leads her to the kitchen by the hand.

Jake, stay the night.

He glances toward the love-seat. I can't.

They're gonna do their thing and I'll be all alone in my room.

Your room?

OK Elizabeth's. Once. You don't want a body to be alone on a night like this, do you?

On such a holy occasion. A day after the Glasby twin's birthday.

Huh?

Nothin'.

How can you abandon me?

The women return and the four shift positions on the parlor chairs, across from the wall of books. Dan dribbles another round of port.

This stuff's good!

This stuff—. Ginny emits a polite chuckle. Jake, Daniel tells me you're a reader.

I've been known —

—According to him you have a mountain a books.

I lot messier than these—

—Vida and I have a book club. You're welcome any time, if you'd like—

—I'm not allowed.

Don't listen to him! He can come any time, but he prefers not to. Some a our members drive all the way up from the city—that's how into it they are.

A bunch a old biddies!

You shush—. Jake, I'd like you to come.

Vida works her plate with a sterling fork. She sets it down, finishes chewing, wipes gravy from her lower lip with the corner of her napkin, which she then rests again on her lap. She lifts her glass, tilts the stem, declares, Merry, merry! then sniffs, sips, waits, and swallows. I agree with Ginny, she comments finally. Join us, Jake. We could use some fresh blood. He observes legs forming on the side of Vida's goblet. By the time she takes her last sip her plate has been cleaned and Ginny rises, positions herself next to her, strokes her hair as she leans forward to take her plate. She pulls a package from the top of the sideboard, wrapped and bowed, and hands it to her.

I thought we're not doing this anymore, remarks Vida. Said we all got enough stuff—isn't the what you told the family?

Do we? Have enough? queries Dan.

I hope it's alright to make an exception. Shall we say it's just a coincidence that I'm giving it to you today? That it's wrapped in this paper, which just happens to be similar to paper others use on a day like this—

—In that case.

The two rise, disappear into the kitchen, then up the stairs.

What d' you say, Jake? Stay with me?

Thus time, tortoise and torturous, hale and hare. Rich in paradox, it travels. At a rate of 67,000 miles per hour. It catapults us with a flaming center. Unconscious for the most part, a type of forgetfulness or unknowing. Prolonged sleep-walking. Readying us for a big sleep, which draws us toward itself the moment we're conceived, birthed in a murk, moving through a haze, bare life papered with religion. For all the hoo-hah, the way people place it on a pedestal, it can be the first to betray you. Like a lover with a wagging tongue.

Here's to you, Fruitcake! To the end of yet another project!

What are we up to? Four?

Who knew you'd make it past one?

Here's to you, too—and Caren! Another kid on the way.

My growing brood.

Your growing wife.

She's happiest that way. We no sooner get used t' a new one before she starts pestering me for the next. Like I'm just stud-service.

And you mind.

Fruitcake, have another beer.

But it's lunch-time.

What d' we gotta do but push a broom? One more beer ain't gonna kill us.

Well, maybe one more—how can it hurt?

Emil reaches for the cooler in the back of the cab, behind Jake's seat. He extracts two cans atop a pile of ice. He snaps the tabs, a sound Jake recognizes well, then hands one over. It's great you an' Dan have become friends.

He is a friend. I think.

So we got a thing in common.

I guess.

He tells me you got abilities.

You mean drawing?

You could say.

Carpentry? What I know I know from you.

I don't mean that, Fruitcake.

What kind then?

—.

I'm gonna kill 'im.

You should. You'n me could a been havin' a good deal a fun all along—

—What do you mean could a?

Think a what we missed.

Missed—what?

You tell me.

An' what about you?

What about me?

What about you'n Dan?

What about us? How d' you think me an' Caren get by? With all them kids. You think this horse-and-pony show's gonna cut it? Six people and one in the oven?

Why not get another job?

And ruin this? What we got? It's how I work. Two-man crew. What d'you say, Fruitcake?

What do I say about what?

Why don' we.

But you're married!

So are you, in a way.

Am not!

—Not the way Dan tells it—

—He's makin' it up.

Just a little fun—and all innocent—no one needs to know.

That's the point—she doesn't!

Nor does she have to. I trust you, Fruitcake.

That ain't the point.

Is that how you felt with Dan? Wha'd you do, gag the guilt reflex?

They got an arrangement.

Did you know that when you went for it?—I heard about Ojo Caliente.

He pressured me.

Oh I'm sure.

It was a failure on both our parts. I'm guessin' you and Caren don't got the same deal.

She understands men.

I'm glad someone does.

I think she'd prefer me'n another dude over me 'n some chick.

Simple's that.

So long's I come home every night. Put out when she wants. Bring home the bacon.... What'd you say, Fruitcake? You in or out? You gonna leave me stranded or you gonna lend a hand? Jake swivels his head, wipes sweat from the window next to him, peers at the finished structure. He hears Emil's breathing intensify, catches him trembling slightly.

Jake turns his gaze toward what's unfolding next to him and Emil reaches forward, strokes Jake's hair, runs his hand along the jaw-line, touches the cheek with the back of his hand, then rests his index on Jake's lip—Sometime you look jus' like a girl—

But I'm—

Emil's attentions shift away, gaze tilted upward, toward the roof of the cab—gimme a hand, Fruitcake.

Biology takes over, that and physics. Plumbing, pipes, and gauges, biding time while pressure builds—Emil emits breaths for words, sighs for directives. Jake observes the facial drama, features of macho pain and school-girl bliss, shut-eyed cruising and wide-eyed anticipation, the long-awaited kiss, array of miens, indistinct in the late-afternoon light, though not so leaden for Jake to miss the big event as Emil begins to tag now this and now that, plays himself out in the blink of an eye, an eternity given the usual nature of the thing, complex and common, a flight finalized in wheels touching down.

Breathing subsides.

Emil stares over the steering wheel then turns toward Jake.

And you a married man with four kids. Pregnant wife.

One on the way.

What about you?

What about me? I'm good—

—Fruitcake—really. Who's gonna know?

I'm guessin' Dan for one. God only knows who else.

I swear, Fruitcake. I ain't gonna tell.

He swore the same.

He must a been drinkin'. Otherwise he probably wouldn' a told. Besides, what's the harm? Look how long it took him to spill the beans.

But he did.

C'mon, Fruitcake.

Jake wrestles with himself.

I mean really, how's it gonna hurt?

You mean who.

I swear I won't tell. Her or Dan.

Then on one condition.

Name it.

Pose for me.

It's freezing!

I mean at my place. Another time.

So it's you gonna tell on me. I seen your drawings. You'll have as much t' tag me on as I got on you.

Then for my eyes only.

At which point Emil nears Jake, reaches past the flap of his jacket and unfastens it, exposing flannel which he unbuttons slowly, the jeans, as though unbinding a gift, the flesh under the tee, darker by comparison to the white of the tee itself.

Soft as a girl.

And yet—

—Nice, Fruitcake.

What does it make you?

The words cap a gesture, many. Just at the moment the show's over, the curtain coming down, Emil pleads that

the two stay together, entangled, as long as animal heat
remains—

....

—Guess we better get back—

—To work, Jake adds profoundly.

—Jus' like doin' it with a chick—

—An' yet—

—With Dan it's different—

—No need—

This was long overdue.

We're here—that's what counts.

Shut up and dig, one a yous at least. There's cops
around—an' this ain' legal.

The ground's frozen!

You gotta get through the crust—

—It's like roots joined arms, trying t' keep us out.

Keep her out!

You try breakin' this shit up.

She brought the shovel, not me—I'd a brought a long-
handle. Better leverage.

It'll get easier once we—

Easy for you to say. How deep we gotta go?

Deep enough. Bro, just shut up an' dig. I'll take over
when you're tire'.

I'm no weakling fellows! I can do it!

Then, be my guest—

Wren proceeds to set soles to the step of the blade, huffing
and leaping, expecting clods to come loose but freeing only
divots from a miserly, frozen earth, which doesn't relish the
intrusion, never mind the nature of the affair, as though
miffed.

Why do we always dispose of our dead down and never up? Up gets all the glory, the space primates tread in trees 'til they started walking bare earth, though I'm sure they fantasized about housing their gods up there, even when they lived in the canopy, far in the sky, ascribing gods to parts unknown and placing the dead and diabolical below, also unknown though they could at least plant their feet there, unlike the province of the birds—for ages human animals plowed what's below but only in the last nano-second in the scheme of things have they gone airborne, and now we're trashing that too.

Oh! Hi!

Officer?

This guy bothering you?

Which guy?

Who d'you think?

No, he's my—

—Why don' you move along, buster. Leave these two alone.

Me?! They're the ones—

You heard me—now skedaddle!

You got it wrong—he ain't doin'—

At which point the cop gazes toward what lay atop the grass, grayed by the moon and oranged by the streetlight when it blinks on—

You know there are laws against this kind a thing. He put you up to it?

I keep tryin' t' say—

—Look, they didn' know—

—Who ask you buster? Look you two, no burials allowed on city property—I'm gonna have t' write you up.

It ain't hurtin' nothin', pleads Wren. No one'll ever know.

Like I say I'm gonna have t' issue you a citation.

This spot is special to my brother—he use to bring our dog here all the time—this'n.

—It was almos' here, corrects Jake. Across the street really. Under the statue—can't bury nothin' there. Or in the gardens nearby. They be turnin' up the dirt over there—

—So we went for the next bes' thing, officer. 'Least she got a good view a the statue from here.

Wren picks up a bundle from below, wrapped in one of her quilting fabrics, drawn with chrysanthemums. She was a member of the family, officer—a person really. Outsize personality in such a li'l body, more'n lots a people. Parents put her down—

—Took forever for us to find 'er—

—Goin' through the bodies—

—This place is special—we won't tell if you don't.

Donald nudges Wren, motions her aside for a parlay, after which she leads the officer back to the squad-car, lights flashing. Jake and Donald, meanwhile, stand over a depression, not yet a burial site near the road but far enough to avoid the syringes, cans, and vials that passersby and druggies discard on their way here and there, in perfect view of *Le penseur.*

The only illumination here normally, beside moonlight, is the street-light, if you can call it that, given how often it blinkers on and off. More to the point though is the light atop the car, casting red, casting blue, in turns, shading violet against Wren's forehead as she continues to grip the handle of the shovel, as though planting a potato.

Even she can' talk her way outta this. Looks like you're gonna have t' take the ticket and shut up about it, Donald tells Jake, who observes the play of light across Donald's forehead, nose, and cheeks.

He approaches the officer who's holding a pad, his pen moving as Wren's lips move, trying to explain the situation. They're yards from Donald, who mans a station beside the divot in the turf and what lies near, away from the cars that pass—

Where in the world is Ojo Caliente? queries the cop, pronouncing the name Oh-Joe after recording it and musing over what he's written. Wren launches into an explanation—

—I been t' Mile High City—my daughter's in college there. But I ain't never heard a that place.

He and Wren continue to exchange small-talk about a tacky tourist town in the Rockies, erstwhile haunt of gold and now molybdenum miners, hunters, skiers, and a former born-again; lots of transients most of all, as anyone can tell, people lost, down on their luck, or just passing through. After an eternity the cop removes the yellow slip under the original, pads with Wren back to the scene where Donald's coat floods red and blue. The cop orders Jake to mail in a check—

—That is unless you wanna show in court and contest it—

—Which I don't suggest you do.

Who ask you?

Really, officer—he's my—

—Zip it.

Jake shakes the man's hand as if to thank him for the citation, and Wren offers her regards to his daughter as he walks away. She slips the receipt from her twin's hand—

—Wow! Fifty bucks!

It's rob'ry.

I'll quote the bastard. Zip it, you two! Donald mutters. Wait 'til he leaves.

The vehicle idles and idles, then idles a while longer, adjacent to the curb as the cop radios dispatch, fills his log then sets it finally to the side, on the seat, below the dashboard, all visible in the artificial light generated above the vehicle—leaving the three to stand like figures in a genre painting by some Dutch guy, about to root tubers from the earth, their task suspended by pigment on canvas.

Finally the vehicle begins rolling, then halts. The cop rolls down the passenger window, leans wide toward the opening and points toward Donald with pistol aim—

—You one lucky bastard—. Count your lucky stars, boy. Getting' away with murder like 'at. At which point he wheels the window closed and peels away, shooting dust and gravel in his wake.

Donald—

Wren embraces him, tries to get him to look at her, but he remains stiff, not unlike the one at his feet.

Jake interrupts, heaving a sigh. Wren, I can't come up with this, I ain't got it—

Donald comes to.

—Who said you gotta? Guy din't give a crap—it's December. Not a lot a ticketin' goin' down and he got a quota.

Jake, I just realized—Donald's right. You're off the hook.

What's that mean?

You're outta state, my man. Asshole can't come after you—

—He was an asshole, mirrors Wren.

She grabs hold of the handle and begins digging in earnest, using the citation to insulate her hands from the metal handle, grown colder after the interruption, until finally the earth yawns enough to accept its charge whether it likes it or not, planted as deep as the season allows.

I wanna go further but I hit sumpin'.

Hit what?

A rock I think.

Should we try an' get it out?

Wren!—Jake!—leave it. We're deep enough.

Don't rocks wanna gravitate to the surface?

It'll be alright—it's cold out here!

Donald, be serious! You think we OK?

This is y'all's thing. But—I'll say it again—it'll be alright.

Wren, Donald's right. It's gonna have t' do. We ain't gonna be digging after no rock.

What if it pulls up? Then what?

It ain't goin' nowhere.

Jake, you jus' want it t' be over, the both a yous. But it's our Moll—

Poor thing—I should a never—

'Nother time—.

The three turn to the figure wrapped in chrysanthemums, a yellow field with white blossoms, chosen from Wren's stash, avoiding pink or blue—she lifts the bundle and bids Donald and Jake to lend a hand in the ritual sense, rest it in the ground, as though planting for the future, which the three do slowly, without opening or looking at what's inside, given they've already seen, perhaps more than enough.

Here's to a giant, comments Wren after lifting off her knees and rising to her feet.

My shadow. Sanity too. In a way.

A guru—she was our teacher, Jake.

For some time the twins wax the way people do at times like this, having waited until then, under the press of elements, to think about let alone address the departed, papering over not a few complications as the occasion demands, the missteps and missed opportunities, misjudgments that seem to loom largest when the chance to express any of that to the living has vanished, in an irreversible way—the tears shed seem as much about opportunities lost as the actual loss, memories of why Molly went as she did, with neither Wren nor Jake in eye- or ear-shot. The weight of knowing you resigned a body to expiring alone. As heavy as the earth pyramiding next to it.

Donald, you wanna say anything?

Me?

Jake—anything?

—.

Wren tosses a handful of dirt into a hole now grown a mile wide and deep it seems, extending further the more soil she and then Jake sprinkle on, when Donald unsticks the edge of the spade where it's adhered to the sod and commences to shovel the pile into the terrain until it's once again more or less as flat as they found it, save for an embossing. He replaces as much of the turf as he can, then tamps it with his shoe, larger and more ponderous than the others'.

Should we put some kind a marker?

You mean like a cross?! Over my dead body.

Who's talking about that? I was thinkin' more a stones. A cairn.

That's gonna attrac' attention—

—But Donald, how will we know where to find it?

Wren—we'll remember.

Jake, you OK with that?

How we gonna forget after all this?

You'd think a deal, principled in its way, a form of barter old as civilization and OK'd by two adults, in private, a pair trading tit for tat, putting the skin of both in the game, so unlike the modern system of currency that commutes paper for services in such an impersonal way—you'd think if the parties went to such lengths to craft such an agreement, of freedom-in-thrall, went out of their way to keep it under wraps to avoid the usual intrusions—executive, statutory, and judicial—you think given all that nothing could go wrong.

Fruitcake, I'll be to your place five-thirty on Monday. We'll take it from there.

She ain't gonna be 'spicious?

She ain't never gonna be up. Not 'til I leave.

Jake exits the cab and begins to untangle a nest of cords, rolling then dropping them in the work-box at the back of the truck.

Shall we state the deal before we go? Only thing that's gonna get me up that early.

The deal.

I just sit there. After that I get my way.

Can you just sit there?

Can you submit?

Once inside the completed structure, the fourth so far, flakes fall on window casings, recently glazed. Here on Frontage Road, just off and well below the interstate, such that on the section of highway between Ojo and Pandemonium a driver might speed by and never notice the row of dwellings, four and counting, that Jake and Emil have constructed single- or double-handed, with one more plot remaining in this makeshift development, if you could call it that. The houses spread across acres.

Even with the highway not far away the silence unnerves. Swallows you. Blankets any arrangement you might have committed to. Doubts you may have about what's proposed, from which something is to be gained and much, potentially, to be lost. Including your livelihood. Roof over your head. Three meals. If things go amiss. Everything you scraped together thus far that you call your own, not unlike the things Jake picks through at the dump.

Snow flakes down. OK then, hour an' a half. Half for you and half for me.

You mean half where I get to call the shots. Half where you do, clarifies Jake.

No saying no, Fruitcake.

No saying no, Emil.
No matter what.
No matter what.

When to yes and when to no a thing without knowing for sure how it's going to play out, like any agreement after you get into it. The things you don't plan on and can never foresee. You try to weigh expense and return. When to say I do and when to back away—especially when one of the parties has already mouthed the words in a different setting, under the eyes of family and friends, church and government, the national census, the education system, medical and legal establishments, the judiciary—the entire panoply of agents of respectability, under the many eyes of cultural surveillance—unlike this-here, which will be maintained and policed by a bureaucracy of two.

Completely under the radar.
Scouts honor?
Scouts honor.
Bet wise and you've cheated fate. Bet wrong and you're screwed.
Either a us can end it any time?
Dumb question, Fruitcake.
I can keep my job no matter what?
That remains to be seen. Whether we do this or not.
Any other articles?
No foolin' around, anywhere, outside your, that is our, place from now on.
Typical.
You're callin' for articles.
You're the one attacked me, just t' be clear. Before god, nature, and anyone who might a passed by.
—That was an hors d'oeuvres, Fruitcake. Can't have that again—
—Even if you feel the urge?

Even if—but Fruitcake!—why the fuss? You got secon' thoughts? Or you just a worry-wart? I got enough a that at home.

Guilty as charged.

No, I ain't a worry-wart! I jus' wanna be clear, since you wanted to spell things out.

Once two hands clasp, calloused and weathered; once two pairs of eyes meet without looking away; once two pairs of lips touch, hands on the move—at that point the two are joined.

Over the ensuing months Jake adds drawing after drawing to a growing stack, setting the most recent aside to be fixed at a more godly hour, after which Emil gets his fill, deprived as he complains he is at home, the unborn child altering life before it ever sucks a breath, stretching Jake's capacity for endurance in the same way Jake stretches Emil's, a man in motion forced to freeze, avoid twitching and scratching, shifting and sighing, complaining too, anything but maintain a set-though-not-rigid pose, a gesture Jake imagined—a trial that Emil endures and repays in kind when his turn comes, putting Jake through his paces too, bespoke in their way—on the hardness scale the two are matched.

I wanna start painting you.

It's your rodeo, Fruitcake. I wanna change things up s'well—what does paintin' mean to me?

It means you assume the same position each an' every time. 'Til the work is done.

Well, we got a deal. But why you wanna do that? Ask a guy t' stare at that same dumb wall, stuck with my thoughts an' nowhere t' go. As though I were dead?

What thoughts?

Mind your business. Tit for tat, Fruitcake. Maybe I'll tie you so you see what it's like.

Thus Jake takes up oils again, inducing rigor mortis in Emil, visit after visit, who again repays Jake in kind, creating a stiff of a different kind and simultaneously making him squirm, cheeks flushed, paying for his or someone's sins, he's sure, the offenses of his fathers, mothers too, coming back to visit him, a math that seems to excite Emil more than anything so far.

What Jake draws from the scenario is that Emil, outwardly jovial and even jolly, eternal jokester and wisecracker, phlegmatic and generous, open and kind, is not without layers, a walking crowd, suiting one way on the street and another here in the trailer, under the protection of an agreement.

An image of a person emerges in oils that began during the construction of house five, mirroring a drama, Jake realizes, that he himself is implicated in, though one of others' creation, a play without any easy resolution. In a sense he puts on a costume only to remove it. A thing that lives under the cushions of the sofa most of the day, which Jake draws out the moment he hears Emil's pick-up come the crack of dawn.

As for the real wife, Jake learns, she's facing a different kind of extremis, prolonged over months until her time nears. By that point Jake's amassed several canvases, different in style, palette, and tone, a collection that shows a working-out as pronounced as whatever's happening in Emil, putting Jake through it, for which he repays his sitter handsomely the next time they meet.

Have you had your fun? pokes Emil. That was difficult today.

Have you? Had your fun?

Sadly.

Sadly?

Too bad we gotta stop, Jake. Go back to our respectable lives—respectability is hell.

That's your thing—none a this is any skin off your hide.

You go t' church for chrise sake.

Think I got a choice?

Don't you? You just got promoted t' deacon, I hear.

That's how I get tanned, Fruitcake. Life does it to us all, one way or another. Only, unlike this, without consent.

It'll be years, decades really, before any of what's taking place here will remotely make sense, if you can call it that, still today, before the situation begins to shed light after the two shed everything, for so long, pre-dawn—actually it'd be years and many miles from here. For now, not just Jake but Emil chalk things up to life, whatever that is, as though paying were a given. Unhappiness.

—Don't we got a choice? Outside here?

Even if we—I—did, Fruitcake, remember the deal. You gotta go with it. Or end it—only freedom, it seems, that you and I got. You still in?

Are you?

You got the power.

You an' me both.

Show me your hands. No, palms down.

Jake flips his wrists, extending the fingers like tree-roots, deracinated and exposed. Suzanne takes one of his mitts and cradles, almost caresses it. Her own hands, knotted and misshapen, chill the calloused undersides not unlike Tommy's behind when the covers slipped off. She toggles back and forth, inspecting now this, now that, then frees them both.

You pass. But you could do with a squirt a lotion—look how dry these are!

The ladies saunter over to scrutinize the cuticles, purpled in places from hammer misses, the skin around and beneath the nails which truth be told he'd never thought about until he moved here, in a winter where dryness causes them to drip blood.

Deacon got you workin'!

Ever think a wearin' gloves?

They all roughed up!

Feel 'em, how leathery.

Jake withdraws his hands, having worked the sideshow long enough. The women assume their places around the table. An array of casseroles, salads, and pastries have been laid out, and Jake unwraps a loaf of bread, removes it from the towel and sets it on a cutting-board next to the rest.

Be honest. You make that? Or buy it?

Bought it for sure—that's my bet.

I vote he bought it too.

I say it's from Safeway.

In fact I made it—

Hones' Injun?

Hones' something.

The door opens and Ginny waltzes in, scattering flakes from her cape before hooking it on a dowel by the door. Looks like we're all here—sorry I'm late. Everyone, this is Jake.

Welcome, Jake!

Dan had a feeling you'd come.

Will he be here?

It's jus' us women—I hope tha's OK.

Jus' us old ladies, Jake, Olivia wheezes.

Standing at the end of the table near the **OPEN** sign, it's back turned street-ward after business hours, Ginny glows. Look't all these treats! An' they smell so good. I brought a few bottles a wine, which I vote we start on.

Hear, hear!

I didn't f'get the corkscrew this time, intones Marge.

Plastic cups are distributed and Ginny reminds the gathered, including the newcomer, what they agreed to read. Were you able to find it, Jake?

I looked—but nothin'.

Lily sits upright in her chair, shoulders rounded, neck set almost perpendicular to her torso. When she speaks she casts eyes to the side rather than swiveling her head. Won't find a copy anywhere up here, Jake.

Lily's right, argues Vida.

I got it at the university, advises Winnie.

Carina opines, I spec' that's the only place you can find it.

Back and forth the conversation goes about where to lay your hands on the reading for tonight, not to mention the rest of the month, which like many of the selections they'll read, Jake will discover, isn't easy to find. Vida remarks that it's a work flying under the radar in this country, for years now. Suzanne adds, Somehow it's fallen outta favor. Ginny suggests Jake look on with Carina for the time-being—Just watch she don't bite. Plastic glasses are filled in front of everyone except Marge, who informed the group she'll stick with water. Now Ginny solicits news before they begin, and Carina announces they're tryin' to get a group going down in the city.

Similar t' the one they started in the Big Apple.

What's that?

After explaining the purpose, something about parents and a flag, rainbow colors, Carina adds that chapters are popping up all over, that it'd be good to get something goin' here too.

Maybe we could sponsor it.

Would the church allow it?

I'm game, remarks Ginny. For obvious reasons. If you get the materials together so we can learn more—Is there anything else?

Since you're not gonna say anything, I will, chides Vida, elbowing Ginny. Our fearless leader's gonna give a talk next week about women in th' ministry.

Marge volunteers to be there, as does Lily and Carina, then the rest, until the suggestion is made to take the church van and go as a group.

Ginny, that's a victory, Olivia comments.

Not t' be the only one, it ain't. A token.

Baby steps.

Why d'you think I'm going along?

Other news is announced, specific to the Mission in Pandemonium but also in town until, no more to say, books emerge from purses and knapsacks, popping on the surfaces of tables that have been configured in the round, almost a circle, large enough to seat the entire group now that Ginny's arrived, leaving barely enough room for a person to squeeze by.

So what did we think?

I ain't gonna lie—I didn't like it, Winnie laments.

Marge opines, It definitely was a challenge.

Couldn't she a made it easier t' follow? Suzanne whines.

But if it were easy, a one-and-doner, would we be here discussing it? Puttin' our heads together? pipes Olivia. Tryin' t' get a bead on what's happenin'? If it were a piece a cake we wouldn' bother—we could read it on our own. Ain't she inviting us to a discussion, challenging us to go back and reread?

To rethink things, agrees Ginny. Including something as basic as how to read.

I agree with that, crows Olivia.

Maybe reading aloud'll help, offers Vida. Jake, you wanna start since you're the new boy?

Is this a baptism? I was never good at reading aloud—I just broke out in a sweat! The ladies smile cordially as he lifts his napkin and fans himself—

—If it's too much to endure—

—I'll do my best—

—Before you do, interjects Winnie. Why the scriggly shape on the first page?

And throughout!

Never seen that before.

They're versions a my initial. The author was thinkin' a me, I'm sure.

I'm sure she was, Olivia.

No doubt, returns Winnie, winking. And all a us here, sittin' in a circle, if you can call it that.

For me they were holes t' crawl in and hide, admits Suzanne. I mean I didn't get nothin' outta this. Couldn't make hide nor hair—

—Holes for sure, smirks Vida.

Maybe they're like weird apostrophes, ventures Lily, scooting up from a slump.

Huh?

Like, *Oooo life! I go to encounter the reality a experience*—or something like that. Or, *O God! How weary and unprofitable is the world!* Or—*O, pardon me, thou bleedin' piece a earth.* Somethin' like that. T' grab attention.

She got mine, Suzanne assures.

Mine too.

Are they blobs? Hollow periods? queries Jake.

That's a loaded one. What would you know about that?

The group breaks up in such a way the focus is lost. Small-talk ensues between groups of two and three, until Ginny intervenes—Jake...Jake.... Jake!—never mind them. You wanna read? It seems the scriggly circles can mean a lotta things, ladies, including the one Jake just mentioned. 'Tentionally or not.

When the monsoon rains arrive the women hunker down in the mountain cabin—

—Actually—can we stop here?

Please.

Why a monsoon? And why a mountain cabin? Why "the women" and not a character? Why the order? Like the women only go to the mountain cabin when the monsoon comes.

Uh, isn't a monsoon a summer thing? Least out here—

Ain't a mountain cabin a special place? suggests Marge.

What's your point?

Somethin' about class? I mean, I can't afford no mountain cabin.

You sayin' something about privilege?

You mean white privilege?

I say that?

Somethin' about privilege then—

—Well, if the shoe—

—If I remember correctly, in that one author we read, rain and—ain't the birds sleeping with open eyes, implying they're—you know—

—Maybe we should read on.

Can we bracket all those ideas and come back to them? remarks Ginny—Jake, can you read?

Water taps as it strikes the rocks, after rivering past the eaves. Trickles enclose the sides of the cabin like a curtain—.

There's the cabin again.

More rain—and water—

—Summer for sure.

Rain drills the rocks, alters their shapes, wears them down until they—

There's your blobs, Jake. Hollowed out. Are they pebbles?

Ain't they both ancient? Pebbles and blob's? First mark humans made, unsteady—I mean, doesn't a blob wanna be a circle?

Wasn't an a X the first shape?

Was it a cross?

A simple line?

Or maybe a blob. One thing I know is like only one artist ever could draw a perfect circle. Is a blob aspiring to be a circle? Perfection?

There are so many blobs throughout here. Like we're being surveilled. Like they're eyes, watching us.

Hotly—

—Like the women are surveilling each other. Observing—

—Ain't blobs multipurpose? In writing and math?

—All those things—maybe. Maybe we can let the crazy Os be for the time being. Jake, can you please continue?

One of the women offers that the sound of water on the rocks reminds her of micturition—

—Excuse me! Mictur-what?—

—I looked it up. Urination—

—Oh god help us.

The women and Jake now break up at the tone of Winnie's remark—

—Yep, replies Olivia.

After Donald arrives from taking the babysitter home Wren pulls down three glasses from the shelf near the sink. To think a all the times we used to come here for Christmas.

You mean the twins' birthday.

God forbid we forgot that.

Where there was food you could always find Moll.

This was defin'ly her favorite room.

Hard t' b'lieve it's ours. Donald rests his keys in a bowl at the end of the counter.

Here's to Molly! Wren enthuses after pouring.

What're you doin' up little girl? Billie enters squinting, rubbing her eyes—

—Did we wake you? Donald approaches the child, strokes her hair, lifts her then takes a seat and rests her on his lap.

What's it like out there where you are? Seem like ages since we visited. You bored yet?

Ever consider comin' home?

I'm bored t' tears. Though somehow I'll stay.

But why? Ain't nothin' t' do out there. How many times can you pan for gold?

That'd be never.

Jake, are you seein' anyone?

Wha'd you mean?

You got a boyfrien'?

Or a girlfrien'? How you stand it? Don't you get horny?

—.

I'd die out there. Man your age should be havin' fun! Sewin' your oats—that's what I'd be doin' if I were—

—If you were what? pipes Wren. What's that s'spose t' mean?

I'm only sayin'…. If I were Jake. No responsibilities. No one to answer to—a free bird with no commitments. Donald fluffs Billie's hair. If I had no one t' worry about I'd be havin' the time a my life.

Is that what you fantasize?

What guy wouldn'?

As though women don't—

—They don't talk about it—

—Maybe we should—

—Don't be so—

—If you say difficult—

—I been drawin' a lot. Paintin' too. Wren I been writin' in that journal you gave.

That's all well and good, but where's it gonna git you? I only hope you don' regret it later, bro. All th' chances you miss because you're stuck in a hick-town, and by choice! Why deny yourself because—I don' know why. Is it that crazy cult, hauntin' you still? The family religion—all into self-denial. That it?

—It's none a our business, Donald.

I dig. But if you see a person passin' up the opportunity of a lifetime, a chance other men would give their right nut for but can't because a choices they made—

—The truth comes out—

—I'm fine you two. Trus' me.

You sure? Don't sound like you're livin' life, pal. If you're not seein' no one…. Or a dozen someones—.

—Jake, you gonna go t' Laurentine?

Huh?!

What about Rauch? Marx? Ro—

—Maybe nex' time.

Don' you miss them? It's been ages.

I miss Cin and Diablo.

They ask about you—they live just two doors down, y' know. We usually take Billie to their house when we have something, but they were busy this evening. They drive the ladies on the block club when we do a hit.

A hit?

When we target a landlord.

With what? Eggs? Toilet paper?

For lettin' a house go t' pot—jus' look outside. We track down the owner an' pay 'em a visit—

What kind a visit?

A visit. With a sign or forty. Somethin' that pops. A bonfire. Anything t' get their attention.

A lotta shouting—. Then he writes about it in the paper.

I'm sure they're glad when you stop. How many people we talkin' about?

It depends—. Forty? If people're busy. But it could be fifty, a hun'ert. Even five hundred once.

So you're there to say—knock-knock—SURPRISE! We love what you've done with the place.

The big shocker is when they spot the media—includin' this guy—I mean they know him. 'Specially when we hit the burbs.

And Cin an' Diablo go along?

They help organize it! Them an' Wren.

We'd never get the ladies there if it weren't for them. We only got so much room in that jalopy a ours.

But seriously. I'm concerned about you. Livin' like a monk. Like you're trying to be a saint in the wilderness or somethin'. D'you even have friends out there?

I joined a readin' group.

You mean there are people who read there?

Surprise, surprise. Me an' a bunch a older ladies.

Oh great. Sounds better by the minute.

He always was a egghead.

Me?

You know what I mean—readin'. Everything you could get your hands on.

—You two—

—You're right, Jake. We trus' you.

Not me! I remember you draggin' your dog to the river.

What's good for you, Donald, may not be—

—Stttttooooppppp, please.

Billie fusses in Donald's lap, signaling she wants to be set down. She squiggles free then makes her way to Wren and motions to be hoisted up.

The three continue to sip their way through first one and then a second bottle, as well as work their way down a joint that Donald produces and Wren passes on. Jake takes a toke or two after Wren has lulled Billie back to sleep.

What about you two?

What about us?

What are you doing besides hitting slum-lords?

Where do you wanna begin?—though we call them landlords. Your twin's a fire-cracker. Hard to keep up with.

Wren?

Never a dull moment, Jake.

I thought you only had to worry about classes.

I wish!—try that and bein' a mom. It's been a eye opener.

What's been?

We thought we were gettin' a deal from Auntie Midge—I mean five grand for this. But we learned they're literally givin' homes away here. Some for a measly buck—a dollar! if you can believe it. They all—not just our place—come with a ton a work. I mean, major. We knew we weren't buying a new home, but we didn't plan on shelling out for everything, roof and boiler—foundation even. We're talkin' major money-pit. No wonder landlords choose to torch a place rather than fix it. Also, the banks won't loan you nothin', not a penny—

—Not if you live in this area. Though they don't mind shellin' out millions to white folks in the burbs.

Like Laurentine, Jake. People who've been here for ages, the ones who stayed, own their homes and stash their savings in the local banks. Those same banks have branches in the burbs where they don't mind dispensing cash like water, which again is really the hard-earned savings of people here—they give it, no questions asked, to people like mom and dad. But anybody who wants to live here—they won't give a penny for them to improve the place. Say it's too risky. So we organized a block-club and got others involved. Formed the Cardinal Road Establishment for Development, or CRED—name's his idea.

First thing CRED did was hit the president's home of the Cardinal Bank and Trust—he was very welcoming—

—You can imagine—

—He was just as happy to see me as the landlords hiding out in white-town.

We picketed the guy, carried signs and did skits—there must a been two hundred that time. In Shagaran Falls— d'you believe it? We tipped off the *Press* and they assigned this guy to cover it. Other media ate it up.

You, Wren?

Wha' d' you mean, You, Wren? Your sister's the ringleader! The guy loved havin' us drop by. Specially there.

He called the cops—

—Thing is, we got his attention.

So you got a loan?

You kiddin'? Like a white guy's ever gonna give in jus' like that—. No, he doubled down. We teamed with twice the number a organizations and hit his house a second time—that's when we hit five hunderd. Again we had the pleasure of having tea with officers—they were thrilled to see us again.

That do it?

Broooo—

Weeeelll! You'd think with that many people. In Shagaran Falls—do that many people even live there?

—He dug his heals in, more'n ever.

Thing is, Jake, when the feds jump in to correct what he and his bad men are doin' wrong, say they'll guarantee loans in the area if they go bad, dude entirely flips. Learns to game the system—trust me! From never givin' a loan to solicitin' people he knows can't pay, knowing the government will eat the loss. He starts bankin' a fortune on fees people pay up front. A maybe-bad bet become a sure-bad bet and the guy is workin' the feds' for real. He made a boat-load that way, no skin off his back.

I can't believe all them loans go bad.

They didn't.

So things're better now?

Bad as ever.

But for us, we no longer got a cracked foundation.

Leaky roof—

—It's just that lots a homes here are stuck in a loop a purchase and fail.

What about city hall?

What about it?

We did a hit at the housing authority, explains Donald. Tryin' t' force them t' demolish the drug dens. That took a while—city hall didn't wanna be bothered. But once the media burn them they flip too. They went from lettin' everything rot to tearin' everything down, 'til we started feeling like we moved to the country—I mean all these Victorian homes that should a been saved were vanishing in thin air.

Giant heaps a rubble, Jake.

We initiated a series a hits t' stop the demoing—

—That was scary! One group'd form a chain in front a th' bulldozers. Another hit the housing authority at the same time, demanding they fix homes instead a tearing them down—I mean it's a city!

We work the feds t' our advantage, playin' real estate agent on our own—

—That's how Deb and Cin got their place.

My fav hit though, was at the parks authority. They're the ones responsible for cuttin' the sycamores on th' block. About fifty a us got branches and marched around city hall, holding them in procession. Funeral. For th' trees. Then we laid 'em in front a the authority's door, one for each tree they cut.

What happen?

First the director refuse t' come out. He send some underling t' placate us. We inform her Channel One was there, that we ain't leavin' 'til we see the director himself. In person.

They also reco'nized this guy in the group.

Director come out?

After waitin' more'n half the day. He emerged all official-like, blathering that these things happen. Mistake in the work order. We said we didn't care, that they needed to replant every one they cut, that we didn't wanna live in the Deforest City.

It work?

You clueless!

But you got trees!

Thing is, Jake, it took forever. Many tries—lotsa hits. We prevailed only 'cause Channel One aired a special—

—Based on this guy's article—

—They videoed the trees all gone. Then they took the viewer on a tour of the director's street with all them elms.

Planting crew show up two days later.

So it ain't totally hopeless.

It's just it's always pulling teeth, Jake. Every little thing.

Fortunately your sister got boundless energy, like she feed off that shit. The dis-comfort a people like that.

Still—

—The trees were a victory. Stopping the demoing. We just need a hundred more like it.

Working hydrants'd be nice.

Fewer strays.

Places for kids t' go after school—keep 'em outta crack dens.

Less truck traffic—they barrel down on their way t' Liberty.

Fewer arsonists—

—It don't end.

We done a lot, but like I say—

—T'answer your question though, city hall's a viper nest. Last thing they care about is us. Not 'til 'lection time.

Jake, who knew Auntie Midge and Gramma Ruby weren't the only white folk in the neighborhood? Dad made it seem that way. But they come outta the woodwork, literally, once we organized, helped with block clubs. Main problem is keeping them from tryin' to run the show, stiflin' other people—

—If she's doin' that, what do you do all day?

Who you think takes care a the monster?

He's being modest. He writes a killer article—many! For *The Forest City Press*, and lately an exposé or twenty for the big paper, in the Big Apple. About the joys of living in a post-industrial, rust-belt city.

Emil repositions himself, plants his feet for leverage, lengthens his torso in an arc, groans as he sets his jaw in a gesture while Jake invents volumes in complementary colors, a spectrum of grays that step forward and recede, waiting on purer tones, occasioning a figure to enliven the plane.

It's been how many months? Weekday mornings and the chance weekend, unplanned, the pair resilient in the returns department, above and beyond the requirements of the contract, the two drawn each in his way after squirreling ideas, caching them to tap next time that they're together. As if to push the limits beyond what the other can take. Because they can—

—Jake. Try as you might to destroy me, I can go on like this forever, Emil enthuses. You're breakin' my butt. But I ain't bored.

Emil stands back, takes in the canvas that Jake pronounced "getting there."

How you know? I mean, to me it's a mess. In part. Completely insane. I mean—what's next to me? I look clear enough. But that blob there, agains' an emerging blue? All these marks, or are the icons?—wha' d' they all mean? He slips his hand down Jake's jeans.

The timer on the stove-top dings. In a sense Jake is only starting to find his groove, despite Emil's critique, the blob intentional, signifying what is an unknown, written in the work, after so much time and so many false starts—it endures. Emil arches his spine like the Persian next-door, cranes his neck in feline fashion then relaxes, bends at the waist and flexes the elbows, hips, and knees, then circles back around the chair that serves as an easel—

—It confuses the shit outta me.

An' yet it feels right—

—Yeah, yeah—talk to the hand. But I admit, you got me. It's this other I don't—

—Think I do?

Jake backs away from the canvas and begins to undress. He runs his hand over Emil's abdomen and the air shifts. Emil extends his arm—

—My turn—

Positions reverse. Jake struggles to get his part right for a partner with particular tastes, a thing clearly in mind, or not, tied to god-knows-what—for a partner shy on direction, as though he enjoys eyeing the other squirm as he figures what he wants, stumbles onto it without him spelling it out, a thing common among couples whether they realize it or not, as though the other should know after all this time;

as though having to say it implies a fault in the pairing; as though it'd ruin the magic the way only words can—Jake reads gestures, plies a part, tries to play a role he knows will shift once Emil perceives he's onto it. Then it'll be off again in another direction, like rebellious clock-work, a free mechanism that mocks the obedient hands on the stove.

Come times-up, before dressing, Emil halts Jake's hand as he reaches for his tee, leads him back to the sofa, sits and leans back, thighs splayed. He bids Jack rest a minute, tells him he deserves it. He dares rest his head against Emil's shoulder, only a moment ago a wordless tyrant. For a time the two remain that way, Emil running his right hand over Jake's torso, pecking his hair.

What gives?

You give, Fruitcake. For which, many thanks—

—Aaaaannd?

She's about to pop.

Congrats.

Who knows what it's gonna mean so far as this.

What's that mean?

Everything changes after a kid.

Like how?

Y' never know.

And?

And it may not work—. This.

You still gotta work.

But there ain't no sleepin' with a screamin' kid. It'll be everything I can do t' drag myself outta bed in time, t' be at the site.

So b'bye paintin'?

B'bye everythin'. For a while. I'm gonna miss it more'n you—trus' me. You been a sport. I mean a dream.

—Your dream. Or is it a nightmare I lived—

—Who knew it was possible?

—She gonna be wantin' it again?

That ain't it—. Jake, I think I'm in—

—Oh god, no. No, no, no. You're not allowed.

Why not? It's the truth, one that slipped in sometime between the handshake and this. Today. I mean, you really are a sport—do you even understand the meaning of no?

—.

Anyway, we knew from the get-go this thing had a shelf-life. Even if we never said it we knew it couldn't last. At least not 'til the next kid on the way—and by that time, who knows?

I guess I wasn' thinking far enough ahead. We left that part unsaid.

Closer the time gets, the more I remember. What comes next—we did say the thing could be dissolved at any time, by either a us. What I didn't plan on is what happen along the way. Inside.

—.

You got me—

—You got me. Many times—. So you can just switch it all off?—Poof! Jus' like that?

You're the poof, Fruitcake, not me—

—.

Emil's trembling. Joke. Who knew there was another way? That you don't gotta choose b'tween Pepsi an' Coke? That you can have both—the thing with Dan. It's pressure gauges. Release valves. Nothin' like this.

You sure?

Be nice. Like we're adults, an' we get t' be kids again.

You call this play?

I do.

Then it's rough—you could a warned me it couldn't last—

—If I only knew. I jus' realize.

Time suspends, hangs limp, despite the stove hands about to mar the mood with its matter-of-fact ding, about to cut everything short as Emil continues to pluck Jake's hair, petals of a flower, physic and poison—I wish I may, I wish I might—

—I know you're in there—

[Hard pounding.]

Your damn truck's here!

[More hard pounding.]

Open this instant!

Emil lifts a slat of the venetians, eyes hotly the tail of a car—

—She's here!

He shouts in muted tones for Jake to clear the stage, remove the sets, costumes, toss everything under the cushions—eat it! Jus' get ridda it! All the stuff! And put somethin' on!

[Continued pounding.]

Uncannily for him, Jake assumes a calm as Emil freaks, attempts to shinny jeans over thighs, slowed by the cruelty of the pounding, shaking Emil to the core—

—Open up!

[More hard pounding.]

At the point Emil abandons the effort to master jeans, underwear, or tee, Jake approaches the door without a stitch, unlocks and calmly pivots it ajar. Caren all but tumbles in, belly out, and in a frenzy surveys the setting, the painting on the easel, things tossed half-under the cushions, lying on the table, counter, and carpet, not to mention the de-facto nakedness of the men.

What in the world?!

It's early.

Instead of a response—true, half- or completely untrue—Jake formulates questions of his own. How d'you find the place? How d'you know he's here? I mean no one can find me, no matter how much I explain—yet here you are! Other comments come to mind but he tables them.

I got spies.

Emil's been kind enough t' pose for me.

My husband! What is he doing here?! Naked! She picks up something on the table. What's this? And, Jake, why are you like that, if you're the one painting—?

Tricky question.

In fact it was the question of the day, a pins-and-needles query on the rack of interrogation. Why the two were both unclad. It wasn't like one could turn to, or on, the other, declare, Oh my god, look—he's—. He's—! Not when you're both in that state.

Emil manages, finally, to slip on his jeans, commando, leaving briefs and tee on the floor. He stands there, barefoot. Jake declines to follow his lead, to cover anything, while Caren detonates other accusations that can't be followed by easy answers. Not in a way that suits convention.

I thought the Dan thing was bad, my good friend Dan, full of information. An' now look! You and him! Like you caught some kind a virus!

Can we talk about it later? At home? I gotta go t' work.

I wanna hear now!

He says he wasn't getting' any 'cause your pregnant.

He said that. An' you believe him.

Actually—.

Emil glances away, slips his shirt and flannel on, one sock then the other, pulls out a boot from under the sofa and stuffs a foot in. He pulls on the other boot and laces it, catching the eyes irregularly like a drunken spider, slipping the aiglets through, too flustered to double-bow the top.

If I weren't like this I'd leave you, Caren blurts, caressing her belly. But what the F can I do?—I mean I'm over a barrel. And you!—she directs a poker-hot eye at Jake—You're done, pal! Workin'. For him—

—But it's a two-man job!

You call him a man, Emil?

But I got deadlines—

—Then what were you doin', monkeying around like this? I mean it's Dis. Gus. Ting!

How'm I gonna survive without work?

You should a thought about that before you went whoring with my husband—my—life!

—But there's nothin' to it!—

—You call this nothin? As though that's possible with men. 'Specially your kind. Preyin' on married—

In the back and forth that follows, tedious and verging on litigious, Jake bargains for the chance to stay on the job another week, not a day longer, long enough to make his rent and time for Emil to hire a replacement.

I should a never agree t' that thing with Dan, dough or no dough.

It ain't his fault. Jake's either.

Then whose is it? Must be mine, of course. It's always the poor—

—Nature's?

Cop-out, Emilio.

But Caren, how's it hurting, you or anyone? You never went without.

You took a vow! Promised to be faithful. Even worse Jake's a big nothin', Emilio, a loser! A zero—I mean scum a the earth! Look at this place! What were you even thinking?

He's definitely somethin'—

Caren shoots her gaze around, peers at the other figure on the canvas.

You call this somethin'?

We all do it.

But is it a subject a litrature?

It's part a life, ain't it? Why shouldn'it be litrature?

I guess, hazards Suzanne. But I don't remember seeing that before.

Ain't that the problem? complains Olivia. We're portrayed as spirits, disembodied, not flesh-an-blood beings that pee—.

Virgins.

Or sluts.

Mmm-hmm—

—God knows, the writer goes there, right off the bat—

—No pussy-footin'!

Jake, you wanna continue?

I think you were picturin' micturition.

How could I forget?

The rivers of rain have an effect on one of the women, who lowers herself and lets go—

Not too graphic.

Primal.

Ain't that the point?

It gets better—Jake, please continue.

The rest coalesce in a loose circle around her as nature does its thing.

Ohhh kaaay.

I guess we ain't in Kansas no more—

—That's clear.

Just in case anyone was wondering.

I think it's beautiful, remarks Ginny.

You would! quips Winnie, and the group erupts.

Seriously. Why the hell not?

There's the loose circle again, adds Carina.

A daisy chain a women watchin' another one pee.

The question is why?

You mean the circle?

No I mean the voyeurism, watchin' a woman squat an'—y'know.

It's in-your-face.

Or is it life, plain an' simple? Wha'd' you think women do 'round the world without flush toilets. Runnin' water?

She saying that?

I doubt the author—with all our mod cons—

—Is it about freedom? I mean from shame? Our bodies? Aren't we told to hide things like that? Pretend it don' exis'?

I remember thinkin' the nuns I had in school never peed, ventures Jake.

We all thought that.

So what does it mean the woman pees in such a communal way? And why the configuration around the action, so to speak?

Jake, do men watch each other—y' know?

That a real question?

The women laugh.

—You're a guy, ain't you?

That's debatable.

Carina.

The group breaks in another laugh.

Then yeah—. They more than perform it.

That's happening here too.

Is it erotic?

Oh my—

Or is pee a blessin'? questions Lily.

A blessing?

I mean, if we don't, we die.

Like tears for the psyche?

I wasn't sayin' that, god knows. Though I wish I did. The group erupts at Lily's comment.

So it's a catharsis?

The physical kind. It's about the body—fuck the mind.

Lily!

I heard a guys who—

—I don't wanna know.

Who invited this guy?

Yeah, who invited you, Jake? Titters travel in a wave around.

It's not disgusting, hazards Vita. Doesn't that get to the author's point?

Which is—?

Not sure, a course. But ain't she challenging notions of the body in history? Women most of all? Not just about the body in general but the female body especially?

And that's supposed to be cleansing? Cathartic? Or, god help us, erotic?

—There ain't nothin' erotic here.

Says who? challenges Vida. Yet again the women erupt. Look what she says in the next paragraph. Let's see....

The rains passed the women celebrate the darkness under the stars.... They follow, chain after each other, ... cardamom and saffron...parsley fenugreek fennel and clove...lavender and vetiver scents the air, the hair of the women. Moans and whispers—

I mean. It's a orgy—how many times you find *that*?

And yet it's not.

It's sensory for sure, Ginny opines. Maybe sensual. All

them female bodies, scented, chasing each other. If it ain't flat-out erotic it's close.

Take that, Uncle Walty!

I agree. It's the author's response to him, to adhesion, the all-guy thing—ain't that what we said he called it?

I don't see how you can read the second paragraph without it commenting on the first, wheezes Lily.

Huh?

Again, does it need to be one thing? Even if it's pointedly about women, I don't see why her point can't be universal.

—.

We're only on page one, worries Marge.

And so the convo moves and stalls at the same time. The agreement was to cover the first quarter of the book, but the women are stuck on the first page, lumbering over the words, parsing each more carefully than anyone thought possible, never mind necessary, as they stumble through the text at the Happy Looker, a kind of home, where meanings of words come alive more than plot, more than a narrator can labor over given the urge to keep the ball rolling, though suffice it to say they're translating a translation of a translation of sorts—of another woman's experience—imagination, effort, and struggle—to capture a complex thing and convey it, inducing a combing on the part of the women, and Jake, who found in the slow, plodding scrutiny an urge, and an opportunity, namely to locate the book in earnest, finding himself hooked as he struggled to catch up. He envisions in it the chance to motor down to the Mile High City, a thing he hasn't done since he arrived in Ojo Caliente, and a thing locals take pride in pooh-poohing, disparaging it and the majority of people who live there. The unrushed gate of the conversation prompts the women to take yet another look at what seemed opaque upon first reading but which, as with everything, grows and even looms in encountering it as a group—they'll take another look next time at what Ginny insists is the most important part, the part they're stuck on, framing what's to come and laying out themes—

—It's a window—

—It gives you something to think about! Suzanne opines.

To wince at, chuckles Marge

To celebrate? Carina ventures.

If you're into that kind a thing, Marge returns.

Even if you're not, argues Lily. It ain't a voice you ever get.

As if we needed it.

Maybe you—we—do.

Here's to hearing her out, toasts Vida, and the women raise their cups, including Marge, who lifts a glass of water.

It never fails after a rupture in routine, or an agreement gone wrong, that the thing that appears lost, the thing that hinged the parties together, tethered them on a road toward something unknown, that that thing paradoxically remains. At the time though, it doesn't look at all like that—it's clear it's over. Naked as that. Leaving only post mortems, questions about what went wrong, what was overlooked? You're left with an animal staring you in the face. A crack. Rift or breach, seemingly permanent, with little hope of a suturing things anytime soon, A with B. It stands as one of life's cruelest tricks that when you're in the throes of it one of the first people to circle back, into your life after having been out of it some time, is the very person you want to see least.

I stopped to let you know Caren delivered.

She did all right.

The two study each other through a slit.

C'n I come in?

It was an unusually bright day. Paper white blossoms on the apricot tree in the drive flash like doves exploding. The sun hangs over the Top Hat restaurant.

I'm not sure.

Five minutes?

Like I say, I'm not sure.

Once inside, after surveying the space from his spot near the door, as though Jake painted a line of Xs beyond which Dan knows not to tread, the latter takes in the space as if it were once his own, a place he felt welcome at one time, day or night. How often had it been?

You're not your usual.

Is there such a thing?

I haven't seen you in a month a Sundays.

Who's countin'.

I'm sorry for what happened.

You are.

I mean b'tween you'n me.

There's nothin' b'tween you'n me. Never was—you're married. To a minister.

Wanna walk some?

I gotta find work.

Emil asked me t' tell you he'll pay.

He means you will. You could a just called.

He asked me t' come in person. Told me t' say he's sorry.

Great. Now leave.

Can we walk a bit.

Here?! On Main?

Down by Clear Creek, atop a giant erratic that must've tumbled into the water during the Ice Age, a spot where Jake has taken to eating lunch on days off like this, refusing to be cooped up inside, the run-off from the high country roars, paralleling the highway, rumbling through the canyon, making it difficult to hear let alone speak—

—BE MY FRIEND. AGAIN!

AS IF YOU WERE MY ENEMY—

—YOU KNOW WHAT I MEAN!

NO! I DON'T!

DON'T BE DIFFICULT, JAKE! I DIDN'T COME TO PLAY GAMES!

YOU SEEM PRETTY GOOD AT IT TO ME!

It's as though the river dispreferred a conversation like this between former bed-mates, roiling the setting with so much negativity, around rocks, conifers, and air. The water complained from a distance, but not so far you could overlook the point, the taste of spray as it lofted, forcing the two to move—

—Oh my god that's better. I couldn't hear myself let alone you. Jake I said I'm sorry. I know you got a bug up your behind. I mean you just fell outta my life.

Number one I don't got a bug up my behind—maybe you do. Number two, I'm through with you.

I'd like to fix things.

Today of all days.

I've been meanin' to—

—But you didn't. You stole a part a me and I wan' it back.

So you blame me.

Who else. She said she had spies.

I didn't take nothin' from you. If anything I gave—

—You gave nothin'.

You know better.

You blabbed.

All those times I was with you, times I was with him, I got the idea you two—

Look where it got me. Without a job. A good gig.

I worried if I said something t' you directly you'd blow a gasket. I guess I misread.

Did you.

But Jake—I was right—

About what? I ain't one t' talk. Not like you.

I'll take that as a yes.

That's 'cause no don't exist in your book.

Why should it? The world is already too stuck on no.

The Whistlean Theology.

Can I see you?

No.

Not even t' give you updates?

I need t' think about it.

Maybe I can help you outta your present mess—

—I don't want your help. They must be raisin' a thousand houses in the city, every day. Emil used t' talk about it, that if cash money were the only thing—

—Have I tol' you how bad he feels.

What good's that do?

So I was right.

He said it'd be between him 'n me. That it was all innocent. Win-win. What could go wrong?

He an' I, we tell each other everything.

I'll make a note a that—

—Maybe you'll feel different someday.

Or not. I don' know how I feel now.

I was thinkin' you and me and....

You're worse than obtuse.

She'll get over it—she's been here before.

—.

I was thinkin' the three a us—

—Ha!

Think about it. It could be good.

Not a chance.

Why not? Isn't that what it's all about? Gettin' what you need?

Yesterday a bomb went off. Today you come with a proposition.

I've seen her get over it.

I gotta get a job.

Los Pajaritos

Stetsons score the sky, low-lying and flat, itching to pierce through. Tall glasses of water, booted and belted, hoisted by heels, topped by a dimpled dome. They tower over you, these guys, threaten to crush as they move in steps dainty and strapping. Lines of machos advancing in waves, moving as one 'til they break into a wheel, revolving, inside the room, turning as couples promenade now in two-step, arms intertwined in ranchers' knots as the music cycles them above the floor, up to the point the entirety splits, only to rejoin in rows without missing a beat.

To be ginned and watching from the sidelines, giants jammed in a box while the air, normally dry in these parts, humidifies, condensing sweat on foreheads and brows, walls and ceiling. Varicolored hankies trail from pockets, wipe sweat on dancers and wall-flowers alike, a locker-room in motion.

The wheel spins. Some drop off, returning to cocktails on shelves running the perimeter, dip like birds at a prairie pond, check their reflections in the glass spanning the wall. Then they couple in again when the DJ modulates the tune, first slowly, almost imperceptibly, causing a kinetic mess until, wonder of wonders, a melody takes shape and the men double up, fast as road-runners, twirling like twizzle-sticks confined in a glass, individually and as a group in quick rotation around the floor, in an astonishing choreography, to Jake at least, whose fascination is with the lack of accidents, the mechanical efficiency of thighs moving between thighs and boots grazing boots without tripping up—how long does it take? As if this were a master class. Though the kingpins—the room's full of kingpins—appear average, and diverse, normal save the clear skewing toward height.

I ain' ever gonna get it.

Why sure y'will—wha'd y' say y'alls name was? Was it Jock?

That's a good one.

The merry-go-round of bearded figures rotates, losing a few of their numbers but gaining others back, and then some, within the first few bars of a recognizable tune, the dance-floor lassoing out, temperature spiking, odor as well.

Bum, Bum, Bum, Bum
Bum, Bum, Bum, Bum
Bum, Bum, Bum, Bum

Jock! C'mon. You gotta try.
Oh my god no!
Mind if I do?

Mr. Stardust, spin me a dream
Handsomest thing, I'd like if you please
Beam me a man to kiss me all over
And put an end to our days as rovers.

In this room packed with Romeos, in this studded–and-buckled Araby of the west, western weeds are a requirement, body hair and boots, not to mention a knack for the dosy-do.

Mr. Stardust, I've been on my own
I want a man to make me a home
So twirl your magic wand at me—
Mr. Stardust spin me a—

—Jock, join me!

The man, whose name Jake didn't catch after three tries, causing him to give up rather than annoy, seems unhearing or uncaring, disappears into a whirl while Jake remains anchored to the margins, nursing a gin, observing, before he sees somewhere in the synchrony of bodies not his new acquaintance but someone he can't place—I mean. Is this one a them Ginny-moments when you think you know, only to find out—? The guy sparkles with the best of them, lifting and lilting around the floor, moustache dancing atop his upper lip—is that what's throwing me? Clutching his partner with a head equally lofty, the two kicking legs deftly, arms switching over and under, roping first one and then the other.

Jake drifts back toward the bar, far enough to be hidden but close enough to catch the action, something he's sure wouldn't be possible in the Forest City in a million years. It was as if he dropped on another planet, peopled with clones of his neighbor in Ojo save a diversity of skin, macho to the teeth but with tastes poles apart, courting each with a spin.

How would Jake know about this place if some guy hadn't handed him a flyer from a copy of *Out Front,* used and crumpled, which he'd fished from the trash on Colfax? He squirreled the copy back to his trailer, pored over it, including the ads. It was one thing to know in general terms that these places exist—he learned about them in religion class at St. Andrej's of all places—and another thing to ball up the courage to barge through the door. Or slink in as the case may be, with some guy you met in line but don't know from Adam. Now inside, it was like being tornadoed into Oz, smack on the dance-floor, the crowd twistering. Here approaches a cowboy, aimed right for you, rendering the scene even more surreal—he's been threading his way after hugging the bar, overlooking the floor while waiting for a drink. He reaches out his hand in a manner that can only be described as courtly.

Would you please do the honor of joining me in this dance?

'Fraid I don'—

Y'all gotta start some-time.

Still—

—This helps. The man hands Jake a drink, full to the rim.

The music pulsing from the speakers makes it unlikely to hear let alone chat or carry on a conversation—the place isn't designed for that. Eyeing only. So as not to be impolite Jake tosses the plastic stirrer on the floor and downs the drink in a swoop, a Romeo-special, due to nerves, daring-do, or a practiced gesture.

—Lookit' you! Wan' another?

I got a long way t' drive.

So that's a yes?—

—Why not?

Jake whisks back to the bar and is resupplied, then is drawn to the maelstrom by a hand. He can't help but notice the I-could-swear-I-know-you face as it flashes in his direction, urging him to keep working at the name, despite how fleet he is and deft at showing off such an airy gait, despite his size. The stranger Jake's with, in a loose sense, positions himself in front of him after the outer ring breaks, and having set his drink on a shelf he whizzes Jake away, forcing him on a curve toward mastering the basics, frustration outed at the top of his lungs, as his partner whirls him around. After many revolutions Jake begs for a break, pleads to stop, and the two toddle off, the other reluctantly, amps besting conversation until Jake is led to an anteroom he didn't know was there.

Once inside he recoils. All manner of action unfolds in several states of undress, rendering what's happening on the dance-floor tame, or is it foreplay?—I mean, why wait 'til you get home, I guess? Jake's urge is to flee, but his hand is gripped.

Let's hang out.

I guess that describes it.

Wanna?

We jus' met!

So?

For good or ill it's impossible to talk in here too. The stranger looks crestfallen. Then why don't we watch a bit?

You mean here?

God knows there's enough to see.

More'n I—.

Then OK, let's watch out there.

Out the two snail, Jake trailing the cowboy, hand gripped tight as if they were an item, until they stumble into the man that Jake sorta recognizes, sorta doesn't.

I know I know you.

Henny, that's so tired.

No!—I do!

The cowboy interposes himself, Jake's sudden date, for now at least, and who knows how long. Wanna do the floor?—

—Your toes'll thank you if we don't—

Name's Polly—

—Polly...Polly—

—Heath here.

I'm Jake.

They're all speaking at the top of their lungs. Just follow me! booms Heath. What I do! He takes hold of Jake with a sturdy hand, steeled by the force of the booze, his steps purposeful. Jake attempts to ape his moves but time after time lands on two left feet.... Almost falling onto Polly, standing to the side—that's it! it clicks in the middle of a promenade—Polly! Miss Purebred. AKA Miss Morphous—a course. Who just happens to be monitoring me now as I circle the room, marking me to the other she's with, as if to say, That's the one. Polly gives in to the most obscene gesture, according to Florrie at least, namely pointing, though granted she's fast as a flicker, almost to the point of indistinguishability. Still Jake caught her in the trough of heads and torsos opening up, the two like prairie dogs on the look-out for coyotes.

Am I the only one in street clothes? Ratty shoes and socks? Same ones I wear t' work? The ad didn' say nothing about no dress code.

After begging off another dance, requiring a whole new kind of movement, Jake trails Heath off the floor. Buy you another? After squeezing through the swarm at the bar, Heath plants his lips on Jake's. He extends his hands inside his jeans and cups Jake's behind, drawing his hands up and apart, slipping—

Ohhhh Kaaay!

And I thought Romeo—the anti-Peacoat, my lamb—who I thought I lost in the press of flesh until—speak of the devil. Who knew what a couple of drinks and a bit of bumbling could do, turn this guy into a fly on a corpse—

Ohhhh Kaaay, pal. You need t' come up for air.

The disappointment on Heath's, and Peacoat's, faces is palpable, for different reasons, but for all Jake's protests—You ain't much into small-talk, are you?—Jake feels trapped and, quite frankly, too drunk to do anything.

Is this common?

But the man, who struggles to remember Jake's name, has made a claim. You go Tiger, Polly yells in Jake's ear as she slides by. You had me fooled!

When Heath's hands surface, tongue too, creating a clearing where his hat towered, making way for the lights pulsing from every point on the ceiling, Jake spots Polly spying him, what's just gone down, Heath's hands slipping now in front, then back—Polly's partner stands behind, the two commenting on the action—but saying what? Something about a fading moment in a room filled with couples in fading gestures, fading attire? Her eyes are riveted on Jake.

She approaches.

How long've y'all known each other?

Never mind.

This is Kitty. We're roomies.

Heath puts his arm around Jake in a gesture that says, I been workin' him ladies, so don' get no ideas. But Polly seems less interested in rustling Jake than taking it all in.

Y' know, Alicia was here. Earlier. Too bad she didn' hang around t' see this. She waves her index finger as though it were a wand.

Where is he then?

With L'Dell. Ain't a'zackly her scene.

Sorry I missed 'im! Tell 'im hi f' me?

You can be sure we will. We'll tell 'im ever'thin', girlfriend. Don' you worry.

Thank you? Tell him I'm learnin'.

Henny, learnin' what?

Howta dance.

Girlfriend, you got a loooong way.

Thanks f' tellin' 'im that.

What's big sister for?

On which note Polly pivots, bunny-hops away, she and Kitty both, while glancing behind.

Jake we wanna talk.

I got the book!—I hope you ain't gonna kick me out. I even read it! An' I brought another loaf, cleaned under my nails—take a look!

Much obliged—Carina, will you do the inspection?

She gently takes Jake's hands one by one.

Checks out.

Do I got a sticker on my forehead? Why y'all lookin' at me like that?

The women erupt—

—I'm sweating!

Again the women break into a chorus—

Relax, coaches Marge.

After the group is seated Carina rests her hand on Jake's shoulder—

—What?!

We wanna talk to you, repeats Ginny. We been talkin'.

Nice of you t' include me—

—We think you should leave Ojo Caliente—

Leave Ojo?

—The mountains—up here, blurts Winnie. Altogether.

Why'd I wanna do that? I'm just starting to feel—

—Then you def'ly gotta go, asserts Lily.

'Makes no sense.

Would someone just tell him? orders Vida.

We think you sh' be in school, bleats Olivia. We decided.

School!! Last thing I wanna—

—Trust us, insists Suzanne.

You're gonna fritter your life away—an' so young—

Unlike us, laments Marge.

—I'm not so sure, I mean—

—Listen t' Ginny. Olivia. Alla us—we're serious.

We know—

But—school?! My father's a factory worker. He got by.

Doesn't sound like it from what you've said, quips Winnie. You wanna end up that way? Hatin' the world and everyone in it cuz you flubbed your chance?

Or never got one.

How many times you say he could a been a doctor? A whole other person—.

Speaking a painting, adds Ginny.

Were we?

We've seen enough to know. No excuses.

It's hot in here, ain't it? More twittering. I never thought a—god forbid! I thought I was done with all that—and I have no money!

You need t' take loans like the rest a us, insists Carina.

I'll be payin' the rest a my life.

Prolly not—

—Even if you do. Be worth it.

It changes you, Ginny remarks. More'n religion.

Lily, what d' you think? Help!

They're right a course. What're you gonna do, swing a hammer the rest of your life? Be a framer-slash-painter in your seventies with nothin' to show? Including workin' knees and elbows?

I can still paint an' draw. Look how many painters—

—That was then, pipes Olivia.

Pack your things. Vamoose. Move to the city—get the hell outta here. You'll still be welcome any time—

—You, me, an' Winnie can drive up together, offers Marge.

—We'll still count on you for street actions down there—

The paddy wagon'd be lonely without you.

Yet again the pulse ramps up. Liquefying the body, terra firma in an earthquake, all undone. The heart moves between beats, in waves, and you sucked in, lost, sound vibrating, organs tethered to speakers in a space packed to the gills. Other bodies also blind, gyrating, bending, splaying, eardrums straining, heads nodding, shirtless and careening, slithering, colors rippling down skin in streams, flesh against flesh—and Jake among them.

Tee soaked.

No way I'm gonna bare myself like them, not with my carpenter's tan, among pumped and bronzed torsos, people's whose lives are worlds apart from mine, from what I do every day. Like I'm the only one that works. But here I am, again, after how many months, with yet another stranger, so many they begin to feel familiar in their strangerness. Like I'm married to a crowd. Never the same body twice, in committed succession. David's packs them in like Charlie's, the cowboy bar, especially on a Friday now that the wheels of work don't revolve the next day. For me at least.

This is the ritual, the observance—the rubbing—against bodies perfect in many ways. Expert at schmoozing, executing a lure, an invitation to sojourn on a strange bed, mingle with a foreign body, and yet in most cases unable to leave with a working number. Anything to break the spell, the solitude suffusing that tin can in Ojo, like a cloud a propane when the heater's on the fritz, a couch-wide trailer dwarfed by natural serrations closing around the town.

How many women has Jake seen stumble up the landing of his neighbor's, and yet how many has he dragged to his own? When you tell someone where you're from they ask, What state's that in? By which they mean not only a geographical place but a frame of mind, some ex-province or alternate zone.

A bunch a hicks up'ere, ain' it?

On a Sunday morning at 8:00, Jake trails regularly up the foothills, alone in his car after a night with what feels like a drifter, on the avenue of life at least, scrambling for comfort. For the moment the beat is just getting started, and for once Jake is here with an actual and not an ad-hoc date, a rare find who traded a real, legitimate number, wonder of wonders, and here he is in the flesh, though who knows for how long?

Darnell owns the floor, drawing the attentions of several mustached giants, hirsute wonders just nearby who bump and grind him, behinds poking naked through chaps, the muscle-bound who impose themselves between the two of us. But others jostle, elbow, and behind him too, Jake's tee absorbing the run-off of so many backs, chests, arms, and foreheads as they jockey here and there in Darnell's direction, his tee a sponge sopping the DNA of everyone nearby.

If only Emil were here. Him or Ginny—she'd be fun. Emil with his respectable, vowed life, upright with their expanding brood. Outnumbering, I wager, the number of offspring this entire lot will ever father, a crowd in the hundreds working to a state of arousal as intense as any Emil will experience. Without me. All that work, and yet they eke out another every year. Will any end up on these floor-boards someday, in a different generation? Gyration?

No doubt they'll pray to god for another, yet again, while I work on my unborn self. A being yet-to-be with no divine to supplicate, beg, cajole, or harangue. Some foreign connection to sustain me another week. Unlike Wren and Donald with their familiar night-after-night, tensions notwithstanding. They were content to stop at one—a mistake if you go with Donald's mother's point-of-view, the need to make up for lost time. Maybe there's a stray father in this crowd too, another Heath—

—Can I speak to Heath, please?

Bette Davis Eyes blasts in the background.

Is there a Heath here??? the lady on the phone yells over the music and loud chatter.

Jake can hear women cackling. Oh Heee-eeath! titters one. Heath, baby! chortles another. Give Heath my number, encourages a third. A fourth echoes, Anyone know a Heath gettin' his nails did?

The woman picks up the phone after setting it on the counter. No Heath here!

The line cuts.

No Heath there. As Jake returned the number to the shoe-box stuffed with dead-ends, he muses about the conversation they had in the back of his car.

Wish I could invite you t' my place—come 'ere.

I gotta go.

Only four cars remain in the lot, one of which is a yellow Fiat, there in the corner. The lights of the bar went dim some time ago. Jake slides closer to the passenger door and glances outside. He listens as the man beside him slips his jeans over his thighs and midsection then extends a zipper up. He reaches into a pocket and extracts a set of keys.

Yer married. An' you got kids.

I never said tha'.

I god all th' luck.

Is wad id is.

If you weren' married with children, would you a asked me over?

I never said that was the case. But if it wasn't, then yes. Maybe. Gimme yer phone nummer an' I'll give you mine. When kin we do this ag'in?

Darnell leads Jake by the hand, deeper into the crush. He doffs his tee and jams it in a back pocket where it bobs like a tail as he spins, confined by the press, the earthy smell reaching a pitch as heightened as the music. He encourages Jake to remove his shirt too, and when Jake demurs he cajoles, C'mon, loosen uppa bit! He grasps Jake's tee by the sides and whisks it in a single, spit-fire motion during which Jake, unthinking, raises his arms toward the ceiling and a disapproving god, never mind a disapproving Peacoat, until his upper torso, naked, moves in the moist air, coursing perspiration. Darnell stuffs Jake's shirt into his other pocket, and it tosses around as he shakes, spins, and wriggles, edged onward by a wave from behind.

Look't you with yer muscles, mister! Where you get them?!

Jake smiles and looks away.

Lemme feel 'em—

—'S no big thing—

—Buddy, you s'prise me. Hiding all that!

Darnell can't help himself. He drags his hands over Jake's chest, shoulders, and back, surveying a kinetiscape, ever in motion as the music pounds, humping his groin against Jake. He responds in kind, liberated now, a bridge having been crossed—in the past when he faced another on the floor it's as though an abyss separated them, but now, just like that, it's been breached.

Yer a firecracker! Darnell enthuses, leaning forward and shouting in Jake's ear. He moves away and Jake leans close, pressing his palm against his chest and muttering in Darnell's ear, Or just a cracker.

In the pulsing lights, blinking spots and surging strobes, revolving mirror-balls fracturing colors and shattering hues, cascading, shooting, and dripping from walls—in that vortex Jake perceives the side of Darnell's mouth rise despite itself. He kisses Jake on the lips, then lifts his gaze toward the artificial sky. The two press flesh by accident and design. Jake takes note of the novelty of the thing, he can't recall in the near or distant past the phenomenon unfolding: he's having fun.

The two turn, contort, leap and flail, Jake bending over and Darnell spooning from behind, the two sambaing in sync, Jake resting his head on Darnell's shoulder as though he'd ever done that before, until the positions are reversed. Since Jake left Laurentine he couldn't remember a time he'd fantasized for a minute about Harry and Florrie seeing him in his life out here. Until now. *Ecce filius tuus!* In his element. Finally. To think a week ago he stood in a cracker-box shower in a cracker-box trailer, tears washing down the drain, trickling into a river that slides from the Rockies, caused by the realization he was destined to share his life with a cadaver, or a ghost of such, albeit animated and ubiquitous, tracking his every step, a zombie that manages to slip behind you everywhere, including here, without having to shell out the cover to get in, a disembodied stiff— there he is in the crowd, keeping an eye on me and—who knows?—Darnell too. Having said that, in the spectrum of things Jake's a pale stand-out. And yet this moment with Darnell is shaping up to be one of his most enjoyable, unless you go back to the vital Peacoat days, so unlike the glum, humorless one staring this way.

So this is what it comes down to, Jake lamented in the shower, water running lukewarm. To me and that thing, eyein' me naked or dressed, no matter where I go. The water in his eyes sears more than the water on his back as he surveys a desert spreading out. How long's a life? Sixty? Seventy? Eighty years? And how old am I? To think of traveling that expanse of time with a figure no one but me sees or recognizes. Will it age with me? Or will it remain ever young? In a sense. The slow-blinking version of a body washed on a beach, bloated, hoisted on a gurney, the lights from the ambulance washing it red and blue on what turned out to be a night from hell, the very fillip for coming all this way.

Alone.

Or so I thought.

Only to discover I have a ward for life, apathetic and interested, humorless among the revelers here, refugees like me from the life out there, battered and bruised, though not defeated. Darnell sees me and I *see* him. In the flesh. As I say the only one whose number, scratched at last call—must a been a month ago—corresponded with the real thing. The truth in numbers. And to think when I called I was about to hang up, practiced as I was at running into dead ends, cul-de-sacs, until a real person piped on the line, author of the script I held.

To think too of the effect it had after so many tries. Never mind Darnell didn't fully recall who I was, or even having given me his number, that my efforts to recreate the scene didn't help—it's immaterial. Never mind either that he might've altered one of the digits were he not three sheets to the wind, thereby slotting it for the shoe-box with scraps of paper piling up like flakes in a blizzard, trapped in drifts between two trailers. For whatever reason, here he, we, are, in the flesh and mutually surprised. Him at what lies under these duds and me at the beauty of the skin he lives in—Wren, I feel you.

For someone with a real and not some trumped-up reason to complain he's adept at a good time, slipping here and there among the bodies, including mine. Like an otter.

The music, having fallen into a mix of neither this nor that, a no-man's-land of recognizability, neither song nor beat, has slowed the floor to a crawl, confusing the motions and emptying it of revelers.

Prolly as good a time as any t' tap a kidney. I'll be back.

I'll be over there.

Untethered, Jake returns to a glass he set against the wall some time ago and which by some miracle hasn't disappeared. He sips, draws in the sweetness—You'll take a what? A pop??? What's that?! The bartender, buoyant with balloons for arms, backs away as if Jake is jerking him around, as if he'd requested PCP, LSD, MDA, or any of the other substances like it circulating the room, he'll later uncover. The order doesn't compute, and there's at least a dozen men in line, waiting, maybe twice that. Jake attends the bar-rail as though clinging to the gunwale of a ship, eyeing the bartender as he moves from man to man in a game of eyes, scratching up bills from the bar with his paw as they remain fixed, never missing a beat.

I'll take a gin and tonic, he roars into the ear of the other bar-man, also pumped like a parade float. That works, finally—how many tries does it take to realize there's no pop in these parts? The bartender shifts to the side, fills a glass with ice then dispenses first alcohol then fizz, lands it on the bar, nabs the money that Jake has learned to hold outstretched in advance, then does an about face. The bartender splays his thighs in front of the register and presses a series of buttons before the drawer dings open. Though a five-dollar bill will do in change he thumbs through that many singles and slams the drawer of the till, plops a quintet of bills on the bar, then leans toward Jake and gives him a kiss with his eyes.

Thank you. Veeeery much. Jake's eyes meet his in a disarming way. The man pulls away and Jake takes up four notes that are plastered, wet, to the surface, then after a moment's thought leaves a companion—the power of a look.

He backs away.

Fancy meetin' you here.

Oh my god! Ain't you afraid a bein' seen?

Why should I?

I just thought—

—That people like me can't have a little fun? Can I buy you a drink?

I already got one. An' I gotta drive.

So do I—we all do. Maybe someone'll take you home an' you won't have t' worry.

Is that what yer after?

—.

It's a long way t' Pandemonium.

Dance with me, Jake.

I'm with someone.

You're with someone? Oh. Well you can still dance with me. He won' mind I'm sure.

Dan leads Jake back into the fray of bodies naked from the waist up—Glad t' hear yer gettin' around. Look't you without a shirt, he shouts over the music.

I ain't really. Gettin' around.

Could a fool me. The smell of liquor on Dan's breath is clear to Jake and no doubt anyone nearby—Jake, if you ever wanna hook up—

The music pulses.

I'll make a note of it.

Your place or mine—it's all good.

I wonder where my date went—

—He prolly hooked up with someone in the men's roo—

—What a thing t' say. We're here on a date—

—You know how men are!

Oh, sorry! Didn' mean t' barge in.

Jake feels a more than deliberate pinch on the behind, throws his eyes open wide as mirror-balls. He turns instinctively in order to discern the culprit, determined as he is now that he's here on a proper date and that he's had enough of the liberties men take—I mean, enough's enough!—causing him to pivot in a huff, a complete one-eighty, the lights blurring as he swivels head and torso until they land on a dimly familiar face, eyes blinking, smiling slyly, even as he continues to move, gaze fixed, causing Jake to stop in his tracks. Afterward, when he'll attempt to pickle the moment in his brain, just as it was, fashion a bronze of it, he won't remember if he twizzled around and latched on or if he played the cool cat, as if to say, Oh, it's you. Whether it was he who embraced Tommy first or Tommy who embraced him, the gritty details lost to time. The two break from the music as Jake breaks from Dan— it's Tommy, alone and away from Polly and L'Dell.

You're here.

I am.

I been hearing about you—here an' there.

Don't b'lieve any of it—

Communicating is hard at this decibel level, the noise of so many revelers and the music to attend to, what with Dan having just stalked off and Darnell—where did he go? And Polly and Kitty, L'Dell too, Tommy's surveillance team— won't they be attending soon? The distractions audible, requiring the two to draw mouths to the porches of each other's ears, over-shouting sound and sense. Back and forth they rattle, Jake mindful of a window—how long I got to go for it? But it's Tommy who takes the first step.

Wanna hang out?

You jokin'?

¿Dónde?

Huh?

When's good for you? And where?

Now—t'night. My place.

Tommy reaches toward Jake as though they've been married a lifetime, pets him the way a husband strokes his mate, terrain familiar with age—known like his own skin.

It's complicated.

Por supuesto, amigo. Siempre. Pero todo está bien.

Huh?

Yer with someone. I saw. Looks like yer havin' a ball—

—I'd rather be with—

A chat on the dance-floor, Jake moving with Tommy until he wheels around to find Darnell directly nearby, at which point Tommy bids his leave, tagging, ¡Te veo pronto! in Jake's ear. The two break off, leaving Jake to resume the evening with Darnell in a proximity equal to before, though different too, the night having been thrown a wrench or a life-saver, the two gyrating until Jake blurts, I ain't feelin' well.

That's sudden.

Yeah—I don' understand it.

Then y'all take care—s'been real.

I'll call ya.

Tracking up the mountain on I-70, Jake considers the longest ride of his life. He's made this trip many dozens of times by now but it seems to lengthen further out, the further he goes. At the trailer finally he paces back and forth despite the hour, as though he just woke up an hour ago and he's full of pep. He sighs, breathes heavy, arranges cushions on the couch at the front a dozen times, stashes the stack of letters from Florrie that have been gathering on the counter, unopened, in the silverware drawer, tidies up the mess of plates, bowls, and forks that have piled in the sink over the past few days, scolds himself for letting them go, and as he's picking up a pair of socks and jeans beside the bed a door opens of its own accord.

I can' believe I'm here. Tommy peers from front to back as though revisiting the House of Youth.

Never mind.

Anything t' drink?

Jake fetches two beers from the fridge that he's been stocking lately and pops the lids. Froth runs from one onto the carpet before he can catch it. Through the window over the sink he glimpses shadows moving atop the bed in a room next-door, two figures forming the silhouette of a spider on its back, or is it an upturned crab? A cat sits briefly on the landing then shoots away. Tommy hovers over Jake, a head taller than before, I swear, swigs from the bottle between advances, sets it on the counter then takes it up, alternating back and forth.

Tommy—

—Silencio.

The two sway to an internal music, hands tracking sense, experience too, an old routine now new, pausing and reaching for bottles, swigging, once and then again, a tango of bottles and bodies, alternating glass and flesh. A rooting, type of germination, bedding, whetting tongues with saliva and beer, furrowing deeper.

It's like we just met.

Silencio.

Like we never did this before.

Silencio—

—Like I'm nervous.

Silencio, Jake—

Time suspends, grows long and unhurried, enlarges over a series of gestures until the two blanket themselves in darkness as they morph from the kitchen with its single bulb, down a short hallway now magically lengthened, Jake nearly tripping three times as though advancing toward death on an altar, a lamb nearing its end at a sodden pace, blanching along the way, backing, thumping into the door where the two remain—is it an hour?—three?—until Jake angles his arm back and wheels the knob, bursts the door open from the pressure of the two slanting against it, almost tumbling into a space that the June moon—look!— has prepared, blued it with light, having ensconced itself in the sky and refused to budge, sending the sun packing, prolonging the night beyond its usual length, now that Tommy's returned, the two moving progressively to a beat different than the one coming from next-door as though a gauntlet has been thrown, challenging them to a duel of gestures and gesticulations, pitching caution to the wind.

Down fall the clothes like last year's needles on an evergreen—no more peek-a-boo partialities but the whole, the real, thing, which Jake has fantasized about how many times and that now stands there in front of him in the irrevocability of the flesh. Up kneel the bodies on the silvered sheets, the moon morphing its glow, a blend of conifer and mildew in the air, the two facing each other, lips pinging, echolocating, the press of cocks, bellies, chests, and chins—it is possible to be nearer still?

If the body exists normally as a landscape ringed by a border, a split-rail fence that stands until it collapses, at which point the feral roam in in a free-for-all—to think of him wrapped in leather that day in December, lost to, actually repelling me—what was that? That get-up. Is it going on a year or is it two? Now here he is, we two, naked to the skin, folded in a furry warmth, him shaking mildly as though once again we're two strangers, granting me the freedom to explore the cheek, the full-fluffed beard, plank of the forehead that I'll walk off any day, the warm, unstrained lips that pair neither too soft nor tautly, forbidden tree of the neck, the apple I enjoy without guilt, the shoulders, pecs, and arms walling me in the grass-covered patch that runs and resolves into the terrain of the stomach, abdomen, a trail pointing me to a mound of black where I pillow my head, the growth furring the balls resting on the thighs into a no-man's-land to be explored in the course of time; thighs, hirsute, calves and shins equally black, obscuring the ankles, feet and toes, all nosed, lipped, and tongued by me as he transitions from kneeling to prone, taking it in until it's his turn, the gentle way he moves until he doesn't, taking charge, flipping me, splaying then tonguing me, buttering me up for when he makes his move—

—Easy, tiger.

The letting up and letting in as I tip over the fence, succumb to our status as a unit, two-as-one in a different kind of dance, one in which he adjusts, angles me this way and that until he inverts me, never parting. While the two across the way appear to compete in pain and bliss, Tommy mumbles, Jake.... I'm in—

—No joke—

—I mean I'm *in*—

—In how?—

—*In* in—

—That news?—

—Big—

—Big what?—

—News—I'm in—

Without parting he's lifted me off the bed with freakish strength, maneuvered me until his back caresses the sheets, making me wish I were in their place, his head cushioned and me on a mountain, a spike driven through an eye, ignited and uncomfortable in some Zen way as Tommy thrusts, pulling my thighs lower as he moves—

—I'm *in* Jake—

The soft tones of his voice, the prayerful ejaculations, supplications to the pleasure goddess to prolong the moment, as though pleading for a hue that don't fade, a blossom that don't brittle, balmy blue and coolest orange light of night and dark of day, Tommy tugs on my nipples as he thrusts, and I groan as he raises up only to drop me down to meet him, as though ticking off a to-do list he's been planning on getting to for ages, our lips meeting, tongues, beards, as he continues to perk my nipples, redden them and, like the bedsprings about to shoot into flames, furnishing Tommy the bounce he desires as he gains momentum.

Jake I can't—

—Wait for me—

—La vida es demasiado seca the longer I wait—look what you do—just you—

I press my abdomen into his and we're insects with eyes locked like the two next-door, I imagine, the bed of hair on the stomach calling me to lie down, lighting a fire as he moves, whetting my desire until the two of us are same-paging the moment—

—It's no use—

Tommy exhales, his body rigidifies, thighs lengthen, feet frot the sheets, sliding from the mattress below while I collapse—Me encanta esto, mi amor.

Huh?

I'm in Jake—te amo.

No, no, no, don't say that—it would be the only line Jake understands in Tommy's idiom. Not unless you mean it.

He wants to file a protest—too soon!—too soon!—but he reconsiders, remembering how things can percolate in an absence, ferment and grow, so he decides to silencio, lips betraying his usual principles, busied as they are at the moment, avoiding, despite himself, interjecting a fly in the ointment for the eternity Tommy lies there, the two umbilically attached in a moment that would layer itself over in the course of time, a coated complexity that needs to be unpacked starting in the not-too-distant future the way the mind has a knack for enshrining moments like this, that is to say bliss, for isolating and even decontextualizing it, bare skin against bare skin, Tommy still leaching his spirit and me admitting, with discussions to come but stifled for now as we pant, leaving contemplation for laxer times, the two of us in Molly's gray universe, beyond the hoohah of exteriors.

Tengo hambre.

We're two hombres?

Ha! True! But no. I said I'm famished.

It was Tommy who broke the nocturnal spell, tracking out of bed, naked hulk leaning toward the window, peeking through the blinds—

Oh my god, the sun!

Jake eyes him crashing the venetians closed then drawing them open again, allowing the outside in. He peers left and right. Este lugar es loco! The black wings across the back, an angel in America, beast too, gathering above and along the crack of his behind, dispersing around the sides of the torso. The rails of muscles running on either side of the spine and up the neck. The lines like rivers where hair gathers and runs down the lower arms—

—Necesito un café, amigo.

At the Ojo Diner, kitty-corner from the trailer, Tommy peers into Jake's eyes from dark-roasted beans. The clatter of dishes is enough to wake the dead or the never-slept. Neither notices the glances of the locals as Tommy fondles Jake's hand. Sight of dark coffee and cream, drinking it in. When the waitress arrives with her pad she susses the situation then glances toward the register. The two broaden then narrow their eyes—

—Wha' kin I git you boys?

Tommy slips his hand away from Jake's and takes the menu. What you gonna have, amigo? But before Jake can order Tommy turns to the server.

No come carne—he indicates Jake.

¿De veras? Podrías haberme engañado.

Sé amable.

Wha' kin I git you then?

I'll have what he's having, without the meat.

You mean the same thing.

Over a double order the conversation is stuck in reverse, a replay of not just the previous night but the past year, two, or is it ten? That ain't no reg'lar gestation period, Jake remarks while the two recount with an elephant memory the first brush at Dodgson, the encounter in Pandemonium with Polly and L'Dell, several phantom sightings and near misses in between, reports from Polly and Kitty, all occasioned by chance or a divine, kind or nefarious who knows? Jake avers he'd been unmindful of Tommy the whole time.

Tell me you didn' think a me.

I didn' think a you.

See how you are.

And now what?

¿Como? Now what—what?

Leftover yolk darkens and hardens on plates, pressed and spread here and there by forks and crusts of bread, pigments on a palette.

The door flops open and Jake's neighbor swaggers in, trailing last-night's date, the one with the healthy pipes vying with his, the hair atop both of them scrambled like an order of eggs—

—Hey, dude. Long night, eh?

Likewise.

Hope we weren' too—

—Ditto. The man's date presses her breasts against his upper arm, embraces it, smooths back the dyed tangle then looks out the window in the direction of the mine.

Sorry about that dust-up you had, dude. With that guy's wife—

—Not sure what you—

—Chick was mad as a hornet!

Jake clears his throat.

The man glances at Tommy then Jake. Name's Derrick—
hey, pal, let's talk sometime.

The two disappear into the corner booth, slouching low
on the banquette. The woman angles against him as he pops
a cigarette and lights it.

What was that about?

Long story.

Are you a home-wrecker?

Not by design.

What comes next, amigo?

A hike?

We didn' sleep a wink!

I know a place—

The two gather green-backs and set them on the table
when all of a sudden Peacoat, who retreated while the
pair were thumbing their noses at the day, the minute they
stepped out of the trailer, comes gliding in the door in a
fashion, making it impossible to tell if he slipped through
glass or coat-tailed a diner through the door. He perches
himself on the banquette behind Tommy sporting his usual
frown, turning around and peering occasionally, directly at
Jake.

I guess it'd be good to get out a bit. For me a hike is like
a mailman strolling on his day off.

It's the place I go when I want to be alone in nature, if
you know what I mean. Totally private.

It's a brazen day, not long before the solstice when things
commence heating up in earnest. Clear Creek trips over
the pair's feet as they stand on the bank, tumbling from
fourteeners in the direction of Golden, an iridescent ribbon
threading rocks the size of hunting hideaways, looping and
curlicuing lower from Loveland Pass, seventy miles to the

plains where it connects with the Platte, the river they say is too thick to flow and too thin to plow, and yet this feeder here can't help somersaulting over itself, sloppy and wet and spitting mist, the water effervescing atop boulders while the hesitant pair waits to cross, boots and socks dangling from their hands, foam whitening everything, including the dark skin of the rocks poking through.

Into that froth Tommy and Jake step, having left the pick-up in the parking lot, if you could call it that, just off the road. Down they descend with legs naked from the knees, their cuffs rolled higher and higher as they traverse the stream. The water rises, reaching Jake's upper thighs, darkening them both.

It's freezing!

Woooooooohoooooo!!! Tommy's smiling as he observes Jake pause. Puedes hacerlo, amigo! You can do it!

I've seen ouzels plunge into the middle of Clear Creek in January, when it was minus fifty out. T' think it's June—nearly summer!— and still so cold. How do dippers do it?

Wanna carry me across? I see you got the guns.

You're the one brought me here. ¡Vete, amigo!

I guess I always forgit that it's so cold!

Tommy grasps Jake's hand and tugs, encouraging and steadying him against a current that could sweep the two away in a blink, through the deepest part where the river, pregnant with runoff, rises to their crotches.

Once on the other side the two slick water from their shins, shake like sheep, don their boots again and ascend toward a series of erratics perched on the valley's flank. When they reach what appears to be a granite wall they halt long enough for Jake to recount the history of the Utes in these parts, centuries past—They were over-nighting here in this canyon, for how long? Hundreds? Thousands of

years? Just yesterday? On this very spot. Without speaking,
the pair begins to undress as though the land demanded
it, ordered them to show themselves. Did the Utes shelter
under this very rock, away from the nosy sun, the way we
are now?

It's one thing to doff your second skin in the dark, and
it's a whole other animal to peel the layers in bright day, late
on a Saturday morning, like two teens on a dare. The once-,
twice-, thrice-over in the glaring sun, reacquaintance after
a hiatus—they were birthed in the open air and here they
are again. Tommy stretches out and his shadow shrinks in
the light. Cars whisk below, hyping the danger and thrill,
day-trippers and week-enders heading to and from the city
at a clip, competing with the Creek.

The dilemma of a single vehicle, in this case Tommy's
pick-up, in a lot. The tendency of a loner like that to attract
passers-by, craning their necks to get a view from behind
glass as they whiz through the canyon—Think the fishing's
good here? Hiking? The view? Someone else thinks so.
First one then another four-wheeler crunches into the set-
aside on Rte. 6, a swelling in the road large enough for two,
three cars max. Jake and Tommy peer down as people step
from vehicles, gaze left and right in search of what's to
see. It's not just any car but a pick-up, Jake imagines them
saying. So should be local, a tip-off for any city-slicker. And
yet clearly no angler can be seen flashing her line in the
flow. No one stumbles on the oversized rocks, chucking
boulders behind like dice, defining chance, but still the
group persists. Jake and Tommy spy them through cracks
in the erratic, standing in a state of nature, jeans drying in
the sun as they ogle the newcomers, wondering how long
they'll stay, if they'll stay or move on.

The only onlooker really—intruder would be unkind—
is Peacoat, who observes things with a ubiquitous eye,

hedging on divine. He's getting bolder, Jake can tell. Soon he'll wanna join—my god.

What is it, amigo?

I was just thinkin'.

A what?

A someone.

Someone I know?

From my past.

You mean the one that guy Derrick was talkin' about at the restaurant? One who cheated on his wife? Tommy sticks a finger in Jake's ribs.

Stopppp. No, a past-er life than that. 'Fore I came here.

How many you have?

A thousand? Or just one. Not sure.

Estás loco—

—Loco I get. Past lives follow you.

No sé—I don' know what in the worl' you mean—

Peacoat advances or wills himself closer, leans his forehead against Tommy's shoulder. The sight of the two paired like that. After all this time Jake has become nearly accustomed to his appearance, the rotted mass and leathered skin, split in places and jellying out where the clothes are shredded and falling away, eyes hollow, black as bears' dens, lips ashen and devoid of warmth, the very penis he cradled once, battered by elements—all that and more have become familiar to the point Jake can finally look without wincing. Until now. To view a form like that juxtaposed to Tommy, the picture of vitality, eyes that absorb everything, or almost—they were the feature Jake remembered most from their encounters, the way they peer at you without slithering away, two eddies you can skinny-dip in, clothes whisked away after a trek, the cool water, the will never to get out. Peacoat's, by contrast, have dried up. They're two vacancies—Jake never looked at him so clearly before.

Tommy's willingness to abandon talk and get down to business, following what happened only hours before, complicated by a presence he knows nothing about.

I must really be tired, amigo.

Look't you! "Amigo."

When I don't sleep I see things.

Then let's chat. Tell me what you been doin' since I saw you that time in Pandemonium, a million years ago. I'd rather get it straight from you.

Tell me what you been doin.

Workin'?

Workin' who?

Be nice.

Peacoat drops his head in Tommy's lap. Tommy's feet are crossed, his arms behind him. He's leaning back on his palms under the cool of the erratic. The sight of Peacoat's head near his crotch, resting.

You gettin' at somethin'?

Far be it from me—Jake, I wanna see you.

Can you ever see more than this?

Y' know what I mean. Reg'larly.

Oblivious to the figure curled in his lap, Tommy reaches forward and tugs Jake's nipple.

Jake returns the gesture.

Wha' d you say?

Hikers have braved the flow below and are heading higher, toward the ridge. These two here, sheltering in the shade while their clothes sun, apart from them, are unaware of their advance, even though the intruders haven't been climbing in silence by any stretch—

—Oh!—

—Oh!—

—Ohhhhh!!—

—'Scuse us!

Tommy and Jake glance at each other, then at their unannounced guests. Again it's one of those circumstances when it wouldn't work to remark, My stars! Look! At him—like that!—not if you find yourself in the same way. The shorter hiker takes her partner's hand, a man whose beard is almost as thick as Tommy's, stature nearly as tall, and leads him from the circumstances before them, as do three more couples, a group of eight threading their way toward the crest.

To think a the times we seen them. In men's magazines. Novels—read what they do. Got the dope on reels, the down 'n dirty. Learned about it in health class whether we wanted to or not. Caught it on the silver screen.

It ain't like they were looking for it—.

Neither were we—just sayin'.

The two move on, pay no heed to the glances in their direction on this sunny Saturday in June.

I don't think either a us is a choir boy.

I ain't intersted in no choir boy. 'Toy buscando un hombre d'verdad. Pero—

—Huh?

Para mi no hay problema.

I don' know what you just said, or what you been doin' all this time.

Verdad.

Huh?

Tommy reaches forward and boxes Jake's chest a few times, nearly tipping him over and waking Peacoat in the process, who for once appeared to be pacified, laying in Tommy's lap. Now he sits up straight, alarmed, as if capable of emotion. He stares at Jake as if to say, What gives!? while a magpie perches on the surface above, strangely rattled too. He lifts off, sails into the air, and leaves a trace on Tommy's thigh as he wings away—

—See what you get?

Tommy takes the side of his thumb and rubs it over the hairs, scraping the sludge and depositing it on Jake's thigh quicker than he's able to shy off, barefoot over the rock and lichen, rough against the skin, prying eyes above be damned. Too late. He plucks a couple leaves from a scrub oak and sands the spot then returns to the shadow of the erratic, which lengthens as the sun moves from its lookout overhead, a motion Peacoat has been following, drawing farther toward the rock face after having been interrupted. Would he simply disappear if the sun never moved, like a vampire destroyed by light?

You're evil.

Don' blame me, amigo—blame that one up there. He missed.

Now Jake boxes Tommy's chest, while remaining rooted to the spot—there's no chance of upending him. He tugs Tommy's penis as if it were pointing in accusation.

Did the Utes play these games? Did they spar unclad, go for it? Was it forbidden or did it go without saying, no big deal? Grabbing a man's vulnerability then holding it. The way cemetery visitors rub or even knock off that part of a memorial figure, god, angel, putto, or other allegory in stone. Was it prudery that hammered off so many, so carefully rendered? Eroticism? Or just mischief? Is there a repository of sheered-off members somewhere?

Here's the Real McCoy, there for the tugging, which now Tommy does in turn, giving Jake a pull, and now the two control each other in a sense. Peacoat retreats as if in fear, presses himself against the side of the erratic, the sunlight waning, prompting Jake to lay where Peacoat's rested, inducing the two to nod off for what seems like a moment but in reality lasted some time.

Jake stirs. We better go back.

Go?! We haven't started.

It's gettin' late and we gotta climb down.

Ain't that what we come for, niño? A little night fun?

Tommy stretches alongside Jake, which he tolerates for a time until he rises and comments, Seriously, we don't wanna get stuck here at night. There are critters.

As if Tommy didn't know.

Back at the trailer the two sprawl across the bed and crash into sleep. The vital version of Peacoat lies pressed against Jake—

Let's leave, make a start some'ere.

But where? Won't we just be taking our problems with us? Wouldn' it be better, Jake, t' face the music here, take what comes our way, so long's we're together?

Peacoat slithers atop Jake, the two warm-skin to warm-skin, youth to youth, face to face, lips about touching.

Somewhere where we wouldn' have th' baggage we got here—we c' make a clean break.

But, Jake, our friends—our world—they're all here in the Forest City.

Peacoat lifts then rests Jake's calves atop his shoulders. He makes his move in a single, steady motion—Wherever you wanna go, I'll go. I ain't gonna leave—I just don't know why—

—Never?—

—Nevvvveeerr.

Jake rides a wave of pain and pleasure, the situation they're forced to deal with a finger in the eye—

Then in that case—

—Anywhere, Jake—you'n me. I'll stay or go, wherever you do—I wanna be there—

—Jake!

Huh!

You're havin' a nightmare!

Low light filters through the blinds from the west, away from Main Street. Tommy's propped up on his forearm leaning over Jake's torso, obscuring everything but the spectral version of Peacoat—is it a fake?—there in his usual corner, the antithesis of the one in the dream—

—Actually, it wasn't such a bad—

—But you were crying—and look—

—Must be lack a sleep.

In bed officially that night, after Jake and Tommy attempt and quite frankly come pert near reprising events of the preceding night, re-enlivening or resurrecting them, the working parts—after which Jake peers at the stars beyond the window, at news billions of years old, almost as ancient as the Big Bang itself when the universe began inflating, a part of it morphing into the Milky Way, over eons, white splattered against the sky in a pattern like stepping stones— to think of what it says about these past few hours, less than a day.

The other Peacoat sits atop the dresser in the corner, ever awake, but it's the original Peacoat Jake remembers as he peers at the white shot across the blackness, lights that reflect on the surface of skin or the clear of the eye, stationary and in motion, burning, white and black, the dark of Peacoat's flesh in his vital days not that long ago in star-time, the stars fallen on him, on Jake, and now Tommy too.

The vital Peacoat, the memory of which is an antidote to the waterlogged residue, present as his zombie-cousin, seemingly unthinking and unfeeling but capable of shearing guilt all the same—that Peacoat can still pack a punch. Synchronous with the moment Tommy packs a punch most of all, the moment when Jake flies from himself, the fake Peacoat doubling down at the messiest of moments, unseen until all the excitement, attesting to the elbow grease of memory—when he makes the scene it's not without a punch of his own. Elements of the past flood back like stars on his belly, chest, and thighs, after which the anti-Peacoat stares in vengeful glory.

If I could only re-enliven you, mister, whoever or whatever you are. Instill life again in those eyes, throughout, stars that once peered inside me like no one ever will. Unlike the way you're peering now, incapable of the same though still a lure, hooking me as though you were the real deal, despite the fact you'll always be what you are. The Unpeacoat. One I can't expunge—rolled, flopped, on the beach, after living underwater for how long?

Wasting me inside.

As Tommy motors over the mountain, drunk from another night without sleep, Jake nears the specter. Zombie. Walker or apparition. It's been difficult to look him in the eye lately, if you could call it that—more often than not when Jake glances toward it it averts its gaze, as though it can't look at him. But now the latter examines the grim mien and tattered clothes, leathered skin, emaciated penis and deformed feet, victims of a lake, events set in motion by a body who walks free, having given the slip to the eye of the law—the power of a collar. The will to look the other way, not get to the bottom of things, including why Peacoat gazes away now from such a broken posture.

You know how I feel. How I always will. Deep down.

Jake reaches toward the presence but it shies away, startled.

You were the first—Romeo was a mistake. Not worth dying for.

It's as if pupils peek now where an emptiness was, as though the figure wills them there. Black as fire-pits where light flamed once, heat emanates from them, as though a spark remains hidden, never to be extinguished—

You taught me—

Liquid trickles down.

—How to—

Is it poison? Residue from the lake?

—To whatever degree I'm capable—

Again, Jake can't help but approach the thing, frighted and cornered, until he slips away again, a hunted sparrow evading a net.

It should a been me, not you—the two of us together. Anything but what it was.

The thing moves around the end of the bed, toward the other side.

—For what it is, I'll forever be in your debt.

Realizing he's headed for the door, shambling over the head of the bed, Jake backs up and shuts it in, imprisoning the two.

—As long I live you'll always be here—Jake touches his chest. Including after I'm gone.

The thing climbs over the bed toward the window.

—But I gotta—

Round and round the two trek after each other, like the progenitor of a monster after his creation, until they switch roles, unable to come to terms let alone halt. The goal isn't to erase the thing—that's impossible—one that, truth be told, comforts as much as it horrifies. It isn't to throw an inkwell in its direction like it were a common demon. Poke your eyes out so you can no longer view it. Rid yourself of its presence by taking your own life—it may be on the other side. Strangle or slash it—useless. Expose it to the sun until it bubbles and burns. Confront it with a cross, rosary, or garlic. All the tactics people resort to, and all bootless.

Jake leaves Peacoat sitting on the far corner of the bed, having come to an impasse. He steps out and into the morning air, exhausted from the lack of sleep. His boss will comment that he was an even more useless piece a shit than usual, that he should a stayed home rather than bothered to make a show—

Too much pussy last night?

Sage perfumes the air. Jake approaches a bush near the edge of the tiny trailer court with its wheeled units lined in succession. He breaks off a branch and weaves the end into the beginning, twists the branches and inserts other weeds as well from the rock garden.

Back inside he draws toward Peacoat who attends him at the door. He backs away as Jake enters, the nose of pine always in the air now mixed with sage. Jake lights the wreath and flames shoot up, giving birth to a trail of smoke which he directs through the trailer, back to front, covering every inch, nook, and cranny, on the verge of hacking as he circulates around the place, recalling as he does the water-logged journey the thing underwent, the elemental bludgeoning because of his association with him, Jake, the truth that really binds him here. He lets it go. Wishes it a peaceful journey to where it's headed—hopefully a land of peace.

The fire burns, billows smoke, then subsides, heat trailing still. Jake removes a hanger from his closet, embraces a shirt draped on it, draws in the smell, touches it to his lips—

—.

In the tiny yard a Fiat wide, between his and the trailer to the north, Jake sets the shirt on the weeds, sprinkles kerosene over it, and sets it on fire. The sight of plaid flaming orange and blue, then black, a pattern decayed. The tiny green wedged between the dwellings grows cavernous—

Todos los Animales

THE APARTMENT WITH ITS THREE BEDROOMS and equal number of tenants, officially, as in on the lease, hosts six on a slow night. On weekends it can be two or three times that, arranged in shifts because a night is long, on weekends especially, starting as it does at tea dance and extending to brunch the following day. In most parts of the city that kind of traffic would trigger the authorities, but on Capitol Hill, not far from Cheesman Park, people take it all in stride. They compete. It defines the neighborhood, this Greenwich Village or Castro of the Queen City, remarkably complaint-, and crime-free, what with all the eyes at all hours of day and night. With the endless coming and going, the parade of bodies drifting from bars and bathhouses on foot, bike, or car, entering not just the apartment here on Josefina but hundreds or thousands like it—with all that activity the streets don't sleep. Earning the area its moniker, a reference to those Sodoms and Gomorrahs on the coasts, east and west—people gravitate to their own.

But from where? Local suburbs for sure, bastions of religious fervor, Wheat Ridge and Arvada, Westminster, and Aurora, but Ojo and Pandemonium too. Individuals who pilgrimage and remain put for the most part, pursuing a living smack in the center of town, away from the margins to this tolerant core, paradoxically, a reversal of a century ago, the new margins now the center, the center the new margin, where truths secrete themselves from neighbors, spouses, and sometimes one's own self.

But they come from more far-flung places too, Cheyenne and Tulsa, Dodge and Rapid City, Casper and Trinidad. The Queen, or Mile High, City is a Mecca for freedom-seekers from land-locked states, conservative for the most part—they come as choir-boys and evolve into something else, altering politics in the process, jobs, clothing, and demeanor too, once they get the hang of it. The gay life. Many have crossed the threshold of 52 Josefina Avenue in the years since Tommy, Polly, and Kitty adopted the place. Tommy, Jake will learn for a fact now, has been no slouch in the numbers race, confirming his intuitions, totals that would put Jake to shame. He's sucked the air of liberation in this 1920s-Berlin-cum-1980s-Queen-City, burning a different kind of midnight oil than Jake when he's lost in a book. He's taken his turn with dozens, hundreds, possibly even thousands, escorting them every night of the week. Twice on weekends. He's a walking encyclopedia of details about the body that he's in the habit of glossing with Polly and Kitty, an endless discourse on dimensions.

'Til lately.

Until he met, or re-met, Jake.

That cooled his jets, causing not a little consternation on the home-front, to wit in Polly and Kitty both.

What in the world are you doin', sissy? Throwin' in the towel? Committin' suicide?

You ain' old enough!

Takin' a breather, I guess.

You're not allow! We got a lifetime agreement, and you got a long way t' go—! T' make up for los' time.

Sissy, ain' this what we fought for? The freedom to decide—. There ain't no law.

Lying upstairs on Tommy's bed, Jake takes in the conversation. Judging by the sound, never mind the passion, of what's expressed in English, Spanish too. From what he can tell, the number one goal seems not to exclude anyone within ear-shot from taking it all in.

Well, when you find someone—

Some*one*?!

You mean some dozen?

No some-one.

Tommy adopts a pose of nonchalance, contrasting Polly and Kitty's vibe, who continue to confront him with more than a hint of concern, disregarding the softness—worse, the vulnerability—on Tommy's part—

—No agreement's forever. You got a go with what feels right.

Later that evening it was that line that Jake latched onto, hankering for clarification—

Maybe they're right—maybe I'm robbing you of a life. A person shouldn't have t' change. Not that much, by the looks of it.

What if it's a change I wanna make?

Including ruinin' the family?

That was already in the works. Since I told them about you. It sealed my fate, my future with them.

Jake's concerns knot tighter. Truth be told when Tommy revealed to him his last name, first thing that popped in Jake's head, he remembered, was, That'll fix 'em! Meaning Harry and Florrie. And they thought Donald—. In a sense nothing could give Jake more pleasure. At least Donald's native tongue is English. His parents were born here. Unlike Tommy's.

Little did Jake know how deeply rooted Tommy's line goes in what people refer to as "This country," much deeper than Jake's for sure, who are upstarts by comparison. Jake assumed, falsely, that anyone like Tommy, speaking the way he does, the hundreds of thousands living in the barrios and suburbs, in and around the Mile High City, staffing stores, unloading trucks, running schools—mayoring the city for Chrise sake—had to be fresh from the south side of the Rio Grande. A boat-load of assumptions, no matter how flawed, flooded his brain the moment Tommy revealed his surname that time, laid it out bare, full-frontal, conditioned as his thinking was by Harry, Florrie, and Laurentine most of all, all unchallenged until Tommy came along by chance or fate, driving home the point in his inimical way, about what end was up and what was down.

Sitting around the table with Tommy, Polly, and Kitty the next day, in a rare break in traffic so to speak, all of that is still to be absorbed. How could Jake have anticipated such a front-row seat to a culture cast as foreign and never seen on an episode of *Jim Doney's Adventure Road,* about a version of domestic soil older than the Forest City. Almost the entire east coast. Here's a culture omitted from the broadcasts, including a version that parties every night, hosting gentlemen-callers, female-female too, and many a mix, downing a string of cocktails before hitting the dance-floor in a circuit of clubs, the point of which is to land a big fish, two, and sometimes three. A regimen Tommy's room-mates, and he too, adhered to in a pact almost like religion, until Jake came on the scene.

For his part, in order to fit in the best he could, Jake developed a tolerance for alcohol, swallowed substances the acronyms for which he never heard of, capered 'til closing, blew out his ears, in becoming a party animal. Unlike Kitty and Polly, whose motto was Never the Same Man Twice, Jake adhered to Tommy's insistence that the two return together, alone, night after night. In that way they competed with the racket from the adjoining rooms. Unlike them, he and Tommy woke knowing the name of the person across the pillow with some degree of certainty.

Alicia, you can't believe what I dragged home las' night!

Pray tell.

Sissy, she was fine. Older. Daddy type—she still sleepin'. Cute as a peanut.

Speaking of nuts, Jake thought, you're gonna be the toughest one to crack. Polly, she—her preferred pronoun—and Kitty, harbored doubts about the whiteboy from—is it Pencil-vania? That where you're from, Jake? Or is it another planet?

Sashaying into our lives, she implied. Endangering the good thing we had going. A longstanding agreement: As Many as Possible.

Anything but a Repeat.

Quantity over qual—.

Until Tommy comes down from the mountain, from Dodgson Reservoir, then Ojo Caliente, spouting this and that about some gringo in a string of words too indelicate to repeat, up to today, spending night after night, for how long has is it been? An eternity?

Sissy, you must get so bored, eating the same thing day after day.

Guys, I'm sittin' right here.

Henny, I don't care if you're sittin' on the pot—Polly's gotta tell it like it is.

Tommy tugs his beard. No digas eso. No es amable.

Pero—no offense, henny.

At which point a man lumbers down the stairs, bracing himself on the railing as he descends, then heads to the table.

Well I'll be—

—Small world, eh Jake?

You know each other?

Maybe.

Maybe not.

Si*ssy*, here he is. A good time if ever there was one—trus' me! Dan lifts Polly's hand and kisses it, as though bowing to royalty. Here's my Jack a Hearts—what did you say your name was again? Sure knows how to jack a girl. Straight t' her heart.

That was fun—. Dan shoots Jake a look. Fancy meeting you here.

Polly offers Dan a coffee—Help yourself—and to whatever left-overs are still in the pan. After Kitty's scooted over on the bench, opening a space for Dan to rest, Polly continues to enthuse about her night.

No need to tell everything—Dan again shoots an eye toward Jake. Some things are better left unsaid.

But henny, talkin' about it's the best part! I don't often bring home older men. What do you do for a living? I'm guessin' you're a suit. A CEO.

I guess school-teacher, jumps Kitty. Look't the hands, how soft. Never worked a honest day in his life—

—You're not far—

—I'm used t' men with calluses—

—I should be going.

But, henny, we got the whole rest a the day! After which, then you can split.

I gotta get home.

Got it. She'll be wonderin' where you are.

Prob'ly not.

As Dan squirms Jake wonders how he'd behave if he, Jake, weren't there—

Gatita, will you show this man the door since he's so rudely rejecting my imperial presence? Off with his head!

When Tommy proves impervious to Polly's view that he's gone monastic, dead down there, she begins to work on Jake. The third month in, before Jake moved to the Queen City from "that crap-hole in the hills," as Polly called it—that's when it became clear they either had a new room-mate half the week or lost one just as many nights.

Polly pulls out the big guns.

Henny, ya gotta protect yourself. She ain't use t' regular fare, an' she could very easily bolt on you. Leave you high and dry. I mean, y' gotta look out for Numero Uno, sweetie. Otherwise you gonna get your little Illinois heart hurt.

Thanks for caring. Who knows how things're gonna go?

I think you put a spell on him—I mean he ain't hisself.

I ain't got powers over no one.

Kitty pipes, Alicia and us, we family, Jake—we go way back.

So happy to hear.

We made a pact we'd always keep things the way they are.

I don' know what t' say.

Somethin' t' keep in mind, sissy.

Jake didn't think it time to express his view that change is the only enduring thing, the heart of life, that if you care about someone, anyone, you'll pay someday; that it's best to take what comfort you can in the moment because who knows, once you blink; that if you're foolish enough to care do it at your own peril; that you'll get your guts ripped out and handed back mangled—if you don't lose your guts entirely. He figured it'd take a novel to explain, god knows more than a boozy bar-chat, even if these two were to give a damn. Discussing it in full would leave him with an even raspier throat, not to mention soul, than he had already.

Moreover if Polly's intentions were debatable, so were Jake's toward her, quite frankly, including anyone of her kind, lumping her and Kitty in a category the way he did. It posed a problem, squaring them with Tommy, aka Alicia— what in the world was that about? Convenience? Custom? Carelessness? Anything but convention.

It would take time before Jake could formulate a theory about the Pollys of the world, after he'd shed a heap of old chestnuts that he carried in his pocket at the time. All he knew then is that when he, Jake, proved stubborn and refused to disappear, Polly remarked in frustration one day, Henny, if you ever hope t' keep him you gotta work on that get-up!

What's wrong with what I got on?

Polly bowed her head, peered over her glasses, raised her eyebrows as she squared Jake in the eye then lowered her gaze over his body, scanning it—

—Whaaat?!

Henny, where t' begin?

Manuel!—Tommy caught the drift of the conversation from the kitchen.

—Me llamo Polly, señor. Por favor. Pero Alteza to you.

Well, Alteza—no seas una perra—

'Toy una perra, verdad. Tell Miss Thing here that.

—What's wrong with what I got on?

I like you best without clothes, niño—don' listen.

With a stirrer, Polly swishes alcohol and ice, then sucks.

Relly, we should go shoppin'. The two a us.

Can I go?

OK, Gatita, you too—we'll fix you up, henny, won't we Kitty?

Polly, stop!

We'll make you a lady, assures Kitty. What you think, Alicia?

I think you should both lay off.

Henny, there ain't no worries about layin' with Jake—lo siento, niño—

You're on! I'll go shoppin' with yous. Might be fun.

Then henny, we are on. Polly and Kitty high five, causing the latter to spill her drink.

Make her pay—Kitty points at Polly. She shits money an' can afford it.

I ain't payin'! I'm the one should be paid. Cash money. A lot of it. For services rendered—

—You render services, all right.

Henny, I'm the best!

The two a you—

She's rollin' in dough.

Polly lifts the front of her wig and removes a wad of bills resting under the weave. Is this what you mean? You never know when a girl's gonna need t' remove herself from a jam.

Su Alteza Real.

Your Royal Hindness, adds Tommy out of sight.

I am La Duquesa Real—don't forget it underthings. I mean underlings. Polly poses in front of her throne, does an about-face, reaches down to steady herself then shifts up her dress. Kiss it, commoners!

There's too much to kiss, your duchy.

Talk about Air Apparent.

Nailed it, niño—

—It's been that a thousand times, Sis*sy*.

Ten times that, mos' likely.

Polly unmusses her gown and sets down an empty glass. Are we gonna dance or are you jus' gonna stay home and admire my backside? Let's vamoose, vermin!

Tommy's already at the door, leading Jake onto the stoop by the hand and pausing, planting a kiss while remarking, They mean well.

Jake swivels Tommy around. The two bow their heads toward Polly as she ducks under the door-frame.

Girlfriend's gonna leave this dreck here. These rags. All of 'em. They ain' clothes. And god knows fashion. If they are they're from the House a Blineness.

Be nice. And don't look at me that way, burnin' to say something.

Henny, I'm burnin' and itchin' both.

The sales associate shoots Polly a look before turning to Jake. He receives the bundle Polly amassed from the floor of the dressing room, balling it in a loose, dissipated lump, along with the bundle Jake was ordered to bring from Ojo, the tee off his back, the whole nine yards, including the corduroys with the elastic waistline. Multicolored socks worn through at the toes and heals both. Clogs that Polly labeled a crime against humanity. Underwear she averred gave up the ghost a decade ago.

Get rid a it all. This too! Polly turns over a garbage bag puffed with the duds Jake left at Tommy's so he didn't have to pack a bag each week, in the same way Tommy left spares at the trailer up the hill. This should a never been allowed on a rack let alone you, henny. You're a thousan' times better off naked—not that I wanna see you that way. She lowers her head and peers over her glasses.

If you say so.

If Miss Morphous says it, believe it, henny. Typist. Stylist. Best lay west a the Mississippi. East of it too. The whole damn country.

B'lieve it, Jake, mews Kitty. Take a look a yourself!

Trailing the duo as they thread their way to the exit, Jake comments, Clothes are meant to come off. No one said they had t' be designer.

Polly halts. That's heresy, henny. Take it back or off with your head! If you can't go runnin' around here the way you and Alicia do back home—whether we—she gestures toward Kitty—wanna see it or not—then you can at least knock 'em dead.

But knocking others dead wasn't the sense Jake got when he glimpsed himself in the three-way mirror near the door, despite a series of efforts—endless outfits—casual separates that can be easily mixed or matched, he learned, without having to consult Polly or Kitty first or, god forbid, Tommy, who clearly can't be trusted given the way he tolerated Jake 'til now in "that mierda you call clothes." Tommy having been barred from tagging along, against both his and Jake's objections, Jake was reduced to sampling garment after garment alone, practically with strangers, including print after print, pant after pant, shoe after shoe, captive to Polly's glossing on the subject not just of sartorial correctness but history too, from the past half-century, starting with the divine goddess, Miss Gabrielle Bonheur, to that damnable revolution, the sixties, examples of which hang still in far too many closets, in the most criminal way, including on Jake's backside until Miss Morphous, aka Purebred, aka Peachum set him straight.

You mean gayly forward, Gatita corrects her.

Your're an intern on fashion from this day forward, even if you're without a pot t' piss in.

Jake brushed the comments aside, throughout the day, and he continues to do so as Polly praises her hand-work, What a trans-formation! Just look't you! Henny, you are totally welcome. You're a member a the human race now at least, no longer a chimp in rags. We only gotta work on that mess on yo' head!

Then cocktails.

Kitty, that for sure—after all this work?

My hair's been this way for ages.

Henny, that's the problem. G'bless Tommy. He recognizes a charity case when he sees one. Then leaves it to his sissies t' do the dirty work—

—Are you sayin'?

Hen, did I say anything'? All I'm sayin' is he got a saint's heart—at least that's what he wants people t' believe. Includin' you.

We know better!

What's that suppose' t' mean?

I didn't hear anything—did you, Gatita? You must a been buck naked the day you met!

Like Alicia fell in a hole.

She always fallin' in a hole.

She wouldn' a paid this one the time a day if he saw him dressed.

Back and forth they compete, leaving Jake to chuckle politely so as not to look the spoiled sport as he surveys himself in the glass—*How can I leave here lookin' like this?*

Henny, we just gettin' started. We still got the hair. Apart from that dirty ol' mop it's the best you ever look.

If I were a bird.

Sissy's gonna go crazy.

I think she's gonna cry.

That's what I'm afraid a.

Wear it with pride, girlfriend.

Don' let it wear you.

Jake lifts his arms, feels the seams of the fabric, his torso snug in geometric forms silk-screened across his chest. The tee moves stiffly up and down, hemming in the armpits, ribcage, and abdomen, skin tight. The lower hem tucked out of sight under a belt holding up pants that are tapered around the ankle, the reverse of bell-bottoms, chafing as he walks, more a straightjacket than a second skin. The only consolation is it's as sheddable as a laundry sack once he's home.

Now you don't have t' be ashamed t' go out—take it from Miss Polly.

Now you can tell everyone with pride that you're a Member of the Tribe.

That you eat at Mary's—

—That you're one a Judy's girls—

—I mean, you look so much better!

It was clearly unworth the effort to argue—what was done was done. What was spent, spent.

After the second make-over the three sit on the terrace of The Mining Company—

—LOVE the hair.

Richard is a genius with scissors.

It wasn't my choice.

Own it, girlfriend.

So glad we had this time together—

—A whole day without Tommy!

What could be better?

What's that supposed to mean?

Girlfriend, I hope you know what you're gettin' into.

I don't understand—

—Jus' be sure to look out for Numero Uno like I says. Kitty taps Jake's chest with her middle finger as she speaks.

But Tommy's a lamb!

Dream on, girlfriend.

Shows how little you know. And yet you're practi'cly at the altar.

I don' know what you mean.

It's your life, henny. But like I says, know what you're gettin' into.

He ain' no picnic.

But y'all have been together for ages. Why would—

We onto him—

—He can't play his games with us. But you're green, henny—

—He's gonna make mincemeat a you, you don' watch out.

And so the conversation continued, the two speaking venom about someone Jake is becoming more than attached to, without a single buzzer or alarm going off. Did the electricity fail? The usual red flags fly off? How can his radar be so broken? That's what Jake wondered as Polly and Kitty harpy on, tongues loosened by alcohol, spilling the family T, filling in a history, stories about Tommy that didn't fit the person Jake knew—and after all this time.

When it came time to drop Jake off, having dropped more for a wardrobe, haircut, and drinks than he thought possible in a year let alone a day, he bids thanks—

—From the bottom a my heart.

Never mind he couldn't wait to undress.

Jake struggles to tote the number of shopping bags from the Fiat. He sets them down as the neighbor wheels by, slowing and crunching the gravel, until he stops.

You get in a accidin'?

Jake tugs on the hair above the mullet. It'll grow out.

You look—special. Like from another planet. Hope it don't kill yer love life. It's a rare evening when Derrick is driving home alone.

You gone monastic or something?

Huh?

Where's your date?

Dude, night's young. Where's your friend?

He'll be comin'—

—I been meanin' t' tell you…. I'm movin' down nex' month.

I'll miss you, though I don' know why—you tried t' palm your cat off on me.

Damn thing. Lotta good it do, no matter how many times I try. Ladies like 'er. Or she's use t' me. Stop for a drink 'fore I go. You'n your pal.

The man's beard has exploded since Jake moved in, lengthening and filling out. He skids into his usual spot and disappears in the darkness. While the two were talking another vehicle pulled in behind Derrick and sat there, passengers inside. Neither budged, and Jake paid no mind really—he thought most likely they're day-trippers, waitin' t' park, illegally, despite the PRIVATE PROPERTY—NO ENTRY sign. They're holdin' out 'til I leave so I won't shoo 'em away.

One cracks the door and sets a foot on the gravel.

She passes one way, then the other removes herself and splits in the opposite direction, toward the trailer by the road. Jake's preoccupied with corralling bags, and mail tumbles from his hand—

—Oh. My, God. Jake!?

Huh?

Jake!! Who would a ever—?! Just a sec—

Indistinct because of the light over the mountain, casting the figure in silhouette, the woman scuttles toward Main, cries, C'mere!—C'mon back! She waves her arms then waits beside the road, her foot directed toward Jake, alternating gazes between him and the other, still lost behind the dwelling—You ain' gonna believe it! I walked right past!

I don' b'lieve it. The voices are unmistakable. If it weren't for the sound Jake would have passed them both—he leaves his things in a jumble by the car.

No way!

What're you doin' out here? It's a helluva long way!—I mean—

—We came t' see you! Among other things. Cin embraces Jake with trepidation, as though he were a phantom. Here you are, in the flesh, after hearin' so many—you know we live next-door to Wren! That how people dress out here?

Look't your hair, Jake! Your outfit! I wouldn' a guessed in a million—

—It ain't even you!

Long story.

Must be! You're not the Jake we knew!

Be nice.

I'd rec'nize the voice though. Anywhere.

Inside the trailer the space shrinks with the three filling it out. Jake draws a chair from the dinette, and Cin remarks she prefers the floor, which the three decide to do together as though they were on the shore of the great lake, jostling for position, the women leaning close, propped against the sofa, until Diablo lies out and rests her head in Cin's lap.

I can't believe we're here!

Me neither—

—How d'you think I feel?

We didn't know how we'd find you, if we'd find you— thought we'd just wing it. You were in such a state when you left. And now look't you—

—A phoenix—

—More like a bird a paradise, Cin chuckles.

You seem different too.

Like you, we got outta Laurentine.

We take care of Billie when Wren and Donald need a break.

What about Rauch and Marks? And Romeo? Do you hear from them?

They moved to the Big Apple. And he's in Laurentine, where he'll always be. Him and your cousin.

What's he doing?

Drinkin' like a fish. Gunnin' for daddy's money. Three kids and another on the way.

Jus' what he wanted.

Jake, I go by Debra now. No more Diablo—that was Rauch's thing.

That might take a little time, 'fore I get used to it. You still Cin?

I go by Cinthia.

Pleased t' meet you both.

And is it still Jake? Jacob? God knows you don' look like no Jake I knew.

Worse thing is, I got nothin' else t' wear, practically—they threw my wardrobe out, all four things.

Who'd do a thing like that?

Someone tryin' t' help. Or not. I ain't sure.

Peacoat's mom gave us a few a his shirts t' bring you—she didn't know what to do with them. We brought 'em with.

Keep 'em. Please.

The door pops open and Tommy slides in, along with L'Dell. The look on his face vanishes when he spots the women, splayed across the floor in a loose triangle, colonizing it, an oddity given the seats untended. The trio grunt to a sitting position, prop to semi-verticality, then upright until they're on their feet. Tommy doesn't wait for Jake to do the honors, he looks each woman in the eye as he presents himself.

Encantado de conocerte. Pleased to meet you.

I'm L'Dell.

We go way back, Debra remarks, gesturing toward Jake, an odd comment when you consider they haven't known each other all that long in the scheme of things—is it four, five years? And yet experience makes it seem like three or four times that, if not more, a truth not questioned by anyone present. It hasn't been that long really, Jake considers saying, until the past floods in—

—Yeah, we go way back.

Tommy an' me too, asserts L'Dell.

Jake considers what Cinthia and Debra have toted, unbeknownst to them, a parcel inseparable from their persons, memories coiled inside and ready to strike. I mean I trekked fourteen hundred miles to flee all that, flee them, and here it is, they are, completely out of the blue.

It's true we go way back. But here we are. Different people now, it seems, the three of us.

Talk about diff'rent, Jake! What'd Polly do t' you?!

You tell me.

Well at least you got your old clothes, remarks L'Dell.

You mean a bin at May Company does. Prob'ly all in a dumpster now.

We'll go back an' return this stuff—how much you buy?!

You mean how much did she buy?

With your money, no doubt. L'Dell shakes her head.

Who is "she"? queries Debra.

She meant well. I think.

Is there a place to get a bite?

Seated at Las Dos Mujeres, Cinthia remarks that Peacoat would a loved the place. The guitar music. The colors.

Jake's tempted to say he's been here many times. Until tonight.

Who's Peacoat? wonders Tommy.

Later, Jake intercepts.

You mean he hasn't told you?

Let it go.

Someone we knew—

—So you're gonna do it anyway.

A dear friend a the three a us. But—Jake's special friend.

Special friend? remarks L'Dell. Sounds juicy.

You never mention him before, niño, observes Tommy. Funny name.

I can't believe Jake never told you, marvels Cinthia. They were the subject of a great deal a gossip where we come from—they were even in the paper.

Can we give it a rest?—

—That's fine. I'm just surprised, given—

—Yeah, given, piggybacks Debra.

—What brings you out west? asks L'Dell.

Debra and Cinthia gaze at each other. The latter peers out the window while Debra picks up a menu and peruses it.

If you don't wanna tell—

—Can we catch up on Jake first?

Well, he's sitting right here, Jake complains. He rests his hand on Tommy's thigh and the two lean in. Their lips meet, once, twice, three times, causing the others' eyes to widen at the approach of the server—

— Ladies an' gen'lemin. What can I git you?

Haven't been called that in a while—maybe never—

—Me either—

—Which is the lady, and which the gentleman?

—Bean tacos, asserts Tommy. What about you two? Are you like Jake—is it a Forest City thing?

Huh? Steak fajitas for me.

So you haven't gone to the dark side—

—Same for me, remarks Debra. Steak Fajitas—Jake, we just got back from India.

I've been there! asserts L'Dell. Actually I studied there.

We're Buddhists now, Jake.

That I never got into—it's refreshing to be around real girls around this guy—L'Dell motions toward Tommy. What a nice surprise. I'm used to being outnumbered.

I get it, returns Cinthia. Back in the day we were the tokens—we worked in a factory together.

Men here are party animals—

—Only here? inquires Debra.

These girls think a one thing an' one thing only. OK, me too—I admit. But they got me beat. If I could ever get my husban' outta the house I'd live a different life, but c'est la vie. I feel safe with my pal here. Meanwhile, India—

—We stayed in an ashram in Varanasi, near the ghats. The haunt of the Beats.

Not quite table talk in this country, eh?

And yet it's hard not to talk about it, anywhere, insists Cinthia.

They do haunt you, admits L'Dell.

What is it? blurts Jake

You mean what are they? corrects L'Dell. The very thing you ladies are trying t' forget.

Debra explains about the pyres, flames burning twenty-four seven, burning male bodies that is, never female, in a tiered system; how women's bodies are weighted with stones and laid in the river, animals too, polluting the Ganges; how none of that stops people from bathing in the sacred—

—But that's a Hindu, not a Buddhist thing, corrects L'Dell.

That's intense, comments Jake. You were right—it ain't dinner talk.

It ain't nothin' you girls wanna dwell on—actually it's the last thing—

—It ain't just them, counters Cinthia. It's tough, for anyone, 'specially anyone who hasn't seen it—

—Here in Marlboro Country most of all, asserts
L'Dell.

—I know what you mean, remarks Debra. After seein'
it practically every day—we were there six months—.
You sorta get used to it?—Like you almos' don't notice
it? It becomes a part a life.

—As if that were possible for an American to get
their head around, agrees L'Dell. I remember the luxury
hotels overlooking the ghats. Fountains with brilliant
rose petals, red as lips, floating on them. People dining
in plush digs, just above the bodies. Like you say, bathers
and boaters on the water. People picnicking. All the
while the fires burn, twenty-four hours a day, like you
said, three hundred and sixty-five days a year—

—You saying you numb to it? Tommy asks.

Yes an' no.

It is possible?

It'd be too much for me, yelps Jake. I don't think I
could do it.

It almos' was for me, admits L'Dell. At first especially.
An' I can take a lot.

Places like that serve a purpose, opines Debra.

I studied in Rajasthan, squawks L'Dell, attempting
to be heard over the music which shifted from a single
guitar to a Mariachi band.

Over several volleys shouted at a larynx-straining
pitch, Cinthia and Debra learn that L'Dell spent time
in Jaipur learning block-printing in a textile factory,
that she apprenticed in carving her own stamps, and
that common sense forced her to leave finally, when she
realized how much was involved, and for so little pay,
when what she needed was a job—I'd give anything to
go back if I could.

We get it, remarks Debra.

Not to change the subject—but Jake, comments Cinthia. We're reading Nigel Gray in the car—we take turns—

—Talk about a guy's guy, blurts Jake. The way he talks about women. Girls. Broads. Devil Ladies. What in the world could interest you in him?

He went t' India. He's a Buddhist too.

They all did, all the Beats—so what? All that rot about dharma, running naked, Siddhartha, hummingbirds, Freddie, the bird dog, Joey, the cat—Nigel has a fit when he sees a dog chained—he even says dogs are smarter than people, before he and Ziggy orgasm over pork an' beans. Liverwurst. Mountain oysters. About what a godsend it is to scarf down a steak after a hike—India and the Buddha didn't do crap for him.

Jake, that's judgy.

What kind a Buddhist talks about the oneness of being and looks the other way when he eats?

Way too judgy, agrees L'Dell.

Did you eat meat at the ashram?

Course not.

Case closed.

Hola!—I have no idea what y'all are talkin' about!

Nothin', love. Forgit it. By the way, I couldn't even order a bean taco when I first came here. But I can now. When the old owner was bought out I convinced the new one there was no need for stock, that water would do.

I guess that's a good thing?

Whatever works, Jake.

His and Tommy's lips meet, and again the eyes of Debra and Cinthia morph into dinner plates—

We ain't in Laurentine, quips Debra—

Jake, one more thing about Mr. Nigel Gray—sorry Tommy. He's in love with Ziggy, even though they go on about the ladies.

¡Cuéntame más! Tell me more!

The book's a love letter—to Ziggy, we're sure. Nigel's happiest when they're together, lost when they're apart—and the end—mind if I read it?

Now?!

Here?

She just happens to have a copy in her purse, deadpans Debra—

—He writes...tup, tup, tup...here it is! He writes, *but Ziggy, you and me forever, we know, the two of us, We're ever youthful, We'll forever weep! On the lake our reflections rise in a heavenly mist, and god, I love you man, I mean I really mean it. I've fallen in love with you....*

Like he's a god—

—Lemme me finish. He addresses god too, through Ziggy. I mean, the whole book's for Ziggy, an alias for Bob—it's the only reading that fits.

—He cloaks what's really goin' on in flowery rhetoric, about god and buddha, dharma—the whole nine yards. Deep down it's a love affair between two men.

Deep down. On another guy—

—Tommy.

Guys are hopeless—

Cinthia and Debra wait while Tommy and Jake kiss like repeater rifles, the kind you hear in the back-woods east of Laurentine come fall, along the Shagaran.

Maybe you'll write a book about me someday, niño. A love letter. Like that.

We heard you're making furniture or something—

Ha! Not quite. I build homes. Use t' be just me'n another guy. We built five up here—or almost.

Es tan macho, ¿qué no?

Huh?

Mi niño es so butch.

I'm on a regular crew now, building developments in town.

You mean ticky-tacky?

That about describes it. Not unlike Laurentine.

What happen to the gig up here?

How long you got?

Niño, you never tol' me why you quit.

It was quite the arrangement. While it lasted.

Who talks about work as "quite the arrangement?"

Did the work dry up?

Somethin' dried up—my luck most of all.

Do you b'lieve it? Our little Jake. Building houses.

An' t' think we use t' make fun a him for slackin'—

—I got a dime, do tell—apparently he tells me nuttin'.

—All old news.

Jake we thought a you all the way here—my god th' crosses—

—Everywhere! All across the country!

You tryin' t' make me sick?

You would a loved it once in a blue moon, you an' Peacoat both.

There's that name again—

—It wasn't our thing—paradin' it—

—Ha! Could a fooled me—

—Others were into it. But not us—

—Like I'm into you, niño? Again the two kiss, making no small stir not just at the table but the restaurant given the wandering eyes, leaning in and trading whispers—Were you religious once?

Hasn't Jake tol' you anything? wonders Cinthia. He was a wild 'n crazy born-again!—

—A rah-rah holy roller—

—Niño, you?!

Apparently not anymore, comments L'Dell, rolling her eyes. Not from what Alicia tells me.

Who's Alicia?

Me llaman Alicia.

You?!

Godless to the core. Him an' his boyfriend here—

—He and Peacoat were as well. Boyfriends. Right under the min'ster's eyes—

Oh my god, cracks L'Dell. Y'all can't help yourselves—

—Why not tell why you come all this way?

The food arrives and the waitress sets three plates in front of Cin, Debra, and L'Dell, each sizzling and sputtering audibly, visually, over which Tommy insists, I wanna hear more 'bout Jake an' this other guy—and the preacher!— Do I gotta worry? He reaches under the table and slides his hand between Jake's thighs—Así que mi diablito was a goody-two-shoes.

Jake runs his palm over Tommy's wrist, arrests it while rubbing the hair—You, shush.

No you don' gotta worry, assures Cinthia—

—Please, don't—

—The guy died—

—OK. He didn' jus' die—

—Wha' does that mean? alerts L'Dell, now genuinely perked.

—Can I get you another round a beers? On me—drink up, ladies! That means you, Jake. How else am I gonna know anything about you? Apparently he never tells me nada.

Diablo, shush. You too, Cin.

It's Debra.

I think Diablo fits.

And it's Cinthia.

Jake takes up his fork then sets it down. He commences folding his napkin into a knot too tight to unfold. He picks, tears at it, creating a tattered mess next to his plate.

He never told you nothin' about Peacoat? What about Romeo?

Who's he?

Dead. To me at least. That's what.

They were live wires at one time—

—Stop!

Why run from it, Jake?

Diablo—

Debra—

—How can it be, niño? That you haven't said nothin' about them.

Ms. Lee.

Well—Debra—Cinthia—maybe you'll tell me—.

Is it hot in here?

Where did you two meet? wonders L'Dell, gazing at Cinthia and Debra.

Before you tell, I wanna hear about these two guys—was it serious? I mean, niño, why didn't you say any—?

—Why don' you tell about your life, pre-me? I just get bits and pieces from Polly and Kitty, 'til you shush them too. I get the feeling we'd be here a year in order to start to get the scoop.

Sounds about right, affirms L'Dell.

—Who're Polly and Kitty? Women friends?

In a manner of speaking.

Jake, can I? Cinthia seems on the verge of begging.

Fuck it. It's a free country—

—One a the church ladies turned rat, spilled the beans on Billie an' Peacoat, about what happen before Peacoat disappeared.

Tell me somethin' I don't already know.

Actually, it was two church ladies that ratted, corrects Debra. A couple a old biddies.

As Cinthia relates the story of what the women claimed they saw, Pastor Billy menacing then failing to nab Peacoat when he had the chance, after he fell in the Shagaran, Jake toys with his taco as though disinterested, all the while Debra takes another tortilla from the warmer, tears it in half and returns a half moon in its place, resetting the lid and spooning bits of animal flesh on the surface, portions of veggies and bean, rapt otherwise in attention as Cinthia speaks, rehearsing a story she already knows by heart, silencing Jake finally for all the interruptions until he sits resigned—

Mierda! Tommy replies when Cinthia falls silent. Mierda!

For a time the five say nothing. Tommy orders another round of cervezas.

Mierda! copies Jake, pensively.

After the waitress collects the plates and hands out dessert menus, Jake pipes, I sorta knew in my bones, before I heard all that from Wren, that something was fishy—I felt it. But how can they make anything stick against Billy, a man a the cloth?

How could it possibly be him?—that was the court's sentiment.

His lawyer tarnished Paulette and Marni somethin' fierce—the stories they collected. The insinuations—. Like they were a couple angry dykes—

—Man-haters—

There was nothin' left a them when Billy's lawyers were done.

Along the berm water slides in runnels, making its way toward Rt. 76. Mud slaps the body of Tommy's pick-up, which skids here and there on the untopped road. Clay accretes on tires in ever denser layers the farther we advance.

No te preocupes.

Huh?

Don' wooorrrrry.

How can I not?

Todo va a estar bien.

Huh?

The world gone aslant, down from forests flanking the peaks, angling to the valley in the southwest, cradling the Trampas. The road gashes the mountainside, slashing a line parallel to the river. Homes squat on the right, clay vessels in their way, stuccoed the color of Tommy's skin, the angle relaxes as it opens on a row of fields, segregated and laid side-to-side like cattle huddling against the cold. Behind them the world again slips downward, as is the case with everything in this world, though, granted, at a gentler skew once the land approaches the riverbed, finally, an artery that depends on the mood of the mountains, which, what, with all this rain, has turned flowy.

Usually this time a year, amigo, you can plant seeds in the river, it's that dry. Grow 'em fast enough t' sell en el mercadillo before monsoon arrive.

On the High Road here Tommy remarked if you wanted to get your exercise by walking along Main, you'd be good as done in ten, fifteen minutes. I thought he was exaggerating, but this place invites superlatives. Shortest road. Stoutest dwellings. Tiniest town. Fleetest growing season. Most indolent livestock. Jake would learn in time there were more to add, including pueblo most likely to roll down a valley, the way a marble walks on its own across a floor. Sleep-walking to the Trampas, which in turn stair-steps toward the Rio Grande and then Mexico, in a kind of reverse migration. And yet the town holds, as it has for two centuries. It clings, stubborn as a bighorn perched overhead and snorting at us. Everything about Las Nieves seems off—or so I thought the first I heard of it, stories of events commonplace and bizarre, banal and unspeakable.

Now that we're here it all fits.

A door opens before we roll to a stop—we don't so much park as cease driving.

Vamos, mi amor.

Huh?

C'mon—

—Hola mi jito.

Unlike the entry into Ruby or Miss Glasby's home no bear hugs are on offer here—a kiss on either cheek and words suffice as embrace enough. Having said that there are glances up and down and left to right, in which as much is not said as said. A metal security door clangs behind us.

Mira lo alto que te has hecho!

Pero Abuelita, ha pasado menos de un año—I saw you not that long ago.

Stiiiiill, jito, olvidé lo alto que eres.

She says she forgets how big I am.

I can't forget that.

Tommy reddens.

Y tu barba, es demasiado grande.

She thinks I'm too scruffy.

How do you say, That's not possible.

Again, Tommy's face reddens.

Puedes cultivar maíz en ella.

Tommy feels his beard, strokes it. Pop says I can grow corn in here.

Jito, you should shaaave. ¿Qué estás cubriéndote la cara así?

He likes my beard—gesturing toward Jake with his chin.

¿Qué?

¿Quién?

Tommy obliges Lita with a name.

This is a house for little people like me, which is to say I feel at home here, rooted in the earth, as if dirt rose up and enclosed a space, rooms large enough to accommodate a son and, once he flew the nest, a grandson, during summer, I'll discover, as a kid and in early adulthood, though less and less these days.

¿Qué hace Chék?

The way she pronounced my name it sounded like I were a revolutionary, out to destroy the local order. Does news filter here from the outside, perched in thin air, two-fold thinner than the Mile High City, thinner too than what I breath in Ojo? I mean they don't call it the High Road for nothing.

Él es pintor.
Pintor?! Qué hace de verdad?
Pintor. Like I said.
No es posible.
She doesn't think you're really a painter.
¿Por qué?
Porque no puedes ganar dinero haciendo eso.
She says you can't make money doin' that.
Tell her she's right.
You tell her.
You're right.
I know.
Oh! You speak—
—Sí, claro, Chék. Puedo hablar.
The air is as ponderous as the walls, feet thick, as you can see in window wells that serve as seats, a place to curl and soak up sun, which is suddenly in abundance after the rain, a light that borders on aggressive. As it is, however, only Lita or Pop could settle in one of those openings given how narrow they are, them or a feline, the sole purpose being to ward off the elements, all of which seem to want

in, the nosy sun most of all, noodling for gossip. The effort to keep it out on a hot day, keep the cool in. Cooking odors too—

—¿Tienes hambre?

She wants to know if you're hungry.

Pero te pregunté a ti....

She wants to know if we're both hungry. So.... ?

Sí—does that means yes?

Pero él no come carne.

Abuelita puffs air. Her cheeks bloat temporarily then empty out. She feels Jake's forehead with the palm of her hand to detect an illness or perhaps heal him, una curandera all of a sudden.

It smells amazing in here.

In the kitchen the Tappan imposes itself, it's several burners, larger and older than Miss Glasby's. It's shoehorned between the ice-box and sink, which sits next to a door, opening to a field that slopes out of sight. Jake watches as the woman removes a container from the refrigerator and spoons fat in a skillet. She beckons Tommy to get down three place-settings of the good dishes, not the everyday, plates covered with winter scenes native to—is it Vermont? Grandma Moses' New York? Massachusetts? Nowhere around here for sure. She sets three places on the kitchenette, and I begin to wonder if I'll be served. I seem to be the only one aware of the fuzzy math as she sets a freezer bag on the edge of the sink, holding a stack of tortillas.

Las hice solo para ti.

She said she made them just for me.

The smell of animal fat permeates the room. Shredded strips of beef jump in lard over a ring of blue. Another cast-iron pan, wide and without sides, is set to warm atop another indigo circle that leapt to light after a match was struck.

Él no puede comer estas tortillas.

Ya lo sé. No soy estúpida.

Just before everything is prepared Abuelita removes a bag of store-bought tortillas from the freezer. Cuantas quisiera?

She wants to know how many.

The woman takes a sharp knife and splits off two disks, which Tommy will joke later were as white as Jake's behind, but to Jake are as rigid as the slabs he splintered during his and Molly's stay on the Shagaran a lifetime ago. One by one she warms them over the flames, softening and charring then tossing them on a plate, reserved only for company, out of reach of everyday life, just waiting for a tall, thin, bearded jito to arrive and take them down.

When they finally sit at the table, the three of them, while Pop takes an everyday plate outside, Tommy remarks in a Spanish unique to the area, an idiom slowly dying Jake will later discern, that he's been dreaming of this moment. That there's nothing like it on earth—this!—just this—I can't tell you how happy I am to share it with you, Jake. My favorite place on the planet.

At first Abuelita says nothing. She peers through the pane in the door toward Pop, who's propped on his banco next to the barn, eyeing a huddle of cattle. She scrutinizes Jake, then comments, looking Tommy in the eye, Pero Chék no puede comer nada.

Está bien.

She nudges the tub of margarine toward Jake. Es mucho mejor con eso.

She says try it. It's better that way.

Jake removes the lid and smears yellow across his tortilla then spoons chili relish that Tommy avers is her specialty—And that luckily you can eat. He rolls the tortilla just as he watched Tommy do, and begins to chew.

¡No comas tan rápido!

She says slow down.
Tell her it's so good. I can't help it!
You tell 'er.
Ain't your grandpa gonna eat?
He likes t' be outside with the animals.
There's an animal in here.
You hush.
¡La forma en que hablas!
Jake—.
But Jake isn't focused on his comment or, worse, first impressions. His attentions instead are riveted on the multi-alarm fire in his mouth, flames blazing like the underbrush in a conflagration just over the ridge, not long ago.

Water, he mumbles, doing his best to endure the heat, never mind the terror.

To think that a lowly veg can pack such a punch—

Abuelita pads to the cupboard, removes a glass, fills it with milk, then sets it on the table. Jake wants to pour it over his face, down his throat, but instead manages a sip, intent as he is on maintaining a semblance of cool, unwilling to grant the satisfaction of watching a gringo unable to take it, the heat, eating fire without the courtesy of any notice, never mind Tommy seems unfazed. Jake considers the idea that maybe there are two batches, one mild the other mean, and that Tommy knew which one to choose. Lita proceeds to pull a bag from the fridge and extracts an orange block. She slices strips of cheddar onto a plate and slides it toward Jake.

Sírvete.

From time to time she shoots gazes Jake-ward, which he interprets as a way of gauging the effect of her malignancy. He imagines that everyone who's ever walked through the door has been a known quantity, until here comes Tommy trailed not just by a gringo but Señor Sincarne, which is to say a crazy paddy.

And the story gets worse. It's not that she'd never heard of, contemplated, or hoped to meet a vegetariano—she knew they existed, Jake will be told. It's just—to have one intrude on her life, with her jito, like that. And a gringo. She returns to a bowl of what she calls chili that looks or smells nothing like Florrie used to fix. Where are the kidney beans and tomatoes, ground meat, and green pepper? The Hamburger Helper?

Tommy's fired. To be with you, niño, in this place.

They made up the spare bed with new sheets, cleared out the clutter on it since Tommy was here last, an accumulation of old slacks and shirts that have nowhere else to go when Lita and Pop are in the place alone. There's just room enough for a bed and a path to scoot by, not unlike Jake's room in Ojo, as if licensed just for one. Two if another steals in. Accordingly the pair lies on top of each other, stacked. Abuelita hauled the extra blankets from the armario, resting them on the spread, intending for Jake to take the living-room sofa, the spot where one of Tommy's brothers used to sleep when they visited many years ago.

But Tommy insisted the two share the mattress—Lita, there's no need making up the couch, dirtying another set a sheets. Jake's short, an' he don't take much room.

The two lie shoe-horned in with little space to move, which doesn't hinder Tommy, who's unusually animate, spiked by the mountain air in this erstwhile land grant, laid out by the gobernador in Mexico City centuries ago, a riot of constellations peering through the glass, howls of the coyotes and crickets—it seems the last thing he's capable of doing is lying still, even though the bed, like everything here, complains of age. Its knees and shoulders grouse about this and that, squeaking displeasure every time you move, the heads of the two butting the heads of those in the adjacent room, with only a wall between. Despite the circumstances neither muchacho questions the wall's ability to hold or muffle sound, or Lita's capacity to glean a commotion above Pop's snoring.

Tommy invites Jake to join him in a song of sorts, which the latter tries to croon in low tones, covering Tommy's mouth with his hand occasionally, bringing his to his own, or, when necessary, eyeing Tommy in a less-than-amorous way in an effort to hold the ruckus to a dull roar, lest there be who-knows-what kind of hell to pay.

She already thinks I'm the devil, I can tell.

She likes you niño, *I* can tell.

I don' think so. But even if she did, we don' wanna give no reason—.

But Tommy's on a mission, traveling without headlights down back-roads on a jet-black night, never mind Jake tries to get him to apply the brakes, go just a tad slower to avoid a mess—avoid busting the bed because of Tommy's vigor, drop it to the floor and in the process jar not just the two next-door but la gente de Las Nieves out of sleep.

When his engine finally blows, Jake rests, assuming that's it, but Tommy's inspired by the breeze through the window. He skinnies between the wall and bed and gestures in the moonlight for Jake to follow. The latter resists at first then extricates himself, chains after Tommy, slipping out the door without a stitch. The two pad through the living room, kitchen, and back door, steal through the portal over stones cool to the soles, then out to the pasture.

Tommy flops against brown and green clods, facing a carpet of stars overhead. He reaches up and takes Jake's hand, draws him down lengthwise, and now two pairs of eyes peer into a light-show.

I never seen nothin' like it! I mean, Ojo has stars, but not like this. And t' think we're lookin' at the past.

Huh?

All that up there's old news. Done deals. Every light we see. Traces. Biographies of light that're ended.

Unlike us.

We'll be old someday.

Jake whiffs the earth, a smell that hovers, suspends in air, the bovines grouped in the distance, casting shadows on the lower end of the property where moonlight silvers them, the unevenness of the terrain, which Tommy has become unaware of, naked against Jake, while Lita and Pop slumber not far off, Tommy's only family now, given what passed at the feedlot, the place his family owns and he used to work. Until they found out. He inhabits a scene of abundance contrasting loss—of family and inheritance both—seeing fullness where others would gather lack, loss of comfort, security, and prospect—to Tommy it's heaven on earth here despite what just passed before they set out, events of which Jake is unaware. Tommy's enthusiasm for the setting has a stiffening effect, never mind what just happened back in the room, as if he's swallowed an elixir old men would kill for. To him it comes naturally, as though he were gifted, inspired by the setting, a prohibition, or DNA, challenging Jake in a sense, throwing down a gauntlet he's able to meet despite his reservations and not much coaxing, as it turns out, fired by Tommy in god's own country. It's as if Tommy's infected Jake's brain like the rising moon, slant overhead, perky and full, affecting coyotes too in the distance.

There's no end to the march of stars, an eternity of movement, seeds scattered, tossed across a field wide as the eye can see as the moon paces like a sower in a genre painting across the terrain, casting light on Tommy's behind as he shifts here and there, pants like cows chuffing, owls hooting, horned, the frequent yap and orgasmic cry of a coyote making a kill. There were other sounds to take in if the two were to stop long enough to hear, some coming from inside, difficult to detect in the natural cacophony, the shooting of the Trampas after the rain as it slaps over rocks in its path. From time to time a single heifer lows loud, out of the blue, as if in a dream. Jake can't help but think of Molly's growls as night, limbs twitching. But what do bovines dream of? Hang-mouthed coyotes? Shadowy pumas? Whetted blades? Whatever it is they pipe from time to time, adding their voices to the crickets, owls, and cicadas, an animal empire that owns the terrain no matter what humans think, among which Jake and Tommy lend a sound.

From time to time the barn clears its throat in response to a gust passing through, as if to say, Excuse me? in an antique way. Watch where you're going! I'm too damn old to toy with. It squeaks out a cough in hopes the wind will get the idea, and in the process contributes to the chorus.

In the iffy moment before the sun commits to day, first Jake then Tommy startle awake, trembling, the temperatures having tumbled ten or fifteen degrees since they knocked off. The dip in mercury is common at these altitudes, even at the height of summer, which has a stiffening effect once sleep has done its thing, roughly shaking the two who lay butt-against each other. The light show ended in accordance with insects mumming, and every nocturnal thing. Jake and Tommy yawn in succession. All of diurnal nature now stands at attention, waiting on a sun that's just about to bolt in view, causing moon-worshipers to shoot into lairs. Early-birds can be heard with the thickening rays along a path that extends to the end of the valley.

Like our ancestors at some point, Tommy and Jake realize they're naked, which is to say no longer presentable.

We best skedaddle—they ain't gonna be none too happy to catch us like this.

Tengo frío, niño. Lay with me a bit.

The latter quilts himself over Tommy who senses biology take command for the thousandth time since they arrived, until Jake, skittish and on watch, eases off, leaving Tommy in the lurch—

—We gotta run. Better not push it.

But you're so warm.

Señor—

—Listen to you—señor. What could be more exciting?

Like I say she already suspects me. Whose side you on?

Defeated, his spirits limp, Tommy slouches to sitting. Their lips meet before they gain verticality, pause for a moment to let nature run its course, gild the turf like the gods of autumn coloring Dodgson—they peek in the kitchen window in search of the all-clear. Tommy takes Jake's hand and leads through the back door, over saltillos cooling criminal steps as they pass under an arch, into the living room, then another arch, back to a space with its conventional bed, arraying themselves under the covers, far apart and in conventional postures for two adult men, separate, rigid, feigning sleep.

At the moment the charade is accomplished a rap on the door startles the two out of their wits—You boys asleep?

Tommy plays the good jito, grogs himself to speak, ¿Cuándo es el desayuno?

Voy a prepararlo ahora.

As she fusses Lita appears laconic as los muchachos look on, famished, seated near her command at the counter. In response to whether either one could lend a hand, her reply is terse, una sola palabra. So the two perch, Tommy shrunk from six-plus feet to three, a child scolded, and Jake shorter still. From time to time their feet meet below, their gazes too when Gertrude turns her back. The moment they discern she's about to pivot, limbs and eyes jump back, splicing the two apart.

¿Puede comer pollo?

She wants to know if you eat chicken.

No—

The reply offers not quite the olive branch Jake hoped to muster, for an offense he's sure he'll learn, as if he didn't know already. As it turns out, breakfast serves Jake with yet another adventure, huevos rancheros minus chorizo and pork chili, the kind that smothers Tommy's and Lita's plates, though Tommy picks at it as sheepishly as Jake, the two beset with apologetic eyes. Lita mopes through her meal in stark contrast to a half-day before when she fawned on her jito, patting him with the palm of her hand and gazing at him as though he were the pride of the line.

Now she barely acknowledges him. Any overture toward her in her native tongue is returned with a nonverbal glance or, worse, a single yes or no, in English, the language of thieves, the ones who came to this land with the purpose of pilfering it from her and her ancestors, Tommy's too, la gente who grumble in their graves in the cemetery on the road to town. They trekked to this valley centuries ago in an effort to stem Apache raids, that mobile band not interested in stationary life like the Puebloans, clustered like a necklace up and down the Rio Grande for the most part, including not far from here in Española Valley. The Apache maintained a complicated relationship with their First-Nations kin, pre-contact, not as hostile as gringo books let on, though it became a different story once the Hispanos arrived. Their presence ratcheted up the tensions as the Euros triangulated, reduced matters to us and them. Carrot and stick.

Meanwhile Lita and Pop's forebears, Tommy's too, were no glad-handers, jumping at the offer of free land. They carted dreams of opportunity through work, long before Jake's precursors fathomed this land, the trip here— Tommy's abuelos settled in the surrounding valley, homes ringing a placita ages before whites circled wagons around a fire, also fending off Indians, on whose terrain they also trespassed, even as they claimed it by dint of right. Here in Las Nieves a pueblo grew, replete with a mission, smack in the middle of the Apache's thoroughfare. At times they prevailed, driving the Hispanos back for a time, decades even, until the coast was clear and the Hispanos returned, dusting themselves off and speaking their own brand of Spanish as I say—they dusted off their homes after a long sojourn away, their numbers swollen to force the Apache on an alternate route to sacred terrain, the Rio Grande Rift, one of only a handful on the planet.

That state of tension eased into a biding standoff that lasted until whites barged in with bayonets and rifles, canons, first on the Santa Fe Trail then armed in waves, bulldozing the land into possession, not just the towns along the High Road but the entire state, establishing a system of white justice, that oxymoron, anathema to the locals to this day.

Animus blooms anew each year with the flowering of the apricot trees.

None of that history's lost on Tommy—he's heard it a thousand times. He'll relay it to Jake too one day, Jake who, as the three sit around the table piecing through their breakfast, rests oblivious for the time being, an invader come to covet Lita's pride.

Breakfast over, finally, Tommy bids Jake to take it easy, suggests he'll stay and help with dishes and in saying shoots him a look. Taking the hint, he fetches his book and pencil, tracing a beeline through the field, bounded as it is by brush and stones down to the Trampas where he sets to work, starting below and sketching his way toward the house, drafting a setting, including cows jawing the grass, revolving weeds and what-have-you in their maws, sustaining themselves, their enormous bodies as large as Jake's Fiat, and all on a diet of green. And to think, he muses, humans evolved mostly that way, with four sets of molars meant to munch herbs and weeds, found fruits, caches of grains, nuts, and legumes, for hundreds of thousands of years if not longer, before they turned into domesticators, industrialists, cold-blooded murderers on a giant scale, extincting other species along the way. To have obliterated a veg past from our collective memory, turning to all-you-can-eat meat, devastating the planet, while these guys get by. Jake scribbles a series of portraits, darkening page after page in his sketchbook before settling on one he wants to render in oil back in Ojo, a portrait of the animal Pop had his eye on, the one who will make it to Christmas unlike the others, Tommy divulged, the others slated to become a form unrecognizable to what's standing today, vital and drooling.

Jake takes in the trees, heavy with fruit. To think of the timing, the chance to glimpse the haul to come—how will they do it? Or will they leave it? He shifts his vantage point to the rise above the road, facing the house where they drove in. His goal is to make a portrait of a place that will develop a special, even sentimental and nostalgic feel in his mind and body both, though a total stranger to the place before today, similar but night-and-day different to the way it resonates with Tommy. He jots sketches then full-scale renderings like a photographer profligate with her shutter, advancing frames as though film were free.

At some point he enters the adobe finally, after Lita called out, Wanna glass a water?

Unlike earlier when she avoided his gaze, she peers at him directly.

Snack maybe?

Tommy turns the knob of the bathroom door and slits it open, face flush, as red as the dress on the Infant over the sofa, there in the nicho. He blows, wipes his nose clean before balling up a hankie and stuffing it in his pocket. He nears Jake, embraces him from behind, wraps his arms around his chest brazenly in front of Lita, then runs his cheek across Jake's ear and neck.

Está bien, Lita.

Poco a poco, Tomasito.

The City Different paces south along 285 where it forks in two directions, from a scatter of adobes south of Tesuque, past the flea and opera, to another group of adobes flocking like bush-tits.

On the plaza before the governor's mansion Jake marvels, It's another country!

Lita was right to have us stop, niño. I f'got how old it is. How it look to outsiders.

I never seen anything like it, comin' from Laurentine.

We'll move here someday.

An' do what?

Time'll tell.

The way you think.

Why'd you leave the place you're from?

You wanna move to a mud house?

You mean a mud city.

At the French cafe off the plaza, in the La Fonda hotel, Tommy orders two mille-feuilles. Jake crumbles it like it were shale along the Shagaran, pooh-poohs sweets until the thing reaches his mouth.

Oh. my. god—

—Such a gringo—green-go is more like it—

—I ain't ever eat anything like it.

Back under the portico of the governor's mansion Tommy samples the bracelets, presumably to add to what's already on his wrist, trying them first on his own and then Jake's arm. Artisans sit, squat, and stand around blankets arrayed with silver and turquoise, among whom Tommy seems at home, like he belonged here, communicating what he's after, which more often than not requires a vendor to grab a bag of wares not on view. After much effort and not a little haggling he lands on two he likes, for which he extracts two bills from his wallet—Jake observes as Tommy exposes more green than he's ever seen in one place, let alone carried.

Para ti, niño. Un recuerdo de la Ciudad Diferente where we'll end up someday.

Huh?

A memento. After Tommy demonstrates how to put it on Jake wraps a sterling C around his lower arm and adjusts it in place.

First time for everything. He kisses Tommy in the sunlight and the locals pay no mind.

Heading toward Eldorado the landscape opens up, the road a form of vandalism on the terrain it seems, unhoused and hilly, craggy and pined, the names of the First Nations and Spanish that inhabited it spoken by the signs that roll by. Cañoncito. Cañon de Apache. Valencia. Glorietta. Pecos—

—To think of so much space so close to a city—this must be what Wren was going on about that time when she arrived with Skye.

It speaks to gringos too—oops! Looks like we went too far. Gotta turn around. At the Pecos exit Tommy motors across a bridge atop the highway then ramps in the opposite direction. I guess this place speaks to too many gringos, he laments. That's the problem. They're invading. Again. They ruin their own cities with strip malls an' ugly buildings and wanna get away, only to come an' do the same thing here. Like they can't help themselves, develop every inch of land. Ugly a place. It's not just old hippies anymore but the well-healed, causing a stir among the locals. They think they own—all this.

An' you wan' me t' move here someday.

You'll be with me—.

Jake works the bracelet over the wrist bones.

Pulling up to Skye's, an orchard greets you. Apricots, apples, peaches, and plums ripen on branches, pruned and evenly spaced—

—You made it.

Grama grass feathers the yard, not unsimilar to the half-assed attempt at a lawn you find at Harry and Florrie's, except for the fact that nature's the proprietor. Seeded and watered it. Including scrub cactus and cholla from the road to where the fruit trees take over, leading you to the door and inside, where the air is ten degrees cooler.

You remember Tommy.

How could I f'get?

Tommy blushes.

Skye introduces Beverly. I hope you didn't have a hard time finding it.

As at Las Nieves the sun is held at arm's length, beyond windows that act like mirrors of light and not eyes, aided by the orientation of the structure and the thickness of walls. Jake tags behind Tommy, imagining what it'd be like to live in the space. He pictures the two of them in its footprint, extending to the back with its tall, stuccoed wall and not a soul in view, the gazes of others barred along with the withering sun, moving overhead and denied its nosy bent— Tommy's hand migrates toward Jake's in the gentle way it does on a dance-floor. His white-boy, what Lita was really on about, not the fact that he's a he—she's seen too much to be bothered by that. Until he reminded her the heart's an animal, a feral thing. Immune to culture. History and religion. Tommy cloaked then unjacketed, without pretense in or out of his second skin—as though rutting were always—

—Here's where the magic happens.

In a room sparely furnished Jake eyes a work-bench, a fireplace angled in the corner darkened from use. Tears well up in his eyes for reasons he can't explain, to himself or Tommy, let alone the women, who for all intents and purposes he knows only through Wren—*Why here, of all places?*—

—Are you OK?

Here's where Skye works, comments Beverly,

It seems so neat! Jake sniffs. I pictured something more messy—more muddy.

The saltillos are cool under the feet. Standing around the work bench is an array of tools, plastic bags with shapes underneath, defining them, containers of slip and a wheel that looks like a tiny lazy-susan under shelf on shelf of black and red wares, all behind glass.

Wren said the Forest City Museum acquired a piece—is this where you made it?

You know that museum?

You might say.

A world away from this.

We enjoyed our stay with Wren and Donald at the opening, and after too, remarks Beverly. We met Cinthia and Debra—you know they were just here?

They said they'd stop—

—And to think you're here because of the crazy way we met, your sister and me, Donald, tossing carrots to the last

donkey we got. Too stupid to run away. What would I a
done without them? We had t' put my father in a facility not
long after—he was just startin' to lose it.

A plastic bin marked **DRY ONLY** butts against the wall.
Jake wonders how these lumps will shift into what's on the
shelves, shaped, carved and polished—how will this become
that? From such mean materials—we're talkin' dirt!—to a
museum he knows like the back of his hand.

You and Wren, Skye comments. Two peas.

He says we'll move here someday.

That's concrete, quips Beverly. You mean like next
month? Next year?

Don't you got a say, Jake? queries Skye.

'Parently not.

Mis padres son de Las Nieves. We were just there.

Town that time forgot. Not far from her mother, in Santa
Agata.

Wha'd your people think a this guy here?

They absolutely fell in love, jumps Tommy.

Oh, I'll bet, quips Skye.

On a rare night when Tommy isn't expected, after months
without eating or retiring alone, the reality of the situation
hits home. Jake's home. For how long now? After an
unpropitious start, loaded down as he was with left-overs
from a life, things and people both. Now what's left is sorted
in boxes discarded in dumpsters at Safeway, stamped with
brand-names of dish-soap and diapers, paper towels and
shampoo, large and small. A kind of cartony filing system
into which things are chucked, when not shoved in a trash-
bag. The sorting—

Dear Son,   Oct 19—

I don't understand how you could a gone runnin
off like that, turnin your back on your ma an pa
like that it has really hurt my feelins. To think
a all the things we did for you I gave birth to
you an nursed you and your father and I gave
everything we had to you and your sisters and
this is the thank's we get. If I didn't switch my
hair appointment th day you left I might not a
even know you'd gone. And t think a the effect all
this is had on your father. It was bad enough your
sister got into that mess she did that was like
driving a stake straight into my heart and now
this. I just dont know what your poor old mother
did to deserve this. Your father worked two and
sometimes three jobs just to put three squares
on the table for you and yer sisters every day
and did you even appreciate it. I don't think so if
you did you would a never done this to me. Even
your older sister says that was a nasty thing a
you to do and she is always taking your side in
everything. She says just about every day don't
worry he'll be back I know he'll come back she
says you're finding your self as the young people
say well tell me this how did you get lost. The
only one's you can every count on in this life is
your family I tried to tell you sister that when
I saw the writine on the wall between her and
that one she gone and run off with the two of you
are just as bad the way you treat me and your
father. I mean you passed through my body at
the same time but who would a expect that you
would both stab me in the heart like that though
it was in differen ways. The two of you running
as your father says from what matters most in
life I mean god give us are family for a reason. At
least Diana understands what its about we know

we can always rely on her. Wren is lost to us for
good i guess but your not so far gone you cant
come home any time because you don't have no
one. all you gotta do is say your sorry and we'll
be their. We'll even come down there an pick
you up and drive you home. That's what I pray
for every morning at mass and after I start my
rosary in the evenin that the blessed mother
bring you home to us. When I realize that you
weren't coming back I cried myself to sleep every
night and when it really set in that you were gone
I got the hives like the dickens. My throat start
to close up shut and your father has to drive me
t the hospital and I almost didn't make it threw
it was the same thing that happened when yer
your sister got in the family way with that guy.
Thats what happens when children step all over
there mothers heart noone knows the suffering
a Our Lord like a mother we give and give and in
the end what do we get in return we get crucified.
Just so you know I'm writing this on your
birthday the same day you and you're sister were
born I was the one who endured all that pain just
to bring you both in the world I was 31 hours in
labor you think that was easy. Wren has made
her bed and she's gonna have to lie in it but you
can still change Jake you can mend your ways
cuz you ain't settled I hear and dont have noone.
I called that Geist boy and he said you can even
get your job back that's what a fine young man he
is. He understands the importance a family he's
settle down with such a nice girl and they have
two kids I think already an another on the way.
why else would he give up everything in order to
help carry on the family business. I see his wife
at the early mass on Sunday mornings she's such
a nice girl she's always there praying for the
family. Maybe you can learn from him after all

you were such good friends and for years an he tells me you never even sent him a postcard from down there. It would do you a world of good to find a nice girl the way he done and settle down and start a family of your own God knows that's what we raise you to do. That's what I pray for every morning I have prayed you thru so many things an i'll pray you threw this to.

your loving mother

Jake,   Mar 19—

It was one thing a you t leave without a decen farewell but I didn't know you were cuttin us outta your life fer good. I send you a letter a time ago did you get it, I don't know cuz I never heard back must be half a year a ago I sent it. I don't know what on god's green earth we could a ever done to deserve this from you I mean your father and me everything we ever did was for you n your sisters to. A mothers suffering is bad enough but your makin it clear that theirs no end to it for your dear ole mom. It would be one thing if you kept in touch with your sister or even your old friends but nobody heres from you even though lot's a people tell me they try to contact you including the Geist boy who I saw at the A&P the other day he was with his wife she's really coming due now with there third I think it is when I says to him if he's heard from you he says not one word. Leo tole me the same thing when I run into him at the graden center he says he hasn't heard a whistle from you either like everybody else I've seen never mind your own sister whose very hurt that you haven't seen fit

to write her back. Are you that busy there that
you can't make time to write a word or two t yer
own flesh an blood just to let us know your ok?
You're sister's birthday came and went and she
never got a card from you, your father and I are
on the verge a given up. It's not about the card or
god forbid my birthday or his its the fact that we
hear nothing from you like you died or somethin.
Actually its worse than a death now that I think
a it when you know someone is still here but their
ignoring you it's like a slap in the face. If it has
anything t do with that boy that died some people
are sayin he got murdered by that quack minister
you were followin i tried to tell you. the last i
heard theirs two ladies say he did it he may even
end up in the slammer. It seems like you should
be over the death a that boy by now I mean thats
a part a life. Look at your father his parents were
both with our lord already before he was even
out a high school and did he go runnin away from
the people that took him in no. No he got a job
and married and we had you three healthy kids
by the grace a the good lord no matter how far
you try to go to get away nothins gonna change
the fact that I conceived birthed and raised
you completely outta love. If only every parent
throught about having children the way we did
your father and me we never even thought about
taking precautions because we knew god would
give us the number a children he want us t have.
We had 3 kids by his grace but more an more it
seems like one, 2 if you count molly its enough
to make a grown women cry. You're father tells
me if I believe in god the way I say I do I would
stop crying and pray instead if I really have
faith but its easy for him to say he never was
mucha a church goer he give that up when his
father died but god understands, sure. God luvs

and understands you too, if theres anything in
you're life your not proud of just turn it over to
him and that includes abandoning you're parents
and taking off for god knows where. I didnt even
know what state your in at first all I know is its
somewhere out there, or at least thats what Diana
said she heard from your sister who isnt very
generous with details when she talks about you.
Diana has gone to see her a times or two just to
see if she can find out something but thout much
luck. I didn understand what the big secret is you
must have an address like everyone else because
you gotta live somewhere and yet the way you're
sister acts its like your sleeping in you're car
or something like some rolling stone but I can't
imaging that to be the case. Even in order to get
my letter to you i had to ask Diana t give this to
your sister to mail an i hear its not to you house
but to some box in some town i can't even say. I
think not knowing is the hardest thing if it were
up to me Id hop on a jet plane tomorrow and come
down their myself wherever that is until I tracked
you down but you're father wont let me. He tells
me to hole off that sometimes a man got to get his
head straight before he settles down but what does
he know about a mothers love or the power of a
mothers prayers. I just have one more thing to say
and that is when you lay you're head down at night
know that you have left a grieving mother behind
whose cheeks are been eating away by her own
tears.

   your loving mother

Son hows it going down there. Do you like it are
you finding wat your looking for down there what
ever it is you left here for i hope its wat you hopped

it d be? Ever thing is good here so done you wurry. I wantd to tell you that i thought about it a lot and i come to relize evry man got a rite to find his own way in this big whirl after all you only live wonce. i guess goin down their was you're way aleast thats sumthing i understan now i didn have that kinda optin when i was yourage. Done feal like you gotta come back just to pleas you're old lady who never stops cryin come back when your good an ready utherwise yull alays regret it. You're ol lady she got the hives after you leff but shes bedder now. You know her shell probly try an get you to come back she cant helpit thats how mothers are. done get me wrong i d like that to but mosely i raspect you're rite to do whats rite for you like i say you only pass wonce through this world so make a yourself wat you can wile your still yong make hey wile the son shines like the say. Wen you do come back i loke forward ta sittin down and havin a beer together man 2 man an i loke forwar to hering stories from you're travels their aint no edacation like travel i alays say. I ramember when you were young we use to watch Jim Dunny Adventur Rd. maybe it was that give you the ants in the pants to go mayb its my fault this whol dam thing ha ha. Thatd suit me rite i gess for goin on about seein the worl its somethin my dad alays tought me but then again he was fresh off the bote. He come her from so far away an had to geta job to raze a famly he never did get to travel once he have a wif an kids to sapport jus' like me. Still he tole me once if he told me a 1000 time bess thing you can do is see the worl its betr than schol, samething i tole you tho I niver git th chance. I'm sure youll seddle down hav a wif some day befor you do that do jus' wat you been doin cuz wonce your hitched you're life is over. Thats all i gotta to say excep it

might not hurt if you rote you're ol lady back one
a these days get her off my back with her cryin an
whalin. Jus' a word or 2 or t be rull honest hi will
do it it dosent have to be the constatushun.

Dec 19—
Dear Jake,

I muss be cursed now your sister tells us she's
goin off she's joinin some community in the south
she tells us an not down where we are but way
south practicly the south pole. You poor old dad
an' I are now 0 for three three strikes we're
out what in the worl did we do to deserve this?
Everyone else we know go on about the kids an
grandkids their havin for the holidays and we
got nobody not even gramma Ruby who wasn
even their any more she just sat in her rocker
til I gotta change her you're sister couldna even
waited til after the holidays is over she says
God is calling her an she gotta go. Their not able
to have nothin there no possesions at all but
the cloths on their back she says the good Lord
will provide. She leave her car with us an the
insurnce paymen t worry about, she says take
care a my jewelry an Barbie collection for me will
ya. Some concellation that is to be stuck with a
buncha old dolls but never mine you're dad an
me are under strick orders not to touch them
or her jewelry she better fine them there just
the way she leave em I wanna know is she goin
ther to stay or planning to come back I just done
know but the bottom line is you poor dadn me are
here in this house all alone. Aleast before we had
Molly but your sister put a end to her. She was
so insisten that we put her down then she up an

leaves ain't that sumpin. I grew t like the ol' gal she an me

Do yer ol' mom a favor an drop me a line sometime you now a son is a blessing to a mother.

xoxo

Jan 19—
Jake,

I'm writing to tell you I joined The Community of Christ the Poor and Jake I've never been happier in all my life. This is the bestest thing I ever did. Our spiritual leader stresses that things are what keep us from God and the only way to remove any barrier is to relinquish all our possessions and trust in Him to take care. There are about 50 of us full timers and 20 part timers who come up anywhere from a few hrs to a few wks at a time to spend here at the Comm. It's not a easy life in lotsa ways there's no running water—we gotta pump it from a well—and we gotta use outhouses like in the old days. Just about everything we eat we grow in the Comm garden so I'll be doing a lotta that come Spr and Sum and even Fall. We get up every a.m. at 2 for matins in the Chapel where we pray for peace in the world, that's the whole point of this place to be a prayerful presence. Everyone is so nice and supportive, in so many ways I feel I'm getting the support I never had at home, I mean I never feel like my family is really my family not matter how hard I try to hold it together. This feels more like family to me than anything I've ever experience. Jake I never felt so happy in all my life as I do now living without things, it feels so liberating to let everything go and not worry about it, that is the essence of love Fr. Walker says. He's my spiritual advisor, him and Sister Crozier both. I think one

reason the convent didn't work for me is because
it was too in the world but I have a good feeling
about this place being separated as we are in the
south here. It's coed for one and that feels right. I
am so grateful I found this place did I tell you I've
never been happier in my life?
    Your Sister in Our Lord,
    Diana

On Capitol Hill if you're in the market for a fling you live
in Cheesman Park, Bitch Beach to the locals, referring
to the slap-dash arrangement of towels and blankets
strewn across an impeccably green lawn, bodies arrayed,
oiled and orienting themselves like sunflowers in pursuit
of a tan and a man, both dark, while the palest of pale
attempt to do away with whiteness in a paradoxical twist,
a game of appropriating skin-tones. Meanwhile if you're
already paired, or domesticated, you most likely head to
City Park instead for a breather, a stone's throw and light
years away from Cheesman. Away from the slathering and
snarking, manscaping and maneuvering, one-upping and
eye-balling—Last place I wanna be with you, comments
Tommy, lost in a funk, though no stranger to Cheesman in
the old days, its mid-day pick-ups—Who wants to deal with
all that?
    He sighs deeply as the two stroll northward around the
lake under sycamores set when landscape architects, in an
effort to replicate a giant green back east, sought to stage
the concept here in the west, transfer it from the Big Apple
to the Queen City, a desert at the time, a history lost on Jake
and Tommy as they approach the zoo—
    —Oh—aha. I don' wanna go there.
    Why not! It's famous, Tommy protests.
    All them cages.

It's fun! Didn' you go as a kid?

—That's the problem—even then I knew—

—Check it out!

No way.

Tommy's shift in mood lately is palpable; Jake appreciates the fact he's trying. He's grown semi-accustomed to it by now, Tommy's irritation at most things, a bellicose orientation, so unlike before, that's infiltrated their lives, bedroom too, causing Jake to wonder for a moment if Polly and Kitty weren't right, if Tommy weren't an unknown quantity after all. His mood's dispelled momentarily as he recollects the times his parents brought him here, the memories vivified by the hoots and howls and occasional growls shooting from behind the walls.

From behind the trunk of a sycamore Jake eyes a couple entertaining their brood on the playground beside the zoo exit, assisting them on the elephant slide, the chimp jungle-gym, the merry-go-round with giraffes, hippos, and tigers replicating the animals inside, turned spectacles and performers, captives most of all, the children squealing and squirming, letting it all out after having been told a thousand times, Stay behind the rope!—Don't go there!—You're gonna get your hand bit off! and dozens of other admonishments— nearly as many prohibitions as the ones waged against the animals themselves. Now, however, they at least can cut loose.

Look't Daddy-O, deadpans Tommy.

No way—.

The man under surveillance totes an infant as his wife shepherds four others on the rides, under piped water that arcs across and over, catching young bodies unaware. Though unsmiling she's in her element. He turns around, faces the sun, and his gaze catches Jake. His eyes widen, head swivels over and back, he lifts his index finger toward the sky. He turns to his wife as though she weren't burdened enough and hands her the infant. The two behind the sycamore eyeball him as he frees himself from the bodies darting underfoot. He heads off, ostensibly in the direction of the public restroom, but then like an inebriated bee makes his way in a pattern toward the pair.

Jake! The man looks this way and that then pecks Jake's lips—I can't tell you how glad I am to see you! Such a sight for sore eyes!

Such a surprise, eh?

Emil pets Jake's tee up and down, tweaks his nipple then runs his hand along the zipper of his jeans. He peers at Tommy—Oh! Sorry! My buddy. He kisses Jake fully now while cupping his crotch—

—This is Tommy.

Please to meet you—Jake, too bad we can't—what about over there?

The restroom?!

I'm suppose t' be there anyway.

Jake's face reddens. For his part Tommy cracks the first real smile in an age. He seems almost as perked as Jake.

I sent Ginny an invite for you. Did you get it? Emil kisses Jake again, who cranes his neck backward—You might wanna contact her. It's from him an' me both.

The tall man studies Jake's face as though looking for something, then peers at Tommy.

It is—

—What it is, finishes Tommy.

I see. Yeah I got it from Ginny. He backs away, face flushed. I gotta go—when I saw you I couldn't help—. I hope Dan tol' you everything the way I asked—seem like a century ago.

The pair watch as Emil slips into the crowd, resumes holding the child, runs his hand along Caren's back.

Turn aroun', pleads Tommy. Give us another look.

Dude, don' min' the mess.

Clutter expands as the two speak. Jake's only caught slivers of the place, when the wind blew hard, the door widened enough, or the Persian darted out. Men's magazines and tools, grocery bags and food cartons, juice bottles and coffee cans, slit envelopes and cardboard boxes but most of all beer cans cover the surfaces, indoor-outdoor carpet barely visible, table and counter—everything is topped.

What mess?

I cain't never seem t' find time.

Not with all the entertaining you—

—Next place I'm gonna be better.

You mean at entertaining?

No with—

—I hope it don't crimp your style. You don't got any trouble bringin' home the gals—I hope it's OK to say.

You noticed?

I'm just a pick-up away.

I hope we ain't been too rowdy.

Ditto.

It was just that dude's wife. Chick got pissed! My girl's like, Think we ought a call the cops?

Glad you din't.

So unfortunate. Always is. Chick's old man find out, you got hell t' pay—once I find myself a the end of a barrel, point-blank. But dude's wife find out, it's ten times worse.

—It weren't nothin' like that. And how would you—?

She was shootin' bullets, sure as shit. Whole neighborhood hear, I swear. You find a way t' hook up with the dude 'hind 'er back?

Guess I learn my lesson.

Sorry t' hear.

Just the idea of hooking up with Emil again, Tommy or no Tommy. The lure that doesn't quit. Apart from that I know the dilemma you face when a man like Derrick quizzes you about a man. Whatever you say is flammable. It's—

Sorry, dude. Didn' mean t' rattle you.

Wha' d' you mean?

You're perspirin'.

Toda está bien, as my friend says.

I guess it's only you'n the other dude now, eh. Sounds like you're havin' a good time. Anyway, sorry that other thing end the way it did. You had a good thing goin', judging by the sound a things.

Jake peers away. What I don't get is you.

Me?

Yeah.

Want me t' call you weird-o? Kick you out an' call the cops?

Have me hauled away.

Get a group t' protest in front a your trailer.

Hold up a sign sayin' god hates fags—

—With a finger pointed at your pitcher.

Shouldn't you?

Should I? Want a beer? Derrick points to the corner. Help yourself.

The inside of the fridge is the cleanest place in the trailer. I'm curious.

Dude, about what?

About you.

Derrick tugs his beard, twirling an end that flops on his stomach when he lets go, revealing a line toward his navel. As Jake has so often witnessed through the slit in the blinds, Derrick's shirtless, leaning against the paneling next to the door as though manning it. Slowly and repetitively he gathers his beard below the jaw and strokes it.

I don' know what t' say.

The two peer at each other.

I got a boyfriend—

Shoe on th' other foot?

You could say.

Gimme your hand. Jake extends his right and Derrick cradles, fondles it then traces the palm-lines with a calloused tip, examining the wrist, veins on the back—I've known girl's with manlier skin. You'n your boyfriend got any rules?

I guess we never talked about it—

Well if you do—

The most difficult thing about a squeeze like this unfolding is how to yank yourself free. It's almost like an American movie in that once a gun is flashed there's no going back—sooner or later it's gonna go off, blasting someone, splattering innards everywhere, blood, guts, and brains. Jake tries to think of a picture he's seen where it wasn't the case, one that said no to a shooting once a weapon was produced. As though it bucked biology, physics, and nature broadly speaking. How many times had he, Tommy too, gawked at Mr. America—the name they anointed Derrick with—as he dragged one woman after another here, without muttering, You lucky dog! Meaning the woman. Lucky him too. How many times had they smirked at choruses in the dark as Derrick and the latest got down to serious logrolling? And now Jake finds himself here, on terra incognita, in their place, perched across a guy whose torso curves from the wall to the chair, legs splayed in such a manner he's practically prone. It's a cat-dance that can't last, and doesn't after a rap at the door, separating the two with the speed of the Persian, darting for cover in a storm.

Jake retracts his body and Derrick perks upright, throws a shirt on from one of the many lying around.

He cracks the door.

Jake here?

Derrick widens the opening—Here's the guilty party. Won' you join us? The Persian darts in before Tommy, as Derrick swipes detritus off a stool at the end of the counter. Jake takes the Persian in his lap and she begins to mew.

Beer?

Gracias. Tommy eyes Derrick's shirt, misbuttoned, then glances at Jake. I hope I didn't interrupt.

Beer's in the fridge—help yourself. You didn't interrup' nothin'.

Tommy pops the top off a bottle and swigs. Jake tells me you're movin' down.

Yup. Tired a th' commute.

Jake says all the work's in the city.

He say that?

You find a place?

All set. Trailer Court on Federal.

I know that place! We use t' go by there when I was a kid. Jake an' I are talkin' about gettin' a place too—

—Actually we don't got a choice.

There's a place available by me. I got a pick between two. Nice inside compared t' this.

Niño that'd be loco. T' end up in that place. I always fantasized about the giant cowboy—that the place, in' it?

Yup.

I still got another month here on the lease.

Polly'd be glad to know you found a place.

Don' tell me you're married too—you gotta watch this guy! Derrick reaches forward and rests his hand on Jake's, holding it. Home-wrecker.

Not intentionally—and yep, he'n Polly are married.

Girls gotta watch out for you, Jake. Not sure I approve.

Jake erupts in a fit of laughter, followed by Derrick, the two doubled over, clutching their bellies, leaning to their sides and almost falling off their chairs—Jake has never seen Derrick laugh before, period, let alone like this, nor he him. Whether it's the effect of the beer or something else it seems they're possessed. The expression on his face speaks agony and pleasure at the same time, heavy breathing and a dire attempt to catch his breath, as often happens in a jag like this, a spasm that lasts forever—

—I guess it's a private thing, Tommy remarks, chuckling along—

—Trust me, it ain't private.

The comment sends the duo into yet another jag that lasts until it slowly peters out. Derrick wipes tears from his eyes with the hand that held Jake's just a few moments ago. He reaches for the hankie in his back pocket and blows his nose.

When he returns to himself, the convulsion passed, he raises his beer in a formal toast—Well, it'd be great t' be neighbors with you again, Jake. An' better yet, the two a yous.

[Scene: The traffic circus near The Forest City Art Museum. The grand stairs of the beaux-arts structure are in view, atop which the Thinker rests in reflection, his legs blown out by an art-saboteur. The museum gardens wheel around the lagoon in front of the museum, along a busy thoroughfare; they're sparking to life after their winter dormancy. It's late afternoon.]

Donald: I mean y'all were insane, thinking you could dump a body on the side a the road, in perfect view a the cops.

Wren: It worked out.

Donald: You got a ticket.

Wren: Jake did.

Jake: Which he never paid.

Donald: I'm gonna stop a cop, turn you both in. Tell 'im you're the one.

Jake: Cop had a yen t' bring you in.

Donald: Welcome to my world—

Wren [taking Donald's hand]: This-here is a special place. An' we did'n dump her.

Jake: It wasn't where I wanted, but the museum's got all the dirt locked up in blooms—they turn those gardens all a time. Over here'll have t' do.

Donald: What if they expand the road? What they gonna find?

Wren: They're not gonna do anything a the kind—the road's as wide as it's ever gonna get. The Eries prob'ly set it with their feet. I'd be willin' to bet it hasn't changed an inch since.

Donald: Don' be so sure. They mowed down all them trees on the block, just because some genius read the order wrong. No tellin' what could happen here.

Tommy: Niño, why here a all places? With all this tráfico—what were you thinkin'?

Jake: Wren's right—this place is special. How many times did me and Moll come here—or just over there. I used t' leave her by that legless wonder on the steps while I was inside. You get a view of it from here. Donald, take a look at the road. Think anyone's touched it in a century? You think they sit at city hall wonderin' how to improve it? You're the one live here.

[As the group strolls over the grass inside the traffic circle they sidestep rings of daffodils. Wren struggles to find the exact spot where Molly lies given how different the terrain looks. Back and forth she laces the terrain.]

Wren: Jake, where do you think it is? The ground was frozen then. There weren't no flowers t' throw us off.

Jake [circling the area]: I have no idea! I thought it was impossible t' forget—I still have dreams about that night. I'm sure if we came back in December we'd go right to't.

Wren: I jus' remember how hard the ground was.

Donald: About as hard as y'alls heads! I'll find it.

Wren: Jake, maybe we should a left a marker after all.

Jake: I'd rather struggle.

Cinthia: You could a raised a cairn or somethin'.

Jake: We could a left a neon sign too: **DOG BELOW.**

Donald [sweating in the unseasonable heat]: Chrise. Where the hell is it? It looks familiar an' unfamiliar at the same time.

Debra [taking Cin's hand]: Is it here?

Wren: No, I think it's here.

Jake: What does it really matter, the exac' spot? We're nearby.

Cinthia to Wren: See how he is?

[Despite Jake's resignation the group tries to locate where Molly was interred on a day the family used to celebrate her birth, because having a date for events like it matters, the thinking goes, regardless of its veracity, regardless of whether it relates to an actual, historical event, like Chrissmus or Easter, or Molly's birth. Finally, Tommy stumbles on a spot, standing bang overhead, the only one in the group that Molly never met.]

Tommy [standing in a depression in the soil in the middle of a ring of daffodils, just beside a yellow straggler]: Niño, I felt algo—muy extraño—very strange!—I think it's aquí!

Donald: Dude! We owe you—we could a been here all day—trus' me. With these two?

Tommy [privately to Jake]: Niño, I felt somethin'—

Jake: What was it?

Donald [overhearing]: Maybe the guts a these two—they were spillin' them to the fuzz that night instead a keepin' it zipped.

Jake: What does it matter in the scheme a things?

Cinthia: That's my Jake. Never was a poker-face.

[After commenting several times that something happened—Like electricity, niño, I swear!—the others stand inside a circle of yellow blooms, taking care to avoid the stray next to Tommy's heel, for an amount of time that feels interminable to Donald, who's checking his watch in order not to be late in picking up Billie after school, taking in the memories of Molly on his own terms.]

Debra: Molly's the one discover Peacoat, rolled on the beach. Romeo claimed he did, but I saw Moll there. Several times. I think she even come back t' tell us.

Donald: Oh right—

Cinthia: Don't laugh! I think Deb's right. She kept runnin' over then runnin' back, whinin', and truth be told drivin' us crazy. We thought she wanted attention, for the hell of it.

Donald: Sounds like Sunday night white-people TV.

Jake: T' be honest I don't really remember much about that night.

Debra: No surprise there!

Cinthia: You were wasted. Completely outta it—I mean, over the edge. 'Til the discov'ry. That slap you awake.

Tommy: Pobrecito. Wish I were there for you.

Donald: I doubt it would a helped—he was one crazy cracker back then.

Debra: Moll was tryin' t' tell us somethin'—I mean, it haunts me.

Wren: All water over the dam—.

[Wren takes Jake's hand, then Donald's.]

Debra: Who knows all the things she said or wanted t' say.

Cinthia: If they could only speak—
Donald: —

[The others in the group join hands as well, all except Tommy who stands in the depression in middle, his heel beside a daffodil.]

Wren: Great spirit, thank you for bringing us together— Cinthia and Debra, back from their time at the Ashram out west; Jake and Tommy—to remember Moll—
Donald: She was a dog, so—
Wren *[squeezing Donald's hand]*: For giving more than we were able to appreciate.
Cinthia: Thank you for every living thing that touches our lives. Molly for sure. Flowers around us. Birds overhead, tryin' to drown us out. Grass below. Apple trees, forsythias—

[She gestures with her eyes to the grove around them.]

Debra: Unliving things too. Rocks. Sun and rain. Clouds.
Tommy: —.
Donald: Amen.

[He attempts to extricate his hand, realizing it's the time to go, but Wren grasps it firmly, holding it there for a moment, even as the circle is broken on the other side.]

Wren: Jake, you wanna say somethin'?
Jake: Like what?
Wren: Whatever you want.
Jake *[after standing silent for some time]*: I think I'm good.

[The others disperse and Wren remains with Tommy, who appears glum, glued to the spot as though unable to move. The two stand silent among the ambient noise—birds chittering in the forsythias, the whirr of vehicles, wind through the fruit trees that confetti the grass with petals, visitors in the gardens in front of the museum, panhandlers hitting people up, polite and not-so-polite refusals, a single-engine airplane chugging overhead—all happening while Tommy's lost in thought, tuned to a different reality, not sensing the

hand on his wrist—he and Wren remain that way until the others interrupt—.]

Jake: Wanna go across the street?

Cinthia: We can let them have a moment, can't we?

Debra: Or an hour, if they want—

Jake: I mean, what are they doing? He's not religious—god forbid. Last thing in the world t' say about him.

Cinthia: Spiritual then?

Jake: Helllll no.

Debra: 'Least that's what he says.

Jake: Every chance he gets!

Wren *[beside Tommy]*: I'm glad—

Tommy: I'm not so sure he's glad about me, lately.

Wren: He gets it.

Tommy: Maybe. But it's like he's afraid.

Wren: Molly would a approved.

Jake: You guys *comin'*?!

[After some time the group migrates across the road to the museum grounds, taking in the gardens by the lagoon. The fragrance of cherry blossoms fills the air in the dimming light as they stroll along the beds of tulips and hyacinths. They make their way to the staircase in front of the museum, beside the Thinker. Donald rejoins the group with Billie at his side.]

Cinthia: Why not here, boys?

Jake: Here?

Cinthia: Donald can officiate.

Donald: I ain't gonna officiate!

Jake: How bout if Billie officiates?

Billie: I wanna fishiate.

Debra: Jake, stand here. And you, Tommy, you stand here. We'll reenact the event for the locals.

Jake: But I never even met his parents!

Tommy: Nor me yours, niño.

Donald: It's for th' best, trust me.

Wren [*gesturing toward Billie*]: It's her grandparents.

Donald: Still—.

Cinthia: We choose our real families—

Tommy [*bending down on one knee, taking Jake's hand, and motioning for Billie to come close*] : Jake, will you marry me?

Jake: Oh shit. Do I gotta give an answer—now? Can I think about it?

Donald: Say yes, you idiot.

Jake: Yes you idiot.

[*Debra positions the pair and Wren leans down, bringing her mouth close to Billie's ear, feeding lines the child repeats with enough accuracy to almost hold in a court of law were the world, the country, and the state, another place.*]

Wren [*whispering to Billie*]: Now you may kiss the—

Billie: Kiss.

[*To which the two respond with a vigor witnessed infrequently at official ceremonies, in front of god and everyone, including Billie and the others. Everyone and everything but the law.*]

Debra: Boys, you can come up for air now.

Donald: Let 'em have their fun. God knows they ain't ever gonna get a chance at the real thing.

Wren [*after the two stop kissing*]: Jake, d'you feel different?

Jake: Than what?

Wren: Than before.

Tommy: I wonder too, Jake. How do you feel?

Jake: Well it ain't legal, one. But two, that aside—I gotta admit I do. Then again, it's tough enough without the government in our lives. Not sure I want them buttin' in.

Tommy: Them keepin' outta our lives is even more invasive—it's a ruse. They're there no matter what, tellin' us what we can an' can't do. In our own bedroom for god's sake. Holy rollers holdin' the government hostage, and yet they whine that they're the ones attacked—just because we exist! A hair dresser can't refuse a comb-out for a bigot bride-to-be, but she can refuse to make him—us!—a cake, don't we know. You don' call that involvement?

Jake: Why do we care?

Tommy *[excited]*: What if we ever do wanna be legal someday?

Jake: Like that'll ever happen. Why would we care about a silly piece a paper?

Donald: Tax benefit alone, dude. For starters.

[The group laughs involuntarily, all but Cinthia and Debra.]

Debra: Tommy's right, Jake. Maybe you don' care—good for you. But some a us— *[she takes Cinthia's hand].*

Tommy: Niño, why are you so bull-headed? You afraid a somethin'?

Jake: Ha! You afraid a me strayin'? Like married people don't stray? I got news—. Think a piece a paper's gonna stop that?

Tommy: Fuck you.

Wren: Jake, you used t' say you wanted t' marry Romeo.

Cinthia *[bursts in a laugh]*: You romantic, you—him! Of all people!

Jake: I was young and stupid.

Wren: When things got to a point with Peacoat you used to fantasize about you an' him too—'member? Away from them fanatics, livin' happily ever after. Wasn't that marriage?

Tommy: ¡Hipócrita!

Cinthia: If Rauch and Marks ever heard—

Jake: They never will. Right?

Tommy: Niño, why'd you even do it then, given how you feel?

Cinthia: Who were all those people there?

Tommy: Gracias a todos por venir—thanks for coming, everyone.

Donald: That was wild.

Cinthia: That's one way a puttin' it.

Wren: Beautiful is the word.

Debra: Who were they all?

Cinthia: The older ladies—

Jake: They were from my reading group—or I'm from theirs.

Debra: And the one who officiated?

Jake: The minister at the church in Pandemonium, the leader of the reading group. Her husband was there too—he's also a minister.

Donald: You, Jake? A church-goer? Not again!

Jake: Dream on.

Debra: An' the others?

Jake: My neighbor. My former boss—we built five homes t'gether. Some guy I met in a bar, name Heath, that I got to be friends with. Another name Darnell, my first real date. A friend a this guy's, L'Dell. Her husband almost came but opted out at the last minute—

Cinthia: An' all them guys dressed like girls—?

Tommy [excusing then absenting himself from the group, strolling the paths]: —

Cinthia: I didn't mean to—

Jake: It's gonna take time.

[Wren excuses herself, tracking after Tommy]

Jake peers at the trailer next-door. He wonders at the way a vacancy reveals itself, whether it's written on the surface of a place, apparent to everyone, or if it's a function of knowing its history, who came and went. Either way the exterior of the dwelling confirms it—that he, and an endless string of women—they're all gone now. Split. For good. He gazes at his lap, re-creases the letters that've been amassing for years, unopened, dating to a time not long after he arrived. He slips them in their sleeves and tosses them in a cookie tin.

I guess moving does that, makes you face the music, brave what you put off for a rainy day that never came, until you opt to clear out finally—clear things out is more like it. People. Leave the only home you've ever known except for a car on the side of a river, both on wheels and ready to go at a moment's notice.

A knock at the door shakes Jake to the present. I can't believe you came! I just finished—I was gonna drop it off. Jake hands over a parcel, wrapped in craft paper—

—Oh I wanna see! Ginny removes the tape and covering, stands and studies it for a while—. OK—. As with everything you do it tells a truth. Whether I want it or not.

I hope—

—You definitely got us—his body. Mine. Such as they are—or were. Mione's gonna be appalled. Lizzie's gonna love it. If Dan were here he'd be philosophical. We started a journey together, him and me. Decades ago. You never know where it'll take you, whether you'll carry on or bail. But I love it, Jake—I'm sure Daniel would too, lesions and all—but you didn't spare either a us, naked to the very skin as you like to quote. Beautiful and grotesque.

I wish I could paint you both again.

This was his last hurrah as your model—

—My muse.

Ha! Well you painted him enough. And now me. If he hadn't been so insistent I probably wouldn't a done it, expose myself in this way—the two of us. The ravages of age—gravity—look at my breasts! My thighs. The wear in our faces. I wish Vida would agree to do it. It's a peeling.

An affirmation too.

The goal was to capture something—maybe someday I can paint you and Vida.

That'd be different, for sure—I'd be afraid of what you'd have to say. But it's an interesting idea, Jake. I'll talk to her.

I won't be far—

Yeah, it's not like you're moving back to—is it?—where is it? We'll see each other. Don't be a stranger—Vida and me—you can visit any time. Meanwhile it's interesting to be here—it felt off limits before—it was your and Daniel's turf. We had a rule about that, but that's over. Now here I am.

Here you are. And as you can see—Jake swivels his head around—there's nothin' to it.

Still. He used to like coming—. For him it was a free space, no judgment. Where you two could talk turkey, no matter—. It wasn't like that other situation, which was a guilty pleasure—I hope you've forgiven Caren. Anyway, here's the letter I promised. I hope it does some good—how can they ignore a woman a the cloth?

I'm sure it's all lies.

We'll want to hear about your progress down there—especially now you got the ball rolling—when you join the women next time. I'm glad you listened and are gonna go t' school. If you get too busy and it doesn't happen—.

—I'll be there—

—You never know—

—I will. I promise.

Don't say that. I spent a year in France and came back different. A move does that—reorients everything. Way you see relationships. How do you think Dan and I—. You're already not the person that moved here.

There's been no change whatsoever, I'm sure. I'm a stone.

Ginny and Jake both laugh.

Even stones change, opines Ginny.

What about things now—talk about change. Are you OK?

All the things Jake calls his own, his possessions, he realizes he's only been renting, no matter what anyone might think about property. Ownership. Once the pile is loaded on Tommy's pick-up, the cookie-tin of old letters will make it on as well, albeit at the last minute. Jake thought about burning the letters before dropping the keys at Jeanette MacDonald's, their energy belonging more to the bad blood that ushered him here than his life ahead. And yet there they will be, along for the ride, who knows how long, burdened as they are with a past, distant and near.

—I think you can imagine, remarks Ginny. You're no stranger to loss. Even when paths end something remains. He helped make me what I am, saw a minister in me, more than himself. He pushed me, and unlike most men stepped back so I could shine—I. I do hope you'll stop by—Vida and I'd love that. The other women.

It's amazing Dan and Polly were on the same floor.

—.

—It's good everyone could be together—

—I'm happy about Polly and Tommy reconciling. But it is remarkable they were just a couple doors away. Dan didn't have far to go to see Polly.

It was some event, for which—thank you again. You made it what it was—I mean I owe you.

All bullshit. But who knows—I may hold you to it.

From his reserve of paper for writing Wren, Jake retained a single sheet. After bidding Ginny to a future as unclear as his own, Jake jots lines and encloses them in an envelope also saved for the occasion, a missive he fantasized penning for a while now but one he wasn't sure he'd ever send. It became a certainty only after he worked his way through the unopened stack, aggregated by a rubber-band until it became a minor cache, betraying Florrie's career as a writer of epistles for an audience of one, only to be nipped in the bud by a delayed response—

`Dear Florrie —`

It was Jake's and has become Tommy's habit to part the blinds in order to monitor the traffic in and out of the trailer across the way where the distance is no longer a pick-up but a road wide, if you can call it that. A paseo. Alley or lane. A way—anything but a real road, no matter the name. A graveled surface with a 15 MPH limit, twice or even three times that if your neighbor's tooling home from the bar, pants on fire and a woman in tow. The city's done nothing to crimp his style, curtail the times he motors home, late, nearly every night. The two on this side of the paseo observe as shadows get down to business. Sometimes Derrick's date spends the night, other times he drives her to her car, they assume, to a parking lot not far away—they caught him doing it before. But who knows really? In any event they part together and he returns alone.

This'd be better'n TV, Jake avers. If we had one.

It's sorta sick.

That why your here?

In fact Jake finds Tommy next to him often, hands far from inactive as the two observe things unfolding. It happens now that Derrick fails to draw the blinds, allowing the two to take in a spectacle. At times Jake appears inspired and involves Tommy, who's sometimes game, but most times not, lately. On a rare occasion they invent narratives, arcs and back stories, particularly when the woman is performing for remuneration. Will he go for the wallet or won't he? After she's gone they gaze as Derrick gesticulates, phone to his ear—He's calling his mother, Tommy avers.

Asking her to pray for him, Jake adds.

So he can go at it again t'morra.

Anything but come home to a empty place—. The joys of marriage.

—It don' have t' be that way, niño. Not for us. We get t' define it.

I don' know why women do it.

What choice they got?

Would you say no?

Course not.

Derrick's head is cocked to the side as if noticing something in the middle of the action. The pair have taken precautions to dim the lights before parting the blinds, but the streetlight sheds light that illuminates their faces, bodies, and actions, in strips. Derrick circles around the bed and stands naked in front of the window. Jake and Tommy drop the slats and pull the cord on the drapes.

Wha's he doin'?

Through a tiny slit they watch as he draws the curtains; the stage goes dark. For several weeks Jake swears off looking, then notices the curtains rent again. Again he, and ultimately Tommy, retake their seats on the side of the bed.

After six months in the trailer park on Federal, in view of and in a sense under a giant, fiberglass cowboy, the two attend a pot-luck, invited by a woman Jake struck up a conversation with on an evening walk. While petting her dog, Buddy, he learns she and her husband have lived here for decades, since the development opened. Unlike Jake and Tommy who are renting, they purchased their place as a starter and never left. Louise exhibits the kind of care for her dog that one would for a child, her home too, the nicest in the park, typical of people in the early days when everything was new, though less so for more recent arrivals. She's seen changes, in tenants mostly, from families to single men in town for work, people who for all intents and purposes allow their trailers to go to the dogs. In contrast Louise maintains a sense of propriety about her place. While most of the residents have long given up caring whether or not the skirt has fallen away, revealing the under-workings of their trailers, wheels and what-not, and while most have relinquished a lawn or any semblance of a garden, allowing weeds to run wild, Louise's husband, John, occupies himself with sheering a patch of green with a push-mower, tends their postage-stamp flower beds, a small garden that includes tomatoes and peppers, carrots and lettuce. In fact their fastidiousness inspired Jake to toss a bit of seed around his and Tommy's turf as well. And in a reprieve of his life in Ojo he began to pocket stones on his walks to create another rock garden, along the side, a line broken only by a handful of stairs.

The actual day of Louise's potluck begins badly. Tommy declares he's famished, but when he sits down to eat a cloud casts over, darkens his face despite the unbroken sky so typical in the Mile High City—three hundred days of sun in a typical cycle. Without saying a word he stands, rushes to the bathroom and seals the door. Fifteen minutes pass, the door opens, and he returns to the table.

I kept things warm.

I can't eat.

It's been over half a year.

I don' care if it's a century.

By the time two o'clock drags around Tommy vows he's together enough to mingle, so Jake packs the Mexican casserole that Lita taught him to make, with one alteration—un pecado

she called it, un crimen, to cook sin carne, without meat—
he wraps the dish in towels and sets it at the bottom of a
grocery bag.

Though the event is staged outdoors, under an awning,
Louise invites Jake and Tommy in. The space is small,
predictably, not much larger than Jake and Tommy's place,
but a good deal larger than the couch-wide affair in Ojo
and meticulously neat, especially for its scale. Tommy
would later remark that if they lived there there'd be no
room for an olive, under the bed or sofa, in the closets or
cupboards—a lesson he learned not long ago when he and
Jake cleared out the three-bedroom apartment on Josefina.
It was a truth Jake realized too when he recalled the things
he moved with to Ojo, a carload of stuff that multiplied
during his stay, into a large pick-up's worth, its payload
bulging. Given that, the tidiness of Louise and John's place
is astounding.

For a couple in their fifties, ancient as far as Jake and
Tommy are concerned, it's remarkable how little they collect.
True, the shelves of a curio are lined with a collection of
chihuahuas, porcelain and miniature. And it's also true that
John's menagerie of clown portraits dominates much of the
walls. But other than that the two seem to have led a pared
existence. And they don't seem discontent to boot.

Tommy ducked as he and Jake entered the space.
Generally speaking its age is betrayed only by the wear
on fixtures—handles, knobs, and other features that are
original, including the wallpaper. The tap over the sink
drips, and later Tommy will learn the toilet runs perennially.
The dry air's taken a toll on the doors, sagging and cracked,
conveying a weathered smell.

When the other guests arrive Jake discovers it's mostly
single men and a few women trailing them. Most have
brought six-packs in lieu of food, inducing Louise to hand

John a wad of green, ordering him to fetch a tray at King Soopers.

Cold cuts an' cheese, she orders. Two loaves a white bread.

A half-hour after the potluck's begun Derrick slips into the mix.

This is awkward, Tommy quips.

Where's his date?

They watch as he circulates among the crowd, like Buddy, a schmoozer—unlike them he knows the others. Ultimately he comes around to Jake and Tommy from behind.

Name's Bond. Derrick Bond. Tommy tips his hat, reaches out his hand and Derrick takes it, examines the size and texture of the palm, the lifeline.

So original.

I am an original, cowboy.

The man's face shows all the signs of skin exposed to sun. Deeply tanned, the color masks spots here and there, wrinkles around the eyes and neck, making Derrick look older close up and in the light than he does at a distance or in the dark. More hirsute too in the filtered light peeking under the awning, a bush of hair jutting around the mouth and dangling down, the pelt on the chest made apparent by the buttons left undone, trailing below the beard, fuller than Tommy's, which according to Lita is already animal enough.

In some ways it seems an actor has stepped from a screen, a heart-throb broken through glass, fleshed and in three dimensions into real life. Guapo, Tommy whispers in Jake's ear when Derrick's distracted, and Jake, having lived with Tommy long enough at this point, replies, Sin duda.

It's so weird, t' see 'im in broad day.

And without a woman—what's that about?

After arriving with the party tray John mounts a portable TV on a shelf. The world series switches on and Derrick, immediately fixated on the action like the others, shouts at the screen—

—Damn! He came so close!

Thank god! enthuses John, registering the disbelief on Derrick's face—

Whose side you on?

Back and forth the two dicker, trot out statistics, swear loyalties, until they come to a truce—

—I'm thinkin' I should git me a room-mate too, Derrick remarks, returning to Jake and Tommy. Save me a boat-load a cash. But the place is small, a one-bedroom like yours. Might cramp my style. Also my wife says she don't wanna share with no stranger when she come. Easy for her t' say. She ain't the one havin' t' pop for two places. How' d' you guys do it?

We share a bed, so—

—That's one way. I don' eye no traffic comin' in an outta your place like Ojo, Jake. Place seem dead. Grant'd I'm gone most a the day—

Tommy excuses himself and Jake attempts to fill in— It's just us. He works. An' I go t' school.

What you studyin'?

Painting.

You gotta go t' school t' learn that? I'll show you how fer free. Or gimme the dough. I got a million better ways t' spend it.

I'm not sure about it myself—I was sorta prodded to it. Jake contemplates asking, Would you be willin' t' let me paint you sometime? But he leaves it go—

—You see that?! John interjects, patting Derrick on the butt. The guy toggles to his right, banters back and forth with John, an alien in these parts no matter how long he's been here, a transplant from the east, over a decade and a half older than Louise, who now appears in her element as hostess, chatting up Jake until Tommy returns from the loo, eyes flush.

You'll have t' excuse me, but I ain't sure I can't stay.

But you jus' got here! You can't leave! Louise protests. The day's still young. It's only four an' look't all this food! Tommy replies he'll do his bes' to stick it out a little longer, jus' for her, but he's got stuff t'—

—You sick?

Long story, Jake explains.

Have somethin' t' drink, amigo, remarks Derrick—Lemme get you somethin'. Tommy tries to dissuade him, remarks he hasn't been imbibing lately, but Derrick disappears anyway, returning with not one but two drinks, bright pink, which Louise concocted special for today.

Nothin' like a prickly-pear margarita fer what ails ya.

Like it's a tea-dance.

Buddy this ain't no tea.

Inside joke—.

In fact not just Jake but Tommy too hadn't had a drink this early since before first Kitty then Polly were hospitalized, some time ago now. The rosy hue, so evocative back then, causes memories to bloom, intensifying Tommy's mood. But the couple clink anyway, take in liquid solace, bitter and sweet. After a few sips a smile, rare for him these days, makes an appearance on Tommy's face. The furrow of his brow eases, lengthening out like a figure in a coffin.

As the game intensifies, distracting the attentions of the party-goers who are more and more focused on the TV, Louise's role morphs increasingly into that of barmaid. Jake steps in to lend a hand, he and Tommy both, as what had been billed as a patio party turns into a scene from a sports bar. The perennial favorites from the east are playing, demons or saints depending on your point of view, on the perspectives of migrants from all over the country chasing jobs in the Mile High City.

Derrick, an Oklahoman, argues when John repeats the familiar line you always hear about the team—he counters, You mean it's the house that big money built! That and corrupt umps.

Them is fightin' words, returns John, and Louise pipes, There'll be no fightin' at my party!

Still the jabs fly, not just between John and Derrick but others too, comments that quicken with the action on the black-and-white screen, the men in pinstripes more like lightning-rods than ball-players, fomenters of invective and praise both. For Jake and Tommy, trading empties, cans, and glasses for fresh ones along with Louise, the game matters less than it does to her. The other women present, few as they are, cling to their men, literally and figuratively, though not entirely. Some tussle too about plays on the screen, including Cindy who can land jabs as neatly as Derrick. Like him, and all the other men, she also avoids serving. Occasionally the other women approach Louise, ostensibly to lend a hand but instead for directions to the powder-room. They disappear into the darkness of the trailer only to emerge five or ten minutes later, refreshed, licking ruby lips while letting the screen door flap behind them.

From this vantage point, manicured as it is, the other trailers suggest the transience of the place. They barely pass muster according to the by-laws of the development, yellowing in the front office, enforcement having become lax lately. Derrick's place for one, just down the way, appears in that category judging by the look of things. While Jake and Tommy take everything in, the game comes to a climax behind them. A roar goes up as though a bull had been gored, betraying the manly fascination with blood. Womanly too. The lust for a sacrifice. A loser. After the final out the energy changes. The party-goers begin almost automatically to drift, to Louise's chagrin.

No need to scoot so soon! The evening's still young!

But a spell has been broken. People sneak, lapse, slip off.

Up for a drink? Derrick queries as Louise tries to rope the others back while chasing after Buddy.

Had they not already downed several margaritas Tommy would have declined for sure, and Jake would have followed, Tommy that is. Given the situation though, the two glance at each other.

Your call.

No. 'S up t' you.

I ain' askin' you t' lay tile. It's just for a drink.

As Derrick engages in parting-talk, Jake comments, It feels weird.

For good reason, Tommy returns.

Welcome to my palace, boys.

Quite a place, Jake replies.

He half expects to find the back of a movie set when they walk in the aluminum door, portal to a world he's only visited in his imagination, so far. It turns out to be a flesh-and-blood space after all, similar to theirs only more cluttered. Jake will later call it the pad of a guy-guy, stripped of charm, a good vacuuming too. Elbow grease to remove the fingerprints. Switches and plugs without cover-plates. Shelves, sills, and shutters, all out of square.

I had intensions a cleanin' up my act—

Here's t' not cleanin' up your act—

—Hey, you. Derrick nudges Jake on the shoulder and holds his hand there, squeezing, then pads to the fridge and pops the door, exposing a coffin of light, shelved with beer for the most part, a loaf of bread, pack of sliced cheese, and hot dogs. He extracts three cans, cracks the tops, hands two and raises the third.

Such a host!

Here, buckaroo—here's t' never cleanin' up our act. The three swill standing because there's nowhere to sit, not without moving something.

Where's the cat?

Damn thing took off. Soon's I arrive. God only knows—

—We wondered why—

—I'm so sorry to hear, remarks Tommy.

Is what it is. Tell me 'bout yourselves.

I'm worried about the cat—

—Actually—sorry t' innerrupt—ain't nowhere here for the three of us. Only place t' sit is in the back. Shall we?

The back turns out to be a mattress, flat as a stage, or a raft, around which clutter amasses and flows. A top mattress plopped in the middle of the bedroom, with camo sheets stretched across.

Have a seat, boys. Jake heads to the bottom of the bed where he perches, his back stiff and leg falling to the floor. Tommy takes a position at the head next to Derrick. The two lean against pillows propped against the wall.

Tell me about yourselves, Derrick repeats.

Actually, why don't you tell us somethin' about you? Jake replies. Somethin' we don' know, other'n that you like the ladies.

I do like the ladies—tha's a fact.

Tell us about your woman back home.

How 'bout I show pictures a my kids.

Derrick extracts a wallet, cracked and tattered, sandwiching images of three girls, their faces hidden there for years, maybe decades. This'n looks a l'il like you, pardner—he gestures toward Jake. Don' ya think?

What about your wife? Got a pitcher?

Y'know, can't say I do.

She know about your life?
She no dummy.
Any chance a her findin' out for sure?
What if you found her doin' th' same?
I'd kill 'em both. We got a agreement.
Which is?
She don' ask nothin' about me.
What if you found him cheatin' on you?
What do you mean by cheatin'?
Cheatin's cheatin'.
Depende. We'd talk about it. But we wouldn't kill no one.
Men gotta have it. Women is differen'.
Guess we hang out with different women—
Derrick places his hand between Tommy's legs.
What're you doing?
Your boy's right there—relax. If I could just get my wife—.
Derrick reaches around and plants his mouth on Tommy's, who backs away long enough to peer toward Jake, who raises his shoulders. After which beards, lips, and tongues brush against each other as Derrick manipulates the buttons of Tommy's shirt—
You OK? queries Jake. He comes around and nears Tommy, who gazes toward him. He kisses him below the eyes.
I didn' mean t' bum you out, man.
He's—these things come an' go.
Wanna stop?
Do I wanna stop? De verdad, no. Me gusta. Pero.
That yes or no?
—.

If I could only get my wife—
With another woman or a man?

Jake, think I care?

Tommy hesitates. Niño—

—It's up to you—.

An eternity passes, during which time Derrick caresses Tommy's thigh. He looks at Jake and back at Tommy then extricates him fully from his shirt. Derrick pets Tommy's chest, a prairie in the shadow of a cloud. Tommy stands, circles the bed and disappears in the bathroom, remarking before he shuts the door, Y'all go 'head.

Derrick doesn't wait for any more talk, he begins to remove his jeans, ordering Jake to do the same, until the two sit beside one another unclothed.

You got skin like a girl.

So I've heard, though I don' know what it means.

Means I like it.

Derrick explores with fervor, as if looking for something, while Jake glances at the bathroom door.

Maybe we should wait—

He said it's OK.

You done this before.

Hasn' everybody?

Tommy pries the door open and drops his jeans and underwear in a heap on the linoleum. He nears, resting a knee on the mattress. His eyes are bloodshot, face flush. Jake unsticks himself from Derrick and leans toward Tommy.

—You ain't new at this, Tommy observes after blowing his nose.

Like ridin' a bi-cycle—I got a idea. Up he rises, breaking away, leaving the couple to query each other's eyes, until Derrick returns with three pieces of paper, small as the confetti they drop at a party or a parade, a quarter the size of a postage stamp.

I thought them days were over.

I been savin' them for a special occasion. Let's have a little fun.

Ain't we already?

Think a how much more's t' be had. A great-big-magic world.

May not be the occasion, with him an' all—

Jus' the thing he need!

I dunno.

Trus' me—

Tommy makes his way to his jeans in front of the sink and returns with a foil packet. I'll do that if you do this.

Can't say I got much interest in that.

It's been in my wallet how long?

I like the ladies. Don't that exempt me from worry, like you guys gotta?

Think so?

How long you been—jus' the two a yous?

Doesn' matter. It's this or nothin', Tommy insists.

If you say so—. Derrick sets one of the tabs on Tommy's then Jake's finger.

On three.

Under tongues the tabs hide, followed by a swig, kicking off a waiting-party during which three bodies begin a journey, elevating the temperature in the room, limbs vining, sweat forming in beads at first, then rivulets, streaming down necks, between pecs, backs, buttocks, and along thighs, perspiration gathering on the skin and under armpits, suffusing the space with an earthiness, which, Derrick comments, ain't that different from his lady friends. The fur covering Derrick and Tommy's bodies mats when they press—

—I'm startin' t' feel it, buckaroos. Actually, look't! You got stars 'n stripes 'cross your face, an' ivy's growin' on his— from the neck.

Niño, are the lights drippin'?

You dudes got TVs for heads.

Your chest's on fire, shoots Tommy. He tugs the other two as they kiss—

I'll die if you stop, moans Derrick.

You'll die if he don't, quips Jake.

Tommy erupts in a laugh, the first Jake's heard from him in ages.

Here's to dying!

Derrick rips apart the foil packet. First time for everything, he gasps.

As a bead of mercury drops down Tommy's cheek he reaches back and pulls the packet from Derrick's hand and tosses it onto the hills of clutter surrounding the bed as he and Derrick get down to business. Tommy's eyes widen at the novelty of the situation, the math off kilter after so much time keeping company with a single, apparently-permanent partner, he peers into Jake's eyes for approval and a chorus erupts, a sound akin to laughter and tears, Derrick fanning a slow burn into a fire-storm, profusely sweating, Tommy sandwiched with his hands moving across Jake's chest, stomach, and down below as Derrick's hands also roam. Flames leap for an eternity in LSD-time, the long-burn of the second-hand, the sweeping minute-hand all but halting, snailing time, killing it dead, the two taller ones coaxing Jake in a seemingly choreographed move down, the three stretching out.

The curtains are on fire, Jake pants.

Then I don't gotta leave 'em open for y'all no more, Derrick mutters. Tryin' t' get yer attention.

I'm ice, Tommy remarks, shaking wildly.

Took long enough. T' get y'all here.

Your head's the moon—

I'm about t' fill yer cowboy ass with stars, pardner.

Tommy trembles.

You're a one-man earthquake, buckaroo.

You're one t' talk.

Your skin's cookie dough, Jake. Yours green sod.

Sod you. You're a bolt a velvet. Crushed and purple. Kind my wife bought for her bridesmaids.

Again, as if out of the blue, Tommy begins to shake—

—C'mere you, reaches Derrick, taking him in his arms as tears wash out in a flood. He draws Tommy flush against him, front to front, steadies him, remarks as Jake stretches nearby that butterflies are fluttering from his back, filling the room—

They're from Polly, whispers Jake. I see 'em too!

An ocean's been injected in my eyes, complains Tommy. Chunky blocks a salt, left from an ancient sea. Evaporated. Salt, salt, salt, salt.

Butterflies! It's Polly, love.

Tommy vibrates violently as tears flood out, falling on Derrick's shoulder which has become a loamy garden, sprouting holly-hocks, tall and stately. He spots El Conejo Blanco dancing by and tries to track him, falling in the effort, into a hole, even as he rests his head on Derrick's bicep, swollen from swinging a hammer, hoisting sleepers toward a roof-line. Jake too appears sad and dejected, concerned for Tommy and relieved quite frankly by the other's presence, having been unable to console Tommy these many months no matter how hard he's tried, him or anyone else, except Derrick apparently who's nursing Tommy, their bodies joined.

Tommy sinks into the mattress, beginning a descent, leaving Derrick and Jake to peer from above around an opening. He slides down a tunnel through the earth, tubular like a drill-pipe under a nodding donkey, jigging his way in a dance airy and terrestrial, tracking El Conejo in a tubular fall below the surface, toward el País de las

Maravillas, attempting to catch up with El Conejo who disappears into a chasm, the parameters of which are too distant to discern, Tommy's tears expanding into an inland, underground ocean, monumental and overflowing, briny and bitter. He catches his hair lengthening into tresses, tangled around his face, chest, back, and arms, all caressed in the current. Sensing his unclothed state, swimming in the open for anyone to see, he looks for help—¿Dónde está mi Conejo? I've fallen and I'm naked. He feels himself a new body, aware that something's different, literally, as though what seemed fixed is detachable after all, that he's misplaced it, annoyed to have lost the thing but liberated too—best just to let it go. He swims, kicks, strokes, and paddles, una niña de repente, searching for El Conejo, some sign of where he might be, but instead he eyes Oruga, Liebre, and Lirón, Águila, Tortuga, and Grifo, crowding, darting under the breakers. He tries to catch up with one of them until he nearly crashes—*thud!*—into a wall scribbled with messages, apparently self-scrawled by a hand before some primordial village was inundated, in advance of his misstep into this other dimension, chasing El Conejo and tracked by La Gatita, or so he thought, foreigners, family, or friends it isn't clear under the circumstances, having vanished one by one until finally enough is enough, Alicia marshals her big-girl voice, roars Conejo! Conejo! and in so doing conjures a wave, beckoning him or any soul who can rid him of this accursed sadness. Solitude. Until finally he looks around, susses the situation, flushes the handle on the wall just in view—and then! On the verge of despair, ready to ingest poison or physic, the water flushes out.

A door in the wall swings open. El Conejo Blanco sticks his head out—Su Majestad la Duquesa wants her peluca, her wig, he remarks, as though only one thing in all the world were out of whack.

Come find it!

Once inside the multi-room dwelling, Alicia hunts high and low for the hair-piece, wishing Conejo were there to help given his knack for dragging it off and playing with it. He's been known to withhold the thing from La Duquesa in an effort to get her goat—no doubt he could go right to it. But where is El Conejo?

Alicia searches alone until El Conejo returns and, miffed the thing hasn't been located, orders Lagartija to slip behind the beds, room dividers, under trolleys, pumps, and monitors in hopes that he, or anyone, will find it before La Duquesa's audience arrives—

—She wishes to look her best! La Gatita remarks frantically, appearing out of nowhere.

Do something!

Frustrated by his lack of success Alicia slips out the door and into a hallway that shrinks to elfin size, so small she barely fits, until she lengthens herself out in such a way that her head butts against the opening of a room at the other end. Oruga sits inside atop a mushroom there, puffing away at a funny cigarette the end of which looks to have been twisted.

I been expecting you.

You have? Alicia starts to weep and again water begins to fill the hallway, until Oruga reaches through the opening and bids the girl to take a toke. Long and hard, baby. At which point the floor dries up and Alicia shrinks to normal size, the same as when she spied Oruga before, arrayed like Cleopatra on her bed, pampered as a goddess. She realized Alicia possessed a force she couldn't manipulate or control, occasioning a rush of emotion not unakin to terror, a discomfort solved by a puff, rendering an outsized fear manageable, for Alicia too—standing there defrocked, denuded, and depressed, her long tresses covering much of her torso, all the while Oruga looks on.

Why haven't you come to see La Duquesa?

I—I—was busy. Until ese maldito Conejo Blanco lured—he tricked me.

She's been waiting for you, day after day. It's been so long she's gone and lost her wig. Then she gets wind you're coming and she freaks, ordering Lirón and Grifo to remove her, shouting, Don't let that bitch see me like this! And get that girl a frock!

A nurse passes, smiling at Oruga, requesting if he can Please keep your smoking in the room and not in the doorway, apparently unaware, unbothered, or understanding the herbal nature of the whiff clouding from Oruga's cigarette—

—Ven, Alicia. Fuma conmigo—Smoke another with me.

Having stood there for some time, halting, sheepishly, outside the door, Alicia ponders Oruga's invitation, her guilt-tripping too that's only making matters worse.

Once inside the lounge Alicia joins Oruga atop her mushroom and the two catch up, having seen neither hide nor hair of each other for months. El Conejo Blanco has stolen you from us.

Or I stole him.

Why does it always wash that way? Oruga takes another toke. Here—this can make you big or small, skinny or fat, rich or poor, depending. It can give you a new frock.

I better stop before I again become too large to fit.

The nurse barges in, uncommonly festive given the setting, and announces, Alicia, you've got a visitor! He's been with La Duquesa!

Damn, Alicia! remarks La Sota. We thought you weren't going to show! And with La Duquesa pining for you, demanding an audience.

I'm here now. Or am I dreaming?

It'll do La Duquesa a world a good. An' y' know—

—Sota, not now, cautions Oruga, finishing off his magic cigarette. Main thing is she's here.

Well, young lady, there's a crowd waiting for you, not the least of which is El Conejo. La Gatita. La Reina de Corazones. She's here to officiate once La Duquesa returns to her throne.

Gatita, come in! Has the wig been found?

Sí, no thanks to Alicia! Tú pedazo de mierda! It fell behind the curtain after all, but it'll take time to whip into shape. La Reina's working on it.

La Reina's doin' that?

Sí! God knows you're no good. Alicia could see all of a sudden that La Gatita's fur had grown spots.

At which point Alicia backs away, appalled, remembering her in her youth, before La Duquesa was ever anointed a Lady, without a trace of blue blood, having readied herself for her public, the ceremony for which La Gatita served as the main go-between and Alicia stood representative for the state, Alicia being the one with the wits and words to address the assembly, the event captured in photo albums across the land—

How's she doing?

Now you ask.

How does she look?

How do you think? Imprisoned in a place she'll never leave.

On the night the title of La Duquesa was conferred, La Gatita and Alicia readied themselves for her public in a long process of primping and posing in front of the looking-glass, hopefully to slay but happy just to avoid a disaster, like the wig not holding, during which time Alicia stood waiting for what felt like an eternity while Gatita invoked the wig gods, much the way she summoned the nurse not long ago, that friend-to-all in this place of im/mortality, the designated coordinator of events similar in this Wing of Death, provisioned especially for the likes of La Duquesa, La Gatita, Lirón, and La Sota, doing her best to get La Duquesa presentable, all the while corralling the gathered guests, beckoning them to a ceremony she demanded. The nurse rushed ahead of the throng waiting for La Duquesa, making sure she's set, keeping her royal head propped with a surfeit of pillows, a process which she managed to do only just before the crowd entered her chamber.

Having assembled outside the door the nurse comes through and into the hall to meet the group which includes El Conejo now, joined with Alicia, to whom the nurse remarks beneath her breath, I think we're good now. Although El Conejo had been to visit and knew what to expect, for Alicia it's a different story, being new to the place. She'd heard La Duquesa wasn't quite herself, but she wasn't prepared for what she found. Arrayed on her throne, a shadow of herself. Head shrunken, swimming in the wig. All the foundation in the world couldn't mask a pallor spanning the gray-scale, body emaciated, lips dry and contorted. Like a leaf fallen on a sidewalk in fall, she's blanketed in spots from head to toe—

—Sissy.

The accent on the second syllable is hardly pronounced, though Alicia hears it anyway, similar to the countless times she's heard herself addressed that way, loud and proud on the street, in bars, at Cheesman, King Soupers—anywhere and everywhere La Duquesa ran into an army of formers or currents, as she liked to refer to them. Non-amours as well like El Conejo Blanco.

You look like hell.

Gracias a ti por nada.

Before them the crowd gathers. Machines blip, ping, suck, and click. Some exhale and wheeze. Announcements can be heard on the PA system. El Conejo, always restless during the night hours, wonders how La Duquesa sleeps amidst all the distractions, despite her exhaustion, as though speaking were enough to bring on a nap in the daytime. Her eyes fall shut, then like a lizard's swing open.

Don' tell nobody.

I swear.

Then you're my friend after all.

What's gonna happen.

You don' need t' be no genius to figure it, Princesa. You an' El Conejo are gonna—

—Don' say! Me?! Him?! Now?!

The throng erupts in laughter, having been able to discern Alicia's words, even if they couldn't quite make out the whispers of La Duquesa.

I, La Duquesa, command it. It only took getting El Conejo to—

—Pobrecito. Muchas gracias, Señor Blanco.

It's funny, pipes El Conejo. But all them times I received a blessin' I never ask for or, quite frankly, believe in. Thought it was a waste a breath, water too depending. A blessin's a blessin's a blessin'—a lot a hot air most a all, I mean what's a blessin' from man? But I request now a blessin' from you, Duquesa, for me an' Alicia both.

A god I ain't—ain't it a fac'? La Duquesa turns to La Reina de Corazones who's standing beside Alicia, whose presence was requested as the officiant for the occasion—it was clear La Duquesa was struggling to get words out.

A goddess you are for sure, love. Bless away.

La Duquesa closes her eyes, appears to retreat into herself, summoning the spirit, energy, and words to speak—You go first, she remarks to La Reina de Corazones. I'll listen.

At which La Reina de Corazones summons the revelers to gather closer, circle round the throne of La Duquesa, enfolding Alicia and El Conejo—Oruga y Liebre de Marzo,

Lirón y Águila Pequeño, Tortuga y Grifo, closing toward La Duquesa and La Reina de Corazones, including El Sota de Corazones, La Gatita, todas las animales from the Happy Looker, Debra and Cinthia, who's holding Billie's hand, Wren and Donald—the group stand witness, particularly El Liebre de Marzo whose eyes take everything in as though the proceedings were a dream, beyond comprehension—

—And do you, Alicia, take El Conejo, to have and to hold...'til death—

About to mouth the words, Alicia is shocked to discover El Conejo, of all people, flooding the room with tears now, in a rare display, there being a first time for everything apparently, almost comical given the contortions of the face, the unlikeliness of the event, to see El Conejo, always so buttoned and composed, weep hot, salty tears, which La Duquesa nearly snoozes through, much like the rest of the ceremony, despite her efforts not to miss a thing.

Her eyes roll open, catching things by the tail end—

—Sissy. What's come over you. The attendees erupt in laughter alongside El Conejo, including La Reina de Corazones who's aping El Conejo in turn, warmth spilling down, halting the event for a moment. La Duquesa groans involuntarily, as though pained to her false hair follicles, motioning the proceedings forward. In the absence of words and amidst the cacophony of machines—the ones that drive up the bill every second they're connected, a tab no one will ever receive—noise fills the void. La Duquesa's eyes shutter closed for a time and La Reina de Corazones stirs—

—There, there—I'm together now. By the power invested in me by god, nature, and all those gathered here I pronounce you married for life.

Alicia lifts El Conejo's paw, kisses it, his cheeks, then the lips for an extended period of time as the attendees, including La Reina, cheer, clap, hoot, and whistle, the nurse as well as she guards the door, even as La Duquesa lifts out of herself momentarily, soggy as a leaf.

La Reina glances toward La Duquesa whose wig has tilted forward, fairly low over her brow, then at the nurse. She reaches her hand toward La Duquesa—

—It's a lot. Think we should go?

No! moans La Duquesa, who again falls silent, sinks into the pillow, shut like a rose-of-sharon at dusk. When the nurse checks her vitals she appears alarmed.

Maybe we should move to the lounge down the hall where we have refreshments waiting for everyone.

When the crowd empties out of the room, leaving La Reina, La Gatita, Alicia, and El Conejo, La Duquesa grasps for Alicia then El Conejo's hand—

Bless.

She closes her eyes for some time, then opens them.

Happy now.

Dinner is rolled in by a second nurse, but La Duquesa motions it away.

How you doin', Manuel? Can I git you sumpin' else instead?

If you don't mind. She just needs t' rest a little, returns La Reina, reading La Duquesa's mien.

Alicia motions for El Conejo to lower his head, and the two plant kisses on La Duquesa's forehead, one by one, followed by La Reina. Pancake flakes against their lips, coats them, the way it does La Duquesa's lesions.

Maybe we ought a leave, suggests La Reina.

La Duquesa's hand falls over Alicia's—

—Go. Live—

With the passing of La Duquesa a chain of events stirs into motion, during which other bodies succumb and fall. If they didn't already have them that day, they developed spots that discolor and darken, impossible to hide, for those who normally eschewed pancake especially, unlike La Duquesa, following a pattern of becoming-other, becoming-animal, as though we all descended from a common root. Bodies shrink, skin fades, casts gray, throughout El País de las Maravillas. Torsos wither, revealing skeletal structures beneath what was once vital, healthy, and muscular. Inhabitants that once resorted to diets, diuretics, suppositories, and dancing to fight the battle of the bulge, the down-side of privilege, appeared gaunt. Without effort. Chronic diarrhea and a revulsion for food made it impossible to recoup lost weight, bodies fast-tracking the grave. Several that were summoned by La Duquesa, present at the nuptials of Alicia and El Conejo, fall within a matter of months, including La Sota de Corazones, spouse to La Reina de Corazones, laying her low in her castle in Pandemonium, inconsolable despite all the efforts of Alicia and El Conejo. Among the fallen too, Lirón, Grifo, and—alas—La Gatita herself, tracking La Duquesa's foot-steps, as though summoned to a celestial tea-dance, common fare in the realm of El País de las Maravillas.

Given the sentence upon her though, La Duquesa didn't go without a fight. And, a Rubicon having been crossed in the form of a coupling, nothing could keep Alicia away, or El Conejo, in her last days, a full two weeks.

Gotta know when you're beat, she mumbled.

Last thing t' go's always the mouth, returns Alicia, though La Duquesa is too spent to muster a come-back.

An era dies, Tommy pronounces as Polly sinks for the last time, eyes leaden. Up until then she struggled to remain awake during visiting hours, whenever he and Jake were there, saving energy all day, though in the last few days all she could manage was to maintain a stare.

Tommy comes to, having lengthened into his former self, muscles returned, hair shortened, body hair sprouted, and what-not restored.

Niño.

We were worried.

Talk about a trip. Where's Derrick?

Gone t' get breakfas'.

Some powerful shit, that. Where were you the whole time?

Tracking you, wherever you went.

We gave her what she wanted.

Out the window, above the trees, stands a bow-legged cowboy, stories tall, towering over the entrance to the trailer park. Tommy recalls the excitement of seeing it as a kid, thinking it'd be the cat's meow to live in eye-shot of the thing, on a daily basis, though time and the elements have taken their toll, dispelling whatever charge it may have had. It's almost as if the epidemic, a pandemic really, no matter what the medical establishment called it, has taken hold of it as well, given how degraded it's become, the sun-withered chaps and vest, hat and hair, facial features. Wind and debris have pocked the skin with lesions. Sometime over the last two decades the handle-bar moustache fell off, depriving it of the feature that fired Tommy's boyish imagination most, made it an icon.

All gone.

Derrick returns with burritos for a couple still naked, lying, remarking as he sits on the side of the bed, I mean I been curious.

Doin' it's another story.

Here we are—

—Here we are.

Like we're all-three married or somethin'.

We are at least.

I've been strugglin' to recall th' day, niño. 'Til last night—this morning—it's less of a blur. I'll remember now—we should call Ginny. See how she is.

Derrick, thanks for comforting him.

Following breakfast, the three shower then dress. Henceforth Derrick will return to entertaining his usual guests, whom Jake and Tommy will never see given the blinds will remain shut, permanently. Once in a blue moon Derrick will come knocking or invite them over to reprise events of the previous night, minus the tabs of confetti, though more and more infrequently—nothing can recap what was.

Should we a done it? Jake queries, pushing shut the door of Derrick's trailer.

Let's not overthink it.

Tommy takes Jake's hand. The two turn and look, contemplate what's passed. They pace to their new digs, open and slip in, then stop, pivot, and peer out. They crack the door wide.

ACKNOWLEDGEMENTS

I'd like to thank Channing Sanchez and Linda Warren for reading early drafts of *Ojo* and offering such helpful feedback. I'm endlessly in your debt.

I'd also like to express my deep gratitude to Andrew Keen for teaching me decades ago to love poetry, and language generally, starting with the works of Wilfred Owen. On trips together throughout England literary language and history were the themes, which altered how I view everything, including writing.

Thanks as well to Brad, Moyra, Ringo, and Stan for opening a world to me. Once you know a thing you can't unknow it; the question is how you let it alter your life, and you've altered mine.

I'm also much obliged to Victoria Amador, Rick Rodriguez, and Linda Warren for engaging in public discussions with me about literature that doesn't walk a conventional path. Your generous questions and feedback, your insights, have inspired me to no end. They have me thinking still.

Thanks too to Sonia Sanchez Cuesta for your abiding, smart, tutelage in Spanish, including your help on *Ojo*. To learn another language is yet another way of opening a world, one through which you've been my guide.

Finally many thanks especially to Don Mitchell and Ruth Thompson of Saddle Road Press for making *Ojo* possible. Beside your invaluable direction it's been a pleasure to work with and get to know you both. I extend that gratitude on my behalf but also on behalf of all the writers whose dreams you've birthed into reality.

About Donald Mengay

Donald Mengay grew up in a suburb of Cleveland, Ohio, where he worked in a factory for a time and managed a bookstore. He began writing fiction in his early twenties.

 He taught Queer and Post-Humanist Lit at the City University of New York for over thirty years, as well as English at the University of Paris, Nanterre. During his years teaching he published several articles of queer criticism in academic journals that include among others *Genders, Genre,* and *Minnesota University Press.* He also co-published a book entitled *Dis/Inheritance: New Croatian Photography,* from Ikon Press. *The Lede to Our Undoing,* his debut novel, was the first in this trilogy. He lives in Santa Fe, New Mexico.

Printed in the USA
CPSIA information can be obtained
at www.ICGtesting.com
CBHW031149140924
14207CB00045B/563